LILITH SAINTCROW

DEAD MAN RISING

www.orbitbooks.net

ORBIT

First published in the United States in 2006 by Warner Books,
Hachette Book Group, USA
First published in Great Britain in 2006 by Orbit
Reprinted 2008

A CIP catalogue record for this book is available from the British Library.

ISBN 978-1-84149-467-8

Printed and bound in Great Britain by
CPI Mackays, Chatham, ME5 8TD

Papers used by Orbit are natural, renewable and recyclable
products made from wood grown in sustainable forests and certified
in accordance with the rules of the Forest Stewardship Council.

Mixed Sources
Product group from well-managed
forests and other controlled sources
www.fsc.org Cert no. SGS-COC-004081
© 1996 Forest Stewardship Council

FSC

Orbit
An imprint of
Little, Brown Book Group
100 Victoria Embankment
London EC4Y 0DY

An Hachette Livre UK Company
www.hachettelivre.co.uk

www.orbitbooks.net

To L.I.
Peace. The charm's wound up.

ACKNOWLEDGMENTS

This book would literally not exist without a number of people, starting with my husband, James. Without his constant support, none of this would be possible; he is far better than I deserve even on my best days. Also due for thanks are my two children, who teach me more about being human than any dry book could.

Danny Valentine and her world would not be without my agent Miriam Kriss, who has believed in me since the very first draft, and Devi Pillai at Warner, the editor every writer wishes for. Not to mention Linda Kichline, who spotted the potential in a battered manuscript and continues to be both a true friend and a stellar editor.

Thanks, also, to the ad hoc writer's community in Vancouver and online: the *Write Like You Mean It* group; Carolyn Rose and Mike Nettleton, networkers extraordinaire; Mel Sanders (who gets the biggest cookie); Clyde Holloway, the nicest man I know; Jefferson and Janine Davis, true friends even when I'm rude; and the Mighty F-List, for massaging my brain every morning.

To the music makers who feed my Muse, thank you. Especially Rob Dougan, Garbage, the Eagles, Delerium, and Frou Frou. Writing is much easier with good music.

Almost last but certainly not least, many thanks are due to Chelsea Curtis, coworker, fan, and righteous babe; and Joe "Monk" Zeutenhorst, whose grasp of technology always stuns me.

Last of all, thank you, my Readers. As always, you are who I write for. Let me thank you once again in the way we both like best: by telling you something really cool. Just settle in, turn the page, and let's get started . . .

Quis fallere possit amantem?
—Virgil

Leaving Hell is not the same as entering it.
—Tierce Japhrimel

Since before the Awakening, the world has been aware of the existence of psionics. And since the Parapsychic Act was signed into Hegemony law, the psionic Talents have been harnessed to provide valuable service to mankind. Who can imagine a world without Skinlin and sedayeen cooperating to find new cures for every gene-morphing virus, creating new techniques for alteration and augmentation of the human body? Who can imagine a time when the Magi did not probe the laws of magick and alternate realities, or when Ceremonials and Shamans didn't minister to the needs of believers and track criminals, not to mention provide protection for houses and corporations? Who can imagine a world without psions?

The Necromance's place within this continuum is assured: The Necromance treads in that realm of mystery called Death. At hospital bedsides and in courtrooms, Necromances ease the passing of their fellow humans or provide testimony for the last wishes of the dead. An accredited Necromance's work touches the very mundane world of finance, wills, and bequests at the same time that they peer into the dry land of Death and return with absolute proof that there is an afterlife. Necromances also work in the Criminal Justice arm of the Hegemony, tracking criminals and murderers. A Necromance requires not only the talent for entering the realm of Death, but also the training and sorcerous Will to come back out of Death. This is why accreditation of Necromances is so expensive, and so harrowing for even the Academy-trained psionics whose Talent lies in Necromance.

On the flap opposite you will see several careers where an accredited Necromance can make a difference . . .

—Brochure, *What Can Death
Do For You?*, printed by the
Amadeus Hegemony Academy
of Psionic Arts

1

The cavernous maw of the warehouse was like the throat of some huge beast, and even though it was large and airy claustrophobia still tore at my throat. I swallowed, tasted copper and the wet-ratfur reek of panic. *How do I talk myself into these things? "Come on, do a bounty, it's easy as one-two-three, we've done a hundred of them." Sure.*

Darkness pressed close as the lights flickered. *Damn corporate greed not putting proper lighting in their god-damn warehouses. The least they could have done is had the fluorescents replaced.*

Then again, corporations don't plan for hunters taking down bounties in their warehouses, and my vision was a lot better than it used to be. I eased forward, soft and silent, broken-in boots touching the cracked and uneven floor. My rings glinted, swirling with steady, muted light. The Glockstryke R4 was in my left hand, my crippled right hand curled around to brace the left; it had taken me weeks to shoot left-handed with anything like my former accuracy. And why, you might ask, was I using a projectile gun when I had two perfectly good 40-watt plasguns holstered in my rig?

Because Manuel Bulgarov had taken refuge in a warehouse full of plastic barrels of reactive paint for spreading on the undersides of hovers, that's why.

Reactive paint is mostly nonvolatile—except for when a plas field interacts with it. One plasgun blast and we'd be caught in a reaction fire, and though I was a lot tougher than I used to be I didn't think I could outrun a molecular-bond-weakening burst fueled by hundreds, if not thousands, of gallons of reactive. A burst like that travels at about half the speed of light until it reaches its containment edge. Even if I could outrun or survive it, Jace certainly couldn't, and he was covering me from the other side of the T-shaped intersection of corridors faced with blue barrel after blue barrel of reactive.

Just like a goddamn bounty to hide in a warehouse full of reactive to make my day.

Jace's fair blond face was marred with blood that almost hid the thorny accreditation tat and the spreading bruise up his left cheek, he was bleeding from his shoulder too. Ending up in a bar brawl that alerted our quarry was *not* the way I'd wanted to do this bounty.

His blue eyes were sharp and steady, but his breathing was a little too fast and I could smell the exhaustion on him. I felt familiar worry rise under my breastbone, shoved it down. My left shoulder prickled with numb chill, a demon's mark gone dead against my flesh, and my breathing came sharp and deep, ribs flaring with each soundless gasp, a few stray strands of hair falling in my face. *Thank the gods I don't sweat much anymore.* I could feel the inked lines of my own accreditation tat twisting and tingling under the skin of my left cheek, the emerald set at the top of the twisted caduceus probably flashing.

Tone it down, don't want to give the bastard a twinkle and let him squeeze off a shot or two.

Bulgarov didn't have a plasgun—or at least, I was reasonably certain he hadn't had one when he'd gone out the back door of the PleiRound nightclub and onto an airbike with us right behind him, only slightly slowed down by the explosion of the brawl. After all, the PleiRound was a watering hole for illicits, and once we'd moved and shown we were bounty hunters all hell had broken loose. If he'd had a plasgun, he probably wouldn't have bothered to run. No, he would have turned the bar into a firezone.

Probably.

I'd almost had Bulgarov, but he was quick. Too quick to be strictly normal, though he wasn't a psion. I made a mental note to tell my scheduler Trina to tack 15 percent onto the fee, nobody had mentioned the bastard was gene-spliced and augmented to within an inch of violating the Erdwile-Stokes Act of '28. That would have been nice information to have. Necessary information, even.

My shoulder still hurt from clipping the side of a hover as we chased him through nighttime traffic on Copley Avenue. He'd been keeping low to avoid the patrols, though how you could be inconspicuous with two bounty hunters chasing you on airbikes, I couldn't guess.

It was illegal to flee, especially once a bounty hunter had identified herself as a Hegemony federal officer. But Bulgarov hadn't gotten away with rape, murder, extortion, and trafficking illegal weapons by being a law-abiding jackass who cared about two more counts of felony evading. No, he was an entirely different kind of jackass. And staying low meant a little more time without the Hegemony patrols getting involved in the tangle, which made it him against just two bounty hunters instead of against full-scale containment teams. It was a nice move, and sound logic—if the two bounty hunters weren't an almost-demon and the Shaman who had taught her a good deal about hunting bounties.

My eyes met Jace's again. He nodded curtly, reading my face. Like it or not, I was the one who could take more damage. And I usually took point anyway; years of working bounties alone made it a tough habit to break.

He was still good to work with. It was just like old times. Only everything had changed.

I eased around the corner, hugging the wall. Extended my awareness a little, just a very little, feeling the pulse thunder in my wrists and forehead; the warehouse was magshielded and had a basic corporate security net, but Bulgarov had just walked right in like he owned the place. Not a good sign. He might have bought a short-term quickshield meant to keep him from detection by psions or security nets. Just what I'd expect from the tricky bastard.

Concentrate, Danny. Don't get cocky because he's not a psion. He's dangerous and augmented.

My right hand cramped again, pointlessly; it was getting stronger the more I used it. Three days without sleep, tracking Bulgarov through the worst sinks in North New York Jersey, taxed even my endurance. Jace could fall asleep almost instantly, wedged in a hover or transport seat while I crunched data or piloted. It had been a fast run, no time to catch our breath.

Two other bounty hunters—both normals, but with combat augments—had gone down trying to bring this guy in. The next logical choice had been to bring a psion in, and I was fresh from hunting a Magi gone bad in Freetown Tijuana. From one job to the next, with no time to think, perfect. I didn't *want* to think about anything but getting the next bounty collared.

I would be lying if I said the idea of the two extra murder charges *and* two of felony evading tacked onto Bulgarov's long list of indictments didn't bring a smile to my face. A hard, delighted grin, as a matter of fact, since it meant Bulgarov would face capital punishment instead of just filling a prison cell. I edged forward, reaching the end of the aisle; glanced up. Nothing in the rafters, but it was good to check. This was one tricky sonofabitch. If he'd been a psion it would have made things a little easier, I could have tracked the smears of adrenaline and Power he'd leave on the air when he got tired enough. As it was, the messy sewer-smelling drift of his psychic footprint faded and flared maddeningly. If I dropped below the conscious level of thought and tried to scan him, I'd be vulnerable to a detonation circuit in a quickshield, and it wasn't like this guy *not* to have a det circuit built in if he spent the credit for a shield. I could live without the screaming migraine feedback of cracking a shield meant to keep a normal from a psion's notice, thank you very much.

So it was old-fashioned instinct doing the work on this one. *Is he heading for an exit or sitting tight? My guess is sitting tight in a nice little cubbyhole, waiting for us to come into sight, pretty as you please. Like shooting fish in a barrel.* Sekhmet sa'es, *he better not have a plasgun. He didn't. I'm almost sure he didn't.*

Almost sure wasn't good enough. *Almost sure,* in my experience, is the shortest road to *oh fuck.*

Jace's aura touched mine, the spiked honey-pepper scent of a Shaman rising around me along with the cloying reek of dying human cells. I wished I could turn my nose off or tone it down a little. Smelling everyone's death on them was not a pleasant thing, even if I, of all people, know Death is truly nothing to fear.

Whenever I thought about it, the mark on my shoulder seemed to get a little colder.

Don't fucking think about that, Danny. Nice and cautious, move it along here.

A popping *zwing!* made me duck reflexively, calculating angles even as I berated myself for flinching. *Goddammit, if you heard the shot it didn't get you, move move move! He's blown cover, you know where he is now!* I took off, not bothering to look behind me—Jace's aura was clear, steady, strong. He hadn't been hit.

More popping, clattering sounds. Reactive paint sprayed as I moved, blurringly, much faster than a normal human. My gun holstered itself as I leapt, claws extending sweetly, naturally, my right hand giving a flare of pain I ignored as I dug into the side of a plastic barrel, hurling myself *up*, get *up*, and from there I leapt, feet smacking the smooth round tops of the barrels. My rings spat golden sparks, all need for silence gone. The racks holding the barrels swayed slightly as I landed and pushed off again, little glowing spits and spats of thick reactive paint spraying behind me as lead chewed the air. *He's got a fucking semiautomatic assault rifle up there, sounds like a Transom from the chatter, goddamn cheap Putchkin piece of shit, if he had a good gun he'd have hit me by now.*

I was almost under the floating panel of a hover platform. Its underside glowed with reactive paint, and I could see the metal cage on top where the operator would guide the AI deck through manipulating the dangling tentacles of crabhooks to pick up five racks at a time and transport them to the staging area. A low, indistinct male shape crouched on the edge of the platform, orange bursts showing from the muzzle of the semiautomatic rifle with the distinct Transom shape. He wasn't aiming at me now, he was aiming *behind* me at Jace, and this thought spurred me as I gathered myself and leapt, fingers sinking into the edge of the platform's corrugated metal and arms *straining,* the deadweight of my body becoming momentum as I pulled myself up as easily as if I were muscling up out of a swimtank. Almost overbalanced, in fact, still not used to the reflex speed of this new body, proprioception still a little off, moving through space faster than I thought I was.

Don't hit Jace, you motherfucker, or I'm going to have to bring you in dead and accept half my fee. Don't you dare hit him, you piece of shit.

Gun barrel swinging, deadly little whistles as bullets clove the air. A smashing impact against my belly and another against my ribcage; then I was on him, smacking the barrel up. Hot metal sizzled, a jolt of pain searing up my arm from the contact, then faded as my body coped with the damage. He was combat-augmented, with reactions quicker than the normal human's, but I'd been genetically altered by a demon, and no amount of augmentation could match that.

At least, none that I'd come across yet.

I tore the Transom away and grabbed his wrist in my cramping right hand, setting my feet and yanking sharply down. An animal howl and a crunch told me I'd dislocated his shoulder. Fierce enjoyment spilled through me, the emerald on my cheek giving one sharp flash, the *kia* burst from my lips as I struck, *hard;* ringed fist ramming into the solar plexus, pulling the strike at the last moment so as not to rupture fragile human flesh. My rings turned my fist into a battering ram, psychic and physical power wedded to a strike that could kill as well as daze. The *oof!* sound he made might have been funny if I hadn't felt hot blood dripping down my ribs and the slight twitching as a bullet was expelled from the preternatural flesh of my belly. *Ouch.* It stung, briefly, then smoothed itself out, black blood rising and sealing the seamless golden flesh. Another shirt ruined. I was racking up dead laundry by the ton now.

Of course, I could afford it. I was rich, wasn't I?

Knee coming up, he struggled, but he was off balance and I shifted my weight, hip striking as I came in close, he fell and I was on him; he howled as I yanked both arms behind his back, my fingers sinking into rubbery, augmented muscle fed by kcals of synthprotein shake and testos injections. *Gonna have to pop that shoulder back in so he can't shimmy free of magcuffs. You've got him down, don't get cocky. This is the critical point. Just cuff him, don't get fancy.* He bucked, but I had a knee firmly in his back and my own weight was not inconsiderable, heavy with denser bones and muscle now. The quickshield sparked and struggled, trying to throw me off; it was a sloppy, hastily purchased piece of work—all right for hiding, but no good when you had an angry Necromance on your back. One short sharp Word broke it, my sorcerous Will slicing through the shell of energy—a Magi's work, and a good one, despite being so hurried. I snapped the mental traces aside, taking a good lungful of the scent;

maybe we could track down whoever did the quickshield, maybe not. They hadn't done anything illegal in providing the shield; quicks were perfectly legal all the way around. But a Magi this good might have something to say about demons, something I'd want to hear.

"Jace?" I called into the warehouse's gloom. The sharp smell of reactive paint bloomed up, mixing with dust, metal, the smell of human, hot cordite, sweat, and my own spiced fragrance, a light amber musk. Sometimes my own smell acted like a shield against the swirling cloud of human decay all around me, sometimes not; it wasn't the psychic nonphysical smell of a true demon, but the scent of something in-between. "Monroe? How you doing?" *Jace? Answer me, he was aiming at you, answer me!* My voice almost cracked, stroking the air with rough honey. My throat was probably permanently ruined from Lucifer's fingers sinking in and cracking little bits of whatever almost-demons had in their necks. I sounded like a vidsex operator sometimes.

Apparently I could heal from bullets, but demon-induced damage to my throat was another thing entirely.

"You're so much fun to hang out with, Valentine," he called from below. I tried not to feel the hot burst of relief right under my ribs. The bitter taste of another hunt finished exploded in my mouth, my heart thudding back to a slower pace. My left shoulder prickled numbly, as if the fluid mark scored into my skin was working its way deeper. *Don't think about that.* "Got him?"

Of course I've got him, you think I'd be talking if I didn't? "Stuffed and almost cuffed. See if you can find the control panels and bring this sucker to the loading dock, will you?" My lungs returned to their regular even task.

My tone resumed its normal, whispering roughness. Most Necromances affect a whisper after a while; when you work with Power wedded to your voice it's best to speak softly. "You okay?"

He gave a short jagged spear of a laugh, he was rubbed just as raw as I was. "Right as rain, baby. Get you in a second."

My right hand clumsily fumbled for the magcuffs. Bulgarov mumbled a curse in some consonant-filled Putchkin dialect. "Shut up, waste." I sank my knee into his heaving back. Short squat man, corded with heavy muscle and dressed in a long-sleeved shirt and jeans under his assassin's rig, a long rat-tail of pale hair sliding out from under the kerchief he'd tied around his head like a kid playing minigang. "Unlucky day for you."

The magcuffs cooperated, and I had to hold him down while I popped his shoulder back into the socket with a meaty sound, eliciting a hoarse male scream. The cuffs creaked but held steady, and just to be sure I dug in my bag and retrieved the magtape, spent a few moments binding the bastard's elbows, knees, and ankles; I gagged him too. I was ready when the hover platform's control board lit up, I kept the man down and watched him cautiously while the platform jolted into life and began to glide on its prearranged path. Bulgarov had escaped last year from a seven-person Hegemony police unit that had him down and cuffed; I didn't want to underestimate him.

Four little girls, six hookers we know he killed for sure, three we're not sure of, and eight men, mostly Chill dealers. I wouldn't have minded the Chill dealers, but the kids . . . My rings were back to a steady glow: amber, moonstone, obsidian, and bloodstone all swirling with easy Power.

I surveyed the mess the bullets had made of the reactive barrels as the hover platform glided over neatly-placed racks and rows. Glowing paint dripped thickly under dim sputtering light from fluorescents turned down for the night pulsing outside in all its shades of darkness. *And he killed them slow. Gods.*

I could understand killing when necessary, the gods know I've done my share. But kids . . . and defenseless women. Even a *sedayeen* healer experienced with mental illness could do nothing for this man; he was a pure sociopath. No remorse, no hesitation, no conscience at all; he was neither the first nor the last of his kind the world would see. And probably not the last one I'd hunt, either.

The trouble was, I'd had little difficulty tracking him. Thinking like him. *Being* like him, to catch him.

That was starting to worry me.

The hover platform settled with a jolt and Bulgarov thrashed, making a muffled sound behind the gag. It probably wasn't comfortable, lying facedown on a cold metal platform with a stretched-out, busted shoulder and a bruised solar plexus. I might have broken his nose, too, when I had my knee in his back. At least, I hoped I had. My hand tightened on the neck of his jacket as I finished searching him for weapons, finding the trigger to the quickshield—a pretty ceramic medallion with a Seal of Solomon etched into one side—four knives, two projectile guns, and a little 20-watt recharge plasgun fitted into a pocket on the thigh of his jeans.

I turned the plasgun over in my hand. *Gods.* A tremor slid through me, my teeth chattering briefly. *That close to blowing up this whole warehouse, would have taken a*

good chunk out of the neighborhood here too. You son of a
bitch. Thank the gods you didn't use this.

The assault rifle bothered me, but he could have had it
stashed on the airbike. My tat tingled, ink running under
my skin, and my left shoulder tingled too. I was used to
both sensations by now; did my best to ignore them. I'd
smashed my slicboard into the side of a concrete building.
If I was still human I'd be dead by now.

Jace met me on the platform. He looked like hell, his
clothes torn and his face bloody and bruised. He also
looked chalky-pale under his perpetual tan. I'd have to
healcharm him, or find a healer to do it.

"You okay?" My throat rasped a little, but my voice
still made the air shiver like a cat being stroked.

He nodded, his blue eyes moving over the trussed
package on the floor, checking. I reached down, set my
feet, and hauled Bulgarov up, nodding toward the pile of
weapons. Without the brace of his Shaman's staff, Jace
almost-limped on his stiff knee over to the pile, his sword
jammed through the belt on his rig. It was a *dotanuki;*
heavier than the last sword I'd used. My right hand
cramped again, remembering driving the shattering blade
through a demon's heart as we both fell through icy air
and smashed into the surface of the frozen sea.

Don't think about that. Because thinking about that
would only make me think of Japhrimel.

I winced inwardly as I hopped down to the yellow-
painted concrete of the loading dock, the shock grating in
my knees. I'd gone a whole . . . what, forty-five minutes
without thinking of him? Adrenaline was wonderful, even
if I wasn't sure what the demon equivalent to adrenaline

was. Now if I could just find another bounty as soon as I dragged this guy in, I'd be all set.

"Chango," Jace breathed. "He had a plasgun."

I could have laughed, didn't. The short man was a heavy limp weight, more awkward than hard to carry; I was a lot stronger than I looked. He'd given up thrashing, his ribs heaved with deep breaths. I caught him straining against the magtape and dumped him on the concrete. Drew one of my main-gauches from its sheath and dropped to my knees, my fingers curling in his greasy hair. This close I could see the blemishes on his skin, blackheads rising to the oily surface. A side-effect of illegal augments, he had a pallid moon-shaped face scarred and pocked by terminal acne. Revulsion touched my stomach. I pushed it down, pulling his head back and craning his neck uncomfortably. It would be easy to give a sudden twist, hear the snap like a dry stick. So easy.

I laid the knifeblade against his throat. "Keep struggling," I whispered in his ear, my voice husky and broken. "I'd love to rid the world of a blight like you. And I'm a deadhead, Bulgarov. I can easily bring you back over the Bridge and kill you twice."

I couldn't, of course. Death didn't work like that; an apparition brought back from the halls of the hereafter couldn't be killed twice, only sent back into Death's embrace. But there was no reason for this bastard to know that. I'd seen the files and the lasephotos. I knew what this bastard had done to the little girls before he killed them.

He went limp for a moment, then struggled frantically against the magtape. I held him down, easy now that he was bound, and used the knife's razor edge to prick at his flesh, right over where the pulse beat. "Come on," I whispered. "Struggle harder, sweetheart. I'd love to do to you what you did to the little blonde girl. Her name was Shelley, did you know that?"

"Danny!" Jace's voice. "Hey, I've keyed in for pickup; we've got a Jersey police transport coming to get us and our little package. Want me to bag the weapons?" Did he sound uneasy? Of course not.

Or did he? I might be a little uneasy if I hung around me. I wasn't hinged too tightly these days. Call it nerves.

"Sure. Make sure that plasgun's sealed." My messenger bag's strap dug against my shoulder as I turned my head, objects inside shifting and clinking a little against my hip. A tendril of dark hair fell in my face, freed of the tight braid I'd put in this morning. Bulgarov had gone limp and still as a fresh corpse underneath me.

I resheathed the knife and let him go, his head thudding none-too-gently against the concrete. My hands were shaking, even my crippled right hand, which rubbed itself against my jeans. I was dirty and tired, no time for a shower while I was tracking this bastard, barely time enough for food to keep Jace going, since my stomach usually closed up tight on a hunt. Jace was looking a little worse for wear, but he insisted on coming along. And I was soft enough to let him—after a bit of bitching, of course.

Anything was better than staying at home, staring at the walls and thinking thoughts I would rather not think. Especially since the only thing I seemed able to do while I was at home was research in Magi shadowjournals and stare at the black urn that held a demon's ashes.

A Fallen demon. Japhrimel.

You will not leave me to wander the earth alone, a soft male voice, flat but still expressively shaded, whispered in my head. I shut my eyes briefly. The mark on my left shoulder—*his* mark, the burning scar Lucifer had pressed into my flesh to make Japhrimel my familiar—hadn't faded with Japh's death, just gone numb as if shot with varocain. Sometimes it was like a mass of burning ice pressed into the skin, pulsing every now and again with a weird necrotic life of its own. I wondered how long it would feel like that, if it would ever fade, and how long it would take for the cold burning numbness to fade.

If it ever did.

Goddammit, Dante, will you quit thinking about that?

Distant sirens began at the edge of my hearing, slicing through the rattling whine of hovertraffic. All this reactive paint, and the bastard had a plasgun all the time. What if he'd decided to take a potshot, take us with him?

Would a reactive fire kill me? I didn't know. I didn't know what I *was* now, other than almost-demon. Part demon. Whatever. I was stuck with the face of a holovid model and a body that sometimes escaped my control and moved far faster than it should, and I was taking down bounties like they were going out of style. Gabe called it "bounty sickness," and I wasn't sure she was far wrong.

I'd be home this week for my usual Thursday rendezvous with Gabe in the back booth they saved for us at Fa Choy's. I'd missed it last week. *That's a good thought,* I told myself grimly as the sirens drew nearer and Jace finished bagging Bulgarov's weapons. *Keep that one.*

But what I thought of, as I watched the shapeless lump of the man magtaped on the floor, was green eyes, turning dark and thoughtful, and a long black coat, golden skin, and a faint, secretive tilt to a thin mouth. Goddammit. I was thinking about a demon again. A *dead* demon, at that.

Does a demon have a soul? The Magi don't know, they only know what demons tell them, and the question's never come up. And what am I? What did he do to me, and why didn't I die when he did?

That was a bad thought. Jace brought the bagged weapons over, his injured knee slowing him a little, and gave me a tight smile. "Fresh as a daisy," he said in his usual careless tone. "I hate that about you."

"Fuck you too." It was postjob banter, meant to ease the nerves and bring us down. It was working.

"Anytime, sweetheart. We've got a few minutes before the transport gets here." His mouth quirked up into a half-smile, and he rolled his shoulders back under the leather straps of his rig. But his eyes slid over the man on the floor, checking the magtape. Professional to the last. A handsome blue-eyed man, spirit bag dangling from a leather thong around his neck marking him as a *vaudun* just as the tat on his cheek marked him as a Shaman. He'd cut his hair like Gypsy Roen's sidekick on the holovids, soft and spiky, a nice cut on him. Especially with his lazy smile and his electric eyes.

Despite myself, I laughed. I tried not to; my ruined voice made it sound like a rough invitation, velvet curled under sweating fists. "You're the soul of chivalry, as always."

"Only for you, baby." The sirens were screamingly close. "Wanna carry him outside?"

"Do I get to drop him headfirst?" I sounded only halfway joking.

So did he. "If you want, sweetheart. Make sure you do it on concrete."

. . .

We caught the redeye transport back to Saint City; it deposited us onto the dock amid a stream of normals. I was glad to get off the transport, claustrophobia tends to run in psions. I was also happy to get rid of the whine of hover travel. It settles in the back teeth, hoverwhine, and rattles your bones. Normals can't hear it, but they get itchy on long hover flights too. Of course, it could be because all the normals I've seen on transports are a little edgy at being in a compartment with a psion. For some reason they think we want to read their minds or force them to do embarrassing things, though the gods know that the *last* place a psion wants to tread is the messy, open sewer of a normal person's brain. Without the regulation and cleanness imparted by training, minds can get rank and foul very quickly—and they stay that way. I don't know how normals endure it.

I was wearing my last clean shirt, but the fact that my jeans were dotted with black blood that smelled like sweet rotting fruit might have had something to do with the sidelong looks and not-so-subtle avoidance of normals. Or perhaps it was my rings, glowing faintly even in the gray thin morning light, or the rig with the guns and knives, stating clearly that I was combat trained and licensed to carry anything short of an assault rifle on public transport. Or the holovid-star face with velvety golden skin, and dark eyes set above a sinfully sweet mouth; or the way my right hand twisted sometimes into a claw without my realizing it, cramping up as if it was trying to grab a corkscrewed swordhilt. I missed the feel of a hilt and the clean confidence of carrying a katana; knives just aren't the same. But shattering a sword in a demon's heart isn't the best way to keep your swordhand whole. I was lucky; if Japhrimel hadn't changed me into whatever I was now, killing Santino might have killed me instead of just crippling my slowly-healing hand.

Yeah. Lucky, lucky me.

My skin tingled as we stood there, Jace leaning on his staff—rescued from the hotel room in Jersey—with its raffia twine at the top, small bones clicking and shifting against one another, even though the staff wasn't moving. After a while a Shaman's staff tends to take on a personality of its own, much like any object used to contain Power. There are even stories of Shamans who have passed their staves on to students or children, mostly in the older traditions. Jace was an Eclectic, like most North Merican Shamans; it's hard to work for the Hegemony and only stick with one discipline. Plus, psions tend to be magpies. We pick up a little of this, a little of that, whatever works. The use of magickal and psionic Power is so incredibly personal we'd be fools to do otherwise.

The tingling on my skin was my body adjusting to the flux of Power in the rainy air, the transport well was full so we had docked in an auxiliary outside bay. Rain misted down, a thin barely-autumn drizzle that smelled of hover-wash, the salt from the bay, and the peculiar damp radio-active smell of Saint City.

Home. Funny how the longer I spent chasing down bounties, the more I thought of Saint City as home.

"You coming home?" Jace tapped the butt of his staff against the concrete, but gently. Just a punctuation, not the sharp guncrack of frustration. His wheat-gold hair was beginning to darken and slick itself down with the drizzle; the bruise had faded and I could *see* the faint pulsing of the healcharm I'd laid on him. He'd slept on the transport, I hadn't; but we were both night creatures. Being out in the light of early morning was guaranteed to make both of us cranky. Not to mention he'd need a few hours or so to reaccustom himself to the flux of ambient Power here, we hadn't been gone long enough for his body to set itself to Jersey's Power flux. It was like hoverlag, when the body isn't sure whether it's day or night because of the speed of transport, only harder and if a psion was drained and exhausted enough potentially very painful.

Glancing at the glass doors, I found my voice. Wherever we were going, we could take the lifts down to the street together. If I wanted to. "No, I've got a few things to do."

"I thought so." He nodded sagely, a tall, spare man with a quick famous grin, his assassin's rig easy over his black T-shirt and jeans, the *dotanuki* thrust through his belt and his staff in hand. If it wasn't for the accreditation tat, he might have been a holovid star himself. But there were fine fans at the corners of his eyes that hadn't been there before, and he looked tired, leaning on his staff for support instead of effect. The last ten months hadn't been easy on him. "It's the Anniversary, isn't it."

I didn't think you'd remember, Jace. The last time you saw me do this was years ago. Before Rio. Before you left me. I nodded, biting my lower lip. It was a sign of nervousness I never would have permitted myself, before. "Yeah. I'm glad we're back in town, I . . . well, missing it would be rough."

He nodded. "I'm going to pop in at Cherk's and have a drink before I go home." He tipped me a wink, the patented Jace Monroe grin flashing. That smile used to line up the Mob groupies for him, he never had any trouble with women—as he was so fond of remarking—until he met me. "Maybe I'll get all drunk and you can take advantage of me."

Damn the man, he was making me smile. "In your dreams. Go on home, I'll be along. Don't get too drunk."

"'Course not." He shrugged and stepped away, heading for the door.

I wanted to go after him, walk down to the street together, but I stood very still and closed my eyes. My right hand lifted, almost of its own accord, and rubbed at the numb spot on my left shoulder. Was it tingling more than it had before?

Stop it, Dante. It was the stern voice of my conscience again. *Japh's gone. Live with it.*

I am, I told that deep voice. *Go away.*

It went, promising to come back later and taunt me. I rubbed my shoulder, scrubbing at it with my knuckles since my fingers were curled under and cramped. At least it didn't hurt anymore. Not there, anyway.

I wondered, not for the last time, why the mark hadn't faded with Japh's death. Of course, Lucifer had first burned it into my skin.

That was an uncomfortable thought, to say the least.

Jace was nowhere in sight when I took the lifts down and emerged blinking again into the gray day. Down on the street the drizzle had turned to puddles vibrating with hoverwash and splashing up whenever an airbike or wheelbike went by, the ground hovertraffic moving a little bit slower than usual. The sidewalks were crowded with people, most of them normals intent on their own business, since the psions would probably be home in bed. It felt good to walk, my hands dangling loose by my sides and my braid bumping my back, my boots light on cracked pavement. Bulgarov had been left in a holding cell in Jersey lockdown; the fee for the collar plus the extra 15 percent I'd told Trina to charge was probably safely in Jace's bank account by now. I didn't need the money, as there was plenty left from Lucifer's payoff. Even though I had no qualm about using it, I still flinched internally whenever I looked at my statements or signed on through my computer deck. Blood money, a payment for the life Lucifer had manipulated and cajoled me into taking, even though left to myself I would have killed Santino.

I had *needed* revenge. Lucifer still owed me, both for Doreen's daughter and for Japhrimel. I didn't have a chance of collecting, but still. He owed me, and I owed my life to a dead demon.

I winced, pacing through the rainy gray Saint City morning. The Prince of Hell might still be keeping an eye on me.

I owed him *nothing,* and that was exactly what the Prince of Hell was going to get from me. End of story.

Think about something else, Dante. You've got a lot to brood over. Like Jace.

Jace had given up his Mob Family for me, just handed it over to his second-in-command without a word and signed the papers for cessation-of-ownership. After fighting so hard to get his own Family he'd turned his back on it and showed up at my door.

Dante, you are spectacularly good at thinking things you don't want to.

It took me an hour to get to the corner of Seventh and Cherry. I had stopped at a street vendor's for a bouquet of yellow daisies, and I stood on the south corner under the awning of a grocery store that had been put in two years ago. The times I'd been here with Lewis, there had been a used bookstore across the way.

My pulse beat thinly in my temples and throat, as if I was taking down a bounty again. I clutched the daisies in their plasticine wrap, their cheerful yellow heads with black centers nodding as I held them in my trembling right hand. Coming back here every year was a penance, maybe, but who else would remember him? Lewis had no family, substituting the psionic kids he fostered for a real blood link. And to me, he was the only family I'd known, my caseworker from the time I was an infant until I was thirteen.

If I was anything to be proud of, it was because Lewis had taught me how to be.

Memory rose. That's the curse of being a psion, I suppose. The Magi techniques for training the memory are necessary and ruthless. A Magi-trained memory can remember every detail of a scene, a magick circle, a canon of runes, a page of text. Necessary when one is performing Greater Works of magick, where everything has to be done right the first time, but merciless when things happen that you want to forget.

The prickling in my shoulder had gone down, thankfully. There wasn't much of a crowd here, most passersby ducked into the small grocery and came out carrying a plasbag full of alcohol bottles or synth-hash cigarettes. I stood just around the corner, tucked out of the way close to the wall, and stilled myself, forcing the memories to come clear and clean.

He'd brought me down to the bookstore, a special treat, and the smooth metal of the collar against my throat was less heavy on that unseasonably sunny autumn day. The crisp cinnamon smell of dried leaves hung in the air and the sky was impossibly deep blue, the type of blue that only comes in autumn. Blue enough to make the eyes ache, blue enough to drown in. Lewis had pushed his spectacles up on his beaky nose, and we walked together. I didn't hold his hand like I did when I was a little girl, having grown self-conscious in the last few years. I had ached to tell him something, anything, about how bad things were at school, but I couldn't find the nerve.

And so we walked, and Lewis drew me out, asking me about the last books I'd read, the copy of Cicero he'd loaned me and the Aurelius he was saving for if I did well on my Theory of Magick final coming up at the end of the term. *And did you enjoy the Ovid?* he asked, almost bouncing with glee inside his red T-shirt and jeans. He didn't dress like a social worker, and that was one more thing to love about him. He had given me my name, my love of books, and my twelve-year-old self had cherished wild fantasies of finding out that Lew really was my father and was just waiting for the right time to tell me.

I enjoyed it, I told him, *but the man was obsessed with women.*

Most men are. Lewis found the oddest things funny, and it was only once I reached adulthood that I understood the jokes. When I was young, of course, I had laughed with him, just happy that he was happy with me, feeling the warm bath of his approval.

I had been about to reply when the man blundered around the corner, jittering and wide-eyed, stinking of Clormen-13. It was a Chillfreak desperate for his next dose, his eyes fastening on the antique chronograph Lewis wore, a glittering thing above his datband and looking pawnable. Confusion and chaos, and a knife. Lewis yelled for me to run, my feet rooted to the ground as the Chillfreak's knife glittered, throwing back a hot dart of sunlight that hurt my eyes. *Run, Danny! Run!*

My eyes were hot and grainy. Drizzle had soaked into my hair and coat. I was standing exactly where I'd stood before I'd obeyed him, turning and running, screaming while the Chillfreak descended on Lewis.

The cops had caught the freak, of course, but the chronograph was gone and the man's brain so eaten by Chill he could barely remember his own name, let alone what he'd done with the piece of antique trash. And Lew, with his books and his love and his gentleness, had left me for Death's dry country, that land where I was still a stranger even if I'd known my way to its borders.

I laid the flowers down on the wet sidewalk, as I did every year, their plaswrap crinkling. The bloodstone ring on my third left finger flashed wetly, a random dart of Power splashing from its opaque surface. "Hey," I whispered. "Hi."

He had a grave marker, of course, out in the endlessly-green fields of Mounthope. But that was too far for a student to ride public transport and get back to the school by curfew, so I ended up coming here, downtown, where he had died almost immediately. If I'd been older, combat-

trained and a full Necromance, I could have run off the
Chillfreak or mended Lewis's violated body, held him to
life, kept him from sliding off the bridge and into the
abyss, under the blue glow of Death . . . *if* I'd been older.
If I'd had some presence of mind I could have distracted
the Chillfreak, diverted his attention; wearing a collar
meant I couldn't have used any psionic ability on him, but
there were other ways. Other things I could have done.

Other things I *should* have done.

"I miss you," I whispered. I had only missed two An-
niversaries, my first year at the Academy up north and the
year Doreen died. Murdered, in fact, by a demon I hadn't
known was a demon at the time. "I miss you so much."

Nihil desperandum! he would crow. *Never fear!*

Other kids were raised on fairy tales. Lew raised me on
Cicero and Confucius, Milton and Cato, Epictetus and
Sophocles, Shakespeare. Dumas. And for special treats,
Suetonius, Blake, Gibbon, and Juvenal. *These are the
books that have survived,* Lew would remind me, *because
they are as close to immortal as you can get. They're good
books, Dante, true books, and they'll help you.*

And oh, they had.

I came back to myself with a jolt. Morning hovertraffic
whined and buzzed overhead. I heard footsteps, people
passing by on Cherry to get to the shops, but nobody
going down this side of Seventh because it was apartment
buildings, and everyone was gone for the day, or in bed.
The daisies, a bright spot of color against cracked hard
pavement, glowed under the thickening rain.

"All right," I said softly. "See you next year, I guess."

I turned slowly on my heel. The first steps, as usual,
were the hardest, but I didn't look back. I had another

appointment today. Jace would beat me home, and he would probably already have a few holovids from the rental shop on Trivisidero. Maybe some old *Father Egyptos,* we both loved that show and could quote damn near every line of dialogue. *What evil creeps in the shadows? Egyptos, the bearer of the Scarab of Light, shall reveal all!*

Uncharacteristically, I was smiling. Again.

2

_M_orning had leapt gray into drizzling afternoon when I knocked on the wooden door, the street behind me gathering circles of orange light under each streetlamp. A glowing-red neon sign in the front window—a real antique— buzzed like hovertraffic without the rattling whine, its reflection cast on the bank of yarrow below. I felt wrung-out and a little sore, as usual after a bounty, and the blood on my clothes, with its simmering stink of decaying spicy fruit, didn't help.

The door was painted red, and the shields over this small brick house with its cheerful ragged garden were tight and well-woven. Kalifor poppies vied with mugwort and feverfew, nasturtium and foxglove; there were some late bloomers, but mostly the plants were now merely green or dying back, getting ready for the rainy chill of winter. I smelled the sharpness of rosemary, she must have just harvested her sage too. In summer the garden was a riot of color, the property-line shields smooth and carefully woven, an obvious stronghold. Then again, I'd heard Sierra never left her house. I'd never seen or heard of her around town, and I didn't care either.

No, I came here for a different reason. I blinked against the gray sunlight, wished it was darker. Like most psions, I never feel quite myself during the day; a marker for nocturnalism crops up with amazing regularity in psion gene profiles. When darkness falls is when I feel most alive. At least that hadn't changed, even if everything else about me had.

I was glad I was back in time. I'd missed my appointment last month and been a little out of sorts ever since. I lifted my hand to knock at the door but the house shields had already flushed a warm, welcoming rose color, and the door pulled open. I pushed back a few stray strands of my damp hair and met Sierra Ignatius's eyes.

Her gaze was wide and pale blue, irises fading into the whites, the pupils sometimes flaring randomly. There was an odd film over her eyes; the sign of congenital blindness. Usually blindness is fixed with gene therapy during infancy, but for some reason she hadn't received the therapy then or in later years. Despite that, she moved around her little brick home with an accuracy and assurance some sighted people never achieve. Rumor had it that her parents had been Ludders, but I wasn't curious enough to find out. Her blindness made her, like me, an anomaly; it was probably why I allowed myself to come here.

"Danny!" She sounded calmly delighted, a short thin woman with thistledown hair and a thorn-laden cruciform tat on her left cheek. My cheek burned, my tat shifting. I felt another unwilling smile tug the corners of my mouth up. Sierra looked like a tiny pixie full of mischief, and her aura smelled of roses and wood ash, a clean human smell I somehow didn't mind as much as others. "I wondered if you'd come back. You missed last month."

Behind Sierra, taking her hand off the hilt of her short-sword, was a rangy female Shaman with the kind of tensile grace that shouted combat training and a tat that matched Sierra's. She inclined her chin gracefully, turned on her heel, and stamped away. Kore didn't like me, and the feeling was mutual. We'd tangled over a bounty once, one of her Skinlin friends I'd hauled in for murder and illegal genesplicing. She didn't hold a grudge but she didn't have to like me either, and whenever I showed up for my appointment, Kore took herself upstairs out of the way. I appreciated her restraint.

I would have hated to kill her.

"Sorry I missed last month." I stepped inside, took a deep lungful of kyphii incense and the smell of dried lavender. The air was still and close, and as soon as Sierra closed the outside world out I felt my shoulders relax fractionally. Her front hall was low and dim, candles burning in a niche under a statue of Aesclepius. The walls were wood paneling and the floor mellow hardwood. "I was out on a bounty."

"You've been out on a bounty since I've met you, sweetie. Come on back, the table's set up. What's hurting you today?" She was, as usual, all business, setting off past me with a confident step, faster than I could have gone with my eyes closed. I saw her aura fringing, sending out little fingers of awareness, the perfume of spiced Power trailed behind her, reminding me of Jace. We walked down the hall, through the neat little kitchen with its racks of potted herbs in the window and the suncatcher above lazily hanging on a string. Her counters were clean and the kitchen table clear except for two wine-red place-mats and a vase of white lilies that sent a shiver up my spine. There were few flowers I could see anymore without thinking of Santino.

"Hurting me?" As usual, I pretended to give the question my full attention as she led me into the round room at the back of the house, where a fountain of piled black stones dripped. She stepped down onto the plush carpet and moved into the middle of the room where the table sat, draped with fresh white sheets. *Hurting me? Nothing, really. Only my shoulder. My hand. My heart.* "Not much. I feel pretty okay."

"Liar. All right." She smoothed the sheets, a habitual movement. "What do you want me to work on?"

I shrugged, remembered she couldn't see the motion. Slid out of my coat, hung it up on the peg by the door, and undid my rig with the clumsy fingers of my right hand. "My back, whatever else. Like usual. Just work your magic, that's all."

Sierra cocked her pale pixie head, listening as I hung my bag and my rig up. "Cordite," she noted mildly. "And I can smell that sweet stuff. You got clipped?"

I found myself smiling again. I could remember going months without smiling, before Rio. "You're amazing. Yeah, I'm a little dirty. Sorry." I leaned down, working my boots off with my right hand, then padded to the table in my sock feet. "Do you mind?"

If I had still been fully human, I would have had to chemwash to get the blood off. As it was, only my clothes were bloody; my skin had absorbed the thick black ichor. She, like all psions, could see the staining of black-diamond fire in my aura, marking me as something close to demon; she never asked me to chemwash, figuring whatever communicable nasties I had weren't dangerous to her. It was open wounds she had to watch out for, and I didn't have any of those.

Not on the outside, anyway.

"Of course not. Your back, you said. What about that left shoulder of yours?"

I reached up with my right hand, touched my shirt over the mark. "Leave that alone for right now." It was the standard answer, and as usual, she accepted it gracefully.

I stripped down, left my clothes on the straight-backed chair set to the side, and eased myself onto the thigh-high table, squirming onto my belly while Sierra pulled the sheet up over me. I'd told her she didn't have to leave while I disrobed, most psions are pretty comfortable with nakedness. I wasn't precisely uncomfortable, but taking her up on her offer to give me privacy while I undressed seemed weak. I fitted my face into the facecradle, seeing the carpet below me in the flickering wash of candlelight and my braid swinging to the side, and let out an involuntary sigh.

"I live for that sound." She folded the sheet down low on my hips. The bolster went underneath my ankles to take the stress off my lower back, and I sighed again. "Ooh, twice. Must have been a hard month."

"Yeah. Couple of bounties." I closed my eyes as she rubbed her hands together, heating them up, the warm good smell of almond oil blooming. She didn't scent the oil, for which I was grateful.

"Always working." She laid her hands flat on my back, one right between my shoulder blades, the other at the base of my spine. A few moments of pressure, then she rocked me back and forth a little, gauging the way my body mass responded. "Too tense, Danny. When are you going to learn to loosen up?"

"Perfectly flexible," I muttered. "Got to work to pay you, sweets."

It wasn't true, I had enough money now. I had all the money I could ever want. I didn't need the bounty fees. But oh, gods, I *did* need the bounties.

She moved to the head of the table. Then what I'd been waiting for . . . she leaned in and smoothed both her hands down on either side of my spine, digging into my muscles under the tough, perfect golden skin. I let out another sigh. Her hands were cool and forgiving, my skin warmer than hers because of the hiked metabolism. I shivered with delight as she started the usual routine, kneading at me. My right hand relaxed and dangled off the table as I let go, fraction by fraction, Sierra's hands seeking out knots and nodes of tension.

Gabe had bought me my initial consultation with Sierra, and I'd thought it a frivolous gift even after she bullied and dragged me to the red-painted door at the appointed time. The first two-hour massage had ended with me in a languid puddle, more relaxed than I could ever remember. I'd gone home whistling, arrived at my door in the closest thing to a good mood I'd had since before Rio, and promptly burst into tears on my way upstairs. Thank the gods Jace had been out shopping for groceries. I'd locked myself in the bathroom and had a completely uncharacteristic fit of sobbing, then took a long hot shower. As dawn had risen through my bedroom window, I had fallen asleep for the first time in weeks, a thin restless troubled sleep but sleep nonetheless.

That did it, I was hooked. I came back once a month unless I was on a bounty, and each time it was the same: her delicate iron fingers digging into me, smoothing me out. Hers was a touch I didn't have to fend off or worry about what it cost me. I paid her, she touched me, it was that simple. Even and uncomplicated.

Why couldn't everything be like that?

"Are you staying in town long?" Her voice was soft, if I chose not to talk she would be silent.

"A while. Don't know when the next bounty's coming up." I felt the involuntary quiver go through me. She must have, too, because her touch gentled.

"Too much pressure?"

You couldn't hurt me if you tried, Shaman. At least, not without steel or a plasgun and a whole lot of luck. "No. Not too much." *I wish I knew exactly what I was. I wish Japhrimel would have had time to tell me.*

There I was again, thinking about him. I let out a long soft breath, keeping my eyes closed. "Just thinking," I explained, grudgingly.

"About?" Again, the soft tone; if I parried the question she'd let it drop.

About a demon. About a Fallen demon, a dead demon, that I only knew for a short time but I can't stop thinking about. He won't leave me alone. And neither will the only other man I ever loved, the one that betrayed me so honorably. A ghost I can't have and a man I can't touch, and skipping from bounty to bounty isn't helping any. "About the past."

A soft laugh. She kept working at my back, smoothing down the muscles, moving to one side or the other and using her elbow or the flat of her forearm, her entire weight pressing down through tough skin. "Never a comfortable subject."

That's the understatement of the year, sunshine. "No." I shifted in the facecradle a little, the emerald grafted into my cheek digging into my flesh. She moved to my legs, flipping the sheet aside, and I swallowed dryly.

"You have great skin." Tactful of her to change the subject. The spicy smell of kyphii was stronger now, reminding me of Gabe's house. Gabe loved burning that stuff. "Lucky girl."

"Mh." A noncommittal sound in reply. She took the hint and the rest of the massage was spent in blissful silence on her side and increasingly ill-tempered brooding on mine.

It was the bounties that were bothering me, I tried to tell myself. Jace was beginning to look a little ragged. Ten bounties in under six months, none of them cakewalks, and he hadn't uttered a word of protest. Not only that, but he'd insisted on coming along, and I'd caved each time. Allowing it, expecting it, treating him as if it was the old days when he had taught me how to track, how to let my intuition do the work for me, how to find a mark and stick on him, how to scent the prey and become the thing you hunted, how to find clients that would pay for things other than a legitimate tag but short of actual murder.

Admit it, Danny. You don't want to let him out of your sight. You're afraid he'll vanish and never come back, or that you'll come back to an empty house.

It was uncomfortably close to the truth. The fact that Jace never asked about Japhrimel only made it easier to pretend nothing was happening, that we were just living together. Just roommates with a good thing going, a lucrative bounty-hunting partnership and a carefully charted dance where he moved forward and I retreated, but never fast or far enough.

Was he waiting for me to forget Japhrimel?

It was only a few days, Danny. And he was a demon. He lied to you about Doreen's daughter, about Santino, about Lucifer's plans. What is it with the men I fall for and their aversion to truth?

"Time to turn over," Sierra said softly, and I did while she held the sheet; then she slipped the bolster under my knees and started working on the front of my legs. The sound of water from the fountain in the corner soothed me, just like the smell of kyphii and Sierra's strong fingers. She knew just where the aches were. *What I would have given to know about this when I was human.* But when I was human I never would have let anyone do this to me, even if I was paying them and thus absolving myself of obligation.

She even massaged my abdomen but left my shoulder alone, and I didn't glance down to see the fluid glyph in its pretty scarred lines, looking more like a decoration than a brand, the mark of a demon. *Is it his Name?* I wondered, not for the first time. *Or is it "best opened by this date"? Lucifer put it on me, like Nichtvren mark their thralls. Maybe it's like a brand.* A swift spill of feeling roiled through my stomach, revulsion and heat all mixed into one pretty package. Japhrimel's mouth on mine, his skin against mine, the semaphore of desire that needed no translation . . . My rings flashed, went back to swirling lazily; my aura rang with the twisted black-diamond flames of demon and the sparkles that meant Necromance. I looked like nothing else in the landscape of Power now.

The massage ended with Sierra taking my hair out of its braid and rubbing my scalp. I had never known what kind of tension lurked in the thin tendons and flat muscles over the cranium. It was unreal. By far my most favorite moment of the massage was when she undid my braid; it was like having Doreen play with my hair again.

Doreen. It was turning out to be a day of unpleasant memories all around. I wished Trina at the agency would call in with the news that she'd scouted me another bounty. There *had* to be a job out there that would keep me going so fast I didn't have time to slow down and brood.

And remember. Memory, rage, guilt. The holy trinity, as far as I was concerned. Good fuel, channeled into bounties and justice. Hadn't I ever felt something softer?

Well, we could add shame to the list, couldn't we? My shame, that I was still grieving for a dead demon I hadn't known more than a few days, who had augmented me into something even my best friends had a hard time looking at.

I sighed as Sierra's fingers trailed through my hair, regretfully. "Better?" she asked.

"Much." I made a mental note to tip her 40 percent this time. I opened my eyes, my left hand curling as if seeking a slim sheathed shape. It was a reflex, as if I hadn't just spent almost a year without a sword. My right hand wasn't cramping either. It had straightened out, the fingers relaxed. The mark lay cold and quiescent against the hollow of my shoulder. "Thanks, Sierra."

"No problem. Want some tea, or would you like to let yourself out?"

So tactful. "I'd better let myself out. Thanks."

"You're very welcome, Danny. See you next month." She retreated, trailing the spiky spicy smell of Shaman and the decaying smell of human with her. I took another deep lungful of kyphii and exhaled into the dark air, staring at the white-painted ceiling. The door closed softly behind her, and I rested there against the table for a moment.

See if Trina can find another quick job. Just one more, I told myself. *Then it might be time for a vacation. Close up and magseal the house, go to the islands or something. Start chasing down more Magi shadowjournals and break their codes, see if any of them know what you are. Maybe even see if there's a Magi circle that will apprentice you, even if you are too old. Your initial training's sound, you're not rusty, and who knows how long you'll live now? Demons are virtually immortal unless killed by violence or suicide. Who knows how long I'll be around?*

I hated that thought. It usually waited until the middle of the day while I was trying to sleep, to show up.

All right, Valentine. Get your ass in gear, you need to go home and change. I surged up off the table, taking the sheet with me, was dressed in five minutes and fully-armed in another five. I would let myself out the back door and through the back gate, up to Ninth, cut through the University District to stretch my legs while I did some thinking. I thought best while moving, and that would get me home in time to get some serious trash holovid-viewing in. I tapped my datband, paying Sierra's fee and tacking

40 percent on for a tip; I'd have Trina schedule me another appointment next month.

Outside, the afternoon was wet and fragrant, the smells of Sierra's garden temporarily overwhelming the drowsing stink of Saint City air. I glanced up at the sky, scanned my surroundings out of habit, and felt my shoulders come up under the habitual burden of tension as I stepped back into my life.

3

*T*wo days later, the buzzing sound jolted me out of an uneasy thready half-trance. Jace muttered something next to me, blowing out between pursed lips. I rolled over, checked the clock, and sighed. The cotton sheets tangled around my legs, I'd been tossing again.

Three PM. Another drunken night of watching old *Indiana Jones, Magi* and *Father Egyptos* holovids shot to hell. There had been a letter in the afternoon mail, an un-addressed vellum envelope with a heavy bloodred wax seal. Even as I picked it up, I'd caught a whiff of heavy, spicy scent. *Demon.* My hands had moved despite myself, trembling, and torn the heavy beautiful envelope open.

Careful scripted calligraphy marched across thick linen paper. *Dante. I would speak to you.* And signed, simply, *L.* As if I wouldn't know who it was from.

The Prince of Hell. Lucifer himself, sending me a little note. I'd tried to tell myself I didn't care, tossed it in the garbage compacter, and matched Jace drink for drink.

Not like it helped. I couldn't even get drunk.

Jace muttered again and turned away, presenting me with his broad, muscled back. The scorpion tattoo on his left shoulder blade shifted uneasily, its black-edged stinger flexing. Thin lines of pale scarring traced across muscle hard as tile, marring skin that had never lost its Nuevo Rio tan. He'd collapsed on my bed for once because the room down the hall was too far away when he was that inebriated. Besides, it was almost soothing to hear him breathing next to me while I lay and tried to sleep, achieving at most a half-trance that tried to rest the mind and left me feeling almost as tired as when I started.

Something's up. Instinct raced along my spine, my rings flashed. A golden spark popped from the amber cabochon on my left middle finger. Of *course* something was up, nobody would call me in the late afternoon unless something was up. And no holomarketer would call a registered psion's number, we tended to be a bad return on that advertising dollar. Even though it was illegal to hex a normal out of spite, some of us had a nasty habit of disregarding possible legal action when it came to bloody holomarketing jackals. It was also expensive for corporations to keep the required coverage that would bring a psion out to remove the hex.

My left shoulder ached, a sudden fresh bite of coldness burning all the way down to the bone. If I touched it, I might almost feel the ropes of scar moving under my fingers. I refrained from touching it, as usual, and shifted position, rolling the shoulder in its socket as I shook the almost-dream away. The phone shrilled again, the most annoying buzz I'd heard in a long time.

I scooped up the receiver, cursing at whoever had thought it was a good idea to plug in a phone up here. It had seemed like a good idea at the time. Which meant I

was muttering imprecations at myself. *"Sekhmet sa'es.
What?"*

All things considered, it was as polite as I could get. I
never use the vid capability on modern phones if I can
help it, the thought of someone seeing me inside my own
private house without having to get in a goddamn hover
and come out just rubbed me the wrong way.

Plus, if I want to answer the phone naked, it's nobody's
business but mine.

"Danny." Gabe's voice. Of all the people I could identify
with one word, she was at the top of the list. She sounded
strained and urgent. "Get your ass up. I need you."

I sat bolt upright, dragging the sheet away from Jace,
who made a low, sleepy sound of protest and curled into a
tighter ball. "Where?"

Click of a lighter, inhaled breath. She was smoking
again. Bad news. "I'm at the station. How soon can you
be here?"

I reached over, shook Jace's shoulder. His skin was
cool under mine, my lacquered fingernails scraping
slightly. He woke up a little more gracefully than I did,
sitting up, sheathing the knife he kept under his pillow as
soon as he realized I was on the phone instead of under attack. We were both jumpy; going from bounty to bounty
will do that to you.

"I'm on my way," I told her. "Hang loose."

She hung up. I dropped the phone back into its cradle
and stretched, the ligaments in my right hand cracking as
I tried to spread the fingers all the way. I hadn't been
dreaming, but it had been the closest I'd gotten to real
sleep for a good three weeks, and I didn't like having it

interrupted. Bounties weren't good for resting; sleep usually meant your prey was getting away.

Then again, I've always had bad dreams; the only stretch of good sleep I've ever had was when Doreen lived with me. A *sedayeen* could tranquilize even the unruliest Necromance, and that was one more thing I missed about her: the gentleness in the middle of the night when she calmed me down from a nightmare and sent me back into grateful blackness.

I could count the time I'd spent with Japhrimel, but we hadn't done a whole lot of sleeping.

"What's up now?" Jace sounded sleepy, but he slid his legs out of the bed and grabbed his jeans. I was already across the room, pulling a fresh shirt off the hanger with no memory of the intervening space. I'd blinked through the room again, using inhuman speed. *Got to stop doing that.*

Ten months and counting, and I still wasn't used to it. I remembered just how eerily, spookily *quick* Japhrimel could move, and wondered if I looked the same way when my body blinked through space and my mind tried to catch up. *A piece of my power,* he'd said. *To make you stronger, less easy to damage.*

If it wasn't for that gift I might be dead now. Lucky Danny Valentine, tougher than your average psion.

"Gabe. At the station. Wants us there *now.*" I didn't need to yawn, but I did take a deep breath, wondering where the weariness came from. If I didn't need to sleep, why should I be tired?

Did part-demons need sleep? None of the Magi shadow-journals or demonology books could tell me, and hunting down bounties was cutting into my research time in a big way. But research just gave me too goddamn much time to fret.

"Fuck." Jace yawned, stretched. He stripped wheat-gold hair back from his face, yanked his shirt down, and shrugged into his assassin's rig. Oiled, supple leather; guns, knives—my own hands moved automatically. My right hand throbbed uneasily until I shook it out, joints cracking and popping. I ducked my head through the strap of my black canvas bag and had to stop, taking another deep breath, settling the strap diagonally across my body.

Maybe it was another bounty. I hoped it was another bounty. A big one, a complex one, one that would keep me occupied with the next thing to be done, and the next, and the next.

It didn't matter. I jerked my coat from its hook, shrugged into it. My two main knives rode in their sheaths; the guns easy and loose in my rig, and my rings popped a few more golden sparks. Familiar excitement mixed with dread deep in my belly, tainted the air I blew out between my teeth.

"Did she say anything else?" Jace rubbed his face, yawning again. His aura rippled, the spiky darkness of a Shaman prickling the air. My own cloak of energy responded, singing an almost-audible answer. "I mean, do I need to bring the rifle?"

"No." I plunged my fingers in my bag and checked for extra ammo clips, the plasgun didn't need them but the projectile weapons did. Sunlight glowed under the edges of my bedroom blinds; I felt logy and slow, as I usually did during the day. "Just your staff. If she needed your rifle she wouldn't have dialed, she'd have shown up personally."

"Good point." How did the man sound so casually amused, especially after drinking three quarters of a bottle of Chivas Red? I could still smell the sourness of his body and Power metabolizing the alcohol, running through the depressant, converting the sugars. "Fuck. I think I'm still drunk, Danny."

"Good." I stuffed another two ammo clips into my bag. It pays to be prepared. "That'll keep you relaxed. Let's go."

4

Late-afternoon sun made Jace's hair glow like a furnace. I blinked, rubbing at my eyes, and slid out of the cab while Jace finished paying the bespectacled cabby. The man had taken a fifty-credit tip to get us to the Saint City South station in record time. My stomach was still churning. Thank the gods part-demons didn't throw up often.

Or at least, I didn't, and I was the only one I knew of. It made sweeping generalizations a whole lot easier. I've never been a fan of sweeping generalizations, but I'm all in favor of efficiency.

Jace clambered out, stood next to me as the cab lifted off and zipped into the traffic lanes, its underside glowing with hovercells and reactive paint. I took a deep breath of the stink that passed for air in Saint City, full of the effluvia of dying cells, the cloying smell of decay—my nose wanted to wrinkle. I let out a short whistle, my rings swirling with steady light.

"Would you look at that." Jace scratched at his hairline with blunt fingers. He tapped his staff once, sharply, on the sidewalk pavement, making a sound like two antique billiard balls smacking together.

Gabriele Spocarelli was waiting for us. She stood on the steps of the police station, a short woman, slim and graceful as a ballai dancer, her sleek dark hair cut in a short bob that framed her classically pretty face. There was a faint shadow of crow's-feet at the edges of her dark eyes, and her air of serene precision had deepened—if that was possible. A cigarette hung from the corner of her chiseled mouth, unlit.

Yep. She's not happy. If she'd lit the cigarette it would have been different. But unlit cigarette plus strained, tense shoulders and an aura singing with blue-violet under its Necromance sparkles all added up to a very unhappy Gabriele.

Her emerald flashed a greeting. The tattoo on her left cheek shifted slightly, inked lines running on her pale skin. My left cheek burned, the emerald flickering in response, sending an electric zing all the way down to my neckbones. Power shifted, stained the air with electricity.

I approached cautiously, my right hand starting to ache. It was a normal ache, so I ignored it. She watched us both come up the steps, unmoving, her aura flushed a deep purple-red like a bruise.

Nope. Gabe was not amused.

"Well," Jace said from behind me. "Still as pretty as ever, Spooky. How's Eddie?"

"Monroe." She tilted her head slightly, the only mark of respect she'd give him. Neither she nor Eddie had forgiven Jace his treachery, his connection to the demon who had killed Doreen and damn near killed me as well—but they were civil for my sake. I'd only presided over one short, strained meeting six months ago, where we hashed out that nobody was going to kill anyone else and all accounts balanced. Jace hadn't known that the head of the Mob Family he'd run from was Vardimal Santino, and just this once, we agreed, the circumstances were extraordinary enough that Jace could get a pass.

Well, Gabe and I had agreed. Eddie simply glowered and quit threatening to kill him. We were all a lot happier when just Gabe and I met at Fa Choy's once a week.

Gabe's eyes cut away, as if she couldn't bear to look at him anymore. "Sends his greetings. You made good time."

I shrugged. "What good are ill-gotten gains if you can't use 'em?" The sunlight blurred as my pupils reacted, squeezing down to pinpricks. That was one thing about having excellent demon vision—bright lights were more painful than ever. "What's up? I assume you didn't call me out here to stand around chatting."

"Fuck you too." She tore the unlit cigarette out of her mouth and tossed it into the trash-laden gutter, maybe for effect, maybe because she was too upset to remember she hadn't lit it. If it was a gesture, it was a grand one; my mouth curled up in an unwonted smile, my cheek burning as the tattoo settled again. "Come on up."

We followed her up the steps and into the police station. Old blue linoleum flecked with little sparkles squeaked underfoot. Fluorescents buzzed—they didn't have the budget for full-spectrum lights in the halls where normals worked, and I shuddered at the thought of working under that soulless light day after day. I followed at Gabe's iron-straight back and felt my hands shake slightly with the urge to touch a knifehilt, caress the smooth butt of a gun. It wasn't like her to be rude. It doubly wasn't like her to call and demand my presence. We met once a week, when I wasn't out chasing bad guys, had dinner, carefully didn't talk about Nuevo Rio or demons. Instead, we traded stories about bounties, bullshitted, and kept a careful distance that was as welcome as it was teeth-grindingly annoying. But I couldn't complain. The distance was there because of me.

Because of what I'd become.

My back prickled slightly, uneasy; fine hairs rising on my nape and the coppery tang of demon adrenaline in my mouth. I could feel it trembling on the edges of my awareness, the scorching smell of fate like the kick of hard liquor against the back of my throat.

Just like a bounty.

Up on the third floor, the Spook Squad hung out. They weren't chained in the basement like in the old days—no, now the parapsychic arm of law enforcement had corner offices, a good budget, and decent equipment at last. Computer decks hummed on desks buried under drifts of paperwork, full-spectrum lamps sat on every desk. I saw a Shaman with a staff made of twisted ironwood prop his boots on his desk, leaning back in his chair, his aura swirling red-orange; three Ceremonials clustered at the watercooler, laughing about something. All three of them wore sidearms—police-issue plasguns—and long black synthwool coats, their accreditation tattoos shifting on their cheeks. The air resonated with Power, my rings sparked again. Heads turned as I followed Gabe.

They weren't stupid and head-dead like normals. Even if they couldn't name what it was, they could see the twisting black-diamond patterns staining my aura like geometric flames.

Part-demon. Unique, even among psions. I could have done without the honor.

We reached Gabe's cubicle, and she dropped into her cushioned ergonomic chair. She pointed at the two folding chairs on the other side of her desk. "Take a load off." Her mouth turned into a hard line. The expression didn't do anything for her pretty face, but it would take a lot more than that to make Gabe look ugly. "You want some coffee?"

I shook my head. My braid tapped against my back. "Jace?"

"Chango, I need a beer." He shook his head, leaning his staff against the cubicle wall. The bones tied to the raffia twine crowning the length of oak clacked uneasily. "But no. What the hell's goin' on, Spooky?"

"I've got a case." Her voice was pitched low and fierce. "I need you, Danny."

Now I wasn't just uneasy. I was heading into full-blown *alarmed.* "What for?" I was curious too. It wasn't like her to pussyfoot.

She pushed the file toward me. There were only one or two clear spots, the rest of the desk taken up with paperwork, a nice custom Pentath computer deck, an inlaid-wood box that probably held a mismatched double set of tarot cards (Gabe was secondarily talented as a tarot witch), an in-box buried under more paper, and two dusty, full bottles of brandy perched precariously near the edge. "Take a look."

I sighed, scooped up the file. "You're a real lady of mystery, aren't you." Flipped it open, the smooth manila giving under my black-painted nails. My back wasn't crawling with gooseflesh—for some reason my new demon body didn't have the reflex—but the sensation of prickling on my skin still remained, a human sensation I would have been glad for if it hadn't been so creepy. To feel goosebumps rising under your skin but unable to press through to the surface is weird, like a phantom limb complete with ghost pain and a reflexive shudder.

They were homicide lasephotos. Of course—Gabe was a Necromance. What else?

The first photo was of a man. Or I assumed it was a man, once I took a closer look at the shape. "Anubis," I breathed, as the shapes snapped into a horrible picture behind my eyes. The worst part wasn't the loops of intestine or the pool of blood. The worst part was one outflung hand, unwounded, the fingers clutching air. The arm was a mess of meat flayed off the glaring-white bone.

Gods above, that's gruesome. "Gods above. When was this?"

"Four months ago. Keep going."

Jace shifted slightly, his chair squeaking. He knew better than to ask. I'd give him the file when I was good and done.

I flipped through a coroner's report, a standard parapsych incident report, the homicide report, neatly laseprinted. No real leads, nothing of much interest except the savagery. Finally, I looked up at Gabe. "Well?"

She pushed another file across her desk. With a sinking heart I handed the first one to Jace and took the second; Gabe's eyes were dead level and gave nothing away. "This one's about eight weeks old."

Jace whistled out through his teeth, a long low note. "Damn." From someone who had seen the type of carnage Jace Monroe had, it was almost a compliment.

I flipped open the second file. "Fuck." My voice held disgust and just a trace of something stronger—maybe fear. Paper stirred uneasily on her desk, stroked into motion by the tension in the air.

This one was even worse, if it were possible. The body lay, exposed and raw, spread-eagled on what appeared to be a cement floor. "Look past the body." Gabe's tone was soft, respectful of the corpse on the two-dimensional glossy paper.

It was hard, but I did. I saw the blurred edges of a chalk diagram, right at the very margin of the photo. I flipped to the next one—the photographer had pulled back, and I could see the chalk lines clearly. It was a double circle, inscribed with fluid spiky runes that twisted from one form to another even as I watched. Even through the lasephoto they seemed to hum with malignant force. They weren't symbols I knew.

That's not from the Nine Canons, I thought, and my skin seemed to roughen with gooseflesh again. I was secondarily talented as a runewitch, and the runes that made up the acceptable and studied branches of rune magick were mostly instantly-recognizable to me. Most psions have a good working knowledge of the Canons, since runes have been used since before the Awakening, when psionic and magickal power began to be a lot more reliable and a lot stronger in certain talented humans. A rune used for so many years, for so many psions, is a good shortcut when you need a quick and dirty spell effect. Not to mention the Major Works of magick that required perfect performance of drawing, defining, naming, and charging runes.

I reached up with my aching right hand and touched my left shoulder, massaging at the constant cold ache of the demon glyph through my shirt. "Looks like Ceremonial work, the double circle and runes." My eyes moved over the picture. A pile of something wrinkled lay off to one side. "Is that what I think . . ." *Don't. Don't tell me it is.*

"The fucker flayed her." Gabe pushed another file at me. My gorge rose, I squeezed it back down. *I don't throw up,* I reminded myself. *I hate throwing up.*

I was grateful that thirty years of that habit was hard to break. I scanned the remainder of the second file and handed it to Jace. Then I took the third one.

"This one was last night," Gabe said tightly. "Brace yourself, Danny."

I opened the file and felt all the blood drain from my face.

Gabe watched me, dry-eyed and fierce. Her tension stirred the dust in her office, made it swirl in graceful patterns in the climate-controlled air. This keyed-up, with the sharp powerful scent of Power on her, she smelled like pepper and musk. It wasn't so bad, not like the usual human stink. I'd toyed with the idea of becoming a Tester to keep my hand in, since I could now smell Power and psionic talent instead of just seeing and feeling it with human senses. That sort of work wouldn't give me an adrenaline jag and keep me from thinking, so the application papers still lay on top of my laseprinter, half-finished.

It can't be. I turned to the coroner's report. There it was in black and white, the name of the victim who had been dismembered in the middle of a circle, bones and gristle and muscle torn into unrecognizable shapes, a murder of exceeding savagery all the more chilling because it was done to a psion like me. However shattered and wrecked the body was, there was just enough of her face for me to recognize.

Christabel Moorcock.

A Necromance.

Like me.

5

"Sekhmet sa'es," I breathed, looking down at the photographs. "This is . . ."

"Does it look familiar, Danny? You're way into scholarship these days, can't drag your nose out of books when you're not out trying to kill yourself with bounties. Does it look like *anything* you've read about? Seen before?" Gabe's eyebrows drew together, her mouth tight. She pulled out another cigarette and tucked it behind her ear, the slight smell of dry synth hash mixing with the aroma of the citronel shampoo she used.

I stared at the picture, my eyes heavy and grainy. "No. I've never seen anything like this. I've been studying demons, old legends, Magi stuff. When I'm not working bounties." Tore my eyes away from the pitiless image. "But that's not why you called me down here."

Gabe's voice was heavy. "We've got Christabel down in the morgue. I need you to bring her out so I can question her."

Jace went completely still beside me. On any other day I might have found that funny. Or touching.

I swallowed bitterness. Rubbed at my left shoulder as

if trying to scrub the scar away with my shirt. "Gabe . . ."
I sounded like I'd been punched breathless.

There wasn't much on earth that could hurt me these
days, not since Japh had changed me. Changed, gene-
spliced, molded into something new—but my heart was
still human. It pounded under a tough, flexible cage of
ribs, my pulse thready in my wrists and throat. Pounding
so hard I felt a little faint.

"I know it's hard for you," Gabe continued. "Since . . .
since Rio. Please, Danny. I can't do it, I've tried, there's
just . . . not enough body. Or some kind of wall, some
barrier. I can't do it. You can. Please."

I stared at the photo. I hadn't gone into Death for ten
months.

Not since Nuevo Rio, hunched on a wide, white blazing-
stone plaza running with sunlight, sobbing as I prayed. I
remembered cinnamon smoke drifting in the air, as the
demon's body in my arms crumbled bit by bit.

That was a memory I usually kept to torment myself
during long, slow daylight while I tried to sleep. I shoved
it away, shut my eyes, opened them again. Shapes jum-
bled in front of me, my vision blurring. My god still accepted my offerings, but I had not gone into His halls.

Sekhmet sa'es, *Danny, call it what it is.* My heart
pounded thinly, my eyes unfocused. *You're afraid that if
you go into Death, Japhrimel might be waiting for you.*

"Danny?" The concern in Jace's voice was also equally
amusing and touching. Did he think I was going to pass
out? Start to scream?

Was I? I felt close. Damn close.

I blinked. I was staring at the photo. Gabe was sweating now, tendrils of her sleek dark hair sticking to her

forehead. The temperature in the room had gone up at least ten degrees. The climate control would kick on soon and blow frigid air through the vents. Power blurred out from my skin, Power and heat and a smoky fragrance of demon. Tierce Japhrimel had smelled like amber musk and burning cinnamon; I smelled like fresh cinnamon and a lighter musk. *Demon lite, half the Power, all the nasty attitude,* the humorous voice that accompanied bad news rang out inside my head.

I felt my chest constrict as the vision rose in front of me—ash drifting up from white marble, a hot breeze lifting smudges and scatters of it. Ash and the single, restrained curve of a black urn, left as a final cruel joke.

My right hand twisted into a claw.

I owed her too much to easily walk away from. Gabe was old-school. She'd gone with me into hell and nearly been eviscerated on the way. She hadn't ever uttered a word of anger at my rudeness or my distance or about the fact that she'd almost died because of my hellbent need for revenge on Santino. Or about the fact that I held her at arm's length, refusing to talk about Rio or demons or anything else of any real importance that lay in the air between us, charged and ready to leap free.

"I don't know, Gabe." *Why is my voice shaking? My voice never shakes.* "I haven't gone . . . there . . . for a while."

And I missed it. I missed communing with my god, feeling ever-so-briefly the weight of living taken from me. I made my offerings and kept my worship, and every once in a while when I meditated the blue light of Death would weave subtle traceries through the darkness behind my eyes, a comfort familiar from my childhood.

But still, if I went into Death, what would I meet on the bridge between this world and the next? Would I see a tall slim man in a long dark coat, his golden hands clasped behind his back as he considered me, his eyes flaring first green, then going dark? Would he tell me he'd been waiting for me?

You will not leave me to wander the earth alone. But he'd left me, burned to death, crumbled in my arms. Seeing him in Death's country would make it final. Too final. Too *unbearably* final.

"You're the best, Danny. You can even hold an apparition out of a box of cremains, you've *always* been the best. *Please.*" Gabe never begged, but her tone was dangerously close. She didn't even shift in her chair, leaning forward, her elbows on her desk. *She's ready for action,* I realized, and wondered just how tense and staring I looked. I was bleeding heat into the air, a demon's trick.

It wasn't just that Gabe was asking me. I closed Christabel's file and met her eyes squarely. At least she didn't flinch. Gabe was perhaps the only person that could look me in the eyes without flinching.

She still saw *me.* For Gabe, I hadn't changed. I was still Danny Valentine, under the carapace of golden skin and demonic beauty. She wasn't afraid of me—treated me no differently than she had ever since we'd become friends. For Gabe, I would always be the same person; the person she had dropped everything, leveraged her personal contacts, and hared off to Rio for. She had never even considered letting me face Santino by myself.

I would go into Death just for that reason alone.

I looked away. "What else is going on, Gabe? Come clean."

"Can't fool you, can I?" She shrugged, reaching again for her crumpled pack of cigarettes. She couldn't smoke in here, but she tapped the pack twice, a habitual gesture both soothing and oddly disturbing. I had never seen her this distracted. "It's not much, Danny. If I had anything more to work with . . ."

"Give it up." I sounded harsh, my voice throbbing at the lower registers of "human." The brandy bottles chattered against the desktop, my right hand ached. I wished the alcohol would do me some good. If it would have, I would have reached for it.

"Moorcock was found in her apartment. I searched the place, of course, and found exactly nothing. Except this." She held out a folded piece of pale-pink linen paper.

I took it, the black molecule-drip polish on my nails reflecting stripes of fluorescent light. Actually, they looked like nails, but they were claw-tips, just another mark of how far away from human I'd been dragged. My rings shimmered. They were always awake now, not just when the atmosphere was charged—though the air in here was heavy enough with Power and tension to qualify. I was radiating, and so was she. The line of force between us was almost palpable. Jace, of course, lounged like a big blond cat, smelling hungover and human with a soupçon of musk and male thrown in; spiky, spicy Power contained and deadly within a Shaman's thorny aura.

I caught a fleeting impression from the paper—a wash of terror perfumed like cloying lilacs, an impression of a woman. Necromances are an insular community, for all that we're loners and neurotic prima donnas. We *have* to be a community. Even among psions, the juncture of

talent and genetics that makes a Necromance is unusual. I
had known Christabel peripherally for most of my life.

The paper was torn on one corner. I gingerly opened it,
as if it held a snake.

It pays to be careful.

I looked at it. All the breath slammed out of me again.
"Fuck," I let out a strangled yelp.

Her handwriting was ragged, as if she'd been in a hell
of a hurry. Great looping, spiky letters, done in dragonsblood ink; the pen had dug deep furrows in the paper. Like
claw marks.

Black Room, it said. And below, in huge thick capitals,
*REMEMBER REMEMBER RIGGER HALL REMEMBER
RIGGER HALL REMEMBER REMEMBER—*

There was a long trailing slash at the end of the last letter, daggering downward as if she'd been dragged away
while still trying to write.

I gasped for breath. The lunatic mental image of my
body flopping on the floor like a landed fish receded; I
forced my lungs to work. The world had gone gray and
dim, wavering through a sheet of frosted glass. My back
hurt, three lines of fire; another throbbing pain right in the
crease of my left buttock. *No. No, I don't have those scars
anymore. I don't. I DON'T.*

It took me a few moments, but I finally managed to
breathe again. I looked up at Gabe, who sat still and solemn behind her desk, her dark eyes full of terrible guilt.
"Fuck." This time I sounded more like myself, only savagely tired.

Only like I'd been hit and lost half my air.

Gabe nodded. "I know you went there. Before they had
the big court case and the Hegemony closed it down.

Moorcock was a few years older than you, she actually testified at the inquiry."

My mouth was dry as desert sand. "I know," I said colorlessly. "*Sekhmet sa'es*, Gabe. This is . . ."

"Blast from the past?" For once her humor didn't make me feel better.

Nothing would make this feel better.

I realized I was rubbing at my left shoulder with my wounded right hand, fiercely, as if trying to scrub away the persistent ache. I stopped, dropping my hand into my lap as I examined the paper again. There was a tiny wardglyph at the top of the page, sketched hastily. It held no Power—it hadn't been charged.

Maybe she'd been interrupted by whatever had torn her body apart. Whatever. *Who*ever.

Could a person do this? I'd seen some horrible things done to the human body, but this was . . .

"When did she write this?" *I actually sound like myself again, maybe because I can't breathe enough to talk. Hallelujah. All I have to do is get the wind knocked out of me, and I'll sound normal. Simple.*

"We can't tell," Gabe said. "We had Handy Mandy try it, but she just passed out. When she came to, she said it was too thick and headed straight for a date with the bottle, hasn't sobered up since. It was on Moorcock's desk in her bedroom; she was in the living room when she was . . . killed. There was no sign of forced entry—her shields were still in place, fading but still in place, and ripped from the *inside*."

From the inside? "So it was someone she knew?" I wanted to rub at my shoulder again, stopped myself with an effort that made my aching fingers twitch. I smelled something new on the air.

Fear. A sharp, sweaty stink, as if I were tracking a bounty.

Except it was my own.

Gabe's eyes were darker than usual, the line between her eyebrows deepening. "We don't know, Danny."

"What about the other two victims?"

"They're . . . interesting, too. The first one—Bryce Smith—was registered as normal. Except he lived in a house with some mighty fine shielding, but he had none of those damn chalk marks around his body. And the second, Yasrule—she was one of Polyamour's girls." Gabe's mouth twisted down briefly.

Mine did the same. Polyamour, the transvestite queen of the sex trade in Santiago City. It wasn't her fault, sexwitches were born sexwitches, and the psionic community was too hated as a whole by normals for us to consider shunning our own. Still . . . I was glad I hadn't been born as one of them.

"A normal, a sexwitch, and a Necromance." I shook my head. A stray strand of silken ink-black hair fell in my face, I pushed it back impatiently. "Gods."

"We can't get anything else from the scenes," Gabe said. "That's when your name came up."

Lovely. The cops call me in when all else fails. Am I supposed to feel honored? The sarcasm didn't help. I swallowed sourness again, looked down at the pale-pink paper. Gabe had made no move to take it back.

REMEMBER RIGGER HALL. The writing glared up at me, accusing. I didn't want to remember that place. I'd done everything I could to forget it, to go on with my life.

I wish I could tell her I'd do this just because she asked me. I tossed the paper back onto her desk, as if it had burned my fingers. I wouldn't have been surprised if it had.

The phone shrilled just as I opened my mouth to tell her I couldn't take the fucking case. I *couldn't*. Nothing could induce me to even *think* about Rigger Hall for longer than absolutely necessary. As a matter of fact, I was eyeing the brandy, wondering how much more than two bottles it would take before the liquor would have some effect. I'd lost interest at about six last time. I suspected I couldn't drink fast enough to cloud my Magi-trained, demon-enhanced memory. Not with my fucking metabolism.

"Spocarelli," she snarled into the receiver. A long pause. "Fuck me . . . You're sure?" Her eyes drifted up and met mine, and for an instant I saw through her calm.

There were dark circles under her eyes, and her pale skin had a pasty tone she'd never had before. Her collarbones jutted out, and so did the cords in her neck. She was too thin—and there was something torn and frightened in her dark eyes.

Something terrified. And furious. She was a psionic cop, and something had killed two psions on her watch. A normal, maybe one of the Ludders, gone mad and deciding to murder instead of simply protest the existence of psions? But what normal human could do this *and* tear psionic shields from the inside?

Was it a vendetta springing up rank and foul from the deep filth of the place where I'd learned just how powerless a child could be? What revenge would wait this long and be this brutal? A group, working together? Or one person?

"Keep them off as long as you can," she said finally. "I've got Valentine in here right now. We're heading to the morgue." Another long pause. "Okay. See ya."

She dropped the phone back into its cradle with excessive care. "That was the Captain. The holovids have gotten wind of this."

I winced. Then I opened my mouth to say, *No. I can't do it. Find someone else.*

Instead, what came out was, "You weren't at Rigger Hall, Gabe." I knew her career like I knew my own, like I knew John Fairlane's. Necromances were rare among psions, we listened for news about one another. If Christabel Moorcock was dead, there were only three left in the city, two of them in this very office.

Of course Gabe hadn't gone to Rigger Hall, she hadn't been poor or orphaned.

"No." A flush rose to her cheeks. "I went to Stryker. My mom's trust fund, you know. But . . . Eddie went to Rigger."

Eddie. Her boyfriend. The Skinlin.

He'd gone with us to Nuevo Rio, had almost lost Gabe to my quest for revenge, and been knocked around a good bit himself. And Eddie had been to Rigger—which meant he would have his own nightmares. The net of obligation closed tight around me.

Oh, fuck. "I guess we're going to the morgue."

I was rewarded with a look of relief so profound that I was sure Gabe didn't know how loudly her face was speaking.

Jace made no sound, but he hitched himself up to his

feet, scratching at his forehead under a shelf of tawny hair. He stretched slightly, his aura touching mine, thorn-spiked Power offered in case I needed it. I pushed the touch away—but gently. He didn't sway on his feet, but he did scoop his staff up and twirl it, the small bones clicking and clacking together. The familiar sound did nothing to comfort me.

"Hades," Gabe said, "I was afraid you'd—"

"I won't promise anything. It's been a while. I might not be able to do it, might need to practice before I can get back into the swing."

But I felt the tattoo shift on my face, its inked lines running under my skin, and knew I was lying.

6

The morgue was across the street, in the basement of a county administration building that looked as if it predated the Seventy Days War, graceless crumbling concrete and some oddly-shaped old glass windows instead of plasilica. Fine, thin clouds were beginning to blow in from the bay, and the sunlight had taken on a hazy quality. I could almost taste the barometric pressure dropping. Sudden shifts like that used to give me a headache.

I breathed in the stink of Saint City and once again felt the city press against my shields like a huge animal waiting to be stroked. The security net on the morgue building let us in, the armed guard in the foyer lowering his plascannon. Legal augments rippled and twitched under his black-mirror body armor. He had a chest the size of a small barrel of reactive and a pair of old optical augments set into his cheekbones, mirrored lenses that looked like sunglasses until their polarized magscan capability gave them away. The guard's lip curled behind Gabe's back as he saw us. I toyed with the idea of giving him a grin, decided against it. Gabe wouldn't like it if I got into a scuffle. Not to mention Jace was hungover—why make him fight? Besides, one normal with legal augments wasn't even a challenge, not anymore. Even if I didn't have a sword.

Gabe signed us in at the counter, staffed only by an AI receptionist deck in a gleaming steel humanoid casing. We were given plasilica one-liners to smooth over our datbands, and in we went.

Necromances don't like morgues, but they're bearable. At least inside a morgue there is cold steel and the clinical light of medical science. The aura of dispassionate research helps. Not like graveyards and funeral homes, where grief and confusion and agony and generations of pain dye the air a razor-grieving red. The holovids make it look like Necromances spend all their time illegally digging up bones in graveyards, but truth be told that's the *last* place you'd look for one of us. You'd have a better chance in a hospital or a lawyer's office.

Though hospitals aren't easy either. Any place soaked with pain and suffering isn't easy.

Jace's hand curled around my elbow when we got to the bottom of the staircase, a warm hard human touch. Gabe pushed though the swinging door and we followed her, boots clicking in uneven time over the same blue glittery linoleum as the police station. I didn't shake my arm free of Jace's touch all the way down the hall. The man was stubborn, following me on bounties and picking up after me. I didn't know what debt he thought he was paying.

I didn't even know what debt *I* was paying on now, I had so many due.

I pulled away from his hand as Gabe flashed her badge at the admin-assist behind a sheet of bulletproof. The girl's throat swelled as she nodded, her pink-streaked hair sticking up in the new Gypsy Roen fashion—she had a subvocal implant. Her fingers blurred as she tapped on a datapad. I wondered who she was talking to while she was taking dictation, followed Gabe through the fireproof security door, and swallowed against the sudden chemical stench. *I wish I could figure out how to quit smelling that.*

"Hey, Spooky," a thin geek in a labcoat, carrying a stack of paperwork, called out. "You here for the dead-head?" Then his eyes flicked past her to me, and he stopped cold, unshaven face turning the color of old cottage cheese.

It wasn't as satisfying as it might have been. His stringy hair was cut in the bowl shape Jasper Dex had made popular. It didn't suit him. Neither did the color of his face. His eyes came suspiciously close to bugging out. I wondered why—working in the morgue, he probably saw his fair share of Necromances, between Gabe and John Fairlane.

Then I remembered I was golden-skinned, with a face like a holovid model's and a share of a demon's beauty without the persistent alienness of a demon; my hair was ink-black, longer than it had been and silky, refusing to stay back unless braided tightly, sometimes not even then. I looked like a particularly good genesplice to most normals, like I'd paid a bundle to look like a holovid wet dream.

The emerald in my cheek would just give normals a reason to fear me; an atavistic fear of psions in general and Necromances in particular. Silly normals sometimes mistake Necromances for Death Himself, loading another layer of fear onto the trepidation they feel about all psions.

If they knew how unconditionally Death loved His children, maybe they would fear Him less. Or more. But psions were feared by normals all over the world, just because we had been born different.

"Yeah, Hoffman, I'm here for the pile of meat that used to be a deadhead." Gabe's voice was a slap bouncing off the hall walls. "This is the big gun. Dante Valentine, meet Nix Hoffman."

"Charmed, I'm sure." The dry tone I used was anything but. My voice echoed, not as hard as Gabe's, but casually powerful; I had to remember to keep toning it down *especially* around normals. The effect my voice had on unsuspecting civilians was thought-provoking, to say the least.

"Likewise," he stammered. "Ah, um, Ms. Valentine—"

"Which bay is the body in, Hoff? Caine's?" Gabe barely even broke stride.

"Yeah, Caine's got it, he's in his office. He was doing toxicology." The young man's eyes flittered over me. I knew what he was seeing—a particularly desirable gene-spliced woman—and wished I didn't. His pupils swelled. If I flooded the air with my scent I could have him on his knees, begging without knowing why. Yet another side effect of whatever I was now.

Hedaira, a flat ironic voice whispered in the lowest reaches of my mind. I shut that voice away—it hurt too much to hear it. Why was Japhrimel's the voice I used to hurt myself?

"Thanks, jerkwad." Gabe sailed past him, and I did the same, letting out a deep breath between my teeth. I did *not* sneer. It took some effort.

"You've got yourself a reputation," Jace murmured in my ear. I snorted something indelicate. "Oh, come on,

Danny. You're too cute. Maybe we should get you one of them Oak Vegas Raidon outfits."

"I can't raise the dead in a black-leather bikini," I muttered back, grateful once again because the damnable urge to smile rose again. Gabe's boots clicked on the linoleum.

"A *studded* black-leather bikini," Jace corrected.

"Pervert." The stench of human cells, dying decaying dead, rose up to choke me.

How did Japhrimel stand it? I wondered, and my left shoulder suddenly *burned* as if something hot was pressed against it, scorching the skin, twisting. I could almost feel the scar writhing on my skin.

I stopped dead. Jace nearly ran into me, stopped just in time, the bones tied to his staff clicking together. His Power stroked me briefly, a pleasant touch that would have unloosed my knees and made my breath catch if I hadn't been struggling to make my lungs work, my skin running prickly with demon Power. "Danny?"

"Nothing." These flashes of heat were getting more and more pronounced lately. I wondered if I was going into demon menopause.

There was another, nastier idea. I wondered if the flashes of heat had anything to do with the Prince of Hell.

What a nightmare-inducing thought. Assuming I could sleep, that is. I put my head down, started forward again, lengthening my stride to catch up with Gabe. "Just a thought."

"What kind of thought?" He sounded only mildly curious, his staff tapping in time with our footsteps.

"The private kind, J-man. Back off."

"Fine." Easy and calm, he let it drop. How he managed

to do that I could never guess—it took a lot to ruffle his smooth surface. Maybe it was growing up in a Mob family that did it, made him so hard and blank; impenetrable. Or maybe it was putting up with me. *Why did you hand over your Family, Jace? Just give it up? People have killed to stay in Families, let alone control them. You could have had everything you ever wanted. Why?*

I wished I could find the words to ask him.

Gabe stopped in front of another door. Her bobbed hair swung as she turned her head slightly, a quarter-profile as pure as an ancient marble in a statis-sealed museum case. "Word to the wise. Caine's a Ludder."

I felt my lip curl up. A *genesplice-is-murder, psions-are-aberration, Luddite-Text-thumping fanatic.* They were everywhere these days. "Great. He's going to *love* me."

Gabe opened her mouth to reply, but the frosted-glass window set in the door darkened. The hinges squealed, and I had to kill the sardonic smile that wanted to creep up my face. I had the distinct idea that the hinges were deliberately left dry. *Come into my parlor, said the medical examiner to the hapless police detective.* My right hand tightened, searching for the hilt of a sword. I actually twitched before I remembered I didn't have a katana anymore. My hand ached, one vicious cramp settling into the bones and twisting briefly before letting go. Getting better. It used to ache all the time, now it only ached when I wanted to reach for a hilt and found only empty air.

"Gabriele," the stick-thin elderly man said. His eyes, poached blue eggs over a bloodless mouth and pale powdery cheeks, swam behind thick plasrefractive lenses. His lab coat was pristine, the magtag on his pocket read *R. Caine.* He'd chosen a caduceus logo on the tag; it reminded

me of my own accreditation tat. A mad giggle rose up inside of me, was suppressed, and died an inglorious death
as an almost-burp. "And some company. How charming."

"Afternoon, Dr. Caine." Gabe's voice was flat, mono-
tone. Deliberately noncombative, but slightly disdainful
at the same time. "I presume Captain Algernon has spoken with you."

If he could have sneered, he probably would have. Instead, his eyes lingered on me. The pink dome of his scalp
under a few thinning gray-white strands of combed-over
hair added to the egglike appearance of his head; no cos-
metic hair implants for this gentleman. His teeth were still
strong and sound, but they were terribly discolored,
shocking in this age of molecular dental repair. Like the
dry hinges, his teeth were probably deliberate too. "This
is most irregular," he sniffed. "What is *that?*"

"Dante Valentine, Dr. Caine. Dr. Caine, Dante Valentine." Gabe moved slightly to one side, still between the
doctor and me. I got the impression she was ready to jam
her boot in the door if he decided to try to slam it shut.

"Pleased to meet you." I lied with a straight face, for
once.

His watery blue eyes narrowed behind the lenses.
"What *are* you?"

I set my shoulders. I'd been given the cold shoulder by
a lot of normals, he was going to have to work harder than
that to irritate me. "The proper term is *hedaira,* Doctor.
I'm a genetically altered human." The words stuck in my
throat, dry and lumpy. *Wouldn't you love to know, Doctor.
I didn't ask for this to be done to me. And I have no idea
what* hedaira *even means. The only person who could
have told me is ash in a black urn. When I'm not halluci-*

nating his disembodied voice to flog myself with, that is.
"Although I suspect *abomination* is the term you're looking for. Let's get this over with."

"Who did your genesplicing?" He licked his thin,
colorless lips. "It looks like an expensive job."

*Expensive? I guess you could say so. It cost me my
life and someone I loved.* I felt it like a sharp pinch on
already-bruised flesh. So maybe he *would* manage to
annoy me. One point for the Ludder doctor. "That's none
of your business. I'm here to view a body in a legitimate
murder investigation. Should I come back with a court
order?" My voice made the glass in the door rattle
slightly. *I think I'm behaving badly.* A lunatic giggle rose
up again inside of me. Why did I always have the urge to
laugh at times like this?

Dr. Caine's wiry eyebrows nested in his nonexistent
hairline. "Of course not. I know my duty to the police department. *Despite* their habit of sending me cadavers."

"Why, Doctor, I thought it was your job to deal with
cadavers." I didn't move, my feet nailed to the floor despite Jace's sudden grip on my elbow. I hated the syrupy
sweetness in my voice—it meant that I was about to say
something unforgivable. "Perhaps you should retire."

"Not until I'm forced to, young woman. Come inside."
He laughed mechanically and didn't look pleased, but
ushered us into a small office jammed with a desk, two
chairs, two antique and crooked metal file cabinets, piles
of papers and files, and a thriving blue-flowered orchid on
top of another file cabinet, this one wooden and glowing
mellow with polish. That was interesting. Nearly as interesting was the dry-erase board set on the wall across from
the second door. Dr. Caine's handwriting was spidery, and

it wandered inside the neatly-ruled sections, keeping track of what body was in what bay and what tests needed to be done. At least, that's what I assumed the complicated numbers and letters meant. It looked like a code based on the old Cyrillic alphabet.

"Now I want it to be very *clear*," he said, once we were all crowded in his office, "this is happening against my will, and under my protest."

"Mine too," I muttered under my breath, taking refuge in snideness. Gabe cast me an imploring glance. I shut up.

The good doctor studied me for a long moment. I noticed he had two lasepens in his breast pocket and a capped scalpel too. "The body is of a Necromance." His lip curled. "Cause of death, as nearly as we can determine, was some type of psionic assault."

That was something new. Dr. Caine noticed my sudden attention. "We can tell because of the MRI and sigwave scans." He directed his words at me. "Bleeding in the cortex in characteristic star-patterns. It seems that, just as manual strangulation leaves petechiae, psionic assault resulting in death leaves these starbursts of blood and scarring in the brain."

Thank you for that incredibly vivid mental image, Doctor. I glanced around his office again. I smelled chemical reek, dying human cells, and pipe tobacco mixed with synth hash. So the good Doc was a smoker. Most medical personnel were. His hands didn't tremble, but they were liver-spotted and thin as spider's legs. I imagined his hands on a lasecutter and had to shudder. *He probably talks to the cadavers. And very patronizingly, too.* I glanced up at the ceiling, where the random holes in the soundbreak tiles almost began to run together and make sense. Dust swirled in the air, forming little geometric shapes as the room heated up with four adult bodies in it—and the extra heat I was putting out. Power trembled at the outer edges of my control, straining to leap free. I invoked spread-thin control, clenching my right fist so hard I felt the claws prick my palm. It felt comfortingly like fingernails digging in as I made a fist.

"What kind of psionic assault?" Gabe asked. "Feeder, Ceremonial, Magi, what?"

"I am unable to determine. I was under the impression that was *your* job." This sneer he directed at me. I ignored it. Instead, I studied the dry-erase board, watching the shape of the letters blur as I unfocused my eyes. With it all hazy, I could almost pretend there was a pattern there too. If I spent a little Power, I could probably decode it, my minor precognitive talent turning a randomness into a glimpse of the future.

I came back to myself with a barely-covered start. Took a deep breath. I couldn't afford to get distracted here. No amount of precog was worth even a momentary lapse in attention.

"What else can you tell me, Doctor?" Gabe was in her element. I almost forgot she was a cop; she looked like a wide-eyed med student. Caine preened under her attention. I overrode the urge to rub at my left shoulder. The mark was burning, a piercing, drilling, fiery pain I only felt rarely over the last year. Was it just because I had allowed myself to think of Japhrimel again? Was thinking of him more frequently now?

As if I ever stopped thinking about him, even while I was being shot at by panicked, psychopathic bounties.

"There is a high likelihood that Miss Moorcock was

also sexually assaulted before she was dismembered." Caine's poached eyes glittered. "There was tearing and severe bruising in the vaginal vault. Unfortunately, we were unable to recover any DNA evidence because of contamination by blood and foreign matter in the vagina."

My throat closed again, hot bile rising. *Why do I keep wanting to throw up?* I braced myself. Jace's thumb drifted across my elbow, a soothing touch.

Too bad I wasn't soothed.

Gabe waited.

"There's nothing else," he said finally. I'd have bet my house and the rest of Lucifer's blood money Caine was enjoying this. "We're running toxicology screens and re-analyzing some of the forensic measurements."

"Reanalyzing?" Gabe fractionally raised one eyebrow.

"Either we have made an error, or whatever ripped her into pieces did it simultaneously. Her arms, her legs, her head—all at the same time. As if she was quartered. Are you familiar with quartering, Ms. Valentine?"

His poached-egg eyes rested on me now, his thin mouth curved into the slightest of smiles. I dropped my right hand back down to my side, both my hand and shoulder burning. "I'm somewhat of a student of history, Doctor. I'm familiar with the term."

7

The tiled vault of the body-bay was chilly. Steam rose off my skin as soon as I stepped through the airseals into climate control. I had to spend a moment's worth of attention readjusting—my internal thermostat was set on "high." I ran very warm these days, not needing a pile of blankets like I used to when I was human. That was one thing Jace had been good for during our affair, even though he ended up kicking off the covers. I supposed it was living in Rio that made him so warm.

Nowadays, if he collapsed on my bed it was because he was drunk, and he slept on top of the covers more often than not, or woke when I poked him in the ribs to haul himself down the hall to his own room.

I scanned the room habitually—nothing but the usual security net and countermeasures; the holovid captures set in strips along the ceiling to get everything in 3-D. Steel lockers took up one side of the room, tools hung neatly, racks of equipment and scanners. My teeth ached until I took a deep breath and made my jaw relax.

The tough blue plasticine bodybag lay on the stainless-steel table. The shape was subtly wrong, of course—there were only parts of Christabel Moorcock left.

I was alone in a morgue with a body. My skin roughened, smoothed out. All of a sudden I was more comfortable than I'd been for almost a year. I knew how to do this. I'd been doing this most of my life.

Then what are you afraid of? a cool, deep voice asked inside my head. I shut that voice back up in its little black box. It hurt too much to hear the shading of male amusement, the flat ironic tone of a demon's voice stroking the most intimate of my thoughts. Why couldn't I just let the sound of his voice go?

What *was* I afraid of? Oh, nothing. Except for maybe finding him waiting for me on the other side of Death's bridge, his hands clasped behind his back and that faint smile on his face. The last time I'd brought a soul out of Death like this, Japhrimel had been with me, watching.

The intercom crackled. "Whenever you're ready, Danny," Gabe said from the observation deck outside. This would be taped, of course, since it would be admitted into evidence as part of the investigation. "Just take it slow."

Take it slow, she says, a nasty mental snigger caroled across my brain. *It's not her ass on the line here.*

It wasn't precisely that I was afraid—after all, I still had my tat and my emerald. My patron god still accepted my offerings. I missed the touch of my god, missed the absolute certainty of the thing I knew I was best at. The contact with a psychopomp is so achingly personal for a Necromance. My god would not deny me.

No, I was only afraid of myself.

I reached up, touched my left shoulder. The mark burned

with a fierce, steady ache now. As painful as it was, I welcomed it. It had burned like that when Japhrimel was alive—as if a live brand was resting on my skin. I had never thought nerve-scorching pain could be comforting. The mark would turn ice-cold soon enough as whatever made it heat up faded, and I would be left with the reminder that the demon it named was dead.

Dead, maybe. Forgotten, no. And Lucifer . . .

I didn't want to think about the Prince of Hell.

I had no sword, but my right-hand knife was good steel, and I held it loosely. Two glassed-in white candles stood on a wheeled cart between me and the body. Cool air touched my forehead, caressed my cheekbones and the shallow V of skin exposed by my shirt. My right hand cramped slightly on the knifehilt, then eased suddenly.

I had to look.

I skirted the cart and approached the table with its plas-wrapped burden, the soles of my boots scritching slightly on the easy-to-hose plaslino floor. The silvery drain set below the table gave out a whiff of chlorine and decaying blood.

The intercom crackled again. "Danny?"

You of all people should know that I just can't barge into this headfirst. Though I don't know why, that's my usual style. "Just relax, Gabe. I need to see."

"Danny—"

"I won't touch the body. I'm going to unzip the sheath, that's all. It will make it easier." I heard my own voice, calmer than I really felt; I was a master at sounding like I knew what I was doing.

"For who?" It was a blind attempt at humor, and it failed dreadfully. I glanced up at the observation window, felt my lip curl up slightly. The magshielding in the walls was good, I could only feel them through the window—Gabe a cool purple bath of worry; Jace, spiky, spiced electric honey, every nerve suddenly focused on me; and Caine's dry, smooth, egglike aura, giving nothing away. Blind natural shielding, a disbelief so huge it could protect him from psychic assault. Some normals were like that. They literally wouldn't believe their own eyes when it came to magick.

I wondered what he thought of psions, since he was so disbelieving. Of course, he was a Ludder, he probably thought we should all be put in camps like the Evangelicals of Gilead did during the Seventy Days War. Rounded up, shot, and put in disposal units. Ludders hated genesplicing on principle, but they hated psions with an atavistic revulsion as irrational as it was deep. It didn't matter that we'd been born this way, according to the Ludders we were abominations and all deserved to die.

"Don't ride me, Gabe. It's not recommended." I wasn't amused.

"Then just get this done so you can go home and drink." She wasn't amused either. Guess we were even.

Like drinking will help. I can't even get drunk anymore. My fingers closed around the cold zipper. I drew it down with a long ripping sound.

At least they had put the parts where they were supposed to be. I wondered what was missing—I hadn't looked at the preliminary report yet. The stink of death belched up, assaulting my sensitive nose.

Sensory acuity was a curse sometimes. No wonder demons carried their personal perfume around like a shield. I wished I could. "Christabel," I said. "*Sekhmet sa'es.*"

The air stirred uneasily. There was no dust here, but I felt the Power in the air—my own—tremble unsteadily, like a smooth pond touched by a hover field. Not rippling but quivering, just about to slide free of control and plunge into chaos.

Well. That's odd.

I backed up. I didn't need to see more than her ruined, rotting face. I retreated to the other side of the room, swallowing hard. A snap of my fingers as I passed the steel cart lit the candles. I used to get such a kick out of doing that.

Back before Japhrimel. "Kill the lights, Gabe."

"All right." A popping sound, and three-quarters of the fluorescents went dim. The ones that remained lit buzzed steadily, maddeningly. It was better lit than the warehouse had been. I briefly wondered where Bulgarov was now, if they'd run him through the courtroom and into a gasbox yet. No, it was too soon. I wouldn't need to testify, I'd only done the collar.

Quit dithering, Danny. The bounty's over. Focus on what's in front of you.

I held the knife up, steel glimmering, a bar between me and whatever happened next. "Here goes nothing," I murmured. "Dante Valentine, accredited Necromance, performing an apparition on the body of Christabel Moorcock, also accredited Necromance." *And I hope like hell she has something to tell us.*

"Got it," Gabe said. "Whenever you're ready."

I sighed. Then I closed my eyes. I had no more time to screw around.

It was easy, too easy. I dropped below conscious thought, into the blue glow of whatever juncture of talent and genetics allowed me to see the dead. I wasn't touching the body—I couldn't stand the thought of resting my hand on that plastic—so I expected there to be a time lag, some difficulty, maybe a barrier between me and the blue crystal walls of Death's antechamber.

I was wrong.

Oh, gods, it feels good. My head tipped back, my loose long hair streaming on a not-quite-wind. The chant bubbled up from the most secret part of me, my voice husking on the high accents, Power leaping to fill the words almost before I uttered them. "*Agara tetara eidoeae nolos, sempris quieris tekos mael—*"

So far so good, I thought hazily, then it swallowed me whole.

Blue crystal light rose above me. My rings spat a shower of sparks, my left shoulder blurring with pain. Riding the Power, the crystal walls singing, I reached across space and steel and vibrating air, hunting. Bits of shattered bone and decaying flesh turned bitter against my tongue. Christabel's body was no more than an empty shell, no spark of life still housed in the fragile meat, not even the foxfire of nerves dying hours or days after the event. The cold, stiffening chill of death walked up my fingers with small prickling feet, taunting the ends of my toes.

I opened my eyes.

It was so familiar I could have wept. The chant poured out of me, sonorous, striking the blue crystal walls stretched up into infinity. I wore the white robe of the god's chosen, belted with silver that dripped like chainmail in daggered loops. My bare feet rested on the bridge over an endless abyss; a silver stream of souls whirling past, drawn over the bridge by the irresistible law of Death's renewal. I walked, the emerald on my cheek casting a spectral glow, enfolding me. The emerald's light was a cocoon, keeping me safely on the bridge, preventing me from being flung into the well of souls. The abyss yawned below, the bridge quivering like a plucked harpstring. I did not have time to see if perhaps a demon's soul waited there for me. I had been afraid that he would be here in Death's halls, tied to me. I had been afraid that he would not be here—that mortal death held no place for a demon's soul.

How could my own cowardice have kept me from the thing I loved most, the only place I felt utterly safe?

I raised my head slowly. I could not look, did not want to look.

Had to look.

The god of Death's cipher, His slender dog's head glossy black, regarded me. The same as He always had, since the first time I had ventured fully into the blue glow. He sat on the other side of the bridge, a dog-shape that was only a mask for His true form; the merciful mask that allowed me to come into Death and face the infinite terror of life's ending. Though I was Necromance, Death's touch frightened even me; no finite human likes to face the infinite. And yet, cheek by jowl with the terror was complete acceptance. Death's touch was cool and forgiving, the laying-down of burdens, the easing of pain, the washing-away of obligation and of memory.

And oh, how I wanted to feel that lightness, even as I struggled against it as all living things struggle, clinging to a life that is familiar even if painful. The agony I knew, not the mystery of what lay beyond the well, the secret Death whispered to every mortal thing sooner or later.

I let out a dry, barking sob in the middle of my chant. Power crested, spilled over me, the god reached through me. The place inside me where He lived bloomed again, a hurtful ecstatic flower, and I became again the bridge a god uses to pull a soul from Death.

Pressure, mounting against throat and eyes and the juncture of my legs, sharp pleasure. My head fell back, and a subliminal *snap!* echoed dryly against tiled walls. The chill numbness rose in my fingers, creeping up my arms. "Ask . . . your . . . questions . . ." I said softly, fierce joy rising and combating the chill. I had done it. I had *done* it once again.

The intercom crackled, Gabe's voice staticky and harsh, and Christabel Moorcock's ghost moaned. There was no modulation to the ghost's voice—of course not, the dead don't speak as we do. There is nothing in an apparition's tone but the flat finality of that most final punctuation to the act of living. The longer a body has been in a grave, the more horribly flat an apparition's voice. People have screamed and fainted when an apparition speaks, and sometimes even other psions blanch. I've seen it happen while watching others of my kind work in training videos.

Nobody likes to hear the dead speak.

What's that? Even in my chanting trance I realized something wasn't right. Christabel's low flat moan scraped across the surface of my words, tautened the Power holding the chant steady, sent a cold fiery finger up my back. It was *wrong*. No apparition should sound so . . . horrified.

This isn't right, I thought, but I held the apparition. Held it to the living, the chill starting in my fingers and toes, the cold marble-block feeling of death.

Gabe asked again, and a feedback squeal ripped against my vulnerable psyche. I screamed, Power tearing through me again, my emerald spitting sparks and my rings crackling, showering golden sparks. Tiles shattered, and glass from a fluorescent tube chimed against the floor. I dug my heels and mental teeth in, the chant spilling and stretching, Power bucking, mental threads tearing with sharp, painful twitches.

REMEMBER! REMEMBER! REMEMBER!

For one vertiginous second I felt the caress of cold, mad fingers against my cheek, a blast of something too inhuman to be called thought, carrying undeniable meaning and repeating the single word over and over again. *REMEMBER! REMEM—*

I tore away. The ghost screamed and my knife flashed up, cold steel between me and the hungry thing lunging at me, feeding from the Power I carried.

"Japhrimel!" I screamed hoarsely. My shoulder gave a crunching flare of pain that ripped through my trance. A gunpowder flash of blue flame belled through the air, and my shoulders hit the wall, cracking more tile. Tile-dust and ceramic shards pattered down as more glass drifted to the floor, ground diamond-fine. Sudden dark plunged through the room—only one flickering, buzzing fluorescent remained lit on the far side of the body-bay.

I slid down the wall, blinking, as Christabel Moorcock's dead body sucked the last traces of her hungry ghost back into Death. I shuddered, my emerald burning on my cheek, and could not stop the dry coughing sobs welling up inside me. Tears slicked my cheeks, hideous relief and fresh grief welling up from a place too deep to name.

Japhrimel was not in Death's halls. Wherever he was now, he was lost to me completely.

8

"*F*uck," Gabe said for the twentieth time, rubbing at the back of her neck. "I'm sorry, Danny. Hades, that could have killed you."

I shrugged, using the small plastic stick to stir the coffee-flavored sludge with my left hand. My right lay in my lap, useless and discarded out of habit. The sound of the Spook Squad bustled around us, and I heard a Ceremonial on the other side of the partition dictating into a video-recorder about a suspected-telepath bank robbery. "Don't worry about it, Gabe. I'm a lot tougher than I used to be."

He wasn't there. He's gone. Really gone. I told that voice to go away. It went without a struggle, but promised to return and taunt me the next time I tried to sleep.

At least some things in my life were consistent.

"That's apparent." She sighed, looking down at the heaped files on her desk. One stray dark strand of hair had fallen into her face, shocking in a woman of Gabe's precision. Her sidearm was briefly visible as she rubbed at the back of her neck with both hands, massaging away a constant ache. Her eyes were wider than I'd seen them in a while, but at least she'd lost the cheesy pale color in her cheeks. "Gods. I'm so sorry, Danny."

"Don't worry," I repeated, suppressing the flare of irritation. *She's worried about me, she's my friend, she doesn't deserve my bad mood,* I told myself for the fifth time, leaning back in the chair and shifting my gaze to the bottle of brandy. Gabe had offered us all a medicinal swig and I'd taken it, even though it might have been water as far as my new physiology was concerned. Jace had actually taken three long drafts before capping the bottle and handing it back to her. "At least it tells us a few things."

Jace took a long slurp of his coffee, holding the plasticine cup gingerly. "What does it tell you, Danny?" He sounded only mildly interested. His face was set and white, blue eyes bloodshot and livid. The bones on his staff moved uneasily, one clacking against another. Feverspots burned high up on each cheek.

I appeared to have frightened them both. I supposed when the feeling of relief and crazed joy at daring the borders of Death again wore off, I would be frightened too. But I didn't have the good sense or manners to be scared right now. I felt oddly as if I'd won a victory.

There were only a few things that could turn an apparition into a ravening, hungry, vengeful ghost, most of them having to do with soul-destroying torture before the act of death. Ritual murders—what you might call "black magick," Power gained through the expense of torturing and killing another sentient being—and genocides were high on the list. So was being attacked and contaminated by a Feeder—a psychic vampire. Among a population where Power was so common and so frequently used, it stood to reason that some would develop pathology in their processing of ambient Power and need to siphon off vitality from those around them, feeding on magickal or psionic energy in ever-increasing doses, until they got to the point where they could drain a normal person in seconds and a psion in minutes, depriving them of the vital energy needed to sustain life. Most Feeders were caught and treated while young, able to live out normal lives as psions with early intervention. When an older psion started to exhibit Feeder pathology, early intervention was key as well.

But Feeders didn't tear their prey apart. At least, not physically.

It looked like a ritual murder to me, but it was too soon to tell. Whatever it was, Christabel Moorcock had suffered something so horrible even her ghost was insane with the echoes of the act.

"Well." I propped my boots up on Gabe's desk, picked a sliver of tile out of my hair, dropped it in her overflowing wastebasket. "It tells us we're dealing with some serious shit. That's nice to know. If we can assume we're dealing with a ritual murder, which would be my first guess, it also tells us that whatever was done to her reverberates after death. So that narrows down the type of magick we're hunting. It tells us that someone is very, very determined; it tells us that a lot of preparation and time went into this. So there are some clues lying around. Nobody can work a magickal operation like that with surgical precision; there's always some sloppy fucking mistake. I learned that doing bounties." I deliberately did not look at Jace, though it was an implicit nod to him. He'd been my teacher, after all; had taught me more about bounties in a year than I could learn on my own in five.

"Great." Gabe rested her elbows on her desk, finally

stopping the rubbing at her neck. The white rings around her eyes were starting to go away. I smelled pizza—someone must have decided to grab a quick dinner here. It reminded me I was hungry. As usual. "Caine's having a fucking fit that you destroyed one of his body-bays. The holovids are going to be all over this, Danny. And if word gets out you're working on it, the sharks will go into a frenzy."

"He'll get tax compensation and the Hegemony HHS will step in since his body-bay was destroyed during a routine investigation." My tone sharpened. "And nobody cares what *I* work on."

I was surprised by Jace's snort. He took down half of his scalding coffee in one gulp, reached for the brandy bottle and, apparently changing his mind in midreach, settled back again. The flimsy folding chair squeaked. "Oh, really? You're *the* Danny Valentine, world-class Necromance who retired rich at the top of her game after a hush-hush bounty hunt that nobody can dig up any information on except for the Nuevo Rio Mob War. Of course they're going to eat it up. I'd be surprised if there weren't reporters covering your house already, Danny."

He forgot to mention that I was the Necromance that had raised Saint Crowley the Magi from ashes, as well as worked on the Choyne Towers disaster. And my recent string of bounties had been profiled on a holovid show. Gabe was right, if it surfaced that I was working on the case all hell might very well break loose. Plus, it would be bad for the cops to admit they'd had to bring in a freelancer.

"Fuck." I took a long swallow of the scorching mud that passed for coffee around here. Decided to change the subject. Accentuate the positive, so to speak. "So we've got more information than we had before, and we have a direction."

"What direction?" Gabe asked.

"Rigger Hall." I shivered. "Nightmare Central." *Remember. Remember. Remember.* The memory of the apparition's soulless chant chilled me as much as the thought of Christabel's note. I didn't *want* to remember Rigger Hall. I had done very well for years without remembering. I wanted nothing more than to continue that trend.

Silence crackled between us. The paper on her desk shifted uneasily, stirred by something other than wind.

"What happened there, Danny?" Gabe looked miserable. The chaos of ringing phones and crackle of uneasy Power outside her cubicle underscored her words. The Ceremonial next door swore softly and started over again, I heard the click-whirr of a magnetic tape relay. "The inquiry was sealed, it would take a court order to open it, and that means *more* publicity. I'm supposed to keep this as quiet as possible. Once the press sinks their teeth in, we'll be lucky to avoid a rush of copycats and Ludders attacking psions."

She was right. We would be lucky if nobody found out about it and was tempted to do a little cleansing-by-murder. And the first victim had been a normal. If there was even a *hint* that a murder of a normal had been committed by a psion, people got edgy.

Most psions were well able to defend themselves from random street violence, even the idiots who didn't take combat training. But still, it wore on you after a while, all the sidelong looks and little insults. We were trained in Hegemony schools, tattooed after taking Hegemony accreditation, and policed both internally and externally, but normals still feared us. We were useful to the Hegemony and a backbone source of tax funding as well as invaluable to corporations, but none of that mattered when the normals got into a snit. To them, we were all freaks, and it never did to forget that for very long, if at all.

I said nothing, staring at the brandy bottles and their amber liquid. One bottle was almost empty. Inside it, the liquid trembled, responding to my attention.

Jace hauled himself up to his feet, scooping up his staff. "I'm gonna go check for reporters outside." He was gone before I had time to respond.

I watched him vanish and looked back to find Gabe frowning at me. "What?" I tried not to sound aggrieved, shifted my boots on her desk. My mouth tasted grainy with the glass and porcelain dust from the morgue bay.

"He's upset," she informed me, as if I didn't already know. "What's going on with you two, Danny?"

"Nothing," I mumbled, taking another scalding sip of coffee. "He stays at my house, does bounties with me. He sticks around, but . . . nothing really, you know. I can't." *I can't touch him. I won't let him touch me.*

Her frown deepened, the crow's-feet at the corners of her eyes deepening as well. "You mean you haven't . . ." Her slim dark eyebrows rose as she trailed off and examined me as if I'd just announced I wanted a genderchange and augments.

"I don't know what it will do to him." My left shoulder gave one muted throb that sent a not-unwelcome trickle of heat down my spine. *And he's not Japhrimel. Every time he tries to touch me, all I can think about is a fucking demon. Ha, ha. Get it, fucking a demon?* "Can we not talk about my sex life, please?"

"He gave up his Mob Family for you. Just walked away from it. From everything." *And he's human.* She didn't say it, but I heard it clearly nonetheless. Even someone she considered a traitor was better than me mourning a demon, apparently.

"Rigger Hall," I cut across her words. The nearly-empty brandy bottle jittered slightly on the edge of her desk, paper ruffled again. "I don't know a lot, Gabe. But what I *do* know, I'll tell you."

She stared at me for a long fifteen seconds, her dark eyes fathomless, her emerald sizzling with light. Her aura flushed an even deeper red-purple. "Fine. Have it your way, Danny. You always do anyway." She leaned back in her chair, the casters squeaking slightly, and plucked the cigarette from behind her ear. In blatant defiance of the regs, she flicked out her silver Zijaan and inhaled, then sent twin streams of smoke out through her nostrils. A flick of the wrist, and a stasis-charm hummed into life, the smoke freezing into ash and falling on her desk. It was a nice trick.

I swallowed dryly. "Rigger Hall." The words tasted like stale burned chalk. "I was there from . . . let's see, I was tipped from home foster care to the psi program when I was five. So I would have been there, clipped and collared, for about . . . eight years before the inquiry." I shuddered. My skin prickled with phantom gooseflesh again.

I looked at my right hand, twisting itself further into a claw. It ached, not as much as it had, but still . . . My perfect, poreless golden skin was tingling in instinctive reaction, my breath coming short and my pulse beating hot and thready in my throat.

"Hades," Gabe breathed, a lungful of smoke wreathing her face before falling, dead ash, onto the papers drifting her desk. "Eddie does the same thing. What *happened?*"

"The Headmaster was a slimy piece of shit named Mirovitch." My breath came even harsher. My voice was as dry-husky as it had been right after the Prince of Hell had tried to strangle me. "He was part of the Putchkin psi program. Got a diplomatic waiver to come over and reform the Hegemony program with Rigger as an experimental school. What nobody knew was that he was a Feeder, and had been for some time. He was well-camouflaged, and he didn't want to be cured. Instead, he wanted his private playground, and he got it."

"A Feeder?" Gabe shivered. "Gods."

"Yeah. He was slick, and we were just . . . just kids. It was . . ." For a moment my voice failed me, sucked back into my throat. I set my coffee cup down on the floor beside my chair, feeling the floor rock slightly underneath me. Or maybe it wasn't the floor—maybe I was shaking. "It was really bad, Gabe. If you stepped out of line— if you were *lucky*—you got put in a Faraday cage in a sensory-dep vault. It was . . . A couple of the kids committed suicide, and Mirovitch made one of the Necromance apprentices sleep in the room that . . . He went insane and clawed his own eyes out. They wrote it up as an incorrectly-done training session."

Her eyes were round, disbelieving. "Why didn't anyone—"

"He paid off the Hegemony proctors. Had a profitable little sexwitch stable going on the side, could afford to hand out cash . . . and other bribes. And if any of the kids really pissed him off, he signed the forms to turn you into a breeder." I shivered again, rubbed at my left shoulder, my eyes blinded with memory.

Gods. If there was any justice in the world, the memories would have faded. They hadn't.

Once, my roommate had tried to tell her social worker what was going on inside Rigger Hall's hallowed walls. She'd paid for it with her life. It was ruled a suicide, of course—but sometimes even a kid has the guts to take her own life rather than be pushed into the breeder program.

Roanna's body hung tangled on the wires, jerking as the electricity zapped her dying nerves, smoke rising from her pale skin, her long beautiful hair burning, stinking. The streak of the soul leaving her body, as if it couldn't wait to be finally free—and the sick-sweet smell of flesh roasted from the inside. The Headmaster's fingers dug into my shoulder and knotted in my hair, squeezing, pulling, as he forced me to watch. I did not struggle; I did not want to look away.

No. This I would remember. And I swore to myself that one day, somehow, I would get my revenge.

The spike of pain from my shoulder brought me back to myself. Phones rang, people spoke in low voices. It was a normal world going on outside the cubicle—or as normal as the parapsych squad of the Saint City police ever got, I supposed. I reached for the brandy bottle, uncapped it, and inhaled the smell since the booze would do me no good. The liquid slopped against the sides of the bottle. I didn't even try to hold my hand steady.

Of course, the kids who went to Rigger didn't have anyone to fight for them. We were the orphans and the poor; most of our parents had given us up to the Hegemony foster program as soon as we tested high enough on the Matheson index. The rich kids and the kids with families went to Stryker, with the middle-class families receiving subsidies to defray the costs of a psion's schooling. And of course, you could run up a hell of a debt after your primary schooling taking accreditation at the Academy up north, but that was different. If you didn't have a family or a trust fund, your primary school was the closest Hegemony boarding school to your place of birth. Period, end of story, full stop.

I took another deep inhale. *I am an adult now. I am all grown up. I can tell this story.* "The story I heard goes like this: Finally some of the students banded together. Mirovitch was eerie, he could always tell who was making trouble . . . But some of them got together and . . . I heard they cracked the shields and the school security codes, slipped their collars, and caught him in his bedroom fucking a nine-year-old Magi girl. I heard later— now this is *all* rumor, mind you—that one of the Ceremonial students had turned herself into a Feeder and killed him that way, in a predator's duel." My teeth chattered. Chilly sweat seemed to film my entire body, gray mist threatening my vision. The sound of everything outside Gabe's cubicle seemed very far away. *If you go into shock there's nobody to bring you out. You are stronger than this, you are all grown up now. Focus, dammit!*

The chattering shakes receded. "You can't imagine the fear." I stared at the drift of gray ash on her desk. "Or the things that went on. Some of the students stooged for him. Those were the worst. They would avoid punishment by ratting on the others, and they were sometimes worse than *he* was. The beatings . . . They would turn up the collars and administer plasgun shocks . . ." I'd had scars, before I'd been turned into a *hedaira*. Three thick welts across my back, and a welted burn scar along the crease of my lower left buttock. No more. I didn't have the scars anymore. I had perfect, scarless golden skin.

Then why are they aching? Three stripes of fire down my back, the red-hot metal pressed against my skin, my own frantic screams, the leather cutting into my wrists, the trickle of blood and semen down my inner thighs . . .

I am all grown up. I set my jaw, shook the memories away. They didn't want to go, but I was stronger.

For now. When I tried to sleep, we'd see how far I'd gotten.

"Why would Moorcock write that down?" Gabe stubbed the cigarette out in a pocked scar on top of her desk. Her face was caught between disgust and pity for a moment, and I felt the old tired rage rise up in me. If there is anything in the world I hate, it's pity.

"I don't know." I was miserably aware that phantom gooseflesh was trying to rise through my skin. My right hand twisted even tighter, straining against itself, shaped into a knotted claw. Black molecule-drip polish gleamed on my nails. "But I'm going to find out."

"Danny." She pushed herself up to stand behind the desk, her palms braced, bending over slightly to look me in the face. Her sleek dark hair was mussed, and her eyes were dilated, probably catching my own fear. "If I'd known, I wouldn't have asked you. I wouldn't—"

"But you did." I rose, my chair legs thocking solidly into the peeling linoleum floor. "And I owe you. You've done your duty, Gabe. Now it's time for me to do mine."

I didn't think it was possible, but Gabe turned pale. The color spilled out of her cheeks as if tipped from a cup. "It wasn't duty, Danny. You're my friend."

"Likewise." And I meant it. She had her own scars—four of them, on her belly, where Santino's claws had ripped through flesh and inflicted a wound even a Necromance couldn't heal, though we who walked in Death were second only to the *sedayeen* in healing mortal wounds. I was willing to bet Gabe had her own nightmares too, even if she was a very rich woman who played at being a cop. "Why do you think I came down here?"

No, she didn't play. Gabe was good at what she did, working on homicides for the Spook Squad, tickling the dead victims into telling her who killed them. She had a gift. She was the best detective they'd had in a good two decades, ever since her grandmother retired.

"Danny—"

No. Please, gods, no. Don't let her go all soft on me. I can't take that.

"I gotta go." If I stayed here much longer I'd start telling her other things, things she didn't need to know. Things about Rigger Hall, and things about me. "Call me if anything breaks, I'm going to go start looking around. Can you courier copies of the files to my house?"

"You know I can," she said. "Danny, I'm sorry."

Me too, Gabe. Me too. "See you soon, Spooky." I got the hell out of there.

9

*J*ace was waiting for me downstairs. "You okay?" he asked, as I pushed open the door to the ancient parking garage. There was an auxiliary exit here to the other side of the block, and holovid reporters wouldn't be able to catch us. There was already a swarm of them drifting across the front steps of the station house. I didn't envy Gabe having to give a press conference, but the holovids probably loved her.

"No," I said shortly.

"Rigger Hall." He scowled, stripping his hair back from his forehead with stiff fingers. "Danny."

"I don't want to talk about it." I glanced around the concrete tomb, police hovercruisers sitting dark and silent on their landing legs. They didn't have the roof space to host all the hovers on the top of the building, and they'd had to widen both the main entrance and the auxiliary, but it was good enough. A lighted booth crouched at the far end, with a whey-faced duty officer sipping coffee and pointedly ignoring us inside.

"I'm sure you don't." He caught my arm. "Danny."

Oh, please, gods, not now. "Don't, Jace. I need to go to Jado's. And I need to drink."

"It won't affect you." Why did he have to state the obvious?

Never mind that he was right—my changed metabolism simply shunted alcohol aside. It had no more effect on me than water. I was still too much of a coward to try some of the more illegal options for disorientation and sweet oblivion.

If this kept up I might get a little braver.

"I can try." My face crumpled, matching his.

"Ogoun," he breathed, and took me in his arms.

I was a little taller than I had been, but still able to rest my head on his shoulder, my face in the hollow between his throat and collarbones. I had to lean carefully—I was much heavier and stronger than I used to be. I always took point on the bounties, always worried about him catching a stray strike or bullet.

All the same, I let him hold me for a little while, listening to the echoing sounds of the garage around us. Sounds overlapped, straining and splashing against concrete, a cruiser hummed in with its cargo of a dusted-down Chill-freak for processing.

I sighed and stepped away from him, scrubbing at my left shoulder. It throbbed persistently and I wondered why. It had been cold before, a spiked mass of ice pressed into my flesh—now it was warm, a live fire twisting against my skin. The flash of heat hadn't gone away like it always did.

Had the Prince of Hell started sending me heat waves?

Perfect. Another thing to worry about.

"Don't ask me about Rigger Hall," I told him. "Okay?"

It wasn't fair. He still looked like hell, the back-to-back bounties were hard on him. Yet he hadn't complained. He'd shown up on my doorstep and stayed with me, watching my back as I flung myself into hunt after hunt, not wanting to think. He'd betrayed me once, certainly, not telling me he was Mob and abandoning me when his family threatened to assassinate me unless he came back and did their dirty work. At the time, I had known only the agony of that betrayal. But since Rio, Jace had always come through in a big way. It wasn't fair to him at all. None of this was fair to him.

True to form, he dropped the subject. "You got it, baby. I've got something better to ask you." He tapped his staff once against the old, dirty concrete, making a crisp sound that sliced through the humming whine of hovercells.

"Shoot." I started off toward the exit, he fell into step beside me, his staff clicking time against the concrete. Bones clattered dryly together; the aura of his Power was sweet and heady. No other Shaman smelled like Jace—a combination of pepper and white wine, overlaid with fiery honey. If it hadn't been a human smell, it would have been very pleasant.

"Did you love him?" To his credit, he didn't sound angry, just curious.

My boots didn't falter, but I felt like I staggered. "What?" *Why the fuck are you asking me this now? Because I yelled his name when that thing came for me?* One of the silent hovers sitting obediently on its landing gear creaked, responding to my uneasiness.

I took a deep breath.

"Did you love him? The demon. Japhrimel." I could almost see Jace's mouth twisting over the name, as if it was something sour.

"Jace." I made the word clipped and harsh. "Quit it."

"I deserve an answer. I've waited long enough." Quiet. Not his usual careless, ironic tone.

"What do you deserve? You lied to me about Santino." *Predictable, Danny. Take the cheap shot. You bitch.*

What else could he say? I wouldn't let him defend himself. "I didn't know."

"You lied to me about the Corvin Family." Another accusation. I couldn't help myself. Why did we have to have this conversation *now,* of all times? Why?

"I didn't have a choice. I did what I did to protect you. They would have killed you then. When you were human."

It was the first time he'd mentioned the painful nonsecret of my changed status. How long had he been thinking it? "As opposed to an abomination? You're turning Ludder now? Going to go march in front of a hospital with a 'Genesplice Is Murder' sign?" My voice bounced off the concrete, cold enough to coat my skin with ice. I could crack the pavement if I wasn't careful. It trembled on the edge of my control. All this Power, I wondered if Japhrimel had intended to teach me how to use it, how to keep it from eating me alive.

"You're just what you always were, Danny," he informed me tightly. "Stubborn and bitchy and rude. And beautiful."

"You forgot abrasive, unbending, and cruel."

"Not to mention overachieving." He sighed. "Fine. You win, okay? I just want to know, Danny. Haven't I earned it? Did you love him?"

"Why? What possible *difference* could it make? He's dead and he's *not coming back*, Jace. Let it go." We started up the ramp leading to the airseal that closed out dust and trash from the street, keeping the garage climate-controlled. He matched me step for step, as usual, his longer legs canceled out by my quicker stride and his stiff knee.

"When you let it go, I might be able to." He snapped off the end of each word.

"He's dead, Jace. Let it *go*." I couldn't say it any louder than a whisper, because my throat closed off as if a large rock had come to rest there. *Dead, yes. But gone? No. Ask me if he's the reason I can't touch you. Ask me why I hear his voice in my head all the time. Even if I've finally found out it's true, demons aren't in Death's country.*

"Fine." His staff pounded the concrete in time to our steps, bones now clattering with thinly-controlled anger. "What do you need me to do?"

I swallowed, hearing my throat click in the thick silence. I had called Japhrimel's name and not his. He had a right to be angry.

"You're in?" I sounded surprised. *You've done your duty, Jace. Nobody could say you haven't, you've watched my back since Rio. What the hell does anything else matter?*

"Of course I'm fucking in, Danny. What do you want me to *do*?" Now he sounded as irritated as he ever had, his words colored lemon yellow, acrid.

My shoulders suddenly eased a little, dropping down. I shook out my right hand, hearing the joints pop and snap. I was oddly relieved, a relief I didn't want to examine the depth of any more closely. "I need to go see Jado, do

some sparring and clear my head out if I'm starting another hunt." I glanced over at him. His profile was straight
and unforgiving. "Can you get me into the House of Pain?
As soon as possible?"

If I didn't know him better, I'd think he went pale when
he heard me say that. "Chango love me, girl, you don't
ask for anything easy, do you." He actually sounded
breathless.

"I don't smell human," I said dryly. "I think they'll let
me in. But I need an invite or I won't get anywhere, and
you've got the connections to get me one." *Since you were
Mob.* I swallowed the words. That was history, wasn't it?
*Gods, if I could just let one thing be history, what would I
choose?*

He didn't even hesitate. "Fine. I'll get you an invitation. What'll I do while you're talking to the suckheads?"

"You're going to do some research."

10

Jado lived in the University District, on a quiet tree-lined street that had been eccentric years ago but was now merely deserted. There was little ambient energy in the air here, mostly because of him; his house crouched far back in a landscaped yard. His ancient hot tub stood on the deck on one side, and the meditation garden was pristine. There was even a sand plot, impeccably raked, with a few rough black rocks buried in the smoothness. The aura of peace, of stillness, was palpable.

I rang the bell, then twisted the knob and stepped in. The front hall was bare; no shoes on the cedar rack underneath the coat pegs. I caught no breath of human thought in the place.

Thank the gods.

I worked my boots off, and my socks. I hung up my coat and my black canvas bag; my guns dangling from the rig as I hung that up too. Nobody would dare to touch them here. I didn't even bother with a keepcharm. It would have been an insult to my teacher, implying that I didn't trust the safety of his house.

Barefoot, feeling oddly naked as usual without my

weapons, I padded down the high-ceilinged hall and through the doorway into mellow light, and stepped up onto *tatami* mats. Their thick, rough texture prickled luxuriously against my bare soles, and I restrained myself from rubbing my feet just to feel the scratchiness.

Jado sat at the far end on the dais, his robes a blot of orange underneath a scroll with two kanji painted on it. *Ikebana* sat on a low table underneath the scroll; three red flowers on a long slender stem reminding me of the orchids in Caine's office. I suppressed a shiver, bowed properly before I stepped over the border from "space" to "sparring space."

The old man's wizened face split like a withered apple, white teeth flashing. His bald head glistened, charcoal eyes glimmering in the directionless light. His ears came to high points on either side of his head, and his callused hands lay in his lap, in the *mudra* of wholeness.

He looked like a relaxed little gnome, an old man with weird ears, harmless and slow. "Ai, Danyo-*san*. Good thing no students here."

I bowed again. "*Sensei.*"

"So serious! Young one." He shook his head, *tsk*ing slightly. "Well, what is it?"

"I need to think," I said baldly. Not to mention that sparring was the best way to shake off the chill of death. Sparring, slicboarding, sex—anything to flush me with adrenaline and get rid of the bitter taste of death in my mouth, the lingering chill of it in my fingers and toes. "Look, Jado-*sensei,* can we stop the Zenmo crap and get down to business?"

His hand flickered. My right hand moved of its own volition, smacking the dart out of the air. It quivered in a ceiling beam, a wicked steel pinblade and feathered cap. "You are *most* impatient."

I made no reply, watched him. He stood, slowly, pushing himself up from the floor as if his bones ached. My skin chilled instinctively, I dropped into "guard." He clucked at me again. "What would you like? Staff? Sword?"

"I don't have a sword," I reminded him. "Staff or barehand, *sensei*. Either." *Need to move, need to think, and need to ask you a favor.*

"A warrior should have sword, Danyo-*san*. A sword is warrior's honor."

I was hoping you'd say that. "After the fight, I'll need a sword. Unless you don't think you can take me, old man."

He blinked across the room to the rack of staves, his brown fingers curling around a quarterstaff. My heart settled into its combat rhythm, eyes dilating, every fiber of my skin aware of him. "I begin to think you need lesson for manners," he said gently, avuncular.

He tossed me the staff, and followed a split-second later with a staff in his own slim brown hands. The crack of wood meeting wood echoed through the dojo.

Spin, kick, the end of his staff arcing up toward my face, half-step back, *can't afford to do that with him, he's too fast—*

Wood crackled, he jabbed for my midriff and I swung back, the rhythm of staff striking staff lacking a clear pattern. The end of my staff socked into the floor, and I flung myself forward, body loose and flying, Jado narrowly avoided the strike and folded aside but I was ready, landing and whipping the stave out, deflecting the only strike he could make at that angle. Down into a full split, stave spinning backward—a showy move, but the only one I had. Each moment of a fight narrowed the chain of coincidence and angle, Jado moved in as I bent back. I heard the crackle of my spine as I moved in a way no human being should, front heel smashing into the *tatami* to push me up. My body curved, I landed again and feinted, struck—but his stave was there before me, wood screaming as we smashed at each other.

Propellor-strike, shuffling, my breath coming in high harsh gasps, like flying. Alive. I was alive. The lingering chill of going into Death and bringing Christabel out faded, washed clean by adrenaline, every inch of my body suddenly glowing. *Alive. All grown up and alive.* Another flurry of cracks. We separated, I shuffled to one side, he countered. Then, the first flush of the fight over and neither of us having made a stupid mistake, we settled into feinting; first Jado, then me, him trying to lull me into a pattern, me testing his defenses. I earned a solid crack on the knuckles by being too slow, blurred back, shaking my hand out, staff held in guard. Red-black blood welled up, coated the scrape along my knuckles and vanished, leaving the golden skin perfect.

I still wasn't used to that.

"What is it, Danyo-*chan?*" he asked, standing apparently easy, holding his staff in one hand. Tilting forward a fraction of an inch, testing; I countered by leaning sideways, my staff lifting slightly, responding.

"Old ghosts, my friend." My breath came harsh, but I wasn't gasping. Not yet. "The goddamn school. Rigger Hall."

I'd never told him about the Hall. I wouldn't have been surprised at anything he'd guessed, though. I'd come to him for training straight from the Academy, having heard he was the best; he had known me longer than just about anyone, except maybe Gabe.

He nodded thoughtfully, almond-shaped eyes glittering and sweat gleaming on his brown forehead. His mouth was a thin lipless snarl, I'd scored a hit or two of my own. It just felt so *good* not to have to hold back; humans were so fucking fragile.

Careful, Danny. You're still human where it counts. I swallowed, eased down a little, watching his chest. Any move would be telegraphed there. We circled; another fast flurry of strikes deflected. Sweat began on my skin, trickled down my back. It felt good.

It felt *clean.*

"And so you bring ghosts to Jado, eh?" He grinned, but the smile didn't reach his eyes. Here on the sparring floor, there was no quarter asked or given.

"At least I can't kill you," I shot back.

"Hm." He shrugged, inscrutable as ever. His robes whispered as bare brown feet moved over the *tatami;* he closed with me in a flurry of strikes. Sweat flew, his and mine. *Move move move!* I heard his voice from other training sessions. *No think, move!*

His staff shattered, my cry rising with it to break in the sunlit air. I held my own staff a quarter-inch from his chest. The echoes of my *kia* bounced off the walls, made the entire building shiver. Dust pattered down from the groaning roof.

"Not bad," Jado said grudgingly. I treasured that faint praise. "Come. I make you tea."

Sweating, my staff still held warily, I nodded. "Have you ever seen anything dismember a Necromance, Jado-*sensei?*"

"Not recently." He brushed his horny hands free of splinters. "Come, tea. We talk."

I racked my staff and followed him into the spotless green and beige kitchen. Early-evening light poured in through the bay window. Jado got down the iron kettle and two bowls, and his pink Hiero Kidai canister that held green tea. I hid a smile. The old dragon was gruff, but he loved little pink things.

Maybe humans are little pink things to him too. I had to swallow bile again. My left shoulder twisted with hot feverish pain.

"So." Jado put the water on to boil while I eased myself onto a wooden stool set on the other side of the counter. "You have been called out of slumber, it seems."

"I wasn't sleeping, I don't sleep," I objected immediately. "I'm just not a social person, that's all. Been running bounties."

He shrugged. He was right, throwing myself into one hunt after another was a way of numbing myself. Trying to exhaust myself so I *could* sleep, staving off the pain with furious activity. It was a time-honored method, one I'd used all my life; but as a coping mechanism I had to admit it was failing miserably.

His robe, rough cotton, caught the sunlight and glowed. I filled my lungs—the lingering smell of human was only a tang over his darker scent of flame and some deep, scaled hole, darkness welling up from the ground, incense burned in a forgotten temple. I didn't know what Jado was, he didn't fit into any category of nonhuman I'd ever read or heard about. But he'd been in Saint City for at least as long as Abra, because I sometimes, rarely, took messages from one to the other; little bits of information.

I had never seen Jado leave his home, or Abra leave her shop, and I wondered where they had come from. Maybe one day I'd find out.

It was a relief to smell something inhuman. Something that didn't reek of dying cells, of pain, of eventual abandonment.

Japhrimel's gone, I thought, and the sharp spike of pain that went through me seemed somehow clean as well. "What do you know about Christabel Moorcock? Did you ever train her?"

He shook his head. "She is not of my students." The kettle popped on the stove, heating up. "You wish for a sword, then."

It was my turn to shrug, look down at the counter. I traced a random glyph on the Formica with one black-nailed fingertip. My rings sizzled. The glyph folded out, became something else—the spiked fluid lines of the scar on my shoulder. I traced it twice, looked up to meet his tranquil eyes.

"You have decided to live." Jado leaned on the counter, his own blunt fingertips seemingly arranged for maximum affect. His broad nose widened a little and he seemed to sniff. For a moment, his eyes were black from lid to lid, maybe a trick of shadow as he blinked, his eyes lidding like a lizard's. "Though you still smell of grief, *Danyo-chan.* Much grief."

He's not coming back. Maybe I can grieve instead of trying to avoid it. "I never thought I wouldn't live," I lied. "Look, Jado, it's about Rigger Hall. And I think I need a sword. My hand won't get any stronger if I don't exercise it."

"Christabel." His accent made it *Ku-ris-ta-be-ru*. "She was death-talker. Like you."

With only four of us in the city, it stood to reason he would know. I looked down at my left hand, narrow and golden and graceful. His, brown and square, powerful, tendons standing out under the skin. "I don't think that's what killed her."

A slight nod. "So, you have theory already."

"No. Not even a breath of one. I've got a dead normal, a dead sexwitch, and a dead Necromance who left a little note about Rigger Hall. That's all I've got." *I think it might be ritual murder, but I'm not sure. And until I'm sure, nobody's going to hear a theory from me, dammit.*

"And this means you need sword?" His eyebrow lifted. The kettle chirruped, and he poured the water into the bowls. I watched him whisk the fine green powder into frothy, bitter tea, his fingers moving with the skill of long practice. When my bowl was ready, he offered it with both hands. I took it in both hands, with a slight bow. Black *raku* glaze pebbled under my fingertips. The bowl still remembered the fire that made it strong; I caught the echo of flame even in the tea's strong, clear, tart taste.

We are creatures of fire. Tierce Japhrimel's voice threaded through my memory, slow and silken. I was too busy keeping Jado from bashing me with a staff during sparring, but now the thought of Japh crept back into my head. I had managed a full half-hour, forty-five minutes without pain? Call the holovids, stop the presses, rent a holoboard, it was a banner event.

No. I hadn't stopped thinking of him. I never stopped thinking of him. But he was really, truly, inevitably, finally gone.

"I miss him," I said without meaning to, looking into the teabowl's depths. Now that I knew he wasn't in Death's hall, I could admit it. Maybe. "Isn't that strange."

Jado shrugged, sipping at his own tea. His slanted charcoal eyes half-lidded, and the rumble of our strange paired contentment made the air thick and golden. "You have changed, Danyo-*chan*. I met you, and I saw it, so much anger. Where did anger go?"

I shrugged. "I don't know." *The anger isn't gone, Jado. I'm just better at hiding it.* "I've been doing research on demons. And on *A'nankhimel*. Between bounties, that is." My mouth twisted into a bitter smile. I stared into the tea. "He never really told me what he did to me, or the price he paid for it. I still only have a faint idea—it's so hard to separate myth from reality in all the old books, and demons seem to delight in throwing red herrings across the trail." I realized what I was talking about, looked up. Jado examined the window with much apparent fascination.

I sighed. "I used to work so hard at just staying alive, paying off my mortgage, just jumping from one rock to the next. Now I've crossed the river, and you know what? I wish I was back in the middle. At least while I was jumping I didn't have so much goddamn time to brood."

Jado made a soft noise, neither agreeing nor disagreeing, just showing he was listening. Then his dark eyes swung away from the window and came to rest on me. "Perhaps would be best if you did not pursue your past, Danyo-*chan*."

Remember Rigger Hall. "I'm not pursuing it. It's pursuing *me*. Now I have to find out what Christabel did at Rigger Hall, and what connection the three victims had."

"Why?" He took the change of subject gracefully, of course. If anyone knew me, it was Jado. Even before Rio he had never treated me differently than any of his other students.

How could an old man who wasn't human have made me feel so blessedly, thoroughly, completely human myself? "There's only three Necromances left in the city. Me, Gabe, and John Fairlane. We can't afford to lose any more." Bitter humor traced through my voice, etching acid on a pane of glass.

Jado snorted a laugh as if steam was coming through his nose. "Come, drink your tea. We will find you sword. I think I know which one."

The room at the head of the stairs was just as I remembered. Dying sunlight fell through the unshielded windows, slanting to strike at the polished wooden floor. Dust swirled in sinuous shapes with long frilled wings. The door had been taken off its hinges, a long fall of amber silk taking its place. The silk rippled and sang to itself in the silence.

On the black wooden racks against the wall the swords lay, each humming in its sheath. I glanced down to the space where my sword had hung; it was empty. There were four empty spaces—four of Jado's students, out in the world. I wondered if any of the others had broken their sword in the heart of a demon.

The thought managed to make me feel ashamed. Jado didn't hand swords out to just anyone, and I'd broken the last one. "*Sensei*," I whispered, "is it really right?"

He laughed, a papery sound in the bare room. There

were two *tatami* in the middle of the floor, and he gestured me to one. I folded myself down as his thick-skinned bare feet scraped against the floor. An unlit white candle in a plain porcelain holder sat off-center between the mats. "Ai, even swords come and go. You used Flying Silk well. But now, something else." He paced in front of the swords, their wrapped hilts ticking off space behind him. His long orange robe made a different sound than the silk in the door, I could hear the rattlewhine of faraway hovertraffic. It was soothing.

I eased down onto my knees on the mat, tucking my feet under me. It was quiet here; even the dust was serene. My shoulder settled back into a burning prickle, like a limb slowly waking up. I inhaled, smelling Jado's fiery smell, and wished, as I often did, that I could stay with him. It wouldn't work—he was old and liked his space, and my own neuroses would probably irritate both of us to the point of murder after a while. But when I stepped over Jado's threshold, I was no longer a psion feared by normals, or a Necromance crippled by fear and a clawed hand. I was no longer even a *hedaira,* something that wasn't even alluded to directly in the old books about demons I'd managed to dig up. Here, in this house, I was only a student.

And here, I was valued for myself alone. My skill, my bravery, my honor, my willingness to learn all he could teach me.

"This one." Jado lifted down a longer katana. It was in a black-lacquered reinforced scabbard, probably made by Jado's own hands. The wrapping on the hilt was exquisite, and I saw a faint shimmer in the air surrounding it. I found myself holding my breath.

The first time I had stepped into the dojo after killing Santino my breath had come short, my heart pounding; my palms had not been wet but my right hand had twisted into a painful knotted cramp. Jado had been teaching a group of rich teenagers *t'ai chi* as part of the federal health regimen. I'd waited in the back, respectfully; when class was finished and the young ones gone, he had stalked across the *tatami* and, without a word, took my right hand and examined it, moving the fingers gently. I let him, even though I couldn't stand to let anyone else touch me, shying away from even Jace's unconscious skin when he happened to collapse on the couch in an inebriated haze.

Then Jado had grunted. *No sword yet. Staff. Come.* That simply, my nervousness had fallen away like an old coat. An hour later I had dragged myself sweating and shaking to the water fountain after a hard workout; it took a lot more to make me sweat now, but he'd done it. And that, apparently, was that.

No other man could make me feel so much like a child. If Lewis was the father of my childhood, Jado was the father of the adult I had become. I hoped I'd made them proud.

Jado settled down cross-legged across from me. His thumb flicked against the guard, and three inches of steel leapt free. It was beautiful, slightly longer and wider than my other sword. The steel rippled with a light all its own. "Very old. For some reason, Danyo-*chan,* you delight the very old. This—" He slid the blade home with a click, "—is Fudoshin."

The candle between us guttered into life, a puff of smoke rising briefly before the flame steadied. I smiled at the trick, pretending not to notice, my eyes fixed on the sword.

I tilted forward slightly, a bow expressed more with my eyes and upturned hands than anything else, looking up to meet Jado's eyes. "Exquisite."

He nodded slowly, his bald head gleaming with reflected sunlight. The candle's gleam was weak and pallid in the brightness of day. "You delight my heart, Danyo-*chan*. Fudoshin has been with me very long time. He is very old, and very much honor. But I tell you, it is not very good to give this sword."

More time ticked by, the swords singing their long slow song of metal inside their sheaths. Jado breathed, his eyes dark but lit with pinpricks of orange light, his gaze soft as if he was remembering something very long ago.

I always knew Jado wasn't human, but he hadn't truly frightened me until the first time I'd sat across from him in this room. His stillness had been absolute, not the dozing stillness of a human, but a trance so deep it was like alertness. Now I wasn't only human either, and I found myself copying his watchful silence, as if we were two mirrors reflecting each other into eternity.

Finally, Jado drew in a breath, as if wrapping up some long conversation with himself. "Fudo Myoo is the great swordsman. He breaks the chains of suffering, lives in fiery heart of every swordsman. Fudoshin is dangerous, very powerful sword. He must be wielded with honor, but more important, with compassion. Compassion is not your strongest virtue, Danyo-*chan*. This sword loves battle." He looked up at me, his seamed face suddenly seeming old. "So do you, I think."

I shook my head. A strand of hair fell in my face. "I don't fight without reason, *sensei*. I never have."

He nodded. "Just so, just so. Still, I give you caution, you are young. Will ignore me."

"Never, *sensei*." I managed to sound shocked.

That made his face crinkle in a very wide, white-toothed grin. He offered the sword again, and this time I held my hands out, let him lay the almost-instantly familiar weight in my slightly cupped palms. I felt a shock of rightness burn through me, a welcome jolt not from my shoulder but from the pleasure of holding something so well-made, something intended for me. "Fudoshin," I whispered. Then I bowed, very low, over the blade. It seemed right, even though my braid fell forward over my shoulder and swayed dangerously close to the candle-flame. "*D'mo, sensei*." My accent mangled it, but his loud laugh rewarded me. I straightened, balancing the sword, already longing to slide the blade free and see that gleaming blue shine again. Longing to hear the slight deadly hiss as I freed it from the sheath, the soft whistling song of a keen blade cleaving the air.

Jado's laugh ended in a small, fiery snort. "Ai, my knees ache. Ceremony bores me. Come, let me see if you can still perform first kata."

"It would take more than a few months for me to forget that, *sensei*," I told him. It felt so good to hold a sword again. Complete. *Right.*

"It always takes long time, forgetting anything painful." He nodded sagely, and my eyes met his. We both bowed to each other again, and I surprised myself by laughing when he did.

11

I wasn't paying much attention as I rounded the corner, still loose and easy and smelling of healthy effort. I'd kept my house, and bought the two houses on either side with some of the blood money from the Santino bounty. Knocking the two houses down and building a wall around my place was the best step I ever took for privacy. I'd gotten the idea from Gabe. She inherited her private walls, I had to build my own.

My left shoulder burned with steady hot pain. I wondered if the mark would start to eat at my skin, and the last of my good mood fled.

Lucifer, maybe? What are the chances that he's involved in this mess? But no, there was no smell of demon on Christabel. I'm fairly sure I'd smell that. And this is too much gore for a demon, not even Santino was this messy.

Still, thinking about the Prince of Hell made a slight, rippling chill go up my back. It was fairly obvious he was still keeping an eye on me, for what purpose I didn't like to guess.

Screw Lucifer. He can wait until I've found out who's killing psions.

A click alerted me. I didn't stop, but my shields thinned, and I felt the hungry mood circling my front gate. The defenses on my walls sparked and glittered. The curtain of Power would short out any holovid receiver that got too close.

Oh, damn. Reporters.

They hadn't noticed me yet. The click I'd heard was someone tucked behind a streetlamp, taking stills of my walls. His back was to me, sloping under a tan trench coat, uncoordinated dark hair standing up. Purple dusk was falling, and bright lights began to switch on. He was a normal, and therefore blind to the eddies and swirls I caused in the landscape of Power.

I stood aside in shadow, melding with a neighbor's laurel hedge, and watched them for a few minutes. *Holovids,* I thought, blankly. *What the hell do they want with me? Oh, yeah.* Sekhmet sa'es, *who tipped them off? Less than twenty-four hours on the case and there's already a leak. Wonderful. Perfect. Great.*

My knuckles whitened against the swordhilt. The sword was a slightly-heavier katana, a beautiful, curving, deadly blade in its reinforced black-lacquered scabbard, older than the Parapsychic Act. I had expected it to feel strange to hold a sword again. I'd expected my right hand to cramp and seize up.

It didn't. In fact, it felt more natural than ever to curl my fingers around the hilt. Natural, and painless. I could pull the blade free of the sheath in one motion.

It's not my sword yet. My fingers eased up a little. It would take time and Power before the blade would respond like my old sword had, made into a psychic weapon as much as a physical one.

A lance of exquisite pain through my fingers made my hand spasm around the hilt. I drew in a soft breath, watching the holovid reporters circle in front of my gate, their klieg lights blaring, trying to get a good shot of my house. No hovers—they must have gotten some aerial shots already. *Jace.* Had he managed to slip inside unseen?

I finally cut through someone's weedy front yard and down the dirt-packed alley that had marked my neighbor's property line before I'd bought the place. No reporters back here yet, thank the gods.

My shields quivered, straining. I stopped, staring at my wall; the layers of energy I'd warded it with were flushing and pulsating a deep crimson. Demon-laid shields, Necromance shields, layers that Jace had applied, of spiky Shaman darkness. I calmed the restive energy with a touch and felt Jace inside, his sudden attention stinging against my receptive mind.

It was a bit of work to scale the wall; I'd contracted one of the best construction guys in the city to make it smooth concrete, aesthetic razor spikes standing up from the top. Demon-quick reflexes saved me; I hauled myself up and over with little trouble, my boots thudding down in the back garden. Water tinkled from a fountain, the smell of green growing things closing around me. I inhaled deeply, the air pressure changing—Jace's silent greeting, one psi to another.

When I slid the back door open, stepping over a pile of flat slate tiles I planned on turning into divination runeplates, he met me with a cup of coffee and a grim expression. He hadn't started drinking yet, but the night was young. I didn't stare at him only by an effort of will.

"Hey," I managed. "Looks like we've got company."

"Oh, yeah. Fucking vultures." His lip curled. Mob freelancers hate reporters a little more than the rest of us, and Jace was no exception. There's a reason why psis don't work for the holovids.

Well, besides the obvious fact that they would never hire a psionic actor or talking head. It was illegal to discriminate—but the natural antipathy we felt for the way we were shown on the holovids, mixed with the reluctance of the studio heads to put a psion on the air and lose a chunk of Ludder ratings, equaled no psionic actors. Status quo, just like usual.

"Nice sword." That was as close to a comment as Jace would allow himself.

I shrugged. "Thought it was time I started practicing again. How'd you make out?"

A sudden grin lit his face. "Pulled a few old strings, visited a few old friends. Got you the invite, for tonight. You can take a servant with you, it says. Need me?"

I actually considered it for a few moments, then looked at him. There were fine lines at the corners of his eyes, his mouth was pulled into a straight line, and he was bleary-eyed from too much Chivas, too many bounties, and not enough sleep. His clothes were rumpled, and I saw a shadow of stubble along his jaw. It occurred to me that my friends were getting older.

And I looked just the same, when I could bring myself to glance in the mirror. Golden skin and dark eyes, and a demon's beauty. A gift I'd neither wanted nor asked for.

I shook my head. "I need you to research for me, remember?" Even my hair shifted uneasily; the vision of Jace walking into the House of Pain was enough to make me shiver. I wasn't sanguine about going in there myself.

Despite the fact that nonhuman paranormals had legal rights and voting blocs, they still didn't like to get too chummy with humans. I didn't blame them. "I need to know a couple of things, and you're just the man to find out."

He folded his arms, his tattoo thorn-twisting on his unshaven cheek. "You are a spectacularly bad liar, once someone knows you," he informed me flatly.

"What?" Now I was feeling defensive, and I hadn't even gotten ten feet inside my own back door yet. The papers lying on the closer end of my kitchen counter stirred uneasily, whispering. I wondered if there was another parchment envelope in today's mail.

Pushed the thought away. *Jace, for the sake of every god that ever was, please don't ask to go to the House of Pain. I worry enough about you on regular bounties.* I closed my lips over the words, swallowed them. That was the surest way to piss him off, implying that he was less than capable.

He planted his booted feet and regarded me with the cocky half-smile meaning he was on the verge of irritation. "I won't break, Danny. I've seen worse than this, and I know how to take care of myself. Quit treating me like I'm second-class, all right?"

"Jace—" This was not the conversation I wanted to have with him right now. *Why does he always pick the worst goddamn time to throw his little hissy fits?*

"Maybe I'm not a demon," he said quietly, "but I used to be good enough for you once. And I've kept up my end of the bounties, haven't I?"

He did not *just say that to me.* My stomach turned into a stone fist, heat rising to my cheeks. The windows bowed slightly, rattling, and I took a deep breath. If I blew my own fucking house down it would be even more fodder for the vultures outside. Instead, I pushed past him, gently enough not to hurt him, only sending him backward a few steps. My teeth buried in my lower lip, I stalked through the kitchen, down the hall, and up the stairs.

Halfway up the stairs, Anubis's statue stood nine inches tall, slim and black, glowing with Power inside the altar-niche. Two unlit black novenas stood on either side; I had scattered rose petals and poured a shallow black bowl of wine for him. The wine's surface trembled as I stopped, looking into the niche.

Set to one side, a black lacquer urn glowed. No dust lay against its slick wet surface. No dust ever touched it, and no whisper of the ashes it held ever reached me. I'd spent hours staring at it, I knew every curve of the smooth surface. I had even once or twice caught myself opening my mouth to say something to the urn. I'd drawn chalk circles and tried solitary Magi conjurings out of shadow-journals; altering the runes and circles, trying to find my key to weaken the fabric of reality and call him to me. I'd tried to use my tarot cards and runes—but the answers I got were always fuzzy, slippery, fading. Nothingness, emptiness, dissolution. My own desperate hope managed to make any information I could get from divination useless.

My shoulder burned. But my right hand, clamped around the swordhilt, did not hurt.

Japhrimel. I didn't say it. My lips shaped the word, that was all.

He isn't there, Danny. Stop torturing yourself.

But had he waited for me there before slipping into the abyss?

Don't think about that, Danny. Sekhmet sa'es, *he's gone. He's not in Death. You've seen he's not there. Stop it.*

I just couldn't help myself.

Who would ask the questions for me if I managed to make an apparition of my dead demon lover appear? Certainly not Jace. It was too much to ask even Gabe for, and she was the only Necromance who might conceivably do such a thing for me.

I heard Jace's short plosive curse downstairs. Was he listening? He could probably tell from any slight sound where I was in the house. That is, if he didn't simply *extend* his senses and See me. He could tell I was in front of the niche. I'd caught him standing here once or twice too, usually after I'd spent my days between bounties in the living room staring at the urn's smooth sides, reluctantly replacing it every time. When I wasn't feverishly researching demons, searching for any clue about the Fallen, that is. I didn't know what Jace would say to Japhrimel's ashes. I didn't even want to guess.

Jace could certainly tell I was standing here.

Well, Anubis is my patron, I thought, my fingers tightening. *I never asked Jace to come here.*

You never sent him away either, the pitiless voice of my conscience replied. Was it me, or did it sound like Japhrimel's? Not the level, robotic voice he'd used when I first met him, no. Instead, it was the deep almost-human voice he'd used to whisper to me while I shuddered, wrapped in barbed-wire pleasure and his arms.

I sighed. The fingers of my left hand hovered centimeters from the urn's surface. What would I feel if I touched it now, my senses raw from pulling Christabel Moorcock's screaming, insane ghost out of Death, my body loose from sparring with Jado and sweating out the chill touch of that dry country where Anubis stood, endlessly waiting for me?

I let out a soft curse of my own and continued up the stairs. It was useless to waste time. I had to get ready. If I was going to the House of Pain, I wanted to be dressed appropriately.

Oh, damn. I'm going to have to take the whip.

12

Jace stood in the living room, his arms folded, the portable holovid player bathing the room in its spectral pink glow. He hit the mute button as soon as I appeared. I held the cloak over my arm, a long fall of sable velvet; I'd managed a tolerable French twist with my recalcitrant hair. The earrings brushed my cheeks as I tossed my head impatiently, making sure the long, thin stilettos holding the twist steady were not likely to fall out. It would be highly embarrassing to meet the prime paranormal Power in the city and have weapons fall out of my hair.

Jace looked up, his mouth opening as if he would say something. Instead, he stopped, his jaw dropping further open. His pupils dilated, making his eyes seem dark instead of blue.

"What?" I sounded annoyed. "Look, it's the House of Pain. I can't wear jeans and a T-shirt, much as I'd rather."

"You would have before." But his mouth quirked up in a smile. I felt my own mouth curl in response.

"I'd have never gotten an invitation before. They don't *let* humans in, especially not psis. Look, Jace—"

He was suddenly all business. "Research. What d'ya

want me to find?" He flicked the holovid off, bent down to touch his staff where it lay against the couch, then straightened, his back to me. "I'll bet you're thinking of some*one* instead of some*thing,* right?"

I hate your habit of anticipating me, Jace. I always have. "I need you to find out everything you can about our normal." I rotated my shoulders back and then forward, making sure the rig sat easy. Before, I'd always carried my sword—*no use having a blade if it's not to hand,* Jado often said, but I'd need my hands for other things tonight. My rig, supple oiled black leather, complemented the black silk of the dress and the sword-hilt poked up over my right shoulder. The back-carry was buckled to my usual rig. Drawing a sword is quicker when the hilt is over one's shoulder instead of at the hip, and it keeps the scabbard from knocking into things too. It was a compromise, like everything else.

Chunky dress-combat boots with silver buckles hid under the long skirt. I was unwilling to sacrifice any mobility to high heels; I'd already lose out because of the damn dress. The necklace was silver-dipped raccoon *baculum* strung on fine silver chain twined with black velvet ribbon and blood-marked bloodstones, powerful Shaman mojo. Jace had made the necklace for me during our first year together. He had poured his Power into it, using his own blood in the workings over the bloodstones, his skill and his affection for me as well as every defense a Shaman knew how to weave. I had locked it away when he left, unable to burn it as I'd burned everything else that reminded me of him; but now it seemed silly to go into the lion's den without all the protection I could muster. My rings shifted and spat, shimmering in the depths of each stone. "He's our first victim, there has to be a reason it started with him."

"You got it." His eyes dropped below my chin. The dress had a low, square neckline with a laced-up slit going down almost to my bellybutton; my breasts offered like golden fruit thanks to the shape and cut. The slender silver curves of the *baculum* were a contrast against velvety golden skin. The sleeves were long, daggering to points over the backs of my hands. The effect was like Nocturnia on the paranormal-news reports, a sort of elegant old-fashioned campiness. The guns rode low on my hips, the knives hidden in both the dress and the rig, the bullwhip coiled and hanging by my side. I knew I'd be chafing by the end of the night, and probably missing my messenger bag too.

"Did Gabe courier the files?" I tried to sound businesslike. His eyes dropped again, appreciatively, and then he let it go, straightening and scooping up his staff. The bones cracked and rattled—he wasn't quite as calm as he wanted me to think.

For once, I let it go. Dante Valentine, restraining herself. I deserved a medal. Of course, as careful as I was being, he was too. *Give him a gold star. Give him a medal too. Hell, give him a fucking parade.*

I told that snide little voice in my head to shut the fuck up.

He nodded. "Of course. Over there." He tipped his head.

I found them lying atop an untidy stack of ancient leather-bound demonology books. I would have to visit the Library again soon, make an offering in the Temple overhead and go down into the dark vaults full of ancient books. Maybe this time I would find a demonology text that would give me a vital clue about what I was.

I flipped the first file open, took a few pictures; the second and then the third. Christabel's ruined face stared up from glossy laserprint paper, but there was a good shot of the twisted chalk glyphs. I would probably have to visit her apartment too; sooner rather than later to catch whatever traces of scent remained. If nothing broke loose, that was. "I'm going to have to take the hover," I muttered. "Gods."

"Why don't you take a slicboard?" His tone was mischievous.

"In this dress?" I hitched one shoulder up in a shrug.

"Relax, baby. I ordered a hoverlimo." The grin he wore infected my own face, I felt the corners of my eyes crinkle and my lips tilt up. How could he go from irritating me to making me smile? Then again, he liked to think he knew me all the way down to my psychopomp. "No reason not to go in style."

He sounded so easy I could have ignored the spiky, twisting darkness of his aura. Jace was furious, his anger kept barely in check. I laid the cloak down, the pictures on top of it, and for the first time crossed the room to stand next to him, silk whispering and rustling against my legs.

His blue eyes dropped. Jace Monroe looked at the floor.

I swallowed dryly, then reached up and laid my fingertips against his cheek. My nails, black and shiny, wetlooking as the lacquer of Japhrimel's urn, scraped slightly. The contact rilled through me. My aura enfolded him, the spice of demon magic swirling around us both.

Why must even an apology be a battle, with you?

Japhrimel's voice, again, stroking the deepest recesses of my mind. I had never thought it possible to be haunted by a demon. Of course, if he had truly been haunting me it might have been a relief, at least I wouldn't be torturing myself with his voice. If he was haunting me, at least I would have some *proof* that somewhere, somehow, he still existed.

And was thinking of me.

"Jace?" My voice was husky. He shivered.

Be careful, be very careful; you don't know what it will do to him. The old voice of caution rose. Keeping him at arm's length was an old habit; I still ached to touch him even as the thought made my stomach flutter—with revulsion, or desire, or some combination of the two, in what proportion I wasn't sure.

Oddly enough, I wanted to comfort him. He had suffered my silence and my throwing myself into bounties, playing my backup with consummate skill. He had turned into the honorable man I'd first thought he was.

When had that happened?

"Danny," he whispered back.

"I . . ." Why did the words *I'm sorry* stick in my throat? "I want to know something."

"Hm." His fingers played with his staff, bones shifting slightly but not clacking against each other. His skin was so fine, so dry . . . and once I looked closely I could see the beautiful arch of his cheekbone, the fine fan of his eyelashes tipped with gold. Japhrimel had studied me this intently once, as if I was a glyph he wanted to decode.

Lovely, Danny. You're touching Jace, and all you can think of is a dead demon. "Why did you give up the Family?"

Jace's eyes flew open, dug into mine, oceans of blue. I smelled his Power rising, twining with my own. "I don't need it, Danny," he answered softly. "What good is a whole fucking Family without you?"

If he'd hit me in the solar plexus with a quarterstaff I might have regained my breath more quickly. My skin flushed with heat. "You . . ." I sounded breathless. My fingers sank into his skin, his desire rose, wrapping around me. The threads of the tapestry hung on my west wall shifted, the sound brushing against sensitive air, and for once I did not look to see what Horus and Isis, in their cloth-bound screen, would tell me.

He tore away from me, his staff smacking once against my floor, and stalked across the room to my fieldstone altar, set against the wall between the living room and the kitchen. He'd set up his own small altar next to it, lit with novenas; set out a half-bottle of rum, a pre-Parapsychic-Act painting of Saint Barbara for his patron Chango, a dish of sticky caramel candy, and a brass bowl of dove's blood from his last devotional sacrifice. The candleflames trembled. "Even the *loa* can't force a woman's heart," he said quietly. "Here's your invitation." A square of thick white expensive paper, produced like a card trick, held up so I could see it over his left shoulder.

"Jace."

"You'd better go." His voice cut across mine. "I hear the Prime doesn't like to be kept waiting, and I had to pay to get this."

"Jace—"

"I'll have any dirt on your normal by tomorrow afternoon. Okay?"

"Jason—"

"Will you just *go*, Danny?"

Irritation rasped under my breastbone. I stalked up to him, snatched the paper out of his hand, and heard the proximity-chime ring. The hoverlimo was here. Jace tapped his datband, keying it in through the house's security net. I pulled the shields apart slightly to let the big metal thing maneuver into my front yard. I took a deep breath, scooped up my cloak and the pictures, and stamped out of the living room.

If I hadn't been part-demon, with all a demon's acuity, I would never have heard his murmur. "I had to give it up, Danny. I *had* to. For you."

Oh, Jace.

I shook my head. He was right, I was going to be late. And in Santiago City, you never wanted to be late while visiting the suckheads.

13

After the Parapsychic Act, many paranormal species got the vote and a whole new code of laws was drawn up. Advances in medical tech meant cloned blood for the Nichtvren, enzyme treatments to help control werecainism, protection against human hunters for the swanhilds, and a whole system of classification for who and what qualified for citizen's rights. Most of the night world had come out to be registered as voters, some of them reluctantly. The Nichtvren, of course, having shepherded the Act through after decades of political maneuvering and hush money, came out first of all. In more ways than one—Nichtvren Masters were the prime paranormal Powers in any city, keeping the peace and dispensing swift justice to any werecain, kobolding, or any other nonhuman that flew above the radar and made too much trouble. The Nichtvren were courted by both Hegemony and Putchkin, and if you had to deal with the paranormal in any city, a good place to start was with the suckheads. They had their long pretty fingers in every pie.

The House of Pain was an old haunt. Feeding place and social gathering spot at once, it had been a hub of the paranormal and parapsychic community ever since its inception; after the Awakening, it had closed to humans and started catering exclusively to other species. The Nichtvren who ruled it, the prime Power of the city, was rumored to be one mean sonofabitch.

I wouldn't know. Humans, *especially* psions, aren't allowed in Nichtvren haunts unless they're registered as legitimate indentured servants or thralls. I sighed, settling back against the synthleather of the limo's back seat. Several paranormal species didn't precisely like psions, but we were marginally more acceptable than normals. Psions and Magi had been trafficking with paranormals since before the Awakening, trading their own uncertain skills for protection, knowledge, and other things.

The population growth of humanity had eaten away at the habitat of almost every paranormal species—and even the Nichtvren had reason to fear mobs of normals with pitchforks, stakes, or guns. To the other species, humans were evil at worst, psions a necessary evil at best. They have long memories, the paranormals, and they remember being squeezed out of their habitats by humanity, or being hunted when they tried to adapt. Silence, blending in, and clannishness had kept them viable as a species; the habits held even though they hadn't had to hide for a long time.

A psion could go her whole life without really interacting with a paranormal, even if she was a Magi or an Animone. The few humans who studied paranormal physiology and culture were given Hegemony grants and worked in the academic fields, and some anthropologists even studied paranormals . . . but those were few and far between. Despite the stories of psions being taken in by swanhilds or taught by Nichtvren, it just didn't happen that often. Paranormals were more likely to view humans as food—or a disease. Given how we'd treated nonhuman species throughout most of our history, I don't blame them one bit.

The alley off Heller Street was full of milling people, most with press badges. The Nichtvren paparazzi were out big-time; the gothed-out groupies clustered with them, trying to look exceptional and maybe buy a Nichtvren's notice. A faint, listless sprinkle of rain splattered down. Full night had fallen, orange cityglow staining the sky. I saw the thick pulsing of power on the brick wall at the end of the alley, an old neon sign pulsing the word *Pain* in fancy script over the door. A red carpet unrolled from the door down the alley, and red velvet cords on heavy brass stands kept the crowd back. Two hulking shapes I was fairly sure were werecain instead of genespliced bouncers lumped on either side of the door.

"Ma'am?" the driver asked, almost respectfully. His voice crackled over the intercom.

I came back to myself with a completely uncharacteristic sigh. "I'll be out in a few hours. You'll be here?"

"I've been contracted the entire night," the staticky voice said. "Yours until sunup, Miz Valentine. Do you want to get out now?"

Great. I've got a comedian for a driver. I sighed again. "All right. No time like the present."

He hopped out, then the doorhatch clicked and *fwished* aside. The white-jacketed driver offered me his hand, and I took it, careful to place no weight on it as I stepped out of the hoverlimo, my boots grinding slightly on wet pavement. I smelled night and human excitement, and a dash

of something dry and powerful over the top—I wished
again I could shut down my nose.

Laseflashes popped. They were taking pictures. I
blinked, settling the cloak on my shoulders, shaking the
folds of material free. The papers, tucked in a pocket I'd
thoughtfully sewn into the skirt, rustled slightly. I set my
chin, nodded to the driver—a short, pimple-faced young
boy squeezed into a white and black uniform with gold
braid—and set off down the red carpet. Behind me, the
driver's footsteps echoed, then I heard the whine of hovercells as the limo lifted up to float in a slow pattern, joining
the other hoverlimos and personal hovers already threading through the parking level above the House of Pain.

"Hey, Valentine! Valentine!" Some enterprising soul
called my name. I didn't acknowledge it. Soon all of them
were yelling, trying to catch my attention. I strode down
the carpet, head high, feeling the weight of my hair and
the stilettos caught in the twist. *I hate this.*

If Japhrimel had been with me, he would have walked
with his head up, his hands clasped behind his back, utterly unmoved by the human hubbub. Jace might have
grinned, mugged for the cameras a bit, or caused some
mischief. Gabe would have lit a cigarette, and Eddie would
have snarled. The thought of Jado or Abracadabra dealing
with this was ridiculous enough to be laughable.

But me, I couldn't imitate any of them. I strode toward
the lion's den with no time to waste.

The things by the door were indeed werecain, hulking
bipeds covered with fur, halfway between human and
huntform. I'd taken the required classes in paranormal
anatomy at Rigger Hall and beyond, at the Academy, but it
was odd to see them up close. In the old days they might

have worn clothing or stayed in human form. Now all they wore were ruffs of hair around their genitals. I didn't look.

Instead, I held up the invitation, and dropped the outer edge of my shields. Power blurred, stroking against the building's cold blueblack glow. A radioactive wellspring of Power from Saint City's deep black heart bathed this place. It had been here for centuries, the crackling energy of paranormals gathered in one place seeping into the concrete brick and stone. A heartbeat of music thudded out through the walls.

The werecain said nothing. One of them jerked his chin, motioning me inside. Flashbulbs popped.

I wanted to curl my right hand around my swordhilt. I also wished my left shoulder didn't buzz and burn as if red-hot iron was held just above my skin. Anger curled through my stomach, a welcome thread of familiar heat. I would be damned if I would be treated like a second-class citizen to be hustled into this goddamn place, even if I was human.

I measured both werecain with a slow, steady gaze. *I could take them. I could take them both. I could gut them. I've got a sword again.*

Then I remembered I wasn't just human anymore, but I still didn't back down, holding eye contact and playing the dominance game. It would be a bad start to act weak here at the door.

Finally, one of them gave me a jerky half-bow. "Come on in, lady." His voice, shaped by lips and tongue and teeth no longer human, sounded thick and grumbling. "Welcome to the House of Pain."

I gave them a nod and swept past, my head held high. *Who am I? I would have never done that, before.*

14

*I*nside, a migraine-attack of red and blue lights throbbed, and the music was a slow haunting melody over a pounding bass beat. Nothing I recognized. There was a time when I would have known, back when I used to go dancing with Jace, his spiky aura closing me off from the backwash of crowd-feeling. Inside the House, there was no tang of humans or human desperation, no sweet knifeblade of human desire or straining sex in dark corners; there were no ghostflits riding the edges of the crowd's heat. No blur of alcohol, no swirls of synth-hash cigarette smoke either.

Instead, Power rode the air in swirls and eddies, a lazy bath of energy that made me shiver slighly, my lips parting, my entire body stroked and teased in a hundred different ways. If I'd known—

No wonder they don't let humans in here. A psion could get addicted to this, they could have a whole community of Feeders in here. The overcharge of carnivorous Power in here would addict a human psion faster than Chill would hook a junkie, and they would keep coming back for more—or looking for the same charge out on the streets, draining anyone they could to feel the crackling feedback of Power. I was lucky to be safe behind a demon's shielding, closed off from the dozing, razor-toothed buzzing that could swallow me whole. Good thing I'd left Jace at home, too.

The place was warehouse-sized, and full of bright glittering eyes and long hair, beautiful pale faces, and the massive shapes of werecain. I saw a gaggle of swanhilds in one corner, their feathered ruffs standing erect around their heads, and a group of something I recognized as kobolding in another, downing tankards of beer. Each time one of the squat gray-skinned things took down another pitcher, the others would cheer.

Long floating sheets of material hung from the ceiling. I glanced up, wished I hadn't, and glanced back down. *Cages on the ceiling,* I thought incoherently, swallowing. I couldn't afford to gray out from shock now. If Japhrimel had been here—

Stop thinking about that. The image of a lean saturnine face and piercing green eyes rose in front of me, I shoved it down. Set off across the cement floor. A few steps in, slick stone reverberated under my feet. They'd paved the whole place in marble. The sound bounced and echoed. I shook my head slightly, wishing once again I could shut my ears off, or turn the volume dial down just a little.

The area that vibrated most intensely with power was a booth done in red velvet, facing the bar. I skirted the dance floor, trying not to notice the infrequent pattering drops from the cages overhead, or the bright, inhuman eyes peering at me. The Nichtvren didn't act as if they noticed my presence, but I sensed a few of them trailing me. They dressed in silks and velvets, some of them in ultrahip modern pleather and spiked hair, gelglitter sparkling on pale cheeks. One of them, a tall man in bottle-green velvet with fountaining lace at the cuffs, smiled widely at me, showing his fangs. My right hand curled into a fist. I considered stopping, reaching for my sword—but my legs had already carried me toward the booth, as if set on automatic.

This was dangerous. I couldn't afford to lose focus now.

I blinked slowly, the pain in my shoulder spiking, then easing a little. I could tap into the Power here and blow the whole goddamn place down, if I wanted to. Without even the slightest hesitation or hint of backlash. Now was not the time to be glad that Japhrimel had altered me, but . . . I still felt glad. A little. In a weird, heart-thumping kind of way. Playing with the big boys now, Danny Valentine was in a whole different league.

I stopped in front of the booth. Two men that looked almost human, both with a glaze of Power and the musty, deliciously wicked smell of Nichtvren on them, stood on either side. One of them eyed my swordhilt and opened his mouth to say something. I fixed him with a hot glare.

"Let her in." The voice cut through the pulsing noise. The dance floor seethed behind me, a sharp spiked flare of Power matching a rise in the music's tempo. I hoped my hair wouldn't fall down.

Nikolai, the prime Power of Saint City, leaned back on the red velvet of an antique couch carved to within an inch of its life. An equally antique table rested in front of him, pocked with gaps I recognized as bullet holes. He was tall, broad-shouldered, and dressed in nondescript dark clothing that looked silky. No amount of simplicity could disguise the weltering onslaught of Power he commanded.

I would have been impressed if I hadn't dealt with Power all my life. As it was, I cocked a hip for balance and leverage in case anyone came at me, looked into his cat-sheened dark eyes, and held up the invitation.

He had a shelf of dark hair falling over his eyes, a wide generous mouth, and high sculpted cheekbones. He would have been handsome without the flat shine of his eyes, like a cat's eyes at night when the light hits them just right, and the utter inhuman stillness he settled into. He wore a dark button-down shirt, probably silk, and a pair of loose silken pants, a pair of very good Petrolo boots, and no jewelry.

Beside him, leaning forward with her elbows on her knees, sat a Nichtvren female with a fall of long, curling blonde-streaked hair, her dark-blue eyes liquid and fixed on me. She had no catshine to her eyes, and none of Nikolai's immobility—instead, her fingernails tapped at the air, her lush lips parted slightly, the tips of her fangs showing; she wore a frayed red V-neck sweater and a pair of dark ratty jeans, beaten and scarred combat boots, and a thick silver cuff-bracelet with a tiger's eye the size of a mini credit-disc on her right wrist. She measured me from head to foot, and then smiled, half of her mouth pulling up.

I'm glad someone's having fun. I stepped forward, into the booth through a sticky sheet of Power that snapped shut behind me. Instantly, the noise they called music went down in volume, and I gave an involuntary sigh of relief.

Nikolai said nothing, examining me. It was like being eyed by a wild animal that hadn't quite made up its mind to eat you or simply crush you with a clawed paw.

I nodded at the female, knowing that his Consort was the way into his good graces. Rumor had it she was the only thing in the entire city that Nikolai valued. Rumor *also* had it that he went crazy if he even *thought* someone had messed with her.

Aw, now ain't that sweet. "I'm Danny Valentine, and I'm grateful you agreed to see me, ma'am. Sir."

Anyone who knew me would have expected the words to sound sarcastic. I was faintly surprised they didn't.

Nikolai still didn't move. The Nichtvren female laughed. The deep, husky sound surprised me and made my hackles rise, her eyes flared a dark luminous blue. She was exquisite, and I caught a thread of an odd scent; some type of musk that reminded me of sexwitch over the musty caramelized-dark-chocolate scent of Nichtvren. "Hi," she said. "Sit down. Nik's just in a mood. We have to see a werecain delegation after you, and he finds that unpleasant. Want something to drink?" Her accent was old Merican, the vowels shaped oddly, like they used to be around the time of the Parapsychic Act but before the great linguistic meltdown of the Seventy Days War. So she was old too.

Not nearly as old as him.

I wouldn't trust the liquor in here, lady. I shook my head, let my cloak fall to the floor. It was a good gesture, it showed I had nothing but the ordinary weapons. I settled myself on the couch to their left, easing down gingerly, wishing I could hold my sword across my lap. Steel would be better than empty air between me and these two.

Nikolai finally moved. "What is it you require?" he asked, and the woman's pale expressive hand came down on his knee; the tiger's eye on her bracelet flashed with light. He had been immobile before, now he looked over at her, and a stone would have looked frenetic next to him.

"Be polite, sweetie. She's new at this." The woman rolled her eyes, then rested her elbows on her knees again. "What can we do for you, Miss Valentine?"

Now that was unexpected. I drew the papers out of my pocket, making sure to move very slowly. All the same, Nikolai's eyelids dropped a fraction. A chill, prickling weight of Power covered him.

I don't think I'd ever want to see him pissed off. The thought was there and gone in a flash, I pushed the sudden swell of almost-fear down. I had nothing to worry about, I was here on business, and I wasn't just human.

Am I? What's the protocol for an almost-demon dealing with a Master Nichtvren? This wasn't ever covered at the Academy. Maybe I should write to the Hegemony Educational Board.

I laid the papers on the table, swallowing the choking panicked giggle rising in my chest. "The police have asked me to look into this. Have you ever seen anything like it? I know you'll have access to texts I don't. If you can narrow this down, it would help me immensely."

She scooped the papers up. Nikolai didn't move, but he seemed to give the impression of a twitch. She settled back, moving with preternatural Nichtvren grace, and cuddled into his side.

That managed to make him move. He slid his arm over her shoulders and looked down at the top of her head. My heart slammed into my throat. For some reason, he reminded me of Eddie watching Gabe, his face softening slightly, his eyes lighting up. It was a startlingly human expression on a being who hadn't been human for a long, long time. No man had ever looked at *me* like that.

Would you have noticed, if they did? the deep voice asked me.

I decided to not even dignify that thought with a response. Sekhmet sa'es, *I'm even ignoring my own bloody self. I'm losing my mind.*

Velvet rustled as I shifted uneasily. I wished I could have worn jeans to this. *At least if I'd worn jeans I could have ridden a slicboard.* I licked dry lips and watched as she scanned the pictures, her mouth tightening.

She shuddered, her blue eyes lighting with a flare of something almost-panicked, gone in an instant.

Nikolai's eyes flicked over me.

"Nik?" She held up the papers. "Take a look at this."

He stirred himself to glance, a faint line grooving between his eyebrows, taking the laseprints from her slim pretty hand.

"It's Ceremonial." She moved slightly, her body shifting closer to his. "But I haven't seen this variation. Have you?"

"It stinks of evil, Selene." His eyes lost their catshine for a moment and turned dark. For a moment, there was a flash of how he might have looked as a human man, and I found myself staring, hoping to catch it again.

"Have you seen it?" she demanded, her hand flashing out to catch the other side of the sheaf of paper. There was a long, breathless pause.

"No, *milyi*." His eyes searched her face, still dark and horribly, awfully human. "I have not seen this exact variation. And yet . . ." He trailed off, his gaze moving slow and gelid past me and out over the dance floor. *He looks just like a lion looking over a herd of zebras,* I thought. *Or a pimp checking out a flock of unregistered hookers.*

"You're killing me here, Nikolai." She pushed a dark-blonde curl out of her face. Her lips quirked downward before she smiled. Bits of light from the blastball suspended over the dancefloor flicked over the smooth planes of her face. "Can we just once have some information without it being a huge production?"

Hear, hear, I seconded internally. I'd thought it was going to be a relief to be in a place without human stink. Instead, it creeped me out. My hackles rose, almost-goosebumps roughening my skin. They clustered through the whole building, the Nichtvren, alien as demons, even if originally human. The only way to become a Nichtvren is to be infected, bitten and transformed with a blood exchange; it usually takes two or three exchanges for the Turn to happen. Bones change, the jaw becomes distended and cartilaginous, the eyes transform, able to see in complete darkness, and the thirst races through their veins. It's a combination of retroviral infection and some etheric transfer from Master to fledgling that modern science, for all its biomechanical wonder, can't replicate. They were different from normal humans and different from me, yet I still felt something odd: a type of kinship.

Most of the Nichtvren here had been Turned into something else, altered away from human and into something different. Something more.

Like me.

I wonder if people feel like this when they look at me. I shifted slightly on the uncomfortably hard couch. Velvet rasped against my skirt. The air inside the sticky shield turned chill, pressing against heart and throat and eye. If I'd still been human, this would have made me draw my sword, a feral, bloodthirsty current swirling through the air. I would have looked for a safe wall to put my back to. It felt like someone was going to get hurt.

"It looks like Feeder glyphs." One of Nikolai's hands crept up, touched her cheek. The gesture was so tender, blood rose hot in my cheeks, I felt like a voyeur. His eyes took back the gold-green sheen of a cat's, flicked between the photos and then her face. "Why have I heard nothing of this?"

I shrugged. "It started with a normal, and then a sex-witch. One of Polyamour's girls. Then it was a Necromance. Christabel Moorcock." I quelled the shiver rising up my spine. "They're Feeder glyphs?" Feeder glyphs were illegal except for research purposes. Twisting the Nine Canons to serve a Feeder was heavy-duty magick, lethal to some, it was hard to protect against spells using runes that could bolster a Feeder's talents.

"They appear to be," Nikolai answered, his eyes still locked on Selene's face. She moved slightly, her mouth softening, and I dropped my gaze to the bullet-scarred table. *You'd think Nichtvren would have proper furniture,* I thought sourly, and inhaled deeply to calm myself. My left shoulder eased slightly, not so much of the crunching, living glare of pain. The music outside melded into Retro-Phunk, their *Celadon Groove*. A chill finger traced my spine. The last time I'd heard this music had been in Dacon Whitaker's old nightclub before I'd turned him in for running Chill. When I'd blown back into town after Rio, I'd found out Dake was dead of Chill detox, eaten alive by the drug. It wasn't a pleasant thought, just like everything else I'd been thinking lately.

Nikolai spoke again, his voice slicing the noise like a silvery scalpel through mauled flesh. "This thing killed a *tantraiiken?*"

I had to think before I remembered that was one of the old—very old—words for a sexwitch. Sexwitches used to be rare, their ability to heal and need to live off the etheric and psychic energy raised by sex combining to make them prized paranormal pets before the Awakening. It also contributed to a lot of them getting killed off young in some very nasty ways before they had Hegemony protection. I nodded, the stilettos a reassuring sharp weight in my hair.

"Then you shall have assistance in hunting down the perpetrator." Nikolai shuffled the papers back together with one brisk movement. "You are welcome here, Miss Valentine. When you have dispatched this criminal, come back. It seems my Selene fancies you."

The female rolled her eyes again, a reassuringly human movement. "That's his way of saying you can step in without an invitation," she translated, plucking the papers from his hand and leaning forward to offer them to me. My fingers were numb. I forced my right hand to close around the laseprints and tuck them back in my pocket.

"Thank you," I managed through my dry lips. "Ma'am."

"It's Selene." Her eyes flicked out over the dance floor. It was a glance very much like his, maybe an unconscious imitation, but it still made my skin crawl. "There's the delegation," she sighed. "I think that's all we can tell you. Nikolai's got this thing about anyone messing with *tantraiiken.*"

I don't know why I asked. "Why?" *Curiosity killed the cat, Danny. Just get out of here. Get out of here now.*

She shrugged. It was a beautiful, loose, fluid movement. "Maybe because I used to be one. Stay and have a drink if you like, the bar's got stuff for just about everyone. Come back sometime."

"I might." I made it to my feet, my shoulder throbbing. "Thank you."

Nikolai lifted his hand. "One moment, demonling."

I froze. *He recognizes me as demon? Of course, he's Nichtvren. He can see Power.* If he came over the table at me I could carve his heart out, but she was something else. The hard glitter in her dark blue eyes and the nervous way she twitched was almost scarier than his rocklike stillness. And the Power that cloaked them both was impressive, even if it was nothing like a demon's. Then again, nothing in the wide world was like a demon when it came to Power—except for a god.

And I had no desire to meet any god other than my own, thank you very much. I could even go the rest of my life without having to deal with a demon ever again too.

Now if I can just convince the Prince of Hell to forget I exist.

"I have a library." Nikolai's flat cat eyes looked straight through me. The music pounded behind me. I wasn't sanguine about going back out into the sonic assault. Or about having them at my back. Or about staying in this goddamn place any longer than I absolutely had to. I didn't look up at the cages on the ceiling—but the effort cost me dearly. My stomach fluttered uneasily, and I had never in my life wished to vomit more than I did at that moment. "Among my acquisitions are several texts sup-posedly written by demons. You may find them useful."

Where were you the last year or so when I had time to come and bury my nose in a few books? I nodded. "Thank you." It was all I could say.

I turned on my heel and plunged through the sticky shield, pausing only to scoop up my cloak and swirl it around my shoulders. The music slammed into my whole body like a backdraft from a reactive fire. *Get me the hell out of here. I have got to get out of here; dear gods, get me out of here—*

There was only a millisecond's worth of warning be-fore the lights died. The music failed as well, which was a relief. Instinct sent me into a fighting crouch, and my hand blurred up toward my swordhilt. Sudden dark settled into the walls and floor, I heard whispers and shuffles, the lamplit pricks of Nichtvren eyes firing through the gloom.

I heard something else, too. A low, vicious growling.

My sword whispered free of the sheath. My heart gave one incredible leaping thud, my skin coming alive. I cursed the skirt of the dress even as the demon equivalent of adrenaline flooded my system. Whatever was coming, if anything got near me I was going to kill it.

Oh, yes. This was what I *lived* for.

Screams. Something snarled and soft padded feet slap-ping the floor.

A thundercrack of Power slammed out from behind me, bearing the unmistakable cold acid tang of Nichtvren. "I am *not* amused," Nikolai said softly, the weight behind each word pummeling the air in concentric rings of razor-edged glass.

That seemed to break the stasis. Chaos screamed into

being, snarling and scrabbling boiling through the darkness. Roaring filled the air. I tracked the sound, coming up out of my crouch in a fast, light shuffle, blade whirling, the familiar feeling of racing on the thin edge of adrenaline rising from that old place of instinct and terror. The cloak fell for the second time, it would only tangle me up. My boots squeaked as I half-turned, steel coming up with a faint sound as it clove heavy air.

Tchunk. My blade carved cleanly through whatever it was. I whirled on the balls of my feet, avoiding bloodspray, took the second one with a clash. Low hulking shape, my pupils dilated, demon-eyes taking in every available photon and squeezing the usefulness out of it. There wasn't much light here, even for me.

My left-hand main-gauche, reversed along my forearm to act as a shield, took a hell of a strike. I cried out, more in surprise than pain—the damn thing was *fast*. The emergency lights came up, a wash of crimson stinging my eyes but I was moving on instinct anyway, punching something hairy in the face with my fist braced with the knife-hilt then leaping, landing between two hulking shapes. Quick kick behind one's knee, the hairy shape bellowing and folding down; spinning to engage the other. The smell of blood and wet fur exploded out, gaggingly strong, my shoulder burned even more fiercely. Claws raked up my side, and the whole world seemed to go white for a moment, a sheet of fire blinding me. Black, demon blood pattered on the marble, *my* blood, redolent of spice and sweet rotting fruit. *How did I get into this? I'm fighting off a couple of fucking werecain, bad luck I suppose, I was just in the way. Goddammit.*

It hit me like a freight train, fur and stink and claws.

I smashed up with my left and again; *too close to engage with the sword, get a little distance, move move move.* I took the easy way out, dropping and rolling to scythe the 'cain's legs out from underneath it. The 'cain spun aside, twisting in midair with unholy fluidity, and the scar on my left shoulder blazed into agonized life. My body gathered itself, new strength suddenly coursing through my veins, and I kicked up with both legs, my back curving as momentum jolted me up off the floor and onto my feet. My right foot lashed out, catching the 'cain I'd just tripped on the nose. A flurry in the corner of my eye was another one bearing down on me. Steel flashed. Fudoshin described a sweet, clean arc, deadly steel singing low, and more blood exploded. The 'cain leaping for me dropped, its intestines slithering wetly out as I landed, spinning to feint with the main-gauche and then *cut;* followed with a one-handed side-downsweep that missed because the 'cain was shuffling back.

It was my turn to attack, my wrist turning so the blade fell into position again, every motion as natural as breathing. I bolted forward, boots shuffling and the battlecry rising in my throat; my *kia* shivered the air as I engaged with the werecain again. Its snarl turned into a falsetto squeal as I rammed the main-gauche home between two ribs, then leaned, sword coming in from the side, because the side-downsweep turned naturally into the rib-splitting cut. The werecain gurgled as Fudoshin bit deep—deep enough, I hoped, to cut the abdominal aorta. I twisted the blade against the suction of preternatural muscle, smelled the stink of a battlefield and of werecain blurring together, and the 'cain in front of me slumped away from my sword. I backed up, blood hissing free of shining blade as

I whipped it through the cleaning-stroke; faint blue fire etched itself along the razor edge. The process of making the sword *mine* had begun with the first blood shed together.

I half-spun, ready to take on the next enemy, but as soon as it had begun the fight was over. Dead werecain lay scattered about, the last one flopping until Nikolai casually reached down, Nichtvren claws extended, and tore its throat out.

There were more bodies piled over the red velvet couch he and Selene had just been perched on, and still more bodies further away toward the dance floor. For every one I'd killed, Nikolai had killed three. "Most distressing." His voice throbbed in the lowest register, like a huge pipe organ. It was a voice that could tear through bones and thump against the heart itself, a sound felt more than heard in the crackling silence that followed the death of the music.

"Well," Selene answered, over his shoulder. "You left nothing for me."

"My apologies, *milyi*." He straightened. "Søren will have much to answer for." His eyes came up, dark holes in his face under the shell of crimson lighting. "You fight well, demonling. And you attacked my enemies."

That most emphatically does not *make me your friend,* I thought, clamping my teeth so the words couldn't escape. The *last* thing I needed right now was more trouble. *If I hadn't been in the way they would have ignored me, and I would have been happy to just get the hell out of here.* "Thanks for the compliment," I managed, my jaw set tight as I bent down to wrench my knife free of a werecain's ribs. "Why . . ." I trailed off, not wanting the explanation anyway.

"The werecain are embroiled in a territorial dispute." He straightened as I did, immaculate. His face was a thoughtful Renascence stone angel's, set in its perfection and unremarkable as a statue compared to the welter of Power surrounding him. Selene stood behind him, dyed and dipped in crimson, her hands on her hips. She didn't look happy. "This is the faction unhappy with the decision I was required to arbitrate. I am sorry for the disturbance. I do not like a guest of mine being forced to fight, it reflects badly on me. Accept my apology."

It's hell being top of the heap, isn't it? The merry, sardonic voice inside my head almost made it out of my mouth. There was a time when I would have let it. "Oh. No worries." Then, "Have a nice night."

"It is extremely unlikely." He half-turned to look over his shoulder at Selene, his gaze falling in one swift sweep down her body, as if checking her for damage. "But you have my thanks, demonling. Good luck."

Great. I couldn't help myself. "I'm beginning to think I'll need it," I said, and got out of there while I still could.

15

I had the hoverlimo for the rest of the night; there was no reason not to use it. So I gave the driver Christabel Moorcock's address.

I should have started with the puzzling Bryce Smith, or with the sexwitch Yasrule. I should have gone to salvage whatever traces remained, yet I went to Christabel's. I tried to tell myself I was violating procedure because of instinct, and that the other two scenes were too old.

The hoverlimo spiraled down to land on the roof of her brownstone apartment building at the edge of the Tank District. The driver scurried around to open the door before I could reach for the handle; his eyes were wide and dark. The hoverlimo rose afterward to circle in the parking-patterns overhead.

This close to the Tank District, the smell of garbage and synth hash swirled through the air, mixing with sharp spikes of illicit sex from the hookers prowling the strips and the deep wells of the nightclubs, glittering like novas in the psychic ether. Cool wind touched my hair as I stood for a moment on the concrete landing-pad, feeling the atmosphere of the Tank press against me. If Saint City was a cold radioactive animal wanting to be stroked, the Tank was the pulsing heart of that animal, so fiercely cold it burned. The throbbing that forced vital energy through the rest of the city, through the sluggish brain of the financial district and the arteries of the pavement. The Rathole was buried in the depths of the Tank, a deep pit of vital energy whistling a subsonic note at the very bottom of my sensing-range.

My city. It did indeed feel like home.

My datband got me in through the building's public-access net; Christabel's magsealed apartment was on the top floor. Since Gabe had keyed me into the Saint City police net with access to the scenes, the magsealing parted for me.

The air was stale, tinted with the chemical wash of Carbonel, used to get blood out of fibers. The cleaners had come in to get rid of the blood and matter once the forensic techs had gone through the place; I caught a lingering trace of jasmine perfume and the tingle of a powerful awareness. A Reader had been here to capture every aspect of the scene; it had probably been Beulah McKinley. She did good work, and whatever scene she had processed always held a breath of jasmine.

I wondered if she, like Handy Mandy, had caught sight of whatever had driven Christabel's ghost mad.

The front door had been shattered, splinters peppering the wall opposite and the carpeted hall. Christabel's shields were slowly fading, the giant rents torn in them patched with Gabe's trademark deftness. A shuntline hummed into the street outside to carefully and safely drain away the ambient energy and fold Christabel's shields up so no trace of murder and agony remained to create psychic sludge for other inhabitants of this quiet building. The temporary magseal door shut behind me with a click.

I was inside Christabel Moorcock's house.

The carpet was wine-red. The hall was dark, but I caught geometric patterns painted over the walls; protection charms. I glanced into the dining room and into a bathroom with an amber-glowing fleur-de-lis nightlight. In both rooms the painted walls were covered with an intaglio of protection runes, each knot of safety carefully daubed. They resonated uneasily, the ones near the door spent and broken; long waving fronds of Power flowed toward the front door.

Huh. That's odd.

The entry hall, the dining room, and the two bedrooms were carpeted. The bathroom was tiled, the kitchen and the living room in mellow hardwood. The second bedroom was a meditation room, a round blue and silver rug in the middle and the ceiling painted with a wheeling Milky Way.

Quite an artist, Christabel. I did not turn the lights on yet.

I inhaled deeply. I smelled traces of Gabriele's kyphii-tainted scent, the Reader's jasmine, other faint human scents overlaying a more complex well. Closing my eyes, I shut away all the more recent smells, including the sweet, decaying fruit of the blood drying on my ruined dress.

That left me with a powerful brew of female psion, a healthy astringent scent. Christabel had smelled like molecular-drip polish on long nails, slightly-oily hair, and strong, sweet resin incense. Resin was cheap and high quality, readily available in metaphysical supply stores, and it brought back a swirl of memories from my school days.

So you used schoolgirl incense. A little surprising, but I suppose it isn't any stranger than Gabe and her kyphii. The furniture was overstuffed, no hard edges. Her bookshelves weren't dusty, but there were no houseplants. No pets either, not even cloned koi.

The altar in her meditation room held a bank of white candles in varying heights, and a statue of Angerboda Gulveig Teutonica, glittering gold leaf on Her robe worked with flames and the Teutonica heart symbol. There was another statue set off to one side, a black dancing Kali of the old school, graphic and bloody.

There was a fresh offering in front of Kali, a shallow dish of something sticky that smelled of wine and faint traces of human blood. Also interesting.

Christabel's bed was neatly made. A copy of Adrienne Spocarelli's *Gods and Magi* stood on the bedstand, a ritual knife laid across its cover. The clothes hamper was full of dirty clothes that smelled of lilac powder. A sleek, gleaming Pentath computer deck stood in the corner at a precise angle to her mauve bed. Her bathrooms were spotless.

To go from this order to the chaos of the living room was a shock. Great gouges had been torn into the wooden flooring, and the waning chalk marks on the hardwood were barely visible under a dark stain no amount of cleaning could scrub away. The couch was destroyed, the table reduced to matchsticks. Little drawstring bags of herbs, protective amulets all, hung from the dark ceiling fixture. Splashes of blood had baked onto the full-spectrum bulbs;

I was glad I could see in the dimness. There had been a hell of a fight in here.

I let out a long, slow breath. Both Gabe and a Reader had been here. There was nothing for me to see. Wherever Christabel had allowed herself to truly live, it wasn't here. This place was more like a stage set than anything else.

Paper lay scattered across the gouged floor, the same parchment she had written her last message on. A spilled bottle of dragonsblood ink lay near the entrance to the kitchen. Try as I might, I couldn't find the pen among the drift of chaos.

My own voice startled me. "I'm here." It was a whisper, like a child's in a haunted house. "If you want to talk, Christabel, I'm listening."

Silence gathered in the corners. I felt like a thief, here in the middle of this carefully constructed world. I didn't want to resurrect her mad raving ghost; I wanted some breath of the living Necromance.

None came. Even the flowering stain of thick-smelling violence in the air was smooth and blank, nothing for my intuition to grab onto.

The other scenes won't tell you anything either, the deep voice of certainty suddenly spoke inside my head. I paused, velvet and silk rustling as I turned in a slow circle, my eyes passing over the chiaroscuro of protection runes painted on each wall. *The answer to this puzzle doesn't lie here. You know where it lies.*

I did. The only clue I had likely to unravel this tangled skein was encapsulated in three words scrawled on parchment by a terrified dying Necromance.

Remember Rigger Hall.

"I would much rather not," I muttered, and the air

swirled uneasily just like my skirt. I suddenly felt ridiculous, overdressed, and very, very young for the first time in years.

But if remembering the Hall would keep someone else from dying, I would do it. I'd survived that place once. How hard could remembering it be?

The three stripes of phantom fire down my back twinged in answer. So did the vanished scar along the crease of my lower-left buttock. The scar on my shoulder burned, burned.

My hand tightened around Fudoshin's scabbard. I was no longer weak or defenseless.

"All right, Christabel." My voice bounced off the walls. "You're my best clue. For right now, you lead the dance."

I had the not-so-comforting feeling that the air inside her wrecked living room had changed, becoming still and charged with expectation. As if it was . . . *listening*.

My knuckles were white on the scabbard. My mouth had gone dry, and when I slipped out again through the temporary magseal door I should have felt relieved to leave the scene of the carnage behind.

I wasn't. All I could think of were three little words, chanted over and over again by a shrieking, insane ghost who had once been a woman inhabiting a neat, orderly, soulless little apartment.

Remember. Remember Rigger Hall.

I knew what I had to do next.

16

The night was getting deep when the hoverlimo dropped me off on the concrete landing-pad in my front yard, and I tipped the driver well. He muttered his thanks and lifted off before I reached my front door. The garden rustled uneasily, dappled with darkness and the orange glow of citylight.

My hands were shaking. Not much, but enough that I could see the fine vibration when I held them out in front of me. Even my right hand, that twisted claw that had so gracefully held a sword and defended me tonight, was shaking, the fingers jittering as if I was typing a Section 713 Bounty Report.

I made it inside, shut the door, and leaned against it, scabbard digging into my back. The dress was stiff and crusty with blood along my left side that I noticed for the first time. "*Anubis et'her ka.*" The god's name made the air stir uneasily. "That was unpleasant."

Jace wasn't home. He was probably off digging through public records. Because psions so often worked at night, public buildings rarely closed before two in the morning.

It was a pity. I could have used some easy banter.

I lifted my left hand because my right was shaking too badly, examined the black molecule-drip polish and the graceful wicked arches of my fingers. The fingers flexed, released.

The smell of lilacs still clung to my dress. Lilacs, and terror. The quiet dark inside my house suddenly made the flesh hang traitorously heavy on my bones—slender, arching frames, architecturally different than human bones but not agreeing with demon physiology in any of the books I read. Stuck in between, trapped like a butterfly halfway out of a glass chrysalis and frozen, popped into a kerri jar stasis. I didn't belong here in my old life, had nothing and nowhere to move into despite all my frantic thrashing on bounties. Stopped, frozen between one step and the next like a holovid still.

What butterfly wants to go back into the chrysalis? Or revisit being a caterpillar?

Remember. Remember Rigger Hall.

Bile rose, I forced it down. A rattling tremor slid from my scalp to my booted toes. I could feel it circling, the panic attack deep and needle-toothed, combat and the shock of memory both catching up to me.

Hey, Danny, the lipless mouths of my nightmares said. *Thought you shook us loose, huh? No way. Let's get out the old fears and rattle them around, let's dance in Danny's head and shake her left and right, what do you say?*

"Why am I shaking?" I asked the still darkness of my refuge. Took a deep breath and realized how musty the place smelled. I rarely cleaned anymore, and there was only so much Jace would do. Besides, we were gone all the time, tracking down criminals.

Compassion is not your strong suit. Jado's voice careened inside my skull, echoed, stopped as if dropped down a well.

My left shoulder crunched again. I bent over, retching, my hair coming loose and the stiletto chiming on the hardwood floor. Almost a year of hiding behind the image of a big, tough bounty hunter hadn't changed a goddamn thing.

It never would.

Japhrimel was gone.

The floor grated against my knees and palms, cold and hard. The world went gray. *I'm going into shock. And nothing around to bring me out.* The layers of shielding energy over my home shivered, singing a thin crystalline note of distress, like a thin plasglass curve-edge stroked just right.

"You will not leave me." A voice like old, dark whiskey. Familiar.

My entire body leapt to hear that voice.

I looked up. Saw nothing but my front hall, iron coatrack, the mirror, a slice of warm gold from the kitchen. Jace had left the light on.

"You will *not* leave me to wander the earth alone." The voice slapped at me, yanked me up off the floor, and shoved me back against the door, pressure like a wavefront of Power against my entire body, squeezing around me, forcing away the gray shocky cloudiness.

I'm being smacked around by a ghost. A ripping unsteady laugh tore out of me. I opened my eyes, saw the empty hall again. Fragrant, sweet black blood was hot on my chin—I'd bitten my lip almost clean through. It stung before it healed over, as instantly as any other wound.

"Lucky me," I half-sang. "What a lucky girl, lucky girl, I'm a lucky girl, Necromance to the stars."

"Dante." Merely a whisper, but I felt it all the way down to my bones.

"It's not fair. I want you back." Then I clapped my hand over my mouth, and my entire body tensed, listening.

Listening.

A long silence greeted this. I made my hands into fists. Careful. I always had to be so stinking careful. Had to hold back, so as not to damage the less resilient. The *humans*.

A long sigh, and the voice—more familiar to me than my own, by now—brushed my cheek. "*Feed me . . .*"

I scanned the hall. Empty. The entire house was empty.

No human. No demon. No *nothing*. Nothing in my house but me, dead air, my possessions, and the lingering smell of Jace. Dust, and the smell of stale grief. That was all.

Great. The dead will talk to me, but never the way I want them to. Never the useful way. Oh, no. The dark screaming hilarity in the thought was troubling, but it was like a slap of cold water across the face of a dreaming woman.

I am an adult, I told myself. *I grew up, goddammit. I am all grown up now.*

I peeled myself away from the door, silk rustling around my legs as I strode for the stairs. Halfway up, I stopped so quickly I almost overbalanced and fell on my ass all the way back down.

The niche stood as it always had. No dust on the scorching black urn.

Anubis dipped his slender beautiful head, examining me. The wine was gone.

The god had accepted the offering.

The rose petals were withered too. Dry. Sucked dry.

"This is crazy." My shoulder throbbed. "I've got a killer to hunt down. A killer that uses Feeder glyphs in some kind of elaborate Ceremonial circle. And I can't afford to be haunted by . . ."

But being haunted by Japhrimel was better than missing him, was better than grieving for him. "Are you talking to me?" The urn's gleaming curves mocked me. "Please tell me you're talking to me."

Of course, no reply. Nothing but the still hot air teasing at my face, the statue of Anubis shifting, as if demanding my attention.

I met the statue's eyes. Was it a hallucination, or did the god appear to be smiling slightly?

"I've missed you." This time, I was talking to the god. My voice sounded thin, breathless. It was true. I'd missed the sense of being always held, protected—the god of Death was the biggest, baddest thing around. Even Nichtvren feared Death.

Even demons did.

I always wondered if that was why I was a Necromance. A helpless, collared girl pushed into the Hegemony psi program because of her Matheson scores, an orphan sent into Rigger Hall like all the rest—and in the Hall, you either found a protector or you didn't last long.

Death was the best protector. At least I didn't have much to fear; when I finally died it would be like going into a lover's embrace.

There were whole months of my schooling when I merely endured through the day, going from one task to the next, one foot in front of the other. I would wait for every visit with Lewis, but I was getting older and couldn't see him as often. I had only the books.

At night, I would read by the light of a filched flashlight under my covers, every book Lewis had left me. When I could read no longer, when I finally closed my eyes, I would slip into the blue-fire trance of Death.

That kept me going. I was special, both because Lewis had given me his books and because Death had chosen me. I withdrew mostly into myself after Roanna's death, learning to live self-contained, a smooth hard shell. But I always had the books and the blue glow, twin lines going down into the heart of me, feeding me strength. Telling me I could endure.

I aced every single Theory of Magick class, every single Modern Classics test. I was academically perfect no matter how bad it got, having absorbed Lewis's love of study.

More importantly, I never doubted that I would survive. Lew had given me a primary gift: a child's knowledge that she is loved completely. And though the punishments were bad, some of the teachers had been dedicated, true masters of their craft. There were good things about the Hall—learning to control my abilities, learning who could be trusted and who couldn't, learning just how strong I really was.

And always, always, there was Death.

I was too young to tread the blue crystal hall or approach the Bridge, but I would feel the god's attention, a warm communion that gave me the strength to become self-reliant instead of withdrawing into catatonia or developing a nervous tic like some of the other kids. Sometimes, even during the worst punishments, I would close my eyes and still see that blue glow, geometric traceries of blue fire and the god's attention, *my* god's attention, and I had made up my mind to be strong.

I had *endured.*

And when Mirovitch was dead, the inquest finished, and the school shut down, I went on through the Academy and my schooling up to my Trial, that harrowing ordeal every Necromance must pass to be accredited, the stripping away of the psyche in an initiation as different as it is terrifying for every individual. You can't handle walking in Death until you've actually died yourself, and what is any initiation but a little death? I'd had an edge over every other initiate: I never doubted I would survive my Trial. And afterward, with a few white hairs I dyed to make them the standard black of a Necromance, I'd gone on and never looked back. Never stopped in my steady march, moving on.

But all the time, I hadn't had a goddamn idea what I was marching *toward.* I still didn't, but I knew one thing for sure: I didn't want to go *back.*

And yet that was what Christabel was asking me to do.

"Rigger Hall." My eyes locked with the statue's. "I swore I'd never go back."

You must. The eyes were blank and pitiless, but so deep. Death did not play favorites—He loved all equally. *What you cannot escape, you must fight; what you cannot fight, you must endure.* The god's voice—not quite words, just a thread of meaning laid in my receptive mind— made me shudder, my knees bumping the wall. That had been my first lesson when they clipped the collar on me at the Hall. Endurance. The primal lesson, repeated over and over again. Even later, when I seriously doubted I would get out of some new horrible situation alive, a thin thread of me down at the very core of my being had merely replied, *You will*. And that was that.

I've been called suicidal, and crazy, and fey; I've even been called glory-hungry and snobbish. I don't think that's accurate; I simply always knew I would survive, a core of something hard and nasty in me refusing to give in even at the worst of times. Better to face what frightens you than to live cowering in fear; and if Death frightened me I need only go further into the blue glow of His embrace until even fear was lost and the weight lifted from me.

I had nothing to fear. I kept my honor intact. An honorable person was only as good as the promises she kept, the loyalty she showed. My honor was unstained.

A familiar touch against my shields warned me—Jace coming back, probably on a slicboard. He was dropping in fast, probably to avoid being seen or shot by the holovid reporters outside. I felt the security net slide away to let him pass.

I made it almost all the way down the stairs before my legs started to tremble alarmingly. I slid down to sit, my knees giving out so I thumped inelegantly onto the second step. When Jace opened the front door I was perched on the steps, leaning against the wall, my knees drawn up.

He kicked the door closed. "Danny?" His voice, blessedly normal, *sane,* made me shut my eyes again. I rested my chin on my forearms, braced on my knees, the silken cascades of the dress falling to either side. The wall was doing a damn fine job of holding me up.

Three scars, dipping down my back, and the brand laid along the crease below my left buttock. I smelled the sick-sweet odor of burning flesh again, heard whistling soft laughter and my own throaty screams, felt blood and semen trickling down my inner thighs.

And I heard something else: Headmaster Mirovitch's dry, papery voice whispering while the iron met my skin. I forced myself to stare unflinchingly into the memory, the door inside my head a little ajar, showing me what I'd locked away so I could go on living.

"Danny." Jace stood in front of me. "You okay?"

I lifted my head. His hair was messy, windblown, and his blue eyes were humanly kind. I didn't deserve his kindness, and I knew it.

My eyes burned, but my left shoulder had quieted. It took me two tries to reply through a throat gone dry as reactive paint. "No. I'm not. Get the shovels, Jace. We've got some digging to do."

17

The garage housed garden implements and a sleek black hover, dead and quiescent on its landing gear. This space had been empty before I'd gotten rich. I had always meant to turn it into a meditation room, but I ended up avoiding it and doing my meditating in the living room or bedroom.

I pushed a stack of boxes aside, my hands trembling, and looked up to find Jace watching me, his wind-ruffled hair a shock of gold in the light from the bare full-spectrum bulbs.

"Listen." He pushed his hand back through his wind-struck hair. The motion achieved absolutely nothing in terms of straightening it, only made it stick up raffishly. He looked like Gypsy Roen's sidekick Marbery, all angles and cocksure grace under a shock of hair. "Why don't we call this off and get drunk? Tackle this tomorrow night."

"You might be able to get drunk. I can't." I was surprised by how steady my voice was. The smell of the garage, the hover on its leafspring legs and cushion of reactive smelling of metal and fustiness, clawed at my throat.

"Well, why don't we just fall into bed and shag until we

forget this, huh?" He tried to make it sound like a light, bantering offer. Just like prejob bullshitting to ease the nerves. Unfortunately, his breath caught and ruined the effect.

Oh, Jace. I actually managed a smile, then pushed again. The boxes of files scraped along the floor, cardboard squeaking against smooth concrete. I looked down, saw the wooden door set in the concrete. A round depression in the center of the trapdoor held an iron ring.

"You truly are amazing." Jace propped the two shovels over his shoulder like an ancient gravedigger. "This is right out of a holovid."

Irritation rasped at me, but my retort died on my lips. He was too pale, sweat standing out on his forehead. We were both claustrophobic, and he . . . what was he feeling? If I touched him I would know. Bare skin on skin, I might have been partly-demon but I was still the woman who had shared her body and psyche with him. Almost a decade ago, but that kind of link didn't fade.

Was that why I couldn't quite let go of him? Or was it because he reminded me of the person I had been before Rio, a feeling I couldn't quite remember for all the sharpness of my Magi-trained memory?

"You don't have to come down." I closed my hand over the metal ring. It was so cold it scorched—or was it that my fingers were demon-hot? Dust stirred in the still-hot air; I was radiating again. *I'll never need climate-control again, maybe I should hire myself out as a portable dryer. Rent your very own psionic heater, reasonable rates, sarcasm included.*

"And let you face this alone?" He shook his head. "No way, sweetheart. In for a penny, in for a pound."

Words rose in my throat. *I'm so sorry. I wish I could be what you needed.*

Instead, I wrenched the trapdoor up.

A musty smell of sterile dirt exhaled from the square darkness. I felt around under the lip of the hole. "Probably not working," I muttered. "That would just cap the whole goddamn day."

My fingers found the switch, pressed it, and a bare bulb clicked into life. I let out a whistling breath through a throat closed to pinhole size.

"How was the suckhead convention?" Jace's tone was light, bored. I glanced up at him, suddenly intensely grateful for his presence. If I owed Gabe and I owed Eddie, what did I owe to Jace?

The answer was the same in each case: too much to easily repay. Debt, obligation, honor; all words for what I would keep paying until I took my last breath, and be damn grateful for the chance.

It was better than being alone, wasn't it?

It sure as hell was. "Interesting. He says he's got some books on demons I'm welcome to come by and peruse." I managed not to choke on my own voice.

"You do have a way of making friends." Hipshot and easy, Jace Monroe examined the trapdoor, the bare bulb's glare showing a drop bar and a square of pale, dusty dirt.

"Must be my charming smile." I leaned forward, catching the drop bar in both hands. The dress slithered as I trusted my weight to the iron, pulling my legs in and dropping them, then slowly lowering myself down. Thank the gods my swordhilt didn't snag. I hung full-length for a moment, then dropped the three inches to the dirt floor. "There was a werecain attack while I was there."

He hadn't mentioned my torn dress or the black demon blood crusted on the side of the bodice. I would never have believed him capable of such restrained tact. If I went upstairs to change out of the dress, I would find some way of putting this off.

"I can't leave you alone for a moment, can I." Jace handed the first shovel down, the second. He took his sword from his belt and handed it to me.

"Guess not. I went by and checked out Christabel's apartment." Bits of garden dirt still clung to the rusting metal of the first shovel. The second shovel was new. Why had I bought it? Was my precognition working overtime again?

Sometimes I hated being gifted with precognition as well as runewitchery. Being gifted with precognition is like being shoved from square to square on a chessboard, you're never sure if your intuition is working or if you're just getting paranoid. There's precious little difference between the two. Out of all the Talents, precogs—Seers— go insane the most.

"Find out anything interesting?" He leaned over, caught the drop bar, and levered himself down gracefully. His T-shirt came untucked when he curled down and I caught a flash of his tanned belly, muscle moving under skin. His boots ground into the dirt, and he scanned the unfinished space. "Anyone else would have a *ladder*, Danny."

"You think I come down here often enough for that? And yes, I found out something interesting, at least at the suckhead convention. The Prime and his Consort identi- fied the circles as being marked with Feeder glyphs."

I felt cold just mentioning it. Feeders were nothing to

mess with. It's every psion's worst nightmare, tangling with a Feeder.

Jace whistled tunelessly, taking both shovels from my unresisting hands, leaving me his sword. I was abruptly warmed by the implied trust. "That's . . . well." His sandy eyebrows drew together, his lips compressed.

I studied the perfect arc of his cheekbone, the corner of his mouth. He had always been so very attractive; and his air of self-assuredness was compelling too. I wondered if I'd fallen for him because he'd always seemed so damn sure I would, and my own well-camouflaged uncertainty made his confidence even more magnetic. I had always secretly wanted to be as *sure* as he seemed to be, instead of faking it as I usually did. His façade never cracked, his good humor rarely faded. "What did *you* find out?"

A shrug, a brief snort of frustration. "Exactly zip. Our Mr. Smith was registered as normal on his datband. He worked as a jeweler, but his birth certificate's vanished and his utility bills were paid by a trust."

I pushed past him, glad the ceiling wasn't lower. "What kind of trust?" I'd bought this house partly because of the crawl space being basement-sized; Doreen hadn't minded as long as it had a garden. It had been abandoned and rundown, but the foundations were sound; we'd celebrated the final round of remodeling by throwing a huge party for the Saint City parapsych community. I'd met Jace at that party, though I hadn't seen him again until after Doreen's murder.

Thinking of that made me shiver again. I quelled the shudder, rubbing my right hand against my ruined skirt. Dried black blood crusted the velvet, scraped against my black-lacquered nails.

"A blind sealed trust. No way of breaking in. The same trust that covered the names of his clients under corporate confidentiality. A full search of public records turned up a big fat nothing except for the name the guy's slicboard was registered to." Jace sounded disgusted.

I found the corner at the far end of the house, under a closet I never used. I stopped, my heart pounding. The left side of the dress's bodice crackled with dried blood as I took in a deep breath. My heart beat thinly. "A jeweler with a slicboard? What name?"

"Keller. Just the one word. No last name. Bought at a dealership out on Lorraine that's since gone out of business." His aura roiled with spikes—Jace didn't like being down here either. I felt the warmth of his body across the air separating us as I turned back to him. The smell of peppered musk and honey was soothing even if it carried the decaying tang of human.

"The plot thickens." My voice shook. I reached for one of the shovels.

"Goddamn thick enough already." Jace shouldered me aside. "Let me, I've been up to my elbows in paper and public records for hours. I could use a little sweat. Where do I dig?"

I pointed at the corner. "Just start going down."

He gave me an extraordinary blue-eyed glance. In this corner of the basement, the light was dim enough that I couldn't see the fine lines beginning at the corners of his eyes and mouth.

Unless I concentrated.

I chose not to. Instead, I watched him drive the shovel down and start to dig. The concrete foundations were very close here. The earth was dusty and pallid. Having nothing else to do, I lowered myself down and sat on the ground, shifting inside my rig until the sword rode comfortably, balancing his scabbarded blade across my knees.

"Jace?"

"Hm?" He tossed another shovelful of dirt with a clean, economical movement.

"Thank you." The words stuck in my throat. As if I could ever thank him for what he was doing right this second, digging so I didn't have to.

"Anytime, baby." Another shovelful of pale dirt and small stones. "What am I digging for?"

"Metal. I buried it deep. Really, I mean it. Thank you."

"You're going to ruin that dress." His muscles flexed under the black T-shirt.

I swallowed copper fear, wished there was more light. Shadows pressed thickly in the corners. "It's already ruined. And I'm never wearing a dress again. If jeans and a Trade Bargains shirt isn't good enough, people can go fuck themselves."

"I've always liked you in jeans. That cute little ass of yours." He was beginning to get serious about digging, breathing deep and loosening up. Starting to sweat, drenching the air with the smell of a clean human male having a good workout.

I shivered, looking up at the ceiling. "I'm sorry." It came out as easy as an apology ever had. Which meant it tore and clawed its way out of my chest while I watched him excavating something I never wanted to see again.

His even rhythm didn't stop, but his shoulders tensed. "For what, baby?"

"I'm not very nice to you." *That's the understatement*

of the year, isn't it. I'm a right raving bitch to you. You deserve someone who can at least be affectionate.

If I was telling the truth to myself, I might as well let him in on it.

He was silent for a full three shovelfuls. The hole was beginning to take shape. Chills crawled over my skin. My jaw clenched tight so my teeth wouldn't chatter. "No. You're not." He tossed another shovelful of dirt, didn't look at me.

"You're better than I deserve."

That made him laugh. Jace Monroe had an easy laugh, sometimes used as a shield, sometimes genuine. This one was genuine. "You worry too much, sweetheart. What am I digging for?"

"Metal."

"What's inside?" He was beginning to get a respectable-sized hole. My teeth chattered, since my jaw had unloosed enough to talk. I hugged myself, cupping my elbows in my palms, squeezing, feeling my fingernails poke at my arms. Wished I could go back up into my house and forget about the trapdoor again—bury the memory deeper than I'd buried the rest of everything that had to do with the Hall.

"Books. Other things." I couldn't even pretend to have a steady voice.

"Great. Other people bury bodies, Dante Valentine buries books." He warmed to the work, I could feel the heat coming from him. Human heat, animal heat. Familiar heat.

Why did I feel so guiltily grateful for that warmth? For his mere breathing presence?

"They're going to be useful, Jace." I dropped my head, staring at his sword in my lap. A *dotanuki* instead of the katana I usually carried; he'd had it since I'd met him. A bigger hilt for his bigger hands, more weight, I'd sparred with him before. I'd beaten him even before Japhrimel made me into what I was now. But Jace was dangerous, tricky; he was the type that would take a cheap shot. I used to think it was dishonorable of him.

Now I wasn't so sure.

I trailed my fingers over the hilt-wrapping, catching flashes of Jace as he handled the blade. There were memories locked in that steel. I tapped the scabbard, touched the hilt again.

"Danny, baby," Jace said, "you keep stroking him like that you're going to give me a hard-on."

I glanced up. He was watching me, leaning on the shovel. His eyes were dark and hot, I didn't need a dictionary to read the look on his face. Jace Monroe had never made any secret about wanting me, which had made his abandonment of me all those years ago so much more shocking. And then, Rio, and now this penance he was paying by staying with me, watching my back, and forcing me to live.

Of all the things I had to be grateful for, Jace was probably the biggest. Who else would have put up with me?

"Sorry." I laid his sword aside. *That's it exactly, Jace. I don't know what would kill me, but I think losing Japhrimel was damn close to it. Did you think I'd hurt myself? Is that why you came back?*

He gave me a brilliant, unsettled smile. *Well, what do you know. Claustrophobia strikes again.* "It's okay. I kind of like it. What did you find at Christabel's? Anything?"

I snorted and hauled myself to my feet, scooping up the other shovel. "Nothing I didn't already know. Let's get to work." And I walked toward my grave with sweating demon hands and a sour stomach.

"Chango love me, girl." Jace used his forearm to wipe sweat from his face. "You buried this fucker *deep*."

"Only way to stop the dead from rising." I tossed the shovel. It was a passionlessly accurate throw, ending with the shovel neatly stowed up on the surface, out of the way. The second shovel followed, its blade chiming against the first. I laced my fingers. "I'll give you ten up and hand it to you."

The deep gloom of the hole meant I saw the gleam of his teeth and the whites of his eyes as he grinned a little too widely. "Sounds good. I need a shower."

"Me too."

He stepped into my fingers and I lifted him easily enough, careful not to overshoot. He caught the edge and levered himself out.

One good thing about demon strength, I never would have been able to do that before.

Then I lifted my coffin, an old-timey footlocker from before the Seventy Days War. Hefted it with more ease than I'd lifted him. Something chinked inside, and the sound made a cold shiver trace all the way down my spine. I bit back a moan, it died as a strangled gasp.

Jace dragged it up out of the hole. Then I leapt, catching the lip just like the side of a swimtank, hauling myself up. "*Sekhmet sa'es,*" I hissed between my teeth. "I hate this. I just started this hunt and already I'm six feet deep and sinking fast."

"Keep paddling, baby." Jace yawned. "We gonna fill this in?"

"We'd better." I rubbed at my forehead, feeling gritty grave dirt clinging to my skin. "Let's get it over with so we can wash up."

"We could probably use some dinner too." He stretched, then gamely went for the shovels. I laid my hand on his arm.

He went still, looking down at me.

"You go on up, get washed up. Get something to eat. I'll be up in a few." I don't think either of us believed I was dealing with this well.

"I'll help." He shook his golden head, stubborn, his face streaked with dirt.

"Come on, Jace." I took the path of least resistance. "I'm *hungry*. This way, by the time I get up there I can take a shower and eat something. Okay?"

He examined me for a long moment. "'Kay," he said finally, just like a pouting little boy.

"Thanks." Impulsive, I went up on tiptoe and kissed his dirty cheek. What else can you do for the man that just dug you up out of your grave?

He scooped up his sword. When he was gone the entire cellar seemed to close around me. The darkness seemed full of exhaled danger, my nape prickling, my breath coming short and harsh.

I picked up the shovel, considered it, set it down. The hole mocked me. The dirty, rusty footlocker mocked me. My sword, riding my back, mocked me.

I lifted my right hand. It was actually doing pretty well, not cramping or seizing up. Maybe holding a sword was all it needed.

Instead of using the shovel, I started pushing at the pile of dirt with my bare hands, like an animal. I pushed and pushed, scooping great armloads of sterile earth, shoving it, kicking it. My lips pulled back from my teeth. The dress's bodice, never meant for this sort of treatment, tore. One of the laces snapped, and it took me a few moments to undo my rig and shuck myself out of the dress. Piling my weapons to one side, I tossed the fall of silk and velvet into the hole and continued to fill it in. My new golden skin didn't bruise, but I felt as if it had, all the way down to my bones. My hands shook again, so badly dirt spilled between them, dry pebbles clinking and grinding together. It wasn't until I stamped the earth down with my booted feet that I realized I was making a low throaty noise of rage. My left shoulder throbbed dully and the vanished scars on my back felt as if they'd broken open, bleeding phantom blood. A collage of scars. An art statement made of suffering.

And I *laughed.*

I had, after all, survived everything I'd buried. I had fought so long and so hard, I had taken bounty after bounty, taken on the Prince of Hell himself. What was down here that I needed to be afraid of?

I collapsed on top of the disturbed mound of lifeless dry dirt, laughing until I choked, my knees grating against small pebbles. My teeth clicked together painfully. I hugged myself, bare breasts pressed together, hunching over until I presented a small target. Naked except for my boots, I hugged myself and shook like a rabbit, tasting shock bitter and flat against my tongue as I screamed with dark hilarity.

After all, it was a child's fears I was feeling. There was no longer any need for me to huddle in the corners sobbing, like I used to.

Rigger Hall. Goddamn.

How old did I have to be before the name itself didn't make me shiver? Who did I have to be grateful for— Doreen, who had taught me how to be vulnerable again? Japhrimel, who had taught me that love was not strictly a human phenomenon? Gabe, whose friendship had never wavered? Or Jace, who was still teaching me about who I could trust?

I was grown-up now. Rigger Hall could no longer hurt me.

Then why was the child inside me still screaming? Hadn't I grown past that, fought past it?

It was a long time before I heard footsteps again, Jace's stiff knee giving his gait a familiar hitch. He didn't say a word, I pushed myself up, and thankfully he didn't try to help me, just waited until I got to my feet and offered me a robe I dragged on with shaking hands as I shuddered with tired laughter. I felt like I'd just run through five sparring matches and fought in all three theaters of the Seventy Days War without a break as well.

He'd scrounged a ladder and pushed me up it, then dragged me upstairs. I wasn't unwilling, I just let him lead me. He didn't bother trying to get me in the shower. He just slid the robe off my shoulders and pushed me into bed, worked my boots off, then shucked his clothes, dropped down and held me.

He was not Japhrimel, but he was warm and he was human. I took what comfort he offered gratefully, his naked skin against mine, while every tear I had swallowed during eight years of Rigger Hall broke out of its black box and leaked out of my eyes, shaking me as if an animal made of grief had me in its teeth yet again.

18

He slept heavily, lying on his side, his face relaxed without its shield of good humor. Dirt smudged his cheekbones and his forehead. His hair was stiff with dry sweat and dust. Grime worked into the small, thin wrinkles that were beginning to etch his flesh, the lines that would grow deeper soon. He *was* getting older. So was Gabe.

I lay on my side, my leg hitched up over his hip. He was sweating, grime clinging to both of us even though I never seemed to sweat; I traced his cheekbone with a gentle fingertip. Black molecule-drip polish glinted in the dim light from the hall.

The curve of his lower lip unreeled below my touch. His breathing didn't alter. He was out cold, it had been a long day. And whatever else he was, Jace was no longer young.

I pressed his hair back, gently. Traced his eyebrow, drew my finger down his cheek, the rough stubble of his chin made my mouth twitch. He smelled of human, of decaying cells and honeyspiked Power, of grave dirt and sweat.

I can't be what he wants, I reminded myself for the thousandth time. *I don't even know what it is he wants.*

Then again, I'd never bothered to ask him, had I?

I took my hand away and moved, slowly, infinitely slowly, until we were chest to chest, my face inches from him. His breath mingled with mine, a heady brew of demon, Necromance, and Shaman.

My lips touched his, a feathery touch.

He exhaled. I shuddered. It wasn't like Japhrimel. It could never be like that again. My skin crawled, remembering the screaming, intense drowning of being clasped in a demon's arms. The loathing wasn't for the memory— it was as if my body revolted at the thought of another lover. Mutiny in my cells.

I was pretty sure I could push that aside; I didn't need to enjoy sex. I'd had plenty of sex without enjoyment; I could probably even fool Jace into believing I was having a great time. I remembered what it was like with him before: sex between us was another form of sparring. A chess match, a game, each touch a challenge, the prize in the other's final abdication of control.

Sex as war, as a game, hadn't it been that way for him? Another question I had never asked.

Would I forget he wasn't Japhrimel once I reached a certain pitch of excitement? If I let myself go, did what I wanted to do, what would it do to Jace? I remembered the blinding pleasure, heart straining, lungs forgetting their function, ecstasy wrapped in barbed wire and rolled across exquisite nerve endings. A form of Tantra, sex magick, reaching into the deepest level of genes and psyche to remake me.

Remake. In whose image?

I hesitated, my lips touching Jace's. Would it kill him? Remake *him?* I doubted it. I had no illusions about the amount of Power I had—not enough to rival Japhrimel even when he had Fallen. And yet the research I'd managed to do between bounties had made me no wiser about the exact limits of what I was. I probably wouldn't change him into anything, but I didn't *know.* I knew nothing.

I knew nothing, and I couldn't betray Japhrimel. It was an impossible situation. I needed Jace. I wanted to be kind to him, I had a debt to repay to him and one to collect, and yet . . .

My shields quivered, shuddering restlessly. Someone was coming in on a slicboard, coming in fast, and the quick brush against my shields was familiar, garden dirt and the smell of beer and sweat.

I'd expected him to drop by.

I was up and out of the bed in one motion, grabbing a handful of neatly folded clothes as I ran for the bathroom. It was 3:00 AM, late afternoon for most of us who lived on the night side, and I felt him slide through my shields as I ducked into the shower and twisted the knob all the way over to "cold" as a penance.

It took a little longer than I liked to scrub the grime off, but when I came downstairs, braiding my hair back the way I used to, he hadn't come in past my front hall. I stopped at the end of the hall next to the stairs and took him in.

Eddie slumped against the wall, fingers tapping his staff. There were only three people that could key in through my shields like that: Jace, Gabe, Eddie. Anyone else attempting entry would be denied, whether by the security system or by the cloak of Power over my house, the triple layer of shielding. I realized with an abrupt jolt that I was lucky to have three people I could let into my home with no question. Three . . . friends, people who went into danger for me when they didn't have to.

The net of obligation and duty might trap me, but it also protected me and kept me from falling into an abyss. Which abyss I couldn't quite say, but I had felt its cold breath enough to suddenly be very grateful for the man sleeping upstairs, the woman who had pulled me into this, and Eddie in my front hall.

Shaggy blond Eddie of the hulking shoulders and long hair, the smell of fresh dirt hanging on him like it did on every Skinlin dirtwitch berserker. He seemed to carry a perpetual cloud of shambling earthsmell with him, his blunt fingers seeming too indelicate for any fine work. For all that, Eddie was the most dangerous dirtwitch I'd ever met in a sparring match.

I guess he had to be, to keep up with Gabe.

He wore a long camel-colored coat and a *Boo Phish Ranx* T-shirt strained on his massive hairy chest. I studied him for a moment. He stared back, meeting my eyes for once. Shifting his weight from foot to foot, tapping his staff with callused fingertips, his aura roiling, he made the house shields quiver and my own defenses go tense and crystalline. "Eddie."

"Danny." He lifted one shoulder, dropped it. "Guess you wanna ask me a few."

I shrugged. "Why, you know something?" He said nothing, and my conscience pinched me hard. "Not if you don't want to talk," I amended. It was the least I could give him; the gods knew *I* didn't want to talk about the Hall. An act of mercy, not requiring of him what I wouldn't want to do myself.

But Eddie wouldn't be here if he didn't have vital information. And if it would stop another death, he would force himself through it.

He was as cottage-cheese pale as I'd ever seen him. "Dunno if it's useful, but you better hear it."

I nodded. "Let me get my sword."

"Time was you would'n answer the door without it."

Time was I wouldn't have let even you or Gabe key in through my shields and use the key to my front door, Eddie m'man. Guess I've grown up. "Someone would have to be pretty fucking stupid to come in here and start trouble. If they could get in at all without my approval."

"So you got another sword?" He lifted one shaggy eyebrow. For him that passed as tact; he must have been taking lessons from Gabe.

"Figured it was time I stopped fucking around."

"Amen to *that*," he sniffed.

Dear old Eddie, always dependable. I was Gabe's friend, therefore I was—no matter how sarcastic he got—worthy. That was the thing about Eddie Thornton, if you were all right in Gabe's book, Eddie would go to the wall for you. There was no deception in him, no subterfuge. Either you were worth his support, or he would cut you loose. He had no middle ground.

Gods above, but that was refreshing.

I took Fudoshin down from the peg where my old sword had hung. My bag was already slung diagonally across my body, I shrugged into my coat. "My slic's outside with Jace's. Let's go."

19

We went to the old noodle shop on Pole Street. It was absurdly fitting. The place hadn't changed a bit, from the dusty red velour hanging on the walls to the old Asiano man sitting in the back booth slurping his tea and eyeing everyone suspiciously, a curl of synth-hash smoke drifting up from his ashtray. Two bowls of beef pho later, I was beginning to feel a little less raw.

"Okay." I grabbed a hunk of rice noodles with plasilica chopsticks. Eddie sucked at his beer and blinked at me.

The fishtank in the back of the store gurgled softly.

I took the mouthful of noodles, slurped it down. Beef broth splashed. I had to suppress a small sound of delight—eating was the only thing that gave me any pleasure anymore. Thank the gods I had a hiked metabolism, or I'd be as fat as a New Vietkai whore.

Well, I got enjoyment from hunting down bounties too. But it wasn't a clean enjoyment. Each bounty was a brick in the wall between me and the uncomfortable thoughts that rose when I had too much time on my hands.

Eating, however, was all mine. I didn't have to think while I ate.

"You're still a goddam pig." Eddie grimaced.

"Says the man who eats with his fucking fingers?" I fired back. "Spill, Eddie. I left a warm bed for this."

"How warm?" He smirked through blond-brown stubble. "Jace finally tie you up? Or did he put on horns and a pitchfork?"

I laid my chopsticks down. It had taken me a year to learn to eat with my left hand wielding the silverware. Now my right hand felt clumsy, as if all it wanted to do was curl around a swordhilt. "That's *one*, Edward." My tone made my teacup rattle against the table. "Now why don't you quit being an asshole and tell me what you've got?"

"I might know something." He went even paler, if that was possible. Looked down at the table. Gulped at his beer. I suddenly longed to get drunk. This would be so much fucking *easier* with chemical enhancement.

I picked up the thick, white china teacup. Said nothing.

He squeezed his eyes shut. His hand trembled as he set his glass down. "I was there," he mumbled. "Rigger Hall."

I'd known that, of course. He'd been a few classes ahead of me.

Like Christabel.

Great beads of sweat stood out on his forehead. "There was . . . a secret." His throat worked, his Adam's apple bobbing. "I don't know much, but . . ."

Rigger Hall was full of secrets, Eddie. I felt the glowing metal pressed against my skin again, heard Mirovitch's papery voice. Cleared my throat, set my teacup down. "Eddie . . ." My voice was harsh, harsher than it had to be. The glass of beer rang uneasily. *I have got to get some kind of control over myself.* My left shoulder burned dully as if in agreement. "*Anubis et'her ka,* don't do this to yourself."

His eyes flew open. "You don't tell me what I do or don't gotta do," he growled, leaning back. "I can't go home, I can't fuckin sleep, and people are *dying.* I got to get this done."

I shrugged. My heart beat thinly under my ribs, hammering with impatience and adrenaline combined. Picked up my teacup again.

He took another long gulp of beer. "'S a wonder anyone made it out. I wasn't in it, not the Black Room."

I shuddered. His eyes flew open, as wide as I'd ever seen them. "No, not *that* one," he hurriedly amended. "No, that was the name of the Secret. 'Cause they met in that old shed off the lake. You remember?"

I nodded. Christabel's ghostly screaming rang inside my head, I pushed it away. "I remember." Cold sweat lay on my skin. *Black Room, remember Rigger Hall. That's what Christabel meant.*

His eyes were the eyes of a child reliving a nightmare. "You was in the cage?"

He meant the Faraday cage in the sensory deprivation vault under the school. It had been intended to help telepaths who needed a short-term respite from their gifts. Instead, it had been turned into a punishment. Psions— especially strong ones—can only stand a cage for a very short time before their psyches begin to crack under the lack of stimulation. If you weren't a telepath seeking relief, being in a cage was like being trapped in a black void—no light, no sound, and no access to the ambient Power that fed magickal and psychic talent. It is the closest thing to insanity I had ever known, and I still couldn't step into an elevator without shaking and feeling the walls close in. The cage of an elevator or hoverlift was uncomfortably similar to the cage of Mirovitch's Black Room. "Four times," I replied, husky.

"I had two. Two was enough."

"*Never* would have been enough," I forced out past teeth clenched so tightly my jaw hurt. *If it was before Rio, would I shatter my own teeth and swallow them?* The thought of the sensory-deprivation vault and the cage, and the *blackness* rising through me to eat at the very foundations of my mind—"*Sekhmet sa'es,* Eddie . . ." I swallowed dryly several times, my throat clicking. *Got to get control. Goddammit, Danny, get a hold on yourself!*

"The secret . . . Christabel was one a 'em. I wasn', but I got friendly wi' one."

I waited. He would come to it in his own time. The least I could do was give him a few minutes to work up to saying whatever he had to say.

"Steve Sebastiano," he said finally. Was he *blushing?*

Now I had officially seen everything.

My jaw dropped. "You got friendly with *Polyamour?*" Polyamour the transvestite, one of the most famous sexwitches in the world? The sexwitch rumored to be so fantastic in bed that Hegemony heads and even some paranormals paid just to call on her socially? Her house took a healthy chunk of cash just to be put on the waiting list. Polyamour, who used to be Steven Sebastiano, a few classes ahead of me and already the source of whispers and rumor at school. I heard she'd been tutored by Persephone Dragonfly down in Norleans at the Great Floating House, and done an internship in Paradisse as part of an exchange program.

And one of her sexwitches had been a victim. The piece fell into place neatly, and I felt the little click of intuition inside my skull.

The first link in the chain, the first arc of the pattern, was always the hardest. It would only get quicker from here.

Thank the gods. I don't think I can stand to look at another dead body.

Eddie shrugged, looking down into his half-empty glass. "We was roommates. Bastian was one of Mirovitch's sexwitch stable. Fucked him up royal."

A sexwitch in Rigger Hall? "Fucked up" would be an understatement. "I'll bet. So what happened?"

Eddie's sleepy hazel eyes were haunted, no longer the eyes of a fully grown man. Instead, they were the deep wells of pain in the face of a terrified child.

I didn't need a mirror to tell me my own eyes were just as dark. Just as wide, and just as deep—and just as agonized.

"Mirovitch," I persisted, my throat dry and tight. "Who did him in?"

The Skinlin shrugged. "I dunno. I just know Bastian was in it with Christabel. They had code words."

"Like what?"

"Tig vedom deum." Eddie took down the rest of his beer in two long drafts. He was sweating. I could smell the fear on him, rank and thick and human. Was it any consolation that my own fear now smelled like light cinnamon and musk?

My left shoulder began to throb again, evenly, almost comfortingly. "Part of the Nine Canons. Second canto, line four." I shifted on the vinyl bench, looking down at the remains of my second bowl of soup. *I've lost my appetite. Go figure.* "For sealing a spirit in its grave."

"And for short-circuiting a Feeder." Eddie's bushy eyebrows drew together. He glared at the table as if it had personally offended him.

"Any truth to the rumor that one of the students was a Feeder?" *And why would that have jackshit to do with these murders? Mirovitch is dead. The Hall's closed down.*

"I dunno, Danny." He looked miserable. I didn't blame him.

"There's a lot of shit you don't know." Frustration turned my voice sharp and angular. My teacup rattled slightly, I took a deep breath. Power swirled the air in lazy waving tendrils.

If I didn't know better, I'd say it's gotten stronger. I've gotten stronger.

I shoved that thought as far away as it would go. I didn't need another problem.

His eyes flickered up to my face, slid away. He could barely stand to look at my new face, and my heart squeezed inside my chest. "Don't ride my ass, Danny. I've given you all I got. Now go and get this thing done so I can go home and sleep again."

"Why are you afraid? You weren't part of it."

He shrugged. "Don't look like this thing's too fuckin selective, if it'll kill a normal."

Thank you, Eddie. I realized that was precisely what was bothering me. Why would whoever-it-was kill a normal to start off with? Unless it was practice, a dry run— but that didn't seem too likely. Once you've mastered Feeder glyphs and enough power to charge a Ceremonial Magick circle, dry runs lose their usefulness. The higher up you go, the more everything depends on Working perfectly under pressure—getting it right enough to work the first time.

"Unless the normal wasn't so normal." But the coroner's scans would have caught it, if he'd been a psion. I stared at my water glass, my index finger tracing a glyph on the table. A loose, spiked, fluid, twisting glyph in another magickal language.

A glyph scored into my own flesh. If I kept tracing it, fiddling with it, would I eventually get an answer? A whole year of longing hadn't brought me anything but grief.

Quit daydreaming, Danny. "What are you aiming at, Eddie?"

"Seems like someone's cleaning up some loose ends, don't it? I called Bastian. He'll see you soon as you want." Eddie sank down further in his seat, studying me. "You lookin' better, girl."

"Thanks." I don't think my tone could have been any drier or more ironic. "You got me a personal interview with Polyamour? Just how friendly *were* you?"

There it was again, that flush. I never thought I'd live to see Eddie acting like a blushing teener. I'd planned on interviewing Polyamour anyway, but having an introduction would make it much easier.

"Friendly 'nuff." Eddie reached for the second full glass of beer, downed it in one long gulp, his throat working; smacked it back down with a little more force than necessary. He looked at the two empty steins with a mournful expression, his lips pulled down and his sleepy eyes pupil-dilated and dark under his frowsty, bushy blond hair.

"You want another one?" My tone was uncharacteristically gentle.

"No. Danny . . ." He trailed off, tapped his blunt fingertips on the table.

"What?" I had, for the first time ever since Japhrimel altered me, lost my appetite. I pushed the remains of the second bowl of beef pho away. Took a drink of tea.

"Nothin. Just . . . be careful."

I let out a short bark of a laugh. "Since when have I ever been careful, Eddie?" *I never would have guessed Eddie knew the most famous transvestite sexwitch in the western half of the Hegemony well enough to get me an immediate interview. Wonders never cease in this wide, wide world.*

"You mighta been once or twice. When you was young." Eddie's lips pulled back in a brave attempt at a smile.

"Maybe. When I was young." I set my teacup down, extended my hand over the table. "Eddie? Thanks. It . . ." The words failed me. If I still had nightmares about Rigger Hall, he probably did too.

And if my reaction to having the Hall resurrected were enough to make me laugh like a crazed lunatic into the dirt under my own home, what was Eddie going through? Hadn't we suffered enough, both of us?

"Yeah I did." Eddie looked at my hand. His eyes flicked back up to my face; he extended his own hand, touched fingertips with me. His Adam's apple bounced as he swallowed, convulsively. "I got to be able to sleep again, Danny."

It was the first time he had ever voluntarily touched me. We are skittish about being touched, we psions.

My throat was dry.

I swallowed, and I spoke my promise. "I'll catch him, Eddie. Or her. Whoever's doing this. I swear it."

He snatched his fingertips away. "Yeah. You do that. Word of advice? When you do catch 'em, don't bring 'em back alive. Anything to do wit' Rigger Hall is better dead."

You better believe it, Eddie. "Including us?" I sounded wistful, not at all like my usual self.

Eddie moved, sliding his legs out of the booth and standing up. He tapped at his datband, then looked down at me. "Sometimes I think so." His eyes were still haunted wells. "Then I look at Gabe, and I ain't so sure."

I found nothing to say to that. Eddie stumped away toward the door, and I let him go. I touched my own datband, and found out he'd paid for my dinner.

Nice of him. *Oh, Eddie.*

I sighed and took one last mouthful of tea, rolling it around in my mouth to wash away the taste of fear before swallowing. It would take something stronger than tea to get that taste off my tongue, though.

20

I came in the back way, dropping into my backyard with a whine and a rattle. My board needed servicing. The media vans sat squat and dark at my gate, bristling with fiberoptics and satellite dishes to catch footage if I ever came in through the front door. I toyed with the idea of giving a press conference. It wouldn't help anything, but it would put off what I had to do next.

I let myself in the back door. Jace looked up and yawned, pulling his T-shirt down and buttoning his jeans. His golden hair was mussed, sticking up in all directions, but at least he was clean. "Hey, baby. What did Eddie have to say?"

I shook my head. "Got any coffee? We're going to Polyamour's as soon as possible."

His mouth curled into a grin. "I didn't think you liked bought sex, sweets. And I didn't think a fempersonator was your type."

I made a face at him before I could help myself, sticking my tongue out. He laughed, blue eyes dancing, and I was surprised by the way my heart squeezed down on itself. "Turns out Eddie knows her. They were chums at school. And Poly might know something about this group of students that took Mirovitch down." *I guess that wasn't a rumor after all. I wonder what else wasn't a rumor?*

"Good." He poured me coffee, brought it over. I folded my hands around the cup, grateful for the warmth; both of the cup, and of his concern. "Do you think that's what happened?" Carefully-reined curiosity sparkled behind his eyes.

"It's as good a place as any to start, it's our first break. Eddie's nervous, says if the murderer started with a normal then he obviously isn't too picky about his prey." I stared down into the thick black liquid. I liked Jace's coffee. He was the only one who made it strong enough.

"I know that look." He leaned hipshot against the kitchen counter, cocking his head. Breathless morning darkness pressed against the kitchen window. "What are you thinking, Danny?"

What doesn't bother me about this? It's going too slow. I should have latched onto something before this. "Something about that normal bothers me. Why would he have a sealed trust? Why would he have shields? It doesn't make any *sense.*"

He nodded, tapping his fingers against his swordhilt. Took a gulp of his coffee, made a face as if he'd burned himself. "Yeah, it's weird. And who is this Keller?"

I shrugged. "Maybe Polyamour can tell us."

"You want me to go with you?" He didn't sound surprised, but he did arch one eyebrow. He took another long draft from his coffee cup and grimaced. If it didn't hurt going down, it didn't feel like real coffee to him.

"Sure. I hear Poly likes pretty boys." I caught myself

smiling, tilting my head slightly to the side and regarding him. "She might tell you more than she tells me."

"You're using me for my looks." He mock-pouted.

"I guess so. Does that bother you?" The smile felt natural, so natural the corners of my eyes crinkled.

"Naw." His grin answered mine, widened. "I kind of like it."

The footlocker lay silently in the middle of the living room, dusty with sterile earth. I took a deep breath, regarding it from the doorway the way a mongoose might stare at a particularly poisonous cobra. Jace, behind me, didn't ask what was in it.

I'd waited for false dawn, pearly gray light beginning to flower through the windows. The upswing of hovertraffic buzzed in the distance; Saint City's heartbeat quickened slightly, shaking off dreaming and getting ready for the day. I still waited, watching the gray metal as if it would sit up and accuse me. Jace was absolutely still at my shoulder, obviously curious, wanting to ask, not daring to.

Why was this so hard? I had grown past Rigger Hall. Hadn't I?

I was beginning to think I wasn't as far past it as I had hoped.

I glanced at the tapestry on the west wall. Isis's arms were crossed protectively, and Horus's ferocious Eye gazed serene and deadly. The gods were not actively involved . . . but their backs were not turned either. Whatever I did, they would witness.

That's not as comforting as it could be. I finally took a deep breath. Both my fieldstone altar and my main altar were humming with Power, and the house shields were thick and carefully laid. Nothing could harm me here. This was my home, my sanctuary.

Nothing in there can hurt me now. I swallowed dryly, heard my throat click. The locker's closed metal face taunted me. *Yeah. Right.*

My left shoulder burned steadily. It felt as if the ropy scar was pulsing, sliding against itself, straining. I took the first step into the room and approached the footlocker cautiously, placing each footfall carefully, as if I was on unsteady ground.

I sank down beside it on the hardwood floor, my knee on the thick, patterned rug I used for meditation. I had to remind myself to breathe. The padlock—I used a bit of Power, and it clicked open with a sound like a frozen corpse's jaws wrenching open.

My teeth chattered until I clenched them together. *Strong,* I told myself. *I am strong. I survived this.* I laid the padlock aside and opened the top slowly, hearing dirt caught in the unoiled hinges squeal like a scream.

"Valentine, D. Student Valentine is called to the Head-master's office immediately."

The bright eyes of the kids in my class, all solemn and horrified and squeamishly glad their name hadn't been called. Woodenly reaching my feet, setting my battered Magickal Theory textbook aside; the teacher's—Embrose Roth, a Ceremonial and one of the worse at the Hall—ratty little face gleaming with curiosity, mousy hair pulled up in a tight bun, aura geometric and cold blue. Roth staring at my back as I trudged to the door, her attention like the filthy prick of a rat's claws against my nape.

Squeaking of my shoes against the stairs in the main

hall, heading to the Headmaster's office; the collar far too heavy on my neck. Frantically trying to remember an excuse, any excuse, that would keep me from being beaten or worse.

At Rigger Hall it was likely to be worse.

My fingers trembled, my nails scraping against the metal as I pushed it all the way open.

"Chango, Danny," Jace breathed. "You're pale. You don't have to do this."

Yes, I do. I looked down.

There, laid on top, was the collar, a curve of dark metal.

Waves of shudders rippled down my back. My shoulder burned, a fierce pain I was glad of. It kept me anchored. I'd faced worse than this, hadn't I? I'd killed Santino. I'd faced down the Devil himself.

I didn't have anything to fear from the detritus of my past. I denied the trembling that rose up in me.

"That's a collar." I heard the fear under Jace's heartbeat.

Every psion hates the thought of collars. They're supposed to protect the normals from us, but the deadheads are not the ones who need protection. They are in the majority, no matter how many holovids have psions in their storylines. They make the rules, and those of us with Talent have to dance to their tune. Collars make them feel better, sure.

But there's only so much of being collared a human being can take.

"Shut up, Jace." My voice trembled, but it still sliced the air. The house shields went hard and crystalline, on the verge of locking down as if I was under attack.

I blew out a long breath, tried to make my shoulders a little less tense.

The arc of dull dark metal with circuit etching on one side was dead and quiescent. Without a power-pack and the school security net, it was useless. Still, I handled it as if it was live, flipping out a knife and using the bright blade to lift it, laying it aside. I still remembered the hideous jolts—with a collar live and locked on, a psi couldn't protect herself. It short-circuited most types of Power; the teachers had controls to change the settings in order for the students to practice. The principle behind collars was to keep a psion from harming anyone while she learned to control her gifts.

I suppose it was a good idea—but like all good ideas, someone had found a way to make it go horribly wrong. When a collar was live, a plasgun shock administered from a prod hurt like hell, burning through every nerve, as if you were being electrocuted. It didn't leave much in the way of permanent scarring—not on the outside, anyway.

Underneath was a pad of dirty green cloth, rough synth-wool cut from an institutional bedspread in the long, low girl's dormitory. I flipped that aside, keeping one eye nervously on the collar.

My last school uniform. Plaid skirt, the white cotton blouse dingy with age, knee-socks, the heavy shoes I had always hated. The navy synthwool blazer with the crest of Rigger Hall worked in gold thread. I'd put the other five uniforms into an incinerator, but this one was the one I was wearing when the Hegemony had finished the inquiry and pronounced Mirovitch posthumously guilty. After the inquiry, we were free to wear normal clothes, and the Hall was visited by social workers every week. The psis were uncollared for visits with their social workers, and surprise inspections became the rule. The new Headmistress,

Stabenow, had supervised the closing of the school after my class graduated. The younger students had scattered to other Hegemony schools, hopefully better-policed.

I lifted each item out reverently and laid it aside, still neatly folded. Jace was completely silent.

Tears welled up. I denied them, pushed them down. Invoked anger instead, a thin unsteady anger that at least did not choke me.

Under the uniform, books. Schoolbooks, mostly, each with their brown-paper cover decorated with glyphs done in pen, numbers, notes. And eleven slender books bound in maroon plasleather, with gold-foil lettering on the side.

Yearbooks.

I lifted them out carefully. Some junk jewelry and a threadbare teddy bear were wedged into the remaining space; the teddy's plastic eyes glinted at me.

Lewis had given me the teddy.

I survived, goddammit. I survived because I was strong enough to put this behind me, strong enough to go into Death itself. Don't start feeling sorry for yourself, Dante Valentine. Pull yourself together and do what has to be done, like you've done all your life. Do this. You will only have to do this once.

I decided I could look at this just once. Just this once. I was strong enough for that. I swallowed bile. My rings sparked and swirled uneasily. The mark on my shoulder crunched with pain. I inhaled, smelling dust and must and old things. Felt the phantom blood drip down my back again.

In the very bottom of the locker was the only thing I've ever stolen without being paid to do so. It was a long flexible whip, real leather, with a small metal fléchette at the tip. It was still crusted with rusting stains.

Bloodstains.

Jace exhaled sharply as I touched the whip with one finger. The shock jolted up my arm—pain, fear, sick excitement. I snatched my hand away.

"Roanna," I whispered. "She was *sedayeen*. She tried to tell her social worker what was happening at the Hall, but the bastard wouldn't believe a kid and had a nice little conference with the Headmaster." My voice was flat, barely stirring the air. "Mirovitch whipped her almost to death and then signed the papers to make her a breeder. She committed suicide—threw herself on the fencing with her collar turned all the way up."

"Danny . . ." He sounded like he'd been punched.

I ran the back of my hand over my cheek, bared my teeth as if I was facing a fight. I stacked the schoolbooks on top of the whip, pushed the teddy back in his place, then put the uniform and the sheet of green cloth back. I used a knifeblade to lift the collar up, laid it on top. Closed the top, wincing as the hinges squealed, and let out an unsteady barking breath that sounded like a sob. I flipped the padlock up and jammed it closed, the small click sounding very loud in the stillness. I resheathed my knife and slid my hands under the stack of eleven yearbooks. "Clear off the table in the dining room, will you?" I gained my feet and turned around, the negligible weight of the books in my arms seeming much heavier.

Jace's face was set and white, his mouth a thin line. His eyes burned. Fury boiled in the air around him, his aura hardspiked and crystalline. Despite that, his tone was dead-level. Calm. "They did that to you. Didn't they? I always wondered who made you so afraid."

Afraid? That puzzled me. It wasn't in me to be afraid, was it? I was supposed to *fight.* The classics Lewis had poured into me had taught me that much: the only way to kill your fears was to fight them. *Be as frightened as you want,* Lewis's voice whispered in my head. *Then do what you have to do. That's what he's saying here, in this passage.*

"I got whipped once. Put in the cage four times. B-branded. I was lucky it wasn't more." *Lucky nothing happened that broke me. Nothing big. Nothing I couldn't handle, Jace.*

"Lucky." His aura flushed with fury. "Danny—"

"Clear off a space on the table, Jace. The sooner we get this done, the sooner I can bury this again." *And by the grace of Anubis, I can't* wait *to bury this again.*

He stared at me for a few more moments, jaw working, then turned on his bootheel and stalked away soundlessly. I knew that set to his shoulders, the controlled angry grace. Jace was *furious.* I had only seen him in a rage twice, but both times had given me a healthy respect for his anger. I wondered if I was going to see it again, hoped not.

If he went nova I might draw steel on him, and I didn't quite trust myself with edged metal right now.

I carried the books into the dining room. He moved jerkily, clearing a space on the table. Other texts on demonology and basic Magi theory, drifts of paper where I'd made notes, and the talismans Jace had been working on—he stacked them all to the side, and I put the eleven yearbooks down. Blew out a heavy breath.

"Who are we looking for?" He set a four-book set of

Tierley's *Democria Demontia* on one of the chairs with excessive delicate care. I picked up a piece of fine parchment, a twisted glyph that was Japhrimel's name branded into my shoulder repeated over and over again in different permutations. I hadn't even realized I was doodling it.

I cleared my throat, suddenly more grateful for his presence than ever. I had to force myself to speak quietly. "Well, after we visit Polyamour we'll have some more names. But I want to find out if Christabel's class had anyone named Keller. Can you get my bag and your datpilot? I want to see if there are any Ceremonials in town."

"Hm. Why Ceremonials? You're thinking they might have a connection to this?"

Ceremonial magicians weren't as rare as Necromances or as common as Shamans. They worked with the Nine Canons and the Seven Seals, charging and containing Power in objects, working with talismans, and providing permanent defenses for corporations, not to mention doing theoretical work and research into magick and the science of Power. Most teachers and trainers were Ceremonial magicians.

But there was a simpler reason why I wanted to find out who was in town. I met his worried blue eyes and gave him a smile that didn't feel natural at all. "I want to find out if any of them have gone Feeder."

Because, out of all psions, it was the Ceremonials—those who dealt with the theory of containing Power—who most often turned Feeder in adulthood. And if we had a Ceremonial on our hands who had gone Feeder and was hunting down former Rigger Hall students, the whole city's collection of psions would have to be alerted.

I would need all the help I could get.

21

We were into the third book when the phone rang. I stretched and yawned while I padded into the kitchen. Jace tapped another name into his datpilot, glancing up briefly as I passed him. Late-morning light glowed in the windows. I leaned a hip against the counter and picked the phone up. "'Lo."

A click and a pause, as if the call was on relays. My spine went cold, as if my body recognized the truth before I did.

"Dante Valentine. It is a singular pleasure to speak to you again."

My entire body turned to ice. There was only one being in the entire goddamn world that could strangle me with fear in just two sentences.

The voice was smooth as silk, persuasive, crawling into my head. My phone had no vidshell, for which I was now doubly grateful. If I had to face down the Prince of Hell again, even over a holovid shell, I wasn't sure I would come away from the experience quite sane.

The letter. I'd chucked it into the garbage. I owed him nothing. There was no reason for the Prince of Hell to want to talk to me. I'd done what he wanted, and I'd paid the price. I had screamed as Japhrimel turned to ash in my arms. Wasn't he happy? Wasn't that *enough?*

Why would the Devil call me on the *phone* instead of sending another demon to collect me if he wanted me? He'd done it before, sending Japhrimel and asking me to hunt down Santino, perfectly aware I had my own reasons for wanting that bastard dead.

Anubis protect me. The jolt of fear that smashed through my throat tasted like iron. *What if Lucifer is involved with the murders?*

My entire body went cold. My throat was dry. My hand tightened, digging clawlike fingernails into the countertop. Ceramic screeched under the pressure of my fingers, claws springing free and dimpling the tough tiles. "I can't say the same," I husked, my throat burning with the memory of the Devil's hand crushing my larynx. "What the hell do *you* want? Leave me alone."

"Polite as ever." Lucifer's voice held a weight of amusement I wasn't sure I ever wanted to hear again. "I must speak with your lover, and I am unable to contact him in the usual manner. You will not respond to my missives. Therefore, I am forced to use the human channels of communication."

What the motherfucking hell is he talking about? My lover? Has Lucifer been spying on me? My entire body flushed hot, then cold again; my nipples drawing up, my skin going cold and tight as an icy glove.

"Is this some kind of joke?" I could actually *feel* my temper grow thin and brittle, rage rising to wash away sick, deadening fear. "I don't have time for this, *Lucifer.* You killed Japhrimel, you bastard *demon;* are you calling to remind me? You think I'm going to hand Jace over to you? Get a *life.*" *And he's not my lover either. Though that's none of your goddamn business, is it, you sack of diseased shit.* The cupboards rattled as my voice turned sharp and cool, Power spiking under the harsh, throaty croak.

But the suspicion, once voiced, wouldn't go away. *Oh, my dear sweet fucking gods, is Lucifer involved in this?* My entire body turned to ice. A solid block of ice.

If this was something to do with demons, I was dead in the water. But Christabel's body had held no hint of demon, no scent of spice and dark flame.

There was a pause. "Can it be you have not resurrected him?" The Prince of Hell actually—chalk one up for me—sounded shocked.

I seem to have a habit of nonplussing demons.

My voice was a choked whisper. "Resurrected?" What the hell did *that* mean? Jace wasn't dead. And if I could have resurrected Japhrimel, I would have already done it.

Then I shook myself. Demons lied. The Prince of Hell was no exception. So he'd sent me a little love note, and now he was graduating to obscene phone calls. I had no fucking time for this, not when I was trying to deal with every goddamn ghost from my childhood trying to climb up through the floor and throttle me.

"Go away," I enunciated clearly through the scratching in my throat. "You don't need me, I'm not your errand-girl anymore. Japhrimel is dead, you can't hurt *him* any-more. You're just lucky I don't come after you for kidnapping Eve. Now if you'll *excuse* me, I have real work to do and a killer to catch." I slammed the phone down so hard the tough plasteel base cracked.

I wanted to pick it up again, see if he was still on the line. I wanted to scream, I wanted to dial the operator. *Hello, Vidphone Central? Hook me up to Hell. Tell the Devil he can have me, if he just brings Japhrimel back. Tell him I'll do anything he wants, if I don't have to face this alone.*

Then welcome fury crawled up between the words. *Tell him, while you're at it, that if he's involved with this he'd better say his prayers. Because he's meddled in my life one too many times, and if he's killing Necromances in my city I'm going to see how much demonic flesh my blade can carve. We're even, sure, but I have a score to settle with you, Lucifer Iblis.*

Despite my brave words, I couldn't rescue Doreen's daughter. I stared at the phone, longing to reach through and throttle the Prince of Hell. Why call me now? He'd left me to rot in Rio, stewing in the aftermath of Japhrimel's death and savage guilt that I hadn't been able to save Eve. The fact that Eve was a demon Androgyne— a child I had no hope of raising—didn't salve the ache. Doreen's ghost had asked me to save her, and I'd tried.

Tried and failed. Lucifer had Eve now. That I'd had no hope of fighting the Devil to keep him away from her didn't ease my conscience one iota.

Failed. Just like with Japhrimel, lying dead on the white marble plaza under the hammerblow of Nuevo Rio sun, dead and gone. I kept my hand away from the mark on my shoulder only with a titanic effort of will that left me shaking, sweat for once springing up along my scalp and the curve of my lower back.

I drove my teeth into my lower lip, the sweet jolt of pain shocking me back into some sort of rational frame of mind. Too bad rational never worked where demons were concerned. *Stop it. You don't owe the Devil jackshit, you're free. He can't hurt you now.*

That was a lie. The Devil could hurt me plenty if he bestirred himself to do it.

"Danny?" Jace, from the dining room.

I backed away from the phone, eyeing it as if it would rise up and strike me. Given what I knew of demons, it was a distinct possibility.

"Danny? Who is it?"

I cleared my throat. "Wrong number," I called back, my voice as harsh as if Lucifer had just half-strangled me again. *The same wrong number that sent a letter I never let you see.*

Silence. I glared at the phone, daring it to ring again.

It didn't.

Leave me alone. Leave Jace alone, leave my city alone. You killed Japhrimel and stole Eve, you leave me alone or so help me, I will . . .

What could I do? A big fat nothing. Fat gooseflesh rose rough on my arms, bumps struggling up under golden skin. I took a deep, racking breath in. I couldn't worry about demons now too. *Let's just hope he was playing with me, what do you say, Danny? Just torturing the human, making sure I still know who's boss. Who's keeping an eye on my life in case he needs a goddamn hand puppet again.*

Finally, my shoulders dropped slightly. Why would Lucifer pick *now* to start playing mind-games on me again? I hadn't done any divination for a week or so, but even when I had, there had been no whisper of demons in my cards.

Then again, last time there hadn't been any warning either. And the letter, with its fat blood-red seal . . .

Don't think like that, Danny. You're going to get paranoid, and paranoid is exactly what you do not need. Paranoid people don't think clearly.

Despite the fact that paranoid people usually survived better than the foolhardy, I told myself sardonically. Besides, if Lucifer thought he could use me again, he was going to have another think coming. A long, hard think, preferably a painful one.

"Danny, I think I have something," Jace called.

I swallowed, my throat clicking. Turned away.

The phone rang again. Twice. Three times.

No. My hands shook.

"Danny?" Scrape of a chair, Jace was getting to his feet.

I scooped the phone up, pale crimson fury spilling through the trademark sparkles of a Necromance in my aura. "Look, you son of a bitch—" I began, the cupboards chattering open and closed, a mug falling from a rack and hitting the wooden floor with a tinkling crash.

"Danny?" It was Gabe. "What the hell? Are you okay?"

I swallowed. Jace skidded into the room, his guns out. "I'm fine," I said to both of them. My throat was full of scorching sand. "What's up, Spooky?"

"Saddle up, I've got another body." Gabe was trying to sound flip and hard, but her voice shook. I could almost see her pale cheeks, the trembling around her mouth.

"Where?" I shook my head at Jace, whose hands blurred, spinning the guns back into their holsters. He scanned the room, then stared at me, the question evident in his blue eyes.

"Corner of Fourth and Trivisidero, the brick house with the holly hedges." No wonder Gabe sounded uncomfortable—that was precious close to her own home. "Get here quick, we're holding the scene for you."

"I'll be there in ten." I dropped the phone back into its cradle. "Let's go, Jace."

"You might want to take a look at this first. Are you all right?" His eyes dropped from me to the shattered mug on the floor. Shards of ceramic dust—my anger and fear had shattered the mug, ground into it, compounding injury with insult. It was the blue Baustoh mug.

The one Jace liked, the one Japhrimel had chosen for his use the only time he'd drunk coffee in my house.

Anubis et'her ka. I didn't want to think about it.

"What have you got?" I rubbed delicately at my throat with my fingertips, my nails pricking, claws threatening to spring free. My right hand actually *itched* for my sword-hilt, and the sensation was so eerie I almost couldn't feel relieved that it wasn't cramping.

"It occurred to me to look at the last yearbook that listed Mirovitch as Headmaster, the year he died. Guess who was on the Student Yearbook Committee?" Jace looked up from the glossy blue shards of ceramic, and the question in his eyes remained unspoken. I was grateful for that, more grateful than I ever thought I would be to him.

"Who?"

"Christabel Moorcock."

22

I suppose we had to give the reporters something; besides, it was too hard to talk while on slicboards with the wind rattling and howling around us. So we took the hovercar. The flashes from pictures being snapped bathed the underside of the hover. I glanced out the window, my lip curling, glad of the privacy tinting. Jace drove while I looked through the yearbook from my eighth year at school. "Check page fifty-six," he said, and I flipped through the heavy vellum pages. "Now look at Moorcock's picture."

Christabel Moorcock, known as "Skinny." She grinned out of the page of holovid stills, a tenth-year student with long dark hair and wide dark eyes. She was pretty but alarmingly thin; her cheekbones standing out and her heart-shaped face a touch too long. The cupid's-bow of her mouth was plump and perfect, her eyebrows winged out. The picture was a headshot, it showed only the very top edge of her collar.

Below were the usual lists of interests, including Faerie Ceremonial magick—and a small black mark shaped like a spade in a deck of playing cards. I rubbed at it, thinking it an ink blot, but it didn't blur. "The black mark?"

"Now try page fifty-eight. Steven Sebastiano." Jace's fingers danced over the touchpad, and the AI pilot took over inserting us into hovertraffic. I felt the familiar unsettling pull of gravity against my stomach, swallowed hard. *Can it be you have not resurrected him?* Lucifer's soft, beautiful voice teased at my brain.

Resurrect a demon? It's not possible. But then again, I'd been researching only to try and find out how Japhrimel had altered me. I had never thought that . . . It wasn't possible that I could bring him back, was it?

Was it?

I want him back. That was a child's plaint. I wanted each dead person back. I wanted every person I'd ever loved back.

And I, of all people, should understand the finality of Death.

"Danny?"

I shook myself back into the present, closed the yearbook with a snap, not bothering to check Sebastiano's picture. "You're a sneaky bastard." I tried to sound admiring. "Good work, Jace. I wouldn't have thought of that. Have you looked to see—"

"I haven't made a list yet. But I thought it was worth looking into, seeing as how that's the only link between Christabel and Polyamour I can find in the yearbook."

The year Mirovitch died, Christabel was on the yearbook committee. Why would she leave a mark? If she did leave a mark, that is. It would be stupid. On the other hand, Mirovitch was dead by the time they finalized the yearbook, it came out at the end of the year, after the in-

quest. It's probably nothing, some primary-school bull-shit. Still, it's the only clue we've got. "I wonder who lives on Trivisidero." I looked out the window, seeing the city roll by underneath, its daylight geography gray with concrete and splashes of reactive paint marking hover bounce pads, the towers of high-density apartment buildings scrolling down Lossernach Street. If I focused, I could see the strings of Power underlying every street and building, the green glow of any trees and gardens that managed to survive. And underneath it all lay the pulsing radioactive smolder of the city's heart, seething in a white-cold mass of Power.

"Gabe does." The hover dropped out of the traffic pattern into a lazy spiral.

"Gabe didn't go to Rigger Hall." I reopened the yearbook, scanned the pages, looking for more black marks. "We're going to have to make a list."

"Here we are," he said. "Danny? Who was it on the phone?"

It was the goddamn Devil, Jace. "Nobody," I muttered, my right hand reaching up to massage my burning left shoulder through my shirt. "Gods."

Can it be you have not resurrected him?

"'Kay." We were keyed through the police security net. Jace piloted the hover down to land in the driveway of an immaculate brick house. I remembered the place from walking to Gabe's so many times. The holly bushes outside were green and healthy and the walls behind them covered with the strangely geometric shielding of a Ceremonial. There were other police hovers there, including a squat black coroner's hover.

"Great." I triggered the door lock. "Well, what do you know. Digging that coffin up wasn't useless after all."

I hopped out, the hover's hum diminishing as Jace turned off the drive. The springs groaned a little as the hover settled.

The house was three stories high and immaculate, the gardens largely ornamental. I saw several rosebushes and a monkey puzzle tree. The roof was new, plasilica made to look like slate, gleaming wetly from last night's rain and the afternoon sunlight. There were officers milling all over the front driveway, a wide circular field of crushed white stone. At the top of wide granite steps there was a police guard at the massive wooden front door, two Saint City blues; I saw Gabe's familiar figure come out blinking into the sunlight. She lifted a hand, I saw one of the blues at the door flinch.

My nostrils flared. I smelled fear and blood, and death. And the sharp stink of human vomit.

It must be bad. I stuffed the yearbook in my bag and curled my left hand around my sword, then struck out for the front door, my boots crunching on the rocks. A strand of long black hair fell into my face. I blew it back, irritably. "Yo, Spooky!" I called, as soon as I got to the bottom of the stairs. "I should be home in bed."

"So should I." Her shields flushed purple-red. My own shielding reverberated, answering hers; she stopped and looked down at me as the emerald on her cheek sparked a greeting. "You look different, Danny."

"Must be exhaustion and digging up old bodies." I paced up the stairs, aware that Jace was right behind me. His staff tapped on the granite. My cheek burned, the twisted-caduceus tat shifting its inked lines against my flesh. "What do we have here?"

"Ceremonial." She ushered me past the blues, who both recoiled slightly. I guess my reputation preceded me. It was one time I was glad of it—at least if they were recoiling they weren't staring at me.

The emerald on my cheek burned as I stepped over the threshold, a deep drilling warning. "The shielding's torn." I looked up. "From inside."

Gabe nodded. "Just like the other three. It's Aran Helm."

I remembered him. He'd gone to Rigger Hall too, in my class. He'd been a tall blond babyfaced Ceremonial, with blue eyes and a habit of sucking on his lower lip; I'd had him in a Philosophy of Religion class and a few other electives.

Jace swore. "This is Helm's place?" He smacked the butt end of his staff against the marble flooring, one sharp crack echoing through the foyer. "Gods*dam*mit."

"You know him?" I asked, looking up. Apparently Helm's taste had gone for high ceilings, a coat of antiquated mail on a stand, and a tall grandfather clock that chimed as we walked in. A long, overdone staircase went up to the right. I followed Gabe, my fingers trailing the balustrade. The feel of defenses wedded to every stair crackled against my skin, humming uneasily. I smelled beeswax, and a frowsty scent that told me only one human lived here. Apparently Aran Helm lived alone; in a huge house full of silence and loneliness.

"Ran with him for a while, when I was dating you," Jace replied easily enough. "Worked with him on a couple jobs—did some wetwork together. Never met at his house though. Dodgy."

"Wetwork." *Assassination.* A long time ago I would have been willing to swear there was nothing I didn't know about Jace, but here I was finding out something new. I had balked at doing assassinations, though he'd said it was good money. I hadn't asked what his own jobs entailed; I'd trusted him blindly. "How was he?"

"Good," Jace said. "Cold. Not overly troubled with hesitation." His aura touched mine. I shivered.

Not like me; the only time you mentioned assassination to me I almost bit your head off. How many wetwork jobs did you come home from and climb into bed with me? Did you ever want to tell me, Jace, or did you think I'd never find out? I swallowed the anger. It was ancient history. I didn't have to think about it, did I? Not right now with a killer to catch and the Prince of Hell calling me again.

It was a relief to find something unpleasant I *didn't* have to think about.

"He's up in the bedroom." Gabe's shoulders were tense under her long dark synthwool coat. "It's . . . well, you'll see. Have you got anything so far, Danny? Anything at all?"

It wasn't like her to sound desperate. "I'm going to see Polyamour as soon as possible. It seems Steve Sebastiano was part of the conspiracy that got Mirovitch." I laid it out in a few clipped sentences, including the marks in the yearbook, which were probably nothing but the closest we had to a link. At the top of the stairs Gabe led us down a hall past another two blues standing guard, and I didn't need her to tell me which room Aran was in. The hacked-open door and thick cloying smell of blood spoke for itself. After you've smelled death for a while, the smell of blood stops bothering you much . . . at least, consciously.

The lingering traces of other smells in the air were more interesting. I inhaled deeply—protections, even more protections, laid thick and tight over every inch of wall and floor. A marble bust of Adrien Ferriman, legislative creator of the Parapsychic Act, stood on a blackstone plinth, his familiar jowled scowl apparently directed down the hall.

Laid over that was the raw, new smell of human from the blues, Gabe, and Jace. I sniffed deeply, closing my eyes. Human blood, human sweat, protection magick, and . . .

I filled my lungs. *There it is.* I smelled offal, magick, and the reek of aftershave. I filled my lungs, closing everything else out, even the throbbing burn in my shoulder.

I knew that smell. Dust, offal, magick, aftershave, chalk, and leather.

The smell of the Office. The Headmaster's Office.

I shivered, the shudder going from my heels all the way up to the crown of my scalp. Nerve-strings tight and taut, singing their siren song of bloodlust and the path of the hunt laid in front of my feet. But laid over that shudder was fear, nose-stinging and skin-chilling fear. The fear of a child locked in a room without light.

Be careful, Japhrimel's voice whispered at the very back of my brain. *He cannot hurt you now,* hedaira. *You are beyond his reach.* I felt a warm hand touch my face, an intimate trailing down my cheek, pausing at the pulse in my throat, then sliding down to the curve of my breast.

I came back to myself with a jolt. *What the hell? I didn't smell this at Christabel's. That damn lilac perfume of hers, maybe. Or maybe the scent had faded.* "I can smell it."

"Danny?" Gabe paused before the doorway. "You okay?"

No, I wasn't. I was hallucinating my dead demon lover's voice. But it didn't matter. Getting the smell of the quarry is important in any hunt. And if imagining Japhrimel's voice helped me get through this, I was all for it no matter what price I would have to pay afterward, when the hunt was over and I had to face the fact that he was truly gone.

"I'm fine," I rasped. A pattern was starting to appear under the shape of events. "Let's take a look at Mr. Helm." I stepped past Gabe and looked into the room. "He certainly did believe in protection, didn't he?"

"Either that or he was afraid of something," Jace said grimly. "Chango . . ." It was a long breath of wondering disgust.

I agreed. Past the hacked and battered door was an orgy of blood and bits of what had once been a human body. The chalk marks on the floor were familiar but hurried, scrawled instead of done neatly. The circle was sloppily and hastily finished. Had the killer been interrupted? "Who found the body?" My nose wrinkled. The only thing worse than the effluvia of dying cells around living humans was the stench of rotting ones.

You think that as if you're not human, Danny. I shivered again.

"Housekeeper," Gabe said. "Apparently was paid a good deal to come in and work ten hours a day cleaning this pile. And to keep her mouth shut. The body's a few days old, she wasn't supposed to come into this part of the house very often. Once she found the body, she didn't know whether she should call the police. She brought the question to one of her cousins, who's a low-level retainer for the Owens Family and a stooge for the Saint City PD. He brought it to us. If the shields hadn't already been cracked we would have called you in to crack them."

"Gods." Jace looked definitely green, yet another new and amazing thing. I felt a little green myself. "There's only pieces."

Check that. I wasn't just feeling a *little* green. I felt green as a new crop of chemalgae. Nausea rose, twisted hot under my breastbone. I forced it down. I'd seen a lot of murder and mayhem in my time, but this . . . the smell of blood wasn't bothering me, but the visuals were beginning to become nightmare-worthy.

I should know, I've had my share of wonderful nightmares.

I looked into the bedroom. This was evidently where Aran Helm truly lived. Scattered papers and dirty clothes strewn about, a huge four-poster bed with wildly mussed covers now spattered with blood and other fluids, and burned-out candles in many holders. Between this and Christabel's careful obsessive order, I wasn't sure which I preferred.

I stepped delicately inside the room, wishing once again that I could shut my nostrils down, and saw something.

A human hand, severed at the wrist, clutching a bit of consecrated chalk.

A few more bits of the pattern fell together. "*Sekhmet sa'es,* Gabe. We've got it all wrong. The marks weren't made by the killer."

"What?" Gabe stopped at the door. "What are you talking about?"

"Look." I pointed at the hand. "The victims made the marks. I need a laseprint of these. If I can figure out what they were trying to defend against—"

"You don't think it's human?" Hope and dawning comprehension lit her face.

"I wouldn't say that," I answered slowly. "I can't tell. But if the marks are *defensive,* I've been going about this all wrong." I whirled. "If Jace gives you a list, can you find out who on the list is still in Saint City? And who's still alive?"

"All things should be so easy." Gabe's eyes lit up. She looked a few years younger. "You're sure, Danny?"

"Not sure." I gave the room one last look. "But it's better than any other theory I had. There's something else, too."

"What?" She almost twitched with impatience, and I suppressed the desire to giggle nervously. Couldn't she *see?* Why did she need me to tell her?

"This door's hacked *in.*" I looked back at them, saw Jace was watching me, his blue eyes bright against the shadow of the hall. A deeper shadow slid over his face, and I would have recoiled if my feet weren't nailed in place. When I looked again, the shadow was gone, and I had to chalk it up to nerves.

I was chalking a lot up to my nerves lately. It was a bad habit to get into.

"What?" Gabe's tone wasn't overly patient. I had drifted into silence, staring at Jace, my forehead furrowed.

I shook myself and met her dark worried eyes. "I don't think the attack started here."

23

I was right. We found his *sancta* in the basement, a hexagonal stone room with nudiegirl holoposters gummed to the rough walls. A pentacle was etched into the discolored granite floor—Aran had done well for himself, if he could spend time and Power etching stone. I was uncomfortable looking into the room—after all, a Ceremonial's *sancta* is like a Necromance's psychopomp, the deep place they trust to work their greatest magicks. Apparently, Aran Helm had derived a great deal of his power from sex; it didn't look like he had many partners, however. He must have done a lot of Power-raising with his right hand.

A drawer in a low armoire was pulled all the way out, showing shiny sharp implements. Bloodletters and weights. I sucked in a breath, delicately touching the wood of the drawer with a fingertip. The shiver that went through me wasn't entirely unpleasant—blood and sex, and pain. Good fuel for magick.

And very tempting for demons. Even part-demons like me.

Interestingly enough, there was only one door to the

sancta, and it was hacked open—but from the *inside.* I cast my gaze over the hexagonal room.

Jace leaned in the door. Gabe's voice raised in the corridor beyond, giving orders. Jace's staff glowed golden, a faint light edging it and the bones tied with raffia clicking together. Here in another sorcerer's *sancta,* any Shaman would be uncomfortable. And the lingering trail of terror and bloodlust on the air would only add to that discomfort.

Cigars lay fanned under a twisted statue of The Unspeakable. *So he was a Left-hander,* I thought. That was valuable information—no wonder he'd been in the business of assassination. Left-handers wouldn't sacrifice humans to gain magickal energy, but they *would* sacrifice other things. Dogs, cats . . . monkeys, sometimes. Insects. There was a whole branch of Left-handers that dealt with the power released by killing snakes as slowly as possible, since snakes were living conduits of magickal energy. Cats were popular too, and goats. About the only animal a Left-hander wouldn't touch was a horse, since plenty of Skinlins worshipped Epona and their goddess took a very dim view of sacrificing equines. Of course, there was the question of what to do with the body afterward. The old joke was that a *vaudun* and a Left-hander would both kill a chicken—but the *vaudun* would eat the chicken afterward.

Most of the time, after a Left-hander was finished, there wasn't much of the sacrifice *left* to eat.

A half-bottle of very good brandy sat on the altar too. His ceremonial sword, its blade twisted into an unrecognizable shape, was a two-handed broadsword, pretty but cheap metal. If he did wetwork it was with knife or projectile gun, not honest steel. Aran Helm had used the human deaths to pay for his house, and animal death to fuel his magick.

I wondered if either had troubled him.

"Here," I murmured. "Here was where it started. How could it come from inside?" I turned to the door. Gabe had already repaired Christabel's shielding by the time I got there, but the bits from the door had all been on the *outside,* in the hall. "Christabel's shields breached from the inside? And the other two, the sexwitch and the normal?"

Jace shrugged. "Moorcock yes, sexwitch yes, normal no. That's what Gabe said. I'll ask again if you want." But he stayed there, looking at me, his eyes oddly shadowed and burning at the same time. "Danny, what are you thinking? You look . . ."

"I'm not sure yet." *Why are we so sure the normal's part of this? But I am sure, sure as I can be. It started with our mysterious normal and hasn't ended yet. Something I'm missing, something critical. And Christabel, making marks and shouting "Remember."*

I blinked, knelt down. Caught in the pentacle's deep-carved lines was a glimmer of something. My fingertips brushed stone, and I caught a glimpse of a man who had to be Aran—blue-eyed, his greasy blond hair cut in a flat-top, stumbling back as Power whipped like a serpent from the statue of The Unspeakable. "Was he a very good sorcerer, this Aran Helm?"

I felt more than saw Jace's shrug. "Good enough. Better as an assassin, I think. Otherwise, how would he pay for this?"

"True." It was a fine silver chain, a necklace. The clasp was broken. Attached to it was a charm the size of my thumb from distal joint to fingertip—a silver spade, like on an antique playing card. "Ace of spades." I held it up delicately between index finger and thumb. "I think you're onto something, Jace. Good work." *Stupid to put a mark in a yearbook, Christabel. Why would you do something like that? It's a pity I can't bring you out of Death and ask you.* Shivers rilled up my spine.

One corner of his mouth lifted into a half-grin. "Good to hear it. Can Gabe's team start up in the bedroom?"

"I think so." I made it to my feet, holding the necklace. "We need to go through this yearbook and make a list."

"You got it."

A new thought struck me as I rose from the floor. I paused, holding up the necklace. "I wonder if Christabel had one of these."

Jace turned and murmured to Gabe. She said something, then looked over his shoulder at me. "Danny?"

"Did Christabel have one of these?" I held the necklace up so she could see it.

"She did. So did the sexwitch. I chalked it up to junk jewelry." Gabe's tone was uncharacteristically harsh. No cop liked to miss a piece of evidence.

"The normal didn't have one?" I asked, just to make sure.

"Not that I remember. I'll go through the evidence manifest again, if you want."

"Do that." I stared at the nudiegirl posters on the wall. They fluttered as my attention brushed them. Nothing behind any of them. No way into the room but the door, and the door hacked open from *inside*.

I tore the yearbook out of my bag and stalked for the door. "Gabe. Get me the list. *Everyone* in here who has that mark next to their names. I need to know who's still living and where, especially in Saint City. Send it to my datpilot, will you?"

She nodded. "What's up?" At least she knew enough not to bother me with questions that needed long explanations.

"One of Polyamour's girls was the second body," I said, and watched Gabe's eyes light with comprehension. She was looking more relieved by the second. At least we had a connection, however tenuous; a direction to go in was good news to any cop. "I'm going to drop in on Poly *now*. If one of her girls was downed and she has more bits of the puzzle, she's going to be very nervous, very guilty—or the next goddamn victim."

Gabe nodded. "Go. Go on."

I gave her a quick smile and pushed the yearbook into her hands. "I need this back." *So I can bury it again. Maybe deeper this time.*

"Understood. Now go." Her tone wasn't just a *thank you*—it was relief and gratitude all rolled up together and lit with birthday candles.

Jace followed me, his staff tapping on the marble. The spade necklace dangled from my fist, and I stuffed it in a pocket without thinking. My fingers tightened around the katana's scabbard. *I should have gotten a sword long before this so I could have a blade I could depend on.* A chill finger touched my spine. My rings flashed, demon-fed, and the atmosphere of Aran Helm's palatial house shivered. I reached out without thinking, calming the runaway energy like a restive horse. Helm had put so many layers of protection on his home that the air itself would have

been dead and stifling if not for the giant rent whoever—
or whatever—had torn in the shielding.

*From the inside. I wonder if he invited his killer in.
Why, if he was so obsessive about protection?*

It was a relief to have this puzzle, so I didn't have to
think about Lucifer's soft voice burrowing in through the
phone line. *I must speak with your lover, and I am unable
to contact him in the usual manner.*

I wondered what the "usual manner" was and felt my
skin go chill again.

Can it be you have not resurrected him? Taunting, soft,
and corrosive.

I decided I didn't fear him as much as I had when I was
human—and that was bad. After all, I wasn't a demon,
only a *hedaira,* whatever that was. And even if I had been
a demon, Lucifer was the Prince of Hell.

So maybe the Prince of Hell was starting a new game. I
had to go carefully, or I might be caught like I was last
time. Of course, any game the Devil started was rigged
from the beginning; but last time I'd had no warning
whatsoever. Now at least I *knew* something awful was
about to happen.

Cold comfort, if any.

"Danny!" Jace caught my arm. Sunlight fell down on
the crushed stone. I'd walked out of the house and toward
the garden wall. A few more strands of my hair fell in my
face. My boots seemed rooted to the ground now. "Hey.
The hover's this way."

I blinked at him. "Jace." I'd been so deep in my
thoughts I had literally forgotten about him. The sunlight
was kind to him, made his hair catch fire and his eyes

glow. Had he followed me through the entire house, trying to get my attention? "I'm sorry. I was thinking."

"It's not like you to wander around deaf to the world." He shook his staff for emphasis, the bones clicking and twirling on their raffia twine. "It's that phone call, isn't it." His voice was flat.

Once before, I'd been so wrapped up in my own thoughts I hadn't been aware of my surroundings. Japhrimel had pulled me out of the way of a speeding streetside hover. I had no demon to watch over me now; I gave myself a severe mental shake, pushing away uncertainty. I'd deal with Lucifer after I dealt with this mess.

After I deal with a crazed killer from Rigger Hall, the Devil might almost be a vacation. Black humor tinted my mental voice, gallows humor. The type of macabre humor every Necromance and cop used to distance him or herself from the horror of what people could do to each other with gun and knife and club.

My fingers tightened on the scabbard. "Are you coming with me to Polyamour's?" I looked up into Jace's face.

He nodded. His jaw set, a muscle in his cheek flicked. "Of course. Do I get to play bad cop?"

You'd be better at that than I would. How many other things did I not know about Jace?

Did it matter?

Not to me, not now. Whatever he hadn't told me could stay in the past. What mattered was that he'd given up Rio for me, moved in with me, and stretched his human body to the limits trying to help me. And gods help me, I could forgive him everything for that.

"We're not going to frighten her," I decided. "Not unless I think she's guilty." I touched his shoulder, my hand closing, my thumb moving gently. It was almost a caress. "Thank you. For . . . for everything. I mean it."

His face eased slightly, mouth relaxing into a genuine smile. "Hey, no problem, baby. Hanging out with you is better than a holovid game."

An unwilling smile tilted my lips up even as my heart sank. Jace Monroe, the man I'd thought abandoned me years ago, loved me. But I still couldn't stand the thought of anyone but Japhrimel touching me. If Japhrimel could be resurrected . . . "I'll choose to take that as a compliment. Let's go."

24

Polyamour's was in the Tank District, on the very northern fringe between the Tank and the financial heart downtown. Of course, she had to be close to her clients; and her clients had to be rich. To afford a liaison with Polyamour, or one of her contracted sexwitches, took a chunk of hard cash or credit that Lucifer himself might have balked at spending. She was evidently expecting us, for the security net acknowledged my hover; Jace spent a few minutes tapping on the deck, and the net's AI linked with ours, brought the hover down in a circling pattern to land with a jolt on the roofpad. It was broad daylight, so the roof lot was empty except for one sleek gleaming hoverlimo.

I spent a few moments studying the roof and the shielding. The place was well-shielded, both magickally and electronically; I wouldn't have wanted to crack it. The roof entrance was a sort of small gazebo seemingly made of stone and strung with glittering plaslights; stairs descended. I exchanged a glance with Jace and shook my right hand out. It threatened to cramp. My shoulder eased a little; maybe the thin shell of calm over my deepening panic was fooling the demon-made mark.

We went down the stairs and finally came to a beautifully carved mahogany door. Venus glowed from one half, her wooden face serene; Persephone with her pomegranate on the other. Others might have mistaken it for art, but any Magi-trained psion would know better. The sexwitch's realm was Eros and Thanatos, the life-urge married to the reality of Death itself, pain turned to pleasure turned to Power; that it was offered for clients dispelled none of the mystery.

Some theorists said sexwitches were the bridge between *sedayeen*—the healers—and Necromances, those who tread in the realm of Death. I didn't believe it.

Still, I couldn't dismiss the power of sex itself. No psion who deals with the deepest urges of the body and psyche can.

Sex was the least of what sexwitches offered. Redemption, delight, the chance to play with the deepest and most forbidden of fetishes and fantasies, companionship, vulnerability—sexwitches offered all the power of the physical body to soothe, all the power of sex to enlighten, to loosen, to liberate. It was heady stuff, and people paid in buckets for it, making sexwitch House taxes a top revenue source for the Hegemony government.

Two full-spectrum lights made to look like gaslamps burned behind the silvery lattices of ornate carriage lamps. I inhaled and smelled kyphii, sex, and synth hash.

"Great," Jace murmured. "The one time I go into Polyamour's and it's during the *day*."

I laughed. The sound bounced off the creamy marble walls. "I wonder what these stairs are like when it rains."

"Slippery. But think of the possibilities."

"Slipped disk. Cracked skull." I kept the laughter back only by sheer force of will.

He snorted, a short chuckle. "You have no imagination."

"More like too much." The banter to ease our nerves was so familiar I began to relax fractionally. Then the doors gave a theatric creak as they began to open, a slice of glowing almost-candlelight widening.

We waited, my right hand closing around the hilt of my sword. Jace let out a short sound that wasn't quite a whistle and nowhere near a word. When the door was fully open, it revealed a dimly lit hallway hung with red velvet and decorated with tasteful marble statues. And there, standing in the middle of the hall, was the transvestite Polyamour, the most famous sexwitch of our generation.

She was tall, and her face was as beautifully made as any architectural triumph: caramel skin; long, curling black hair; and amazing gray eyes fringed by thick charcoal lashes. She had long aesthetic legs, lightly muscled and revealed by a fluttering pale-pink silk dress. Her feet were bare and surprisingly small, the nails lacquered deep blood-red. One dainty ankle was graced with a thin gold bracelet, and gold hoops hung from her perfect ears. High on her left cheek was the inset ruby, aesthetically placed, which any datscan would reveal as encoded with a powerful protective chip. If a plasgun or projectile discharged anywhere near her or if the ruby were removed, the police would automatically be called. A datscan would also reveal her as a licensed sexwitch, immune to several laws applying to other psionics—and worth ten years in a federal prison if she was assaulted. The Hegemony received far too much in tax profit from sexwitches to look kindly on any harm done to them—not like the fifty years before and after the Parapsychic Act, when sexwitches had all but died out due to the abuse they received from being bought and sold like chattel, worse than any other sort of psion.

Her quick intake of breath showed a pair of shallow high breasts under the silk. I wondered if they were augments, or if she'd taken hormone courses.

Her Power reached out, caressed the edges of both my shields and Jace's. The familiar smell of sexwitch—sex and vulnerability and pure sugary musk heat—rolled out from her in waves.

Anubis, she's powerful.

"Dante Valentine. And Jace Monroe." She tilted her beautiful head slightly, an acknowledgment that sent her perfect ringlets cascading. "I thought you would be along sooner rather than later. The holovids just reported Aran Helm's death." Her voice was caramel with a slight astringency, too deep for a woman's but too light for a man's.

I sniffed. Something smelled odd here: a rank edge of fear under all the perfume.

I saw a glint of silver at her throat.

I dug in my pocket, pulled out the broken necklace. The spade swung at the end of it. "*Tig vedom deum.*" My voice stroked the hall, made the velvet hangings flutter. I was forgetting to be careful.

Polyamour actually turned pale and stepped back. She reached up to her sculpted throat and touched her own necklace. If my eyes hadn't been so sharp, I might not have been able to see it in the shifting, dim light. But there it was, a silver spade. I felt a jolt of sick happiness, one more connection sliding into place. I was getting closer. *Are you happy, Christabel? I'm remembering, and I'm dragging other people through remembering it too. Are you fucking happy?*

"You were not a member, but you know." Her voice was less smooth now. Her eyes slid over me again. "I suppose you should come in."

"I suppose we should." I moved down the steps, heard Jace behind me. "The way I see it, either you're part of it or you're a potential victim. If it's the former, I'll get you first. If it's the latter, you could do worse than have my protection."

She laughed, but the sound was unsteady. Polyamour turned on one soft bare foot and started off down the hall. "I was told you were direct. That seems a bit of an understatement."

"One of the victims was a girl of yours." I moved after her, my boots clicking softly. "Why didn't you say anything?"

She cast me one extraordinary dark glance over her shoulder. The sway of her hips under the silk was almost a woman's. I looked back at Jace, who seemed bemused. "You were at the Hall," Polyamour said. "You know the habit of silence can be hard to break. I didn't *know* anything useful about Yasrule's death until Edward brought me the pictures. Then I knew."

"What exactly do you know?" She wasn't moving very quickly. My boots, and Jace's, thudded in the murmuring silence, all sound dulled by the velvet on the walls. The doors closed behind us on whisper-soft hinges.

"Let's have some coffee. We can be civilized, can't we?" She had recovered. Her voice was back to smoothness. But her aura shifted uneasily, and my own Power reached out, caressing her vulnerable edges. Sexwitches were still nicknamed "beggars" in some circles; the natural physiological processing of Power triggered chemical cascades of pleasure in them, endorphins that made them pleading and vulnerable. As a part-demon, I had more Power than most sexwitches ever encountered; if Polyamour wasn't fully-fed she would be distracted, and I would have to be very gentle. If I was careful of my new body's effect on normal humans, I was doubly careful of what I could do to an exquisitely sensitive sexwitch.

Other halls began to open off this one. I caught sight of round couches, spears of daylight picking out details: a large harp, the glowing green leaves of some trailing plant, a sleeping white Persian cat on a round cushion of black velvet. All in all, it seemed pretty tame.

As if reading my mind, Polyamour laughed. It was a practiced sound, with a rill of uneasiness underneath. "These are only the reception rooms. Have you ever been inside a House, Ms. Valentine?"

"Call me Danny," I said automatically. "No. Some bordellos and brothels, but never a House. It's very beautiful."

She accepted the compliment with a queenly nod. "My private quarters are a few floors down. If you don't mind."

"It would be an honor." Something that was bothering me became painfully clear. "Where are your bodyguards? I'd think your intra-House security would be a little tighter."

"What good would bodyguards do if Dante Valentine wants me dead?" Her tone edged on the whimsical. "No. For personal reasons, I'd prefer to keep this meeting private." The end of the hall rose up in front of us and two shielded doors opened, revealing an elevator. I swallowed, my jaw setting, and Jace's hand closed around my elbow. "Besides, I am not without a slight precognitive Talent. It comes in handy."

We stepped into the elevator. Polyamour's aura pressed against mine, the air roiling with Shaman, sexwitch, and almost-demon. The doors closed. There was a time when I would have drawn steel and started struggling to escape such a confined space, but now I set my teeth together and tightened my left hand around the scabbard. My rings popped and sparked. Jace's touch on my elbow loosened for a second, but then he drove his fingernails in savagely.

The bright diamonds of pain were negligible, but they helped.

Polyamour studied my face. In such close quarters, I could see the line of her jaw, too strong for a woman's. There was an old, faint scar running just under her right ear, under the jawbone to the bottom of her chin. Her forehead was a little too broad too. But those eyes more than made up for it. "You're exquisite," she said. "I could get you a ton of work."

I managed a tight smile. Maybe she didn't assume I'd been genespliced. Then again, she could see the black stain on my aura. *Thanks for the compliment. I don't want to look like this.* "Not many would like to fuck a Necromance." *And I can't touch a man without thinking of a dead demon and how he held me.*

Nothing seemed to throw her. "You'd be surprised." The elevator made a soft sound, and the doors opened. Disregarding safety or politeness, I was the first one out, tearing free of Jace's hand but dimly grateful that he had choked up on my elbow.

This hall was plain, wood-floored, and white-walled.

Sunlight poured in from the windows, but gauzy white curtains diluted the force of the light. I blinked, my pupils contracting, and smelled coffee. Polyamour led us through a plain wooden door and into a large comfortable room with a fireplace, a tumbled king-size bed, two blue linen couches, a battered Perasiano rug, and a woman wearing nothing but a collar and long chain standing in the middle of a small kitchenette, pouring coffee from a silver samovar.

"Please, sit." Polyamour strode across the room, silk fluttering, and draped herself across one of the couches. "Diana will bring the coffee."

I lowered myself down gingerly, the sword across my knees. Looked up at Jace, who wore a faint scowl. He stood to the side and folded his arms, *watchdog* written in every line of his body. "I suppose we might start with the obvious," I said. "Someone's killing the members of the Black Room. Why?"

She gave one elegant shrug, the silk whispering as she moved. The naked woman padded over softly, bearing a silver tray. She glanced at Polyamour, who nodded slightly.

"Cream?" the naked woman asked, her breasts moving gently as she knelt to place the tray on a low ebony table. Her pubic fleece was smoky darkness, her hair a long rippling fall of chestnut. She was a sexwitch too, a ruby glittering in her cheek. She seemed utterly unself-conscious of her nudity, almost to the point of parody. Her aura was at a low ember, fully fed, but she still made a subtle, inviting movement as soon as the edge of my aura touched her. "Sugar?"

"Just cream." *If this is a game to see how I react, Poly,*

you're going to be very disappointed. Even when I was human I didn't go in for this.

She looked up at Jace, who shook his head.

The naked woman handed me an antique silver cup full of expensively smooth coffee and chicory, cut with heavy cream. She spent a few more moments preparing Polyamour's drink, handed it to her, and sat back on her heels, waiting.

"You may go, Diana. I will be quite all right. Come back in two hours." Poly waved her away.

The woman bowed, her breasts moving, hair falling forward to veil her face momentarily. Then she rose, looped the chain from the leather collar over her arm, and left, closing the door with a quiet click.

Polaymour seemed to shrink slightly at the sound of that click. "I suppose you want to know how they did it."

I took a sip of the coffee. "This is very nice."

She acknowledged the compliment with a small nod.

Let's get down to business. "The more I know, the better prepared I am to stop this thing."

"I'm not sure you *can* stop it." She crossed her legs, demurely, but a faint sheen of sweat showed on her forehead. I wondered if she'd had her chin laser-treated to get rid of stubble, or if hormone treatments had taken care of it. "It's probably Destiny coming home to roost. Do you believe in Fate, Danny Valentine?"

I shrugged. "No more than the next Magi-trained Necromance."

She gave a coughing little laugh. "That's very funny. I was involved in a conspiracy to kill a Hegemony officer. Are you going to arrest me?"

It was my turn to laugh, a laugh that dropped and shattered in pieces on the wooden floor. "Not fucking likely. Any truth to the rumor that someone turned into a Feeder and took him on in a predator's duel?"

"In a way, I suppose." Polyamour shivered.

My nostrils flared. I Saw her fear, rising in trails that rippled and eddied like heat. A sexwitch's fear is perfumed, and smells like something fragrant and wanting, pheromones pressing hard against anyone in the room. Humans and Nichtvren like the smell, psions are particularly sensitive to a sexwitch's pheromones of fear or excitement; werecain and kobolding aren't affected at all.

And me? It was difficult for me not to look at the curve of her throat where the pulse beat. She smelled like food. She also smelled—just a hint—of amber musk and burning cinnamon, a smell that made me think of Japhrimel's body against mine, his spent, shuddering sigh as he buried his face in my throat, the tang of demon blood burning my mouth. *It's not real. It's only chemicals and Power. She's just scared.*

Her long caramel hand came up and touched the spade necklace. She curled her fingers around it, then broke the chain with a flick of Power, held the necklace up. "They made it stop." Her eyes moved with the spade as it dangled back and forth, glittering. "Or Keller did."

I breathed shallowly, trying not to inhale any more of the delicious, electric, mouthwatering scent. "Keller?"

Her mouth quirked slightly. "Our fearless leader. I . . ." She was trembling. Abruptly, Polyamour swung her legs off the couch, set her coffee down on the tray, and rolled up to her feet. The one quick movement told me she'd had some combat training, and that was very interesting. Sex-

witches don't normally go for combat; fear turns into desire for them, crippling their ability to respond. "You
know," she said tonelessly. "You *know* how bad it was."

I swallowed. The coffee turned to ash in my mouth, but
the taste of it cut through the tantalizing scent. I wondered
if that was why she'd offered it. "I was in the cage four
times. But I know the sexwitches had it rough."

"Oh, rough." She waved a hand, pacing away from us.
I could breathe again, without her pheromones drowning
me. "Rough. We were fucked every which way but loose,
Valentine. That's not *rough*. The rough part was having
that bastard pawing away at your *mind* while he or one of
his cronies stuck whatever they wanted in their orifice of
choice. If you're a sexwitch, you learn early that your
body betrays you—it's your *mind* that has to stay impregnable. Your soul. To have that filthy old maggot fingering
inside your head . . ." Her cascade of dark curls shuddered
as she turned her supple back. She was *shaking*.

"*Sekhmet sa'es,*" I whispered. At least the few cubic
inches inside my skull had been all mine. No matter how
much of a smoking wasteland it became, it was still my
wasteland. What was that old fable?

*Why do you eat your own heart? Because, O King, it is
bitter, and because it is my heart.*

Even in the middle of my blackest moments, I'd had
my books. The hard kernels of immortal stories, each one
a reminder of how deeply Lewis loved me, of how strong
I could strive to be. My books and my god, steady sources
of strength in the impregnable fortress of my head. I *had*
been lucky.

Lucky. I never thought I would think *that*.

Polyamour turned back to us. The beauty of her face

had become harder, more brittle; her eyes were dark
holes. "I learned early that I wanted to be strong. Or at
least have a strong protector. And so, I built this. But
would you believe I still have nightmares?"

"I believe it." My eyes flickered over to the mantel.
Hung above it was a restrained, priceless Mobian print,
the famous black-and-white of the woman's back tattooed
with a rising dragon. I would bet it was the original. The
subtle shades of gray and stippled black were alive to my
demon sight. I could have contemplated it for hours.
"I believe it." *I had Anubis, and you had nobody. Should
I feel guilty about that? Lucky? Or guilty about feeling
lucky?*

"Would you believe I actually felt guilty?" Her throaty,
husky voice broke on the last word. The sharp pinch of
my own guilt settled in, twisted hard. The scent of her fear
still lingered on me, and it took an effort of will to calm
my own racing pulse.

*If I could, Poly, I'd walk out of here and let you get
back to trying to forget all about it. Because as soon as I
finish this, I intend to forget every-fucking-thing that has
to do with Rigger Hall too.* "Poly, I need to know who. I
need to know what you did. And why the Feeder glyphs
are supposed to protect you against it."

She dropped her head, stood with her carefully ringlet-
ted hair around her face. After a moment I realized the
sound in the room was her. She was breathing like a horse
run too hard, her fear rising in waves like heat from pavement. Her aura swirled in blue and violet, trembling,
about to go nova.

I was off the couch before I knew it, leaving my sword
behind. I approached her softly, my own aura stretching;

my rings swirled steadily. When the gold glow of my aura
touched the edges of hers, the result was startling—her
light yearned toward me, the classic response of a sexwitch. They need to feed, either on sex or the power sex
raised; pure Power always raises a sexual response in
them. That is what makes them so vulnerable—their bodies beg for it, slaves to the deepest urges of the body itself.
The smell of her fear rose to drench me, but my own
demon-scent overlaid it, a fiery, smooth kick like brandy
igniting in my stomach.

Gods above, I could get drunk on this.

I'd forgotten how much more I was. How much more
Japhrimel had made me. The outer layer of my defenses
dropped, and a thin, humming sonic note of Power slid
through the air like oil into a glass. Her head tipped back.
Even though she was taller than me I caught her nape and
wrist easily, the demon-hard calluses on my golden hands
from daily knife-drill rasping on her soft skin. Then my
aura closed around her, the full-scale plasgun charge of
power sinking into her veins. Her eyelids fluttered shut
and she moaned, helpless against the riptide.

*Was that what I looked like when Japhrimel changed
me?* I shook the thought aside. Pleasure scraped against
my nerves, sparked through my bones. It *was* just like alcohol, a thorny electric lassitude like the best stage of
every drunk I'd ever been on. Yet I was in control, not
helpless in its grip. Gently, ever so gently, I stroked down
Polyamour's spine with a feather-touch of Power. She
moaned again, the silk of her dress whispering as her hips
jerked forward. I kept one hand steady on her nape, my
skin roughening slightly as the wave of her pleasure
wrapped around me. My other hand touched her chin, her

skin startlingly soft. My fingernails scraped slightly as I traced the scar on her jaw. This close, I saw that her skin was flawless; her eyelids fluttered again, eyelashes as thick and dark as a young boy's.

I could do anything I wanted to her. The thought shook me. I had *power,* more power than I'd ever had in my life. And Polyamour was helpless, as helpless as we had been under Mirovitch.

Shock jolted me out of the haze of sensation. *No. I'm not like that. I want to help her, dammit. I'm trying to help her.*

I exhaled, disengaging, the flow of Power slowing to a trickle. Waited until she stopped trembling and made sure she had her balance. She leaned toward me. I pressed a kiss onto her cheek, smelling the peculiar musk of sex-witch laid over the smell of human. It was oddly pleasing, but now the edge of fear was gone, and so was the buzzing, blurring pleasure slamming through my nerves. *Do demons feel like that when they scare us?*

Had Japhrimel felt that when he frightened me?

"There," I murmured. "Isn't that better?"

She blinked. Consciousness flooded back into her eyes. She tore away from my hand; I let her go, backed up two steps, and paced back to the couch. Jace stood in the same place, studying the Mobian. He wasn't blushing—but I could smell his arousal. It didn't smell nearly as good as hers. My shoulder wasn't burning—the mark had settled back into a dim glow. I picked up my cooling coffee cup, my hand stopping halfway to my mouth. My head suddenly cleared, swept clean by the jolts of sensation.

Can it be you have not resurrected him?
You will not leave me to wander the earth alone.

Feed me.

Sexwitches needed feeding. *I* needed feeding—but thankfully I could use human food. Japhrimel had needed blood. He had visited a slaughterhouse in Nuevo Rio.

I would not have you see me feed. His voice, old and fiercely dark as whiskey. I stared into the coffee. Polyamour stood with her back to us for a few minutes, taking in deep ragged breaths; but her aura smoothed out. When I could talk around the lump in my throat, I repeated myself. "I need to know who. I need to know what you did. And why the Feeder glyphs are supposed to protect you against it."

She let out a clipped little laugh, then swung around to face us. "I'll tell you what I know. You've paid for it, after all, with that little display."

You enjoyed it. But that was unfair. So had I. "For fuck's sake. You could be next, Sebastiano. Quit fucking around with me and tell me what I need to know or I'll leave you to it and track it down from the other end."

Polyamour held up the spade necklace. It glittered, a venomous dart of light. "I'm dead anyway. We couldn't kill Mirovitch, we were just kids. It was Keller's idea that they . . . they each take *some.*" Her hand jittered. The spade danced, more barbs of light spitting. "I don't know all of it, Valentine. My job was to get them into Mirovitch's private rooms past the security. Keller couldn't take *him* on by himself. And nobody wanted to take *him* on in a Feeder duel. Nobody wanted to become a Feeder, hunted down, despised even after treatment. So Keller came up with the idea. They each take a *part.*"

I blinked. *That's part of why the inquiry was sealed.* If word got out that a circle of psions—just kids—had slipped their collars and murdered the Headmaster of a school, especially one as experienced as Mirovitch . . .

That would be even worse than the public-relations fiasco of a school with a Headmaster gone awry. It was publicly more palatable for the Headmaster to abuse the students. Psions were already hated and feared equally in some places, uneasily accepted at best. The Hegemony needed us, we were protected under the law—but publicity was another thing entirely.

My stomach turned sour. It was the reality of living in the modern world, but it still nauseated me. It was more *acceptable* for him to abuse us than for us to turn on him. Because after all, if psions could kill when they were children, where did that leave the adults? Too dangerous to be left alive, maybe. That was the logical extension to that thought, wasn't it?

Jace shifted slightly. I caught his meaning as if he'd laid it in my brain with a telepath's light open touch.

"Keller?"

"Kellerman." Polyamour sighed.

The name didn't ring a bell. "I must not have met him."

Her voice took on a scraping note of sarcasm, elegantly done of course. "I doubt you'd remember it even if you did. He was eminently forgettable."

"Kellerman?"

Polyamour shivered, her hair trembling—I didn't bother to speak softly, and the entire room reverberated, the tray ringing softly against the creaking table, the walls groaning slightly, the curtains over the windows blown back, throwing gauzy shadows over the walls. I wondered if her body was betraying her, if she was fighting the urge to come back and drop at my feet, fawn on me.

I suppressed a shiver. I thanked my gods I hadn't been born a sexwitch or been sent out as a breeder. Or indentured to a colony. Or any of the thousand other things that *could* have happened.

Still . . . it would be so easy to scare her a little, just a very little, and feel that delicious drowning feedback again.

"It was a nickname. Kellerman Lourdes. His parents were Novo Christer, died in a colony transport crash." Polyamour let out a low breath. "What else do you want?"

"Why the Feeder glyphs? And who else was in this?" The pattern was rising from the depths of coincidence like a shape breaking up through smooth glassy water, pieces falling into place. But not enough pieces, and not nearly quickly enough.

"Only Keller knew. We'd meet him in that boathouse on the grounds—you remember that shack? Anyway, none of us knew about anything other than the person we recruited—never more than one more—and Keller. He took secrecy very seriously. I was only recruited to get Keller and the others through the security."

"The others?" *You'd think she'd be spilling everything she ever even thought she knew about this Keller and Mirovitch,* I thought sourly. But she was pale and shaking, only the flush of my power keeping her from collapsing. If memory could reopen the scars on my back and almost force me into shock, echo in Eddie's head loud enough to make him shake even after all these years, and push the fabled Polyamour into losing her careful control, then she deserved a few seconds and all the gentleness I could muster.

Especially since I was almost trembling with the urge to

do something unforgivable, just so I could have a few moments of oblivion. I had never understood bought sex before, *never*.

Not until now.

"I think Yasrule was one of them. Maybe. I don't *know*." Tears thickened her exquisite voice, welling in her dark, haunted eyes.

"You weren't there? How could you short out the security and—"

"*He* liked orgies." When she mentioned Mirovitch, it was obvious; her voice took on a weight of whispery fear and utter loathing that scraped the air and made it bleed. "So I brought fresh meat, and I brought Keller. I had to get close to *him* and—"

"*Sekhmet sa'es,*" I whispered. "Your one recruit and Keller."

She nodded. "Once we were inside, Keller slipped his collar and bought enough time for me to get the security circle down. Then I dragged the meat away—she was a Magi, Dolores Ancien-Ruiz, she didn't know anything. That's why I hate myself. *He* was busy with her while Keller started his . . . plan . . . and I worked on the net." Polyamour held up her caramel hand, examining her shaking fingers as if they belonged to someone else. "I do hate myself for that."

I had to know. "Why?"

Her shoulders dropped and she pulled them back taut again. "Dolores committed suicide two years later. She was eleven when she hung herself."

Shit. I would have wanted to question her too. The thought of an eleven-year-old girl hanging herself . . . I pushed it away.

"I hauled her out of the Headmaster's House. She was screaming. They went past me—they were all wearing sk8 masks, but I thought I recognized Yasrule. And Aran. And Hollin."

"Hollin? Hollin Sukerow?" *Him* I knew, by reputation at least. I glanced up at Jace, who was pale, a sheen of sweat on his forehead. It wasn't a comfortable story. He was vulnerable to Poly's pheromones, too. I wondered what he smelled when she drenched the air with fear.

"The very same." Polyamour's chin lifted, a faint note of challenge. "Are you almost done? I have an appointment I would rather not miss."

As if you have anything more important to do. But it might just have been that she wanted us gone, that she wanted to start forgetting the fear that made her helpless. I made it to my feet, this time scooping up my sword. Paced over to her, avoiding the low table. I don't know what she saw in my face, but she dropped her eyes, her entire body shifting just a few millimeters. It was amazing how she could express complete but grudging submission with such a subtle movement. I wished I had body language that expressive.

Less than a foot from her, I halted. My fingernails scraped her hand as I took the spade necklace from her slackening fingers. This close, with my aura blurring and wrapping around her, she sighed, leaning forward as if she would lay her head on my shoulder.

I stuffed both spade necklaces into my pocket and caught her nape again with my free hand, holding my sword well clear. Polyamour's forehead touched mine. Her skin was fevered, but still not as warm as mine. She exhaled, I smelled human breath, coffee, and sexwitch musk. If I kissed her, she would melt against me, and Jace would be left standing on the couch. It had been a long, long time for me; and she . . .

But I want to scare her. I don't think I could control myself. The thought frightened me, because it was so god-damn tempting, and would be oh so very easy.

What have I become?

Her aura turned gold as I pushed Power into her, more and more and more until she cried out hoarsely, her body shuddering and hips jerking helplessly forward again. My fingers suddenly turned to iron to brace her. "Full-up," I whispered. "Now for a few nights, you don't have to feed. Take a vacation. And stop beating yourself up over Dolores." My own breath caught as I inhaled, struggling for control. Kept it. *I don't do that. I don't use people like that. I DON'T.*

Oh yeah? For once, the snide voice of my conscience didn't sound like Japhrimel. *What about Jace?*

I drew in a deep ragged breath. "Chances are it wasn't you, Bastian. Lots of kids killed themselves rather than handle the fallout from that place. Who knows what she suffered before she helped bring Mirovitch down?" My voice sank into its lowest registers, a throbbing contralto husk, swirling into her skin as I tied mental strings in a complicated knot, sealing the Power into her. For a few days, Polyamour would be free; she wouldn't have to feed. The power-charge I gave her would last longer if she didn't attempt any spells—and if she was attacked, she now had a full charge to fight with. It was poor payment for what I'd just put her through, but all I could give.

One thing was certain. Our killer wasn't Polyamour. Sexwitches didn't turn Feeder. Their capacity to hold a charge of Power was finite; they couldn't feed from anything other than sex. Not only was our killer not Polyamour, but she wasn't implicated in the mess. She was clean.

She gained her balance, and I let go of her neck. "And the next time you need another few days of rest, Poly, you come see me." I forced myself to step cautiously, then turned on my heel and tilted my head at Jace. "We'll let ourselves out."

Jace turned too, preceded me to the door. His hand touched the knob.

"Valentine!" Polyamour's voice didn't quiver. I halted, not looking back. If I looked back I was going to do something I shouldn't. My left hand almost creaked, I clutched the scabbard so tightly.

"You bitch." Now her voice broke like a teenage boy's. "Thank you."

If you only knew how close I was to scaring you, to using you, you might not thank me. "No problem." I touched Jace's shoulder, he pushed the door open, and led me out into the hall beyond.

"We're going to have to do the elevator again," he said. I let out a sharp breath, closing my eyes. My hand dug into his shoulder. He leaned into it. If it hurt him, he gave no indication. "Don't worry, Danny. I'm with you."

It was more comforting than I expected. "Good." My voice was still low, it made a shiver run through Polyamour's House. *That was close. That was so fucking close. And I invited her to call me again. She needs it, every sexwitch needs it.* Loathing crept up my spine, skin-crawling dislike. *No. I can offer her some help. That's all. Payment for what I almost did to her, for what I was tempted to do. I am not a demon. I'm human. Human.*

But that exquisite sensation, the blessed relief from pain, the *pleasure* of smelling her fear, sweeter than anything I'd tasted since being locked in a demon's arms . . .

No. *No.* I was human, goddammit. I was going to stay that way, no matter what. Genesplicing didn't make a human less *human,* and neither would this. Only my body had changed. The rest of me remained the same.

Didn't it?

Oh, Anubis, I prayed, *don't let me be wrong on this one.*

"Danny?"

I let out a ragged breath. "Yeah?" *Don't ask me, Jace. Don't ask me if I can give you any more than what you already have from me. The best thing I can do is finish out this case, however it ends up, and try to find some way to set you free to live your own damn life. I can't do this anymore.*

But once again, he surprised me. "Where we going next? Let me guess. To find Hollin Sukerow."

I opened my eyes again. The mark on my left shoulder throbbed against my skin, and I felt hot fingers trail up my back. Dead fingers. *Japhrimel's* fingers. Had my fear smelled like that to him? Had he loved the smell of my terror? Had it strained his control? I wrestled the thought away with an almost-physical effort, forced it down. "You got it. But first we're going to rendezvous with Gabe."

And as soon as I can, I'm going to see if there's a slaughterhouse in Saint City that will do me a blood vat.

It was a good thought, one that made my heart lighten. The one that came after it made my entire chest sink. *But what if I'm wrong and I dump Japhrimel's ashes in a vat of blood and ruin them? Lucifer lies, and the rest is just guesswork. What if he's taunting me?*

If the Devil was taunting me, he was doing a goddamn good job of it. I would have to finish this goddamn hunt and then find every book I could lay my hands on about resurrecting demons. No more bounties.

I'd grieved long enough, goddammit.

25

The station house was a seethe of activity, and we made it to the Parapsych floor from the underground parking garage without trouble. I guess my hover was known to the cops, because their parking-lot AI deck took care of bringing the hover in. Jace said very little, and his face was thoughtful. I had finally managed to unclench my left hand and convince myself I hadn't just tempted Poly to call me again. I'd only been offering an exchange, fair payment to her for making her remember the Hall.

So what if I felt the lightest touch of sweat prickling along my forehead and under my arms when I thought of her? I didn't sweat easy anymore, it took phenomenal effort that left me numb and hungry to wring water out of my skin. But there it was.

Gabe stalked into her office with a stack of paper to find us waiting for her. Her dark eyes glittered with something close to rage, her sleek hair ruffled. She stopped, seeing us, and tossed the paper on the desk. "Find anything useful?" A slight snarl turned her pretty face feral.

Yeah. I found out that I can get drunk off scaring a sexwitch. How about you, Gabe? "Lots of interesting, and possibly useful." I blinked at her. "What's up, Spooky girl?"

"I made a list of the kids in the yearbook that had that mark. One of 'em I can't find. *All* of the few still living are still in Saint City. The others are dead."

"How many?" Jace leaned against the wall of her cubicle, folding his arms. I tried to tell myself I didn't want to know what *he* smelled in Poly's fear.

Lying to yourself is a bad habit to start when you're a Necromance.

"Nine outside Saint City dead." Gabe's mouth turned down at the corners. "It looks like they scattered to the winds: three of them in Putchkin territory, two in Freetowns, and the rest in Hegemony territory as far away from Saint City as possible."

"Let me guess." I dropped down in a chair and leaned back, closing my eyes. Thank the gods, something else to think about. "The one you can't find is Kellerman Lourdes."

"Sounds like you've had a productive few hours," she said sourly. "Here's the thing: all of the nine are dead. It started in Putchkin territory, then in the Freetowns, then coming closer and closer to the city. Then this last string of killings in the city itself. And nobody's caught on. Guess when the first killing was."

I shrugged, reaching up and rubbing at my temples as if I had a headache. I wondered if part-demons ever got headaches, or if a psychosomatic headache would explain the way my head was pounding. "Tell me." *Not in the mood for guessing games, Gabe. Sorry.*

"Exactly ten years to the day after Mirovitch's death. The victim, Anders Cullam—"

"I remember him." I shivered. "One of Mirovitch's stooges." The phantom scars on my back started to burn, three stripes of fire; the branding along the lower crease of my left buttock gave one flare of pain and then settled down. My left shoulder spread a prickling heat down my chest, velvet fire threading through my veins, soothing me just as I'd just soothed Polyamour.

I was almost happier with a demon mark that was cold and quiescent than one that seemed to have a mind of its own. Especially since I wondered if the mark was reacting to *my* fear. But that was impossible. I was not a sexwitch.

Gabe dropped down into her chair. "He had one of those spade necklaces and a serious case of being ripped limb from limb. The Putchkin police had the case cold-filed after they hit a wall and no other homicides in the city fit the profile. Look, Danny, I don't understand just one thing. The normal, Bryce Smith. How the hell does he fit in?"

It was a small, sour reprieve to have a puzzle to think about. *Neither do I. That's the thing that bothers me the most.* "Don't know yet. Can you pull his records? Everything not covered under the blind trust?"

Gabe shrugged, dug in the pile of paper drifting up on her desk, and retrieved a thick file. "Already did. Let's see. He didn't have one of those spade necklaces either."

"He *was* a jeweler. His slicboard was registered to someone named Keller," Jace piped up. "Guess what Kellerman Lourdes's school nickname was, according to Polyamour."

"No shit?" Gabe shook her head and flipped the file open. "Bryce Smith. Applied for a Putchkin visa as a 'technological advisor,' which would put him in that territory at about the right time . . . hmm. He took someone else with him, but it doesn't say who. Goddamn diplomatic seals." Her eyes came up to meet mine. "Goddamn, Danny. It's good to have you with me."

That managed to bring a weary smile to my face. I leaned forward to take the file. "I live to serve. You have a list of the ones living in Saint City?"

"I do. Seven of them settled here and are assumed alive—"

"Take Polyamour off the list. And Kellerman Lourdes. That leaves five. Is Hollin Sukerow on the list?"

"Yep. Is Kellerman our suspect, Danny?"

I took a deep breath. My brain clicked over into "work" mode, and it was a relief. "I don't know." *I'm working on blind instinct here, Gabe. You keep expecting a miracle.*

Well, wasn't that what blind instinct was? Wasn't that what *magick* was?

"Why are the people in Saint City still alive?" Gabe's eyebrows drew together.

"Because Rigger Hall is located here. That's where it started—so that's where it will stop." The prickling heat from my left shoulder slid down my back, the phantom scars turning to liquid fire and then subsiding. I blew out through my teeth, a whistling tone that served as punctuation. "All right then. Let's get this hover in the air. What are we going to do?" I was slightly surprised my voice didn't shake. I sounded normal except for the throatiness left over from Lucifer crushing my windpipe. Time hadn't taken the sting from that memory—or from any other, for that matter. A Magi-trained memory is both a blessing and a curse; there were so many things I wished I could forget. The list seemed to be getting longer lately. Much longer.

Do you believe in Fate, Danny Valentine? Polyamour's voice, terrified and low. I hadn't really answered her, because the answer was too . . . scary.

For a moment I contemplated telling Gabe that some things *should* be left to Fate, that something was being worked out here, some horrible equation being finished. I wondered what she would say if I told her that I was beginning to see the pattern, and that it was a terrible one, complete in its infinite awfulness.

Then I had another thought, rising like bad gas from the darkest vaults of my mind. They—whoever it was in that dark room after Polyamour dragged away a screaming nine-year-old who had probably suffered more than *any* child should have to face—had fed on Mirovitch, torn him into psychic pieces and perhaps physical ones too, since physical dismemberment would definitely help the psychic mutilation. And now, decades later, they hadn't contacted the police when they felt danger closing in. Instead, they had retreated to their sanctums and drawn circles with consecrated chalk. Were they the same circles and glyphs Keller had altered and used to drain the life out of a monster wearing the Headmaster's clothing?

I was suddenly, chillingly sure that something had risen from those circles and torn them to pieces. Had Christabel wondered if this might happen all those years ago and marked those she knew might be in danger? A Necromance knew that the dead stayed dead, but could she have suspected something would rise from an unquiet grave and . . .

I shook the thought away, my braid bouncing against my back. She hadn't been a full-fledged Necromance at the time. But maybe Christabel had started to wonder about things . . . And maybe she was like me, with a small precognitive talent that had whispered to her to mark her fellow conspirators, maybe as a *fuck you* to the world that hadn't saved them from Mirovitch, forcing them to do the unthinkable to save themselves.

Remember Rigger Hall. Remember.

My hand dropped to my pocket, feeling the small bumps from the silver necklaces. *Maybe I should just let this take care of itself.*

I couldn't believe I'd just *thought* that. It had to be the fear talking.

I didn't even recognize myself anymore. The old Danny Valentine would never have thought so, would never have entertained the notion that perhaps it was better for *this* circle to be closed. That this murderous cycle might best be left to finish itself out unmolested.

No, the old Danny Valentine would know that whoever had killed Mirovitch was due a debt of gratitude, if nothing else.

The old Danny Valentine wouldn't have wanted to scare a sexwitch just to get a few cheap moments of enjoyment either.

Come on, Danny. Think about it. There is a circle being closed here. You get in front of something with this type of momentum and it could run right over you. And besides, this is not your fight, is it? If it's vengeance, it's a vengeance you have nothing to do with.

It was a dishonorable and uncomfortable thought. A thought not worthy of someone Gabe could count on, a thought unworthy of the woman Jado had given another sword, unworthy of the terrified Necromance Japhrimel had tried his best to protect and the woman Jace was even now protecting as best he could.

But still, the thought persisted. Like the Devil's perfumed, silken voice, crawling in the corners of my mind, searching for entrance.

The Devil's voice—or Mirovitch's.

Besides, I had vengeance of my own to mete out. For Roanna, who had tried so hard to tell her social worker what was happening. And for myself, too. For the child I had been.

Eddie's voice floated through my head. *I can't go home, I can't fuckin sleep, and people are* dying. *I got to get this done.*

I looked up at Gabe's worried face. I had no choice. It had been too late the moment Gabe picked up her phone and dialed my number. *In for a penny, in for a pound.* "Do?" I shrugged. "I'm going to go visit Hollin Sukerow. You try to find out more about this Bryce Smith." *Good luck, if he was a tech advisor you can't break the blind trust; it's standard for Hegemony-Putchkin work trades.*

"Do you think he was Keller?" she asked.

It was an idea. It would have been nice and neat, except for the fact that it made no sense at all. Keller was a psion, or he wouldn't have been at the Hall. "I don't know. We don't even know for sure who Bryce Smith was, only that his body scanned normal and had some genelocking they checked to verify identity. Until we find out more, it'd be useless to assume everything. You know what they say about assumptions."

That earned me a sniggering laugh. She was looking

better by the moment. Give Gabe a clear-cut string of probabilities to work, and she was just dandy. Uncertainty and blank dead ends bugged the hell out of her. "All right. You ever thought of working for the cops?"

I rolled my head back, stretching out my neck. "I'm not too good at playing politics and taking orders. I like being a freelancer."

Gabe laughed. It was a low, brittle sound, but better than nothing. "Actually, my ass is gold right now. The Nichtvren are putting pressure on the mayor and City Hall to give me anything I need. Whatever you did when you visited the Prime Power must have impressed him."

"I killed a couple werecain." I rocked up to my feet. *And I'm planning on paying the Prime and his Consort another visit and raiding their library soon.* "I'm going to go visit Sukerow. Can you give me a copy of the list?"

She grinned. "It's already on your datpilot. Hey, Danny?"

I paused, looking up at Jace, who started scraping himself off the wall. There were dark circles under his eyes, and he looked like he needed about twenty-four hours of sleep. I had to remember his limits. "What?"

"Thanks. For talking to Eddie. He came home last night."

I winced inwardly. "No problem, Gabe. After all, you're my friend."

That being said, I paced out of her office, Jace following me. "We heading to Sukerow's?"

I glanced down the hall, unease prickling at my neck. "No. Home. I need to pick some stuff up, and you need some sleep. I'll visit Sukerow, and hook up with you in twelve hours or so. Then we'll—"

"Goddammit, Danny. I can handle it." He sounded irritated. We took the stairs down to the parking level again.

Our boots rang on the linoleum steps, the sound bouncing off concrete walls. I was breathing easier now, but the prickling on my nape meant bad trouble coming.

"I know you can handle it, Jace." I wondered if the excessive patience in my tone was going to piss him off even more. It was damn likely. "I just don't want you to if there's no need. In twelve hours or so I'm going to need you big-time."

"Why?" Faint tone of challenge in his voice. I could sense the tension in him as he slammed down the steps behind me, his staff thwocked the wall with a hollow sound. *Dammit, Jace, let up on me, all right? I'm not having a good fucking day here.*

"Because when I finish with Sukerow and the others on the list, I'm going to Rigger Hall. And I'm going to need you there." My voice was at least as brittle as his. *And when this is all over I also have something I need to do, something that doesn't concern you. Something you wouldn't understand. Something that concerns a blood vat and a demon's ashes, and me praying a whole hell of a lot that Lucifer just isn't yanking my chain again. You can't waste your life on someone who can't give you what you need, Jace. As soon as this is all finished, all over, I have to tell you that. Make you understand.*

"At least let me go to Sukerow's with you. My 'pilot says it's right near here."

I stopped on the stairs and looked up at him. He carried his staff, his sword was thrust through a loop in his belt, and he'd been silent about us for far too long. I'd guessed it couldn't last—it had been long enough to strain anyone's patience. Even Jason Monroe's.

He shoved his datpilot back into the inner pocket of his

coat, his blue eyes meeting mine. There was a time when I would have sworn that I knew every thought crossing through those blue eyes. He'd come after me, and dealt with me being generally unsociable and rude, never losing his temper, not even pushing me for sex. He had simply been there, a comfort and support.

Why? Especially when the Danny Valentine he knew would never have forgiven him, no matter how much penance he peformed. I was no longer the terrified, swaggering, half-cracked Necromance he'd fallen in love with. I was someone else, and so was he.

Who was he in love with, who I used to be or what I'd become? And who was I trying to protect by keeping him close to me? Jason Monroe, or my own silly self?

The stairwell echoed with silence. I balanced my right hand on the round handrail covered in chipped blue paint; my left hand curled around the sword. It had quickly become natural again to have my left hand taken with the slender weight; I could almost forget everything was so different now. I could almost forget the intervening years; I could almost forget Nuevo Rio, the heat, and the ice of the island we had tracked Santino to.

I could almost forget everything when I looked up at him, the faint fans of lines coming from the corners of his eyes, the way he favored one injured knee, the familiar slope of his broad shoulders, and the way his mouth quirked at one corner even when he was being serious. I had imagined, sometimes, how he would look when he got older, back in the painfully intense days of our first love affair. I'd even toyed with the idea of having a kid with him, once the mortgage was paid off. There was still something about Jace Monroe that made my shoulders relax and my mouth want to curl up in a smile. He could irritate me the way no other human being on earth could—and the memory rose of his hand around my elbow in Polyamour's elevator, his fingernails digging in, silently giving me the pain to anchor myself.

I could almost forget everything except the one thing that stood between us, the shadow-ghost of a tall not-quite-man with his hands clasped behind his back, his long Chinese-collared coat smoking with demon power, green eyes gone dark and watching me. The one thing I could never forget, the one thing Jace would never be able to fight his way through or understand his way around.

Japhrimel. Tierce Japhrimel.

But still, my heart ached for Jace.

He's protecting me the only way he knows how. I eased up another step. My right hand closed around his shoulder, carefully, delicately. "Jace," I said quietly, "if there was anyone in the whole world I would . . . be with now, it would be you. The only reason I . . . well, I don't know what it would do to you. The last time I had . . . sex . . . with anyone, it was Japhrimel." My voice miraculously didn't break on Japhrimel's name, for once. I couldn't bring myself to tell Jace that I couldn't give him anything more. It was cowardice, plain and simple; cowardice and need, dressed up as a gentle fiction to spare his feelings. "I'm *different* now. I don't know what it would do to you, and I don't want you . . . hurt. I don't think you're less capable than you were, Jace. I just don't . . . I don't feel weariness like I used to. Or pain. I can go for longer without resting. That's all. It's not because I don't trust you."

Who else do I have to trust? You, Gabe, Eddie. More than I've ever had in my whole life. I loved you, Jace; I still do. The very thought was shaded orange with bitterness. Why couldn't he have stayed with me instead of disappearing? Why couldn't he have trusted that I could protect myself instead of thinking he had to return to Rio to "save" me? *Why?*

I would have taken on Santino, taken on Lucifer himself, for Jace; I would have counted it small potatoes. But now, with the shadow of a demon between us, I could not give Jace what he needed. Whether I could resurrect Japhrimel or not, I couldn't be what Jace wanted me to be. Who I used to be. The woman he'd fallen in love with.

Maybe it was time to let him go.

He looked down at me, his blue eyes dark and his mouth a straight line. "I've never seen you the way you were with Polyamour," he managed, finally. "And I . . . *Chango,* Danny. This is all fucking wrong."

You can say that again. And I wasn't doing Poly any favors, no matter what it looked like to you. "I know." I swallowed dryly. The words I could never say to him, the silences he'd used against me, hung between us; an even bigger wall than the demon who had Fallen and altered me. I settled for giving in. "Fine. Come with me to Sukerow's. But then I want you to get some rest. If I go back into Rigger-fucking-Hall, I need you fresh. Okay?"

He nodded. Some weight he'd been carrying for a long time seemed to slip from his shoulders, and he sighed, pushing his blond hair back with stiff fingers.

It lasted only a moment, the dark caul sliding over his head. I blinked. His face turned into a deathshead, and my entire body chilled, nipples peaking, my breath catching. The stairwell seemed to go dark, the emerald on my cheek spat a single green spark—and the moment passed, my eyes opening, Jace looking just the same. His lips were moving.

"—Sukerow's, I'll catch a few winks. Sounds good."

I stayed where I was, afraid to move, staring up at Jace's face. He looked down at me, his eyes soft, and then lifted his free hand. His knuckles brushed my cheek. "You don't have to explain, Danny. 'Slong as I get to hang around you, I'm a happy man. 'Kay?" There was no hint of sarcasm or of the anger we used against each other. Just simple tenderness, a tone I'd heard Eddie use with Gabe. My heart rose into my throat, lodged there.

The stairwell was empty except for Jace and me. There was no breath of threat or magick other than my own pulsing demon-fed Power and Jace's bright thorny Shaman glow. I swallowed my heart, hearing a dry click from my throat. "Jace, I—"

"We better go get Hollin Sukerow and see what he has to say," he said. "I'll drive."

I nodded, turned on wooden feet, and led Jace down the stairs.

26

Sukerow's home was a ramshackle brownstone apartment building on Ninth. We clambered out of the hover streetside, then the AI deck took the hover up to hold in a parking-pattern. I slid my sword partly free and checked the blade, good bright steel, then blew out a long breath. Moved my head from side to side, stretching out my neck muscles.

Jace examined me, his fingers tapping his swordhilt. He'd left his staff in the hover, and he touched the butt of a plasgun. "You look like you're expecting a less-than-warm welcome."

No shit. So do you. What else could fucking go wrong today? I winced inwardly. It was tempting Fate to even *think* that too loudly. "I've got a bad feeling about this." I glanced up at the building. "According to my datpilot, he's up on the third . . ." The sentence trailed off. *Hang on. What the hell's that?*

The third-floor corner apartment had a fine set of shields blending with the physical structure of the building. Sukerow was a Skinlin, and his balcony was green even this late in autumn. He probably rented a plot in a co-op garden, but would grow some of the more common things at home. As I watched, some leaves fluttered on a breeze contrary to the desultory chill wind swirling anonymous trash along the sidewalk. The shields pulsed, a streamer of energy spiraling through them, and I drew my sword, the scabbard reversed along my left forearm to act as a shield. "*Fuck!*" I yelled. "Call Gabe! *Stay here!*" Then I bolted for the building.

I could have leapt for the balcony, but that would mean using an amount of Power that would react with Sukerow's torn shields, which were quivering and sending out staticky bursts of fear. Instead, I ripped the maglocked security door open with a quick snapping jerk, streaked into the lobby, and started pounding up the stairs.

Second floor. The tops of my toes barely touched every fourth step, demon speed making me blur. My sword whirled and tucked up behind my arm, the hilt pointing down in my right hand, vibrating with my uneasiness. I reached the third floor, kicked the fire door open, and dove into the hall.

Sukerow's door, apartment 305, was slightly open. Yellow electric light leaked out around its borders. I rolled up, gaining my feet, and pounded down the hall.

The next few moments take on a hazy shutter-click quality. First click—a short hallway, a spreading sticky stain of Power dyeing the air with leprous blue light. Linoleum square in front of the door, a welcome mat of twisted and knotted raffia and strands of plasilica. Each knot held a protective charm, and I shatter every single one of them, the entire rug bursting into flame.

Click. Down the short hall inside the apartment, my sword up, blue light twisting on the steel. What would

have taken me months before Japhrimel altered me—
months of pouring Power into the blade, shaping it, sleeping with it, breathing my life into it—is done in a few
seconds, sparks popping, the steel made *mine,* answering
to *my* will. At the end of the front hall, I see hardwood-
looking laminate flooring and the edge of a chalk circle.
The leprous blue light grows intense, a small starlike
point of brilliance.

I see Hollin Sukerow on his knees in front of a thin, tall
shape I had only seen in nightmares for the past two-and-
a-half decades. The tall figure stands, elbows akimbo, silhouetted against the light in its hand, something pulled
from the yawning mouth of the Skinlin's shattered body.

Click. Blood explodes. Footsteps behind me. Raising
my sword, the *kia* sharp and deadly as it had ever been in
Jado's dojo, blowing the glass out of the windows and
stripping the light away, making it stream in twisted livid
flames. My boots skidding on the laminate as I fling my
weight back, trying to stop.

Click. Jace hurtles past me, his own battlecry ripping
the air with thorns, a Shaman's glow suddenly streaming
from him. He moves without thought, heedlessly fast, as
if he's trying to protect me, place his body between me
and the shadow-thing that curls in on itself like paper in a
hot flamedraft. My left hand drops the scabbard, shoots
forward to haul Jace back.

Click. The shape spins, the light gives a glaring flash
like a holovid reporter's stillcam. The iron smell of blood
in the air mixes with a reek of dust, offal, magick, aftershave, chalk, and leather. The scent I know, the scent of
my quarry in this hunt.

I hear a high, thin giggle that dries all the saliva in my

mouth and makes the scars on my back reopen. They
blaze, sharp agony making my back arch as if the lash and
fléchette had just split open my skin for the first time. My
fingers close on empty air. Jace dives, his *dotanuki* blurring upward to slash through the figure.

Click. A coughing roar. Hollin Sukerow's last despairing, choked scream. More blood explodes. Jace yells
hoarsely, his sword ringing in one awful high-pitched cry
of tortured and stressed metal. Backlash of Power fills the
air, smacking at the walls. My boots grind long scars in
the floor as I am flung back, my left elbow crumpling the
edge of a wall and denting the steel strut just under the
plasticine and Sheetrock.

Click. I see the face—pocked with the scars of teenage
acne, dark eyes soulless and mechanical, greasy dark-
blond hair and the wink of silver at his throat. A pad of fat
under each jawline, the ravages of age clearly visible. He
looks oddly familiar, though I don't recognize him.

Click. The leprous blue light gives one last flare. The
stick-thin shadow vanishes. Another burst of that fetid
stench—the rancidness of the Headmaster's Office—and
footsteps run toward the window. A high, piercing giggle
drives me to my knees, the gray of shock closing over my
vision, the mark on my left shoulder squeezing down and
sending red agony through me, shocking my heart back
into beating.

I cough. Time snaps and speeds back up. I hear sirens.

It had taken only a few moments, all told. I crawled
forward, my sword clattering to the ground, and took Jace
in my arms. "—*oh gods*—" My voice sounded small after
the thunderclap of demon Power.

Jace's blue eyes were glazed and thoughtful, the thorny

Shaman tattoo on his cheek stock-still. His body was light—too light—even in my demon-strong arms. Too light because his throat and belly had been torn open, both in one painless gush.

I reached blindly for Power, my rings sparking, but it was too late. He was already gone. Sometimes not even a Necromance can bring back someone whose internal organs have been yanked out; whose throat has been slashed as well. We are the healers of mortal wounds, we who walk in Death's shadow, but this wound I could not heal.

The bathroom stench of a battlefield rose up around me. Hollin Sukerow's body lay inside a messy, uncompleted chalk circle, the Feeder glyphs wavering and a tide of quick-decaying ectoplasm covering everything in its wet slug-trail gleam, steaming as it rotted away. The glyphs tore and twisted—his hand must have been trembling.

And standing beside him had been a man whose face seemed only slightly familiar. But if I paged through my yearbook, I knew where I would find the younger version of that face.

Right next to Kellerman Lourdes's name.

And I knew what I'd seen, even if my eyes were blurred with tears. I'd seen the stick-thin figure of Headmaster Mirovitch, his hands on his hips, silhouetted against the diseased blue light. I had *smelled* him.

Blood and other fluids bathed my arm. "Jace," I whispered. His head lolled back obscenely far, throat slashed all the way down to the vertebrae; the wet red of muscle sliced too cleanly for a blade. The flesh had parted like water; I saw the purple of the esophagus, a glaring white chip of cervical spine.

His sword, the blade twisted into a cockeyed cork-
screw, chimed against the ground as his hand released it.
"*Jace.*" My tattoo burned as I drew on all the Power available to me. The room shook and groaned. Books fell off
shelves, and glass implements broken by my *kia* and the
welter of backlashed Power from the Headmaster and
Keller shivered into smaller pieces. I poured out every erg
of my demon-given strength to do what a Necromance
should do—bring a soul *back,* and seamlessly heal a
hopelessly shattered body.

The light rose from him. I could still see it, the shining
path made by a soul leaving the body, the foxfire of dying
nerves giving a last painless flash. The blue crystal hall of
Death rose around me, my emerald drenching the hall in
swirling green light as I stood on the Bridge over the
abyss. *Jason!* I howled his name, the crystal walls humming with the force of my distress, and then the God of
Death came.

*Anubis stalked to the very edge of the abyss in His full
form, the obsidian-black, smoothly muscled skin of His
arms and legs gleaming wetly. His ceremonial kilt rang
and splashed with light, gold and gems glittering; His
collar was broad and set with more jewels. The god's
slender dog's head dipped, regarding me with one merciless, pitiless Eye, a black Eye that held a spark of crystalline blue light in its orb. He stood at the end of the
Bridge anchored in the hall of Death, the Bridge I had
walked so many times to bring a soul back.*

*His arms crossed, one holding the ceremonial flail, the
other holding the crook. His will stopped me on the
Bridge, my not-self wearing the white robe of the god's
acolytes, my golden feet bare on the stone.* Please! *It was*

*an agonized cry, with all the force of my Will behind it—
the sorcerous will I had learned to use, used all my life;
the will that pushed Power to do my bidding, the will
every practitioner had to create and use if he or she expected to cast any spell. My throat swelled with the agony
of that cry, a physical ache in a nonphysical space.*
Please, no! No! I will give you anything, I will go in his
stead, please, my Lord, my god, give him back!

*The God of Death looked down on me, His daughter,
His faithful servant, and shook His head.*

*Bare, laid open, I struggled against that kind implaca-
bility. I offered it all: my own life, my service, every erg of
power and heat and love I possessed. I could never give
Jace what he wanted from me, but letting him go down
into Death's dry country . . . No. The stubbornness flared,
and for the first time in my memory, my god paused.*

*One hand extended, one finger, weightless, touched the
crown of my head. There was a price for the balancing of
Death's scales. Was I prepared to pay? Was that what he
was asking me?*

Anything, *I whispered.* I will give You anything I have,
anything You ask.

*And Death paused again. I read the refusal in His
ageless, infinite eyes, and struggled uselessly against it.
My cheek burned, the emerald flaring with drenching
light, driving back the blue flame for one eternal moment.
On and on, the strings of my psyche snapping, tearing,
rent . . .*

I was shoved back, pushed out of the space between
worlds, rammed choking and sobbing back into my body.
I cradled Jace's empty husk to my chest, tilted my head
back and screamed again, a sound so massive it was

soundless, rising out of me like light from a nuclear fission. I was still screaming when the cops arrived, still screaming when Gabe fought through the press of sound, her nose bleeding from the wall of psychic agony. She fell to her knees, taking me in her arms. Her human warmth folded around me while I sobbed, mercifully robbed for a short while of every shred of demon power. I screamed again and again with only a broken human voice while I clutched the breathing, living body to my chest.

Breathing, yes. Living, yes. But nobody had to tell me that the soul inside was gone. My demon-given Power had mended Jason Monroe's shattered body in a mimicry of a *sedayeen*'s miraculous ability to heal, but he was dead all the same.

27

I folded my hands carefully around the paper cup while late-afternoon sun slanted over the street. Gabe spoke softly to someone, they were processing the scene. I huddled in the back of an ambulance hover, a brown woolen blanket around my shoulders, my clothing stiff with dried blood and noisome fluids. I shivered, the black liquid masquerading as coffee inside the paper cup slopping against the sides.

It had been the middle of the day, everyone at work, nobody home except Hollin Sukerow. Which was a good thing, my scream and the explosion of loosed Power had taken out a good chunk of the building. Debris littered the street, smoke clearing on the air. It looked as if a wandering shark had just cruised by and taken a big half-circle bite out of the brownstone.

I shut my eyes. Gray shock closed over the darkness behind my eyelids again. Again the spiked warmth from the mark on my shoulder fought it back. Tears leaked hotly between my eyelids, dripping down my cheeks. My tangled hair was full of dust and blood and dirt.

They had taken Jace's body to the hospital. He was breathing, his heart beating, everything apparently fine . . . except it wasn't. It was an empty shell, an empty house, the soul fled but the housing that contained it intact. All the Power granted me by a demon's touch could not change Death's decree.

My sword, tucked up against my leg, hummed softly. I sat on the cold rubberized floor of the ambulance hover and exhaled softly. The whine of a slicboard rattled over the scene, and I realized my lips were still shaping the prayer to Anubis.

Anubis et'her ka. Se ta'uk'fhet sa te vapu kuraph. Anubis et'her ka. Anubis, Lord of the Dead, Faithful Companion, protect me, for I am Your child. Protect me, Anubis, weigh my heart upon the scales, watch over me, Lord, for I am Your child. Do not let evil distress me, but turn Your fierceness upon my enemies—

I stopped, choked on the rising tears, and forced them back down. Just like a kid, crying because a toy had been taken away, sobbing messily and completely.

No. I was not a child. I would never be a child again.

"Thank the gods you're here," Gabe said.

I opened my eyes to see Eddie heeling his slicboard as the cell powered down, ending with the board neatly racking itself against the step of the ambulance hover. "How is she?" For once, Eddie didn't growl or sneer. Instead, he pushed his shaggy hair back from his face and stole a few worried glances at me in between examining Gabe. He didn't even glance up at the hole in the side of the brownstone.

Gabe shrugged, an eloquent movement. "Danny?"

Both of them approached me, Eddie's rundown boots

scraping the wet pavement. His long dirt-colored coat flapped. His aura, smelling of earth and pines, sweat and beer, meshed with Gabe's swirling Necromance sparkles.

I swallowed bile, looked up at their worried faces. Sunlight glittered in my reactive-dry eyes. I blinked.

"I didn't grab him in time. He was moving quicker than I've ever seen him move. He threw himself at Keller and Mirovitch—" I repeated it through the lump in my throat, my voice barely recognizable. Hoarse and wrecked, the voice of a stunned survivor of some natural disaster on the niner holonews. Change the channel, flip the station. Repeat as necessary.

Gabe's hand closed around my right shoulder. She squeezed just a little. "You already gave your statement, Danny. You don't have to."

"I should have caught him." Why did my voice, as hoarse and ruined as it was, sound so young? "I should have caught him." I held up one golden hand. "All the strength Japhrimel gave me, I should have *caught* him." My face crumpled again, soundlessly contorting into a mask. A tragedy mask, the darker half of laughter's coin. The mask I'd seen on so many other faces when a loved one passed on.

Gabe whispered something to Eddie.

"Goddamn." The dark circles under his eyes were almost gone. He looked better. "Look, Danny, I'm gonna take you to our house. We can clean you up, maybe get you something to eat."

"I'll be fine," I said tonelessly, hoarse. "Got work to do. The others on the list—"

"They've been taken to safehouses," Gabe said. "The building security net included stillcams. We've got a few good shots of Lourdes. They're all over the holovids, make the press work for us for once. Someone will call him in, and we'll take him down." Her mouth twisted slightly to one side. "Hard."

It was a promise of revenge, one that should have made me grateful. I felt nothing; the numbness of a razor drawn swiftly through flesh, the breathless moment before the pain starts, before the blood begins to flow.

"Nobody will see him." The ectoplasm had vanished, leaving only a faint shimmer on the bodies; the other victims had been found too late, no trace of ectoplasmic attack remaining. If we'd seen the slimy eggwhite of a *ka* taking shape in the physical world, we would have been more cautious. A *lot* more cautious. "Any more than anyone would see you if you really wanted to stay invisible. And he's . . . I think . . . Gabe, he's got Mirovitch . . . inside him."

"You saw Mirovitch? But I thought you said he . . ." She looked as confused as I felt.

Focus! The sharp stinging slap of the deep voice of my conscience jerked my head up. I'd been staring at my boots. "Gabe. Look. Poly told me that the kids all took a *piece* of Mirovitch. What if Keller took the last piece? Or somehow . . . I don't know. The first death was a decade after Mirovitch's . . . disappearance. Maybe the Headmaster wasn't as dead as everyone thought."

Gabe nodded. Her sleek hair dipped forward over her shoulders. "So he's out for revenge?"

"Revenge, maybe, who knows? But most certainly *collecting*." I waited until Gabe absorbed this, then tossed the cup of coffee into the street. Steaming liquid spilled out. I watched as the steam twisted into angular shapes, dissipated. "I don't know if safehouses are going to be any good. I don't know how he's tracking them."

"You think Mirovitch is *inside* Lourdes?" Gabe's eyes were wide and dark. It was the stuff of nightmares, a psi carrying something like that around. A mule carrying a Feeder's *ka.*

A Feeder, hungry for Power. And instead of feeding from random victims, or having a mild case of being Feeder, Mirovitch was inside Keller, and taking back whatever the kids took from him years ago. Claiming his own. It made sense. The worst, absolutely *worst* type of Feeder. Hungry, hard to kill, and so very close now to collecting the leftover pieces of itself and becoming a full-blown *ka,* moving from mule to mule and draining each one as it went, turning them into soulless zombies—or worse, into Feeders too. A spreading contagion, replicating itself wherever it could.

"I'm guessing it's a *ka,* Gabe. Nothing else seems to fit." My throat stung, my eyes watering from the sunlight. Yes, only the sunlight. "I have something I have to do." Straining for politeness. It was a long reach.

"Danny. Please. Go with Eddie. Get some food. Get cleaned up and come to the hospital. We'll do this together."

I shook Gabe's hand from my shoulder. She backed up half a step, and I saw the sudden flicker in Eddie's aura. "You don't have to worry," I told them both, still in that little-girl voice I had no idea I still possessed. I heard the hurt clearly in my voice, too worn to camouflage or swallow it for once. "I'm not going to lash out at you. You could have a *little* more faith in me."

"I know you wouldn't," Gabe said. "But you've got

that look again, Danny. That scary look that says you're about to go hunting, and gods help anyone in your way."

"That's about right." The ambulance hover rocked a little on its springs as my tone turned chill. Eddie shivered. The wind rose slightly, keening through the broken edges of the brownstone above. "I was too fucking young to kill Mirovitch all those years ago. I should have, I wished I could. I used to dream about it. This time, I'm old enough and armed enough to do it." I looked up at the smoking hole torn in the building. "I need to find out about this Bryce Smith guy—if he was just a cover for Lourdes. What the connection is. We still don't know that."

Gabe nodded. The purposeful milling around the scene continued behind her. Two coroner's hovers lifted off, the whine of hovercells cutting through the sound of the gathered crowd behind the yellow plasilica tape marking off the borders of the investigation. I saw flashes pop, and guessed the holovid reporters were out in force. My eyes followed the hovers as they rose gracefully, then banked and flew away toward the station house and the morgue. Sunlight stung my eyes even more, making hot tears roll down my cheeks. "Hospital." I winced at the childlike breathiness of my voice. "They've taken him to the hospital?"

Gabe nodded. "Yeah. Come with us, Danny."

No. Please, no. "His sword. You don't need that for evidence, do you?"

Eddie made a brief restless movement. I was being rude again.

I was too tired to care. Japhrimel had never told me about the weariness of demons, the weariness of a being that didn't need sleep. A weariness that seemed to sink into every bone, every thought. Or was it a weariness peculiar to *hedaira?* I had nobody I could ask.

I was adrift again, as if I was twelve years old and shipwrecked by the death of the only family I had ever known. Again.

"You know it's yours." Gabe actually looked hurt. "I'm so sorry, Danny. I know you loved him."

My lips puckered as if I tasted something sour. Maybe it was only failure. *I didn't even know that myself, Gabe.* "Thanks." My voice sounded as if it was coming from someone else, someone whose harsh tone was flat and terribly loaded with Power. If the god hadn't temporarily denied me the ability to use the demon Power I'd been granted, I might have leveled the building. Or even more.

Probably more.

Definitely more.

"Don't, Danny." Eddie was uncharacteristically serious, examining me. His shoulders slumped as if under a heavy weight. The wind plucked at his coat, mouthed his untidy hair. "Don't do this to yourself."

Don't do this to myself? Don't DO this to myself? "Who else should I do it to? I'm kind of out of victims, in case you hadn't noticed. Everyone who gives a damn about me dies sooner or later. You should be getting as far away as—"

I didn't realize I was shouting until Gabe clapped her hand over my mouth, stepping close. Her dark eyes—*human* eyes—were bare inches from mine; she was much shorter than me, but I was sitting on the edge of the hover's step, so her nose hovered next to mine, her mouth on the other side of her hand. Her breath brushed my face, and the smell of kyphii and her perfume mixed, driving through my nose. My demon-based scent flared, a wave of musk and spice, and her pupils dilated slightly. That was all.

"Shut the fuck up, Dante," she said softly, conversationally. "We're using your hover. You're coming to my house to get cleaned up, and we're going to the hospital. We'll catch this fucker, and when we do, what we do to him is going to make a werecain kill look sweet and clean. I dragged you into this, and if you want to blame someone, fine, blame me and we'll do some sparring later to hash it out. But for right now, sunshine, you're with us. You got it?"

It was ridiculous. It was ri-*fucking*-diculous. I was part *demon*, stronger and faster than her, with enough power to level a building when a god wasn't stopping me. Hunger began, a faint cramping under my ribs. But hunger wasn't what was making my hands shake so that I had to clasp my sword, *hard*, to keep them still.

I stared into Gabe's eyes, her irises so dark her pupils seemed to blend into them. This close I could see the fine speckles of gold in her irises, and the faint freckles that dusted her perfect patrician nose. Her aura closed around me, the comfort of another Necromance, not seeking to minimize the pain. Her cedary perfume spilled through the shield of demon scent, and I was grateful for it.

Her eyes looked directly into mine.

I have only stared that intensely into one other pair of eyes, and those had been brilliantly green, glowing green. As it was, wordless communication passed through her into me, a zing like an electric current, stinging all the way down to the quick. It was a different kind of communion than the one that passed between me and Anubis, and still different than the alien ecstasy of Japhrimel's hands on me while he stared unblinking through my humanity. No, this was purely female communication, something as deep and bloody as the depths of labor pangs.

And for all I'd never had a child, I still *knew*. Every child knows. Every woman knows, too.

"I'm with you, Danny," she finally whispered. "You owe him being at the hospital. You know what we have to do."

My vision blurred. It wasn't shock, it was hot tears. Gabe's eyes were gentle and utterly pitiless, but still grieving.

I nodded, slowly. Her hand fell away from my mouth, but she didn't look away. She offered me her hand, and I took it gently, my fingers sliding through hers.

Eddie hunched his shoulders. He said nothing as Gabe pulled me to my feet.

Soft beeps and boops from the machines monitoring pulse and respiration filled the air, and a tide of human pain scraped at my skin. Hospitals aren't comfortable for psions. All the advanced technology in the world can't hide the fact that a hospital is where you go when you're sick, and the terminus of getting sick is dying. Even the Necromance, whose entire professional life is bound up with death, doesn't like being reminded that he or she is finite and will one day tread the same path as the clients.

The room was small, but at least it was private. There was even a window, showing the thin sunlight outside and clouds massing in the north. We were up on the third floor, the curtains pulled back, smooth blue plasflooring under our feet . . . and Jace Monroe's body, lying perfect and breathing like a clockwork toy on the tethered hoverbed with its white sheets and dun blanket. His hair glowed in the pale light; he finally looked relaxed and about ten years younger.

The chair sat stolid and empty on the other side of the bed. Eddie stood at the foot, and I found myself next to Jace's hand, looking down.

Gabe exchanged low fierce whispers with someone at the door. She was a licensed Necromance and the investigating detective, and if she said he was dead her word held in a court of law. With two Necromances in the room and an EEG showing flatline, there wasn't any doubt: Jason Monroe was *dead,* and this was a flagrant use of Hegemony medical facilities for no good reason. Still, Gabe made them go away so we could say goodbye to the soulless body on the bed, probably invoking the second clause of the Amberson Act.

I didn't care. Was past caring. I was scrubbed down and wearing Eddie's shirt and a fresh pair of jeans—not Gabe's, she was too small, and I didn't want to ask why they had a pair of pants in my size at their house. My boots were still wet, but at least they'd been rinsed off. My hair lay wet and tightly braided in a rope against my back that bumped me whenever I shifted my weight.

Gabe closed the door with a firm click. I felt the tingle of Power and glanced over to see her place a lockcharm on the handle. The rune sank in, barring the door with its spiked backward-leaning X; simple and elegant like all of Gabe's magick.

Silence fell. She turned away from the door, her long police-issue synthwool coat moving with her. I hadn't taken my coat off either, and we both were fully armed. Add to that a Necromance's reputation for being a little twitchy, and no wonder the hospital staff was nervous. And if it wasn't that, the sudden appearance of holovid crews outside the hospital would have done it.

Gabe blew out between her teeth, met Eddie's eyes. Communication passed between them, like the look Jace would give me when he wanted to ask if I was all right but didn't quite dare to.

Jace. My throat was dry. "Gabe." The word cracked on the air.

"Take your time," she said.

I closed my eyes, tried not to sway. I needed all my courage for this. All of mine, and more. "You could do it." I whispered, helpless to stop myself. "You could bring him back. He could—"

Eddie made a brief, restless movement. Said nothing. But his aura tightened, the smell of fresh dirt and beer suddenly foaming through the room. He was a dirtwitch berserker, if he got angry enough he was well-nigh unstoppable. There was no reason for him to get angry at me, though.

Not yet.

Gabe sucked in a small breath. "You know I can't." Her voice hitched. "He's gone, Danny. Let him go."

Wonder of wonders, calm precise Gabriele sounded choked. As if something was stuck in her throat. My rings sparked dully. I reached down, saw my own graceful, golden-skinned hand. It hovered above the human hand lying on the fuzzy dun coverlet, callused and scraped from hard combat, white scars from knifework reaching up his wrist. There was a time when I would have known every scar, would have kissed each one. "An apparition." My throat was dry as sand. "Just this once. His body's living, he just needs to come *back*."

"You know it doesn't work like that." Gentle, relentless, but there was a sob behind every word. "We have to let him *go*, Danny. We have to."

I never thought to hear my own voice raggedly pleading at a bedside, though I'd helped many a client over the border and safely into death, making sure their families could hear their last words and say their own final codas. My right hand cramped, but only a little, as I reached up to scrub the tears away from my cheeks. I had promised not to cry, hadn't I?

Anubis et'her ka. Anubis, my Lord, my God, please help me. Please, help me.

Nothing happened. I took in a jagged breath freighted with the smell of human pain and Jace's fading peppery scent. Without his soul in the body, the smell of his Power would leach away, just like the perfectly functioning clockwork of his body would begin to atrophy. He was, for all intents and purposes, gone. Pulling an apparition back from the dry land of Death and trying to force it back into the body wouldn't work. If his soul had stayed, miracles could be worked, but Death had claimed him.

The next prayer that rose was tinted blood-red in its intensity, sweeping over my entire body like a rain of tiny needles, clouding my vision.

Japhrimel. That was all, every scrap of longing poured into one single word. I tipped my head back, jaw working, the murdered animal inside my chest scrambling for escape. The mark on my left shoulder began to tingle, prickle, and finally burn, sinking in through my skin as if the nerves there were slowly waking up after a long cramped sleep. *Please, Japhrimel, if you can hear me, help me out here. Help me.*

Then the shame started as I tipped my head back down. Here I was at Jace's bedside, and I couldn't stop thinking about a dead demon. If Japhrimel could be resurrected, I would have resurrected him by now. I wasn't worth either of them, goddammit.

I snatched my hand back. "I can't." The words tasted like ash in my mouth. I lifted my left hand, weighted with my sword, let it drop heavily back down to my side. "Gabe, I c-can't."

Silence. Was she looking at Eddie? Was he looking back, sharing her pain? Pain shared, pain halved. How many times had I leaned on Jace, letting him take my pain, blind to everything but my own selfishness? And yet he'd given up everything, including his life, thinking he could protect me from still more. I stumbled back a blind two steps, and Eddie's arm closed over my shoulders. I flinched, almost ready to drive an elbow into his ribs and duck away, but control clamped down on combat instinct just in time. The Skinlin's arm tightened, and the heavy edge of his coat brushed mine. He was warm, very warm for a human, and smelled most of all like freshly-turned earth.

He said nothing. It was a new world record, Eddie refraining from a snarky comment for longer than ten seconds. A bloody fucking miracle.

Gabe stepped up to the bedside. She had unsheathed a knife, cold steel. It was, after all, traditional. She didn't glance at me. Instead, her pretty face was set and white as she looked down at Jace's still form, its chest rising and falling with macabre regularity. "Would you like to say anything, Danny?" The familiar question, only I was usually the one that asked it.

"You think he can hear me?" I tried to sound brave. But my voice was too high-pitched and breathy, again lacking the terrible velvet weight of demon's seduction or the ruined hoarseness of Lucifer's final gift to me, when his fingers crackled in my throat.

She smiled, still looking down at his face. He looked peaceful, the lines smoothed away and his hair combed back from his face. As if he was sleeping. "The dead can always hear us, Danny. You know that."

And gods help me, but I did. Only the knowledge held no comfort, even for me. My shoulders hunched. Eddie's arm tightened. I swallowed ash, tasted bitterness. "I'm sor—" Gulped down air, tried again. "I'm sor—" And again, the sounds that were choked halfway. I couldn't say it now, when it mattered most of all.

"Gods," Eddie whispered. "Gabe." He was shaking, a fine tremor that leapt to me as if we were both drunk or sick. I think my knees may have buckled, because I leaned into him.

She understood, and moved forward, one pale narrow hand resting on Jace's forehead, the other holding the knife tucked back against her forearm. Her sleek dark hair gleamed in the light, and the sparkles of her aura began to pulse. "Jason Monroe," she said quietly, her voice carrying ancient authority, "travel well. Be at peace."

Noooooo . . . I swallowed the moan, locked my teeth, refused to let it out. Still, a low hurt sound came, whether from me or from Eddie I couldn't tell. Didn't want to know. Gabriele's aura flashed, and for a moment I seemed to see blue flame crawling up her arm. The knife flicked, steel glittering in the weak autumn sunlight, and a sigh echoed through the room. The machines stopped their beeping and booping. Silence rang like a bell through the room, a silence I had heard so many times but never like this, never when I was the one trying to scream and utterly unable to do so.

"And flights of angels sing thee to thy rest," Gabe whispered softly, tenderly. His eyes were closed, but she laid her hand over them anyway, as if closing them. Her aura faded back to its usual sparkles, her shielding humming as it settled into place. Tears glittered on her pale cheeks. The blood had drained from her face, and fresh shame bit me. What had it cost her to do this for me, something I was too weak to do for myself?

Jace. Jason . . .

I managed to find my balance, slowly. Eddie let me go as soon as I pulled away from him. I took the deepest breath of my life, seemingly endless, my ribs crackling as I inhaled, and inhaled, and inhaled. My aura throbbed.

I stepped up to the side of the bed. Gabe didn't look at me. She studied Jace's sleeping face as if the secrets of the universe were printed there. For all I know, they might have been.

Two fingers, tipped with black molecule-drip polish, I touched the back of his hand. Nothing there, not even the low glow of nerves slowly dying out, what Necromances call foxfire. She had done a good job. Her knife sang as it slid back into its sheath, softly, gently, clicking home.

It was too hard to look up. I stared at his hand. "Thank

you." Amazingly, the words didn't stick in my throat. My broken voice sounded like sandpaper honey. The plain beige curtains ruffled uneasily.

Her free hand found my arm and squeezed once, hard. "You're my friend, Danny." She sounded tired. "You understand? There's no debt between friends."

Maybe it's just that the debt gets so high you stop counting it. I freed her fingers from my arm gently, delicately. "Thank you." It sounded more natural now, more like myself. More like Danny Valentine.

Who the hell was she, though? I no longer knew.

"Danny—"

I turned, digging my heel in, my boot scraping on the plasfloor. Then I headed for the door. Two long strides. I heard Eddie move and tensed, but his hand didn't close on me.

The words sent a chill up my spine. "Let her go," he told Gabe. "Gods above and below, just let her *go.*"

It was too late. The door was closed. I was already gone.

28

*I*t was child's play to slip back into my house without the reporters seeing. I came over the wall again, twisting to land lightly on my feet, and brushed my hands off. My lungs burned from running for so long, literally blurring through the streets, moving with a speed close to the eerie darting quickness of a demon. Close, but not close enough.

The god of Death did not bar me from using my strength now.

The sun was sinking, high dark clouds massing in the north. The first of the winter storms, not coming in from over the bay but sliding down the coast. I took a lungful of Saint City air, chill with approaching winter. My garden was ragged, unkempt; I had been too busy running bounties to keep up with the weeding.

I stopped a good twenty paces from my house, eyeing it critically. Bought with Doreen, as an abandoned dump when cheap property was the rule in this neighborhood because of the gang wars and derelicts, paid off completely with blood money, my haven and sanctuary rose above me, glowing with some freak ray of evening light.

I kicked my front door open, the doorframe shattering

and spraying little splinters into my front hall. Choked, had to swallow cold iron. Tears, and grief. And something so huge I was afraid it would choke me.

The shields shivered, each layer of energy vibrating. The layers of shielding Jace had applied were fading; it would take a long time for them to fully vanish without his reinforcing. Months, maybe, if I didn't put a shuntline in and take them down myself. But I didn't have that sort of time, did I?

I stalked into the front hall, into my living room.

The candles on Jace's altar were out, the smell of burned wax filling the air. The dove's blood had splashed up out of the brass bowl, the painting of Saint Barbara rent and tattered.

So Jace's *loa* knew. Of course they knew. The spirits always know.

I looked at the tapestry on the west wall. Isis's face was turned away, and Horus's wings rustled uneasily, threads shifting against each other with soft, whispering, grieving sounds.

A cream-colored flash on my fieldstone altar caught my eye. I approached it slowly, each footstep seeming to take an eon, my boots making hard clicking sounds against hardwood and muffled thuds on my meditation-rug.

Propped against the inlaid wooden box holding holo-stills of Lewis and Doreen, the envelope crouched. Vellum, with its proud screaming seal of red crimson wax, it grinned at me. I resisted the urge to turn in a tight circle—there was nobody in my house. Not now.

The sound surprised me. A low keening hum vibrated in my chest, my back teeth clicking together as my throat swelled with the effort of keeping the scream in.

Lucifer. Dipping his elegant little fingers in my life again. Taunting me. Polluting even my grief. He couldn't stand to leave me alone. Japhrimel was dead, Jace was dead, and the Prince of Hell had just poked me one goddamn time too many.

This has gone too far. This voice was new, a stiletto of steely-cold fury turning in the center of my brain. I stared at the crimson seal, hearing the creaks and flutters of my house as my rage communicated itself through the air, pressing against the walls, touching the tapestries, ruffling the paper. From the kitchen came a dim crash as cupboard doors chattered open and closed, I heard smashing from the dining room and the tinkle of broken glass upstairs. My throat swelled, a stone caught in its center, my eyes hot and staring as I struggled to contain the fury.

There was no containing it. An almost-audible *snap* resonated in the middle of my chest, a locked door shattering open and sterile light flooding out. The circuit of rage snapped closed, and a humming filled my brain.

I. Have. Had. Enough.

The choking wrath eased, turning into sharp clarity. There were things to do. Places to go.

People—and not-people—to *kill.*

I turned on my heel, stalked upstairs. My fingernails had turned to demon claws. I tore the borrowed clothes off as I went, shreds of fabric falling away. I ripped my shirt into pieces, sliced the tough denim of my jeans. I tripped halfway up, my jeans tangling around my ankles. My head hit the balustrade with stunning force, shattering the wood. The sounds that came out of me smashed the plaster from my walls, scorched the paint, made the glass of each picture I'd hung shatter. The noise of plasglass breaking almost managed to cover my wrenching sobs.

I tore the covers from my bed; they still held Jace's scent and mine. I threw them across the room. Then I punched my computer deck. Plasilica broke, my tough golden skin sliced but closing almost immediately, the black blood welling up and sealing away the hurt. Sparks popped, a spray of them from the deck's monitor, little squealing sounds as my rage smashed the circuits.

My demon-callused feet ground in shards of plasglass, since I'd broken the shower door and the mirrors. I got dressed—a microfiber shirt, another pair of jeans, dry socks, my boots were still damp but I pulled them on anyway. I slid the strap of my messenger bag over my head. The necklace I'd worn to the House of Pain went over my head, settled humming against my breastbone.

I dug the two spade necklaces out of my bloody coat. My hair streamed over my shoulders, heavy and soft, the braid had unraveled. The necklaces went into my bag.

Then I strode down the hall to the end. The holostill of Doreen to my right, smiling her gentle smile, fell. The plasglass of the frame shattered in a tinkling burst. I hit the door at the end of the hall open with the flat of my hand; a hollow sound thudding through me.

Jace's room blazed with the last dying rays of sunlight. A golden square from the window lay over his bed with Doreen's blue comforter. I smelled the lingering sweetness of a psion metabolizing alcohol wedded to the smell of human male, and my heart twisted. The lamp by the bed—a Merican Era antique with a base made of amber glass—rattled as I stood in the doorway. I could go no further.

Neatly-made twin bed, plain pine dresser with empty Chivas Red bottles making a collage of mellow glowing plasglass, each tightly capped and with a small light-charm wedded to each one. At night the bottles would glow softly, each limned in gold or blue; it was a trick most often seen in Academy dorm rooms, where drinking was a hobby raised to an art form. The closet door was half-open, showing neatly hung dark clothes, the long low bench where he made his own bullets and prepared his charms and amulets rested along the wall, organized with amulets in different stages of completion, as well as jars of dried herbs and interesting bits of bone and fur and feather. A threadbare red velvet cushion sat precisely placed in front of the bench. His nightstand held a stack of music discs and a personal player, the headphones stowed out of the way; a short wickedly curved knife; and a Glockstryke R4 projectile gun gleaming mellowly in the thick golden light. No pictures or holostills on the walls. His spare rig hung neatly on a peg near the door, as did his old coat, with its several pockets and leather patches against the tough canvas.

I reached out, gently took the coat down, and shrugged into it, switching my sword from one hand to the other. It still smelled like peppered honey that tingled with the memory of thorn-spiked Shaman's aura.

I filled my lungs with the smell of my Power and Jace's, the mixed scent of a part-demon and a Shaman, the bitter smell of my own failure tainting every mouthful, every inch of oxygen. Then I backed away, closing the door gently, as if someone was sleeping in the room beyond.

It was time to pay my toll to the dead.

I turned, went down the hall and down the stairs, stopping at the niche. The statue of Anubis I wrapped in a square of black silk sitting under it, the resultant bundle went into my bag, with a quiet apology to the god. I picked up the lacquered urn, surprised again by its weight. *Oh, Japhrimel. I'm sorry. Gods forgive me for what I have done. Forgive me for what I am about to do.*

My cheeks were wet again. I sniffed, spat to the side. My rings loosed a shower of golden sparks.

Urn in one hand, my sword in the other, I continued downstairs. I looked into the kitchen, at the dining-room table, where the stack of yearbooks taunted me. I'd forgotten to turn the coffeepot off, and it had no shut-off switch. The smell of cooked coffee made my gorge rise.

What rough beast's hour has come at last? I almost seemed to hear Lewis's voice, from the long-ago dim reaches of my childhood. The poem had always made my hackles rise, it had been my favorite. *And where will it be born, after it slouches through my life?*

I looked at my fieldstone altar; at Jace's altar, my couch, the plants he had watered and nursed between bounties because I'd been too busy running headlong from one thing to the next. I took another deep breath, a thin sound breaking free as I exhaled, catching sight of the vellum envelope and crimson seal.

My bootheels clicked on the floor. I smelled smoke.

I drew my sword.

The blade shone blue, runes twisting on the steel, answering my will as if I'd spent months stroking it and pouring Power into it.

Jace . . .

His name choked me. I could not say it.

Anubis had denied me entry into Death for the first time. The Lord of Death didn't bargain, and I couldn't have brought Jace back even with a demon's Power—his body had been too wounded, internal organs pulled out and shredded. It had been hopeless even before I'd spent all my strength in a futile rebellion against Death's decree. A *sedayeen* might have been able to do it right after the initial injury, but I was no pacifist healer. Or maybe Jace's soul had been tired of living, finding itself freed of the body for a moment and bolting away from the cruelty of life?

My failures rose to choke me. I hadn't been quick enough as a human to kill Santino, and if Japhrimel hadn't given up a large share of his demon Power for me he might have been too tough for Lucifer to kill so easily. And even with the strength and speed Japhrimel had given me, I had not been able to catch Jace when he rocketed past me to protect me from whatever twisted sorcery had dredged up Mirovitch to torture seemingly everyone who had survived Rigger Hall.

The glyph took shape at the end of my sword, encased in a sphere of lurid crimson. It was *Keihen,* the Torch, one of the Greater Glyphs of Destruction, a little-used part of the Nine Canons.

I don't love you, I had told him after Rio. *I won't ever love you.*

And his answer? *If I cared about* that *I'd still be in Rio with a new Mob Family and a sweet little fat-bottomed* babalawao. *This is my choice, Danny.* And stubbornly, over and over again, he had proved his love for me in a hundred different ignored ways.

I had never even guessed how much he meant to me.

There was only one thing I could give up, one penance I could pay, for the mess I'd made of everything. If Japhrimel could be resurrected, it was probably too late; he had Fallen. Lucifer's word meant nothing; hadn't he always been called the father of lies? If a Fallen demon could be resurrected and Lucifer wanted him, he could have sent another demon to collect me and the urn, or just the urn. I was part-demon, sure, but no match for a real one.

None of it mattered. All that mattered was that I had tortured myself with hope, when I had known all along there *was* no hope. Japhrimel was never coming back, and neither was Jace. If I survived taking down a Feeder's *ka,* I'd live afterward with the knowledge that I had denied myself even the faintest slim chance of resurrecting Japhrimel.

My toll to the dead: my hope. It was the only penance big enough.

I took my time with the glyph, no shuntlines, no avenues for the Power to follow except one simple undeniable course. The crimson globe spat, sizzled, and began to steam. Vapor took angular shapes, tearing at the air. I clamped my teeth in my lower lip, ignoring the pain, and stood in my front hall, Japhrimel's urn tucked under my arm and the house shields quivering uneasily but calming when I stroked them. The glyph twisted inside its red cage, trying to escape. I flicked it off the tip of my sword, in the hall between the stairs and the living room, and held it spinning in the air with will alone, my sword sliding back into its sheath.

I got a good grip on Japhrimel's urn. I had to hold the glyph steady while it strained like a slippery fiery eel.

I spat black blood from my cut lip, sank my teeth in again until I worried free a mouthful of acid-tasting demon blood. This I dribbled into my palm and smoothed over Japhrimel's urn, the rising keening of the glyph inside its bubble of crimson light beginning to scorch the ceiling. The heat blew my hair back. The paint blistered on the walls, bubbling, and I smelled more smoke.

I tossed Japhrimel's bloodied urn straight up. My sword rang free of the sheath, a perfect draw, the sound of the cut like worlds colliding. Ash pattered down, the cleanly-broken halves of the urn smacking the floor and shattering, but I was already shuffling back, my sword held away from my body. Running with every ounce of demon speed, I reached the door before the bubble holding the glyph . . . burst.

There was an immense, silent sound, felt more in the bones than heard. I spun aside at the door and leapt, but a giant warm hand pressed against the back of my body and threw me clear. I landed and rolling, instinct saving me. I came to a halt panting, my head ringing with flame, my bitten lip singing with pain until black blood coated the hurt and sealed it away.

My left shoulder came alive with agony. I screamed, the force of my cry adding to the explosion that shook the ground. Flame bellowed up, and bits of the garden igniting and crumbling to ash. The heat was like a living thing, crawling along my body, only the shield of my Power kept my clothes from smoking and catching fire.

There. Both the men in my life, gone. I had read, long ago, of the Vikings sending ships out to sea alive with flame, burial barges to go with the dead into the afterlife. Now I sent my house into Death as well as Japhrimel and

Jace. If I was lucky, when I died they might be waiting for me.

The only thing left now was anger. Fury. Rage. A crimson wash so huge it shoved all other considerations aside. Easier to fight than to cry. Easier to kill than to admit to the pain.

And oh, anger is sweet. Fury is the best fuel of all. It is so clean, so marvelous, so ruthless. Eye for eye, tooth for tooth, rage against evil is better than sorrow. Sorrow can't balance the scales.

Vengeance could. And she would too, if I had anything to say about it.

I was already on my feet, unsteady, walking away. I made it to my front gate as the layers of shielding on my house imploded, fueling the Power-driven flames. There would be nothing left but ash and a deep crater. My head rang and my shoulder crunched again with pain. I inhaled, staggering.

I had always wondered what the limit of my powers was. The wall was scorching, concrete turning black and brittle on the outside. My garden was swallowed alive with flame, kissed with choking ash. I dimly heard human screams, and wondered if the shockwave would break a few windows. The gate itself was beginning to melt and warp. It almost seared my hand when I touched it, tough painted plasilica bubbling and smoking.

I opened my front gate, stepped out.

A few enterprising holovid reporters tried to take pictures. I no longer cared. I stalked through them like a well-fed lion through a herd of zebra. Some of them were cowering behind their bristling hovers. Fine hot flakes of ash drifted down. I heard sirens, and thought that the house was past saving. I did feel a moment's pity for my neighbors, but it passed.

It was three blocks before I remembered to sheathe my sword. The mark on my left shoulder settled into a steady burning that was not entirely unpleasant, except for one last flare that stopped me for a full thirty seconds, head down as I breathed heavily, ribs flickering as my lungs heaved. Then I pushed my hair—dry now from the fierce heat, and crowned with tiny flakes of ash—back, and continued on my way. The sun had sunk below the rim of the bay in the west. The column of smoke from my shattered home blazed a lurid orange, underlit by flame.

Night had fallen.

And it was going to be a long one.

29

$\mathcal{F}$our hours later I stopped in a coffeeshop in midtown, ordered five shots of their best espresso, and stood at a table. My sword tucked into a loop on my belt while I tapped at my datpilot. The shop's holovid feed was on, and I saw without much surprise that my house had made the evening news.

I didn't look after seeing the first few moments of scrambled footage: the column of flame going up an impressive couple of thousand feet, making a mushroom cloud of smoke that led some hysterical people to think that there had been a nuclear attack on Saint City. There had been no hovertraffic overhead, since my house was outside the main lanes, and the force of the explosion had been channeled up instead of outward, so apart from some broken windows and traumatized holovid reporters, there was precious little damage to anything other than my house.

Which was, of course, what I'd wanted. Something I'd done right, for once.

I took down the five shots of espresso at once. The mark on my shoulder had settled back to a satisfied glow, spreading over my body like warm oil. I looked at my dat-pilot. The information Gabe had sent was interesting, to say the least: a summary of all the bodies so far, dates of death, and thumbnail digitals of the crime scenes. She'd also had an analysis done of the glyphs, and it was this that I studied, going from one to the next while my datpilot glowed. It took a couple of hours of standing there, my eyes glued to the screen, to really get a sense of how the Feeder glyphs altered from the regular Ceremonial alphabet of the Nine Canons, and how twisting each rune in a particular fashion would serve the purpose of strengthening a psychic vampire. My secondary talent as a rune-witch helped.

I felt the gnaw of hunger just under my breastbone. For the first time, I had truly extended my powers, and I found I was starving. I ignored it, for now.

My eyes felt dry and grainy. I locked my jaw against the slight moaning sound I wanted to make. *Grieve later,* I told myself. *Work now. Grieve later.*

The door to the coffeehouse opened, and I glanced over. Nothing impressive, just a slicboard kid, his hair done in wild spikes of blue and green, wearing three torn, layered Fizzwhackers T-shirts and loose plasleather shorts with a chain for a belt, along with the newest and most expensive gleaming white Aeroflot sneakers. He looked at me with the supreme unconcern of the very young, and my blood turned to ice when I thought I recognized his face. Then the moment passed. He was too young to have been at Rigger Hall. Far too young, and normal besides. Not a psion.

I noticed for the first time that the shop was very quiet, and glanced up. The three employees were trying not to stare at me, and uneasiness roiled in the air. I set my jaw, put my datpilot away, and left, no doubt to their great relief.

Walking through Saint City at night is always interesting, due to the fact that the city rarely sleeps. In some districts, it never sleeps at all except during daylight. I wandered, head down and hands more often than not clasped around the katana's scabbard. I wasn't quite thinking. It was more like a sort of haze, shot through with different crystal-clear images.

Like the corner of Thirtieth and Pole, a hooker leaning against a streetlamp opening her mouth to proposition me but retreating rapidly as soon as she saw my tat, the call dying on her lips as streetlamp light kissed and slid over her tired human face.

Or a neon-lit alley, where I paid the entrance fee and went into a screaming shuddering nightclub, going to the bar and paying also for a shot of vodka I didn't drink; the atmosphere of synth-hash smoke, sex, and frantic clinging as painful as the loud screeching noise that passed for music. Then, turning away from the bar, wandering aimlessly through the dancers and the occasional ghostflit riding the waves of sound and sensation, and finally going out the front door again onto the black streets.

Or a deserted street, wet because rain had started to fall, patterns of street light swimming against the gleaming concrete. Shapes I almost knew flickered through the gleam of the falling droplets as the storm moved in, washing the air clean.

I penetrated the tangle of alleys in the Bowery, the deepest part of the Tank District. They led to the Rathole, and I spent a little while standing on an abandoned shelf looking down into the huge sinkhole that used to be a transport well, watching the little firefly flickers that were the sk8 tribes getting ready for their nightly cohesion of slicboard deviltry and community-building. Each young slictribe kid down there whirling on a slicboard through the ramps and jumpoffs was a star, reactive paint glittering as they swooped and yelled with joy; I felt the meaning of the patterns of their chaotic dance tremble at the edge of my understanding.

The idea swam just under the surface of my mind. I always thought best while moving, and this aimless back and forth did qualify as moving. I had read once that sharks in the ocean's cold depths couldn't stop swimming or they would drown.

I understood.

Dawn came up in a glow of rose and gold, the storm passing to the south after having dropped its cargo of water. I found myself up on a rooftop in the University District, the spell of night wearing off and the furnace of the sun breaking free of Earth's darkness. I saw dripping trees in Tasmoor Park below me, heard the hovertraffic overhead take on a new urgency to begin the day, felt my dry burning eyes wanting to close.

When the sun had been up for a while, I got up from lying on the wet, cold concrete of the rooftop and climbed down the rusty fire escape to the alley below, and went in search of a callbox. It took some doing—on this edge of the U District the last riots had destroyed a few callboxes, and phone companies were loath to put more in when everyone had datpilots with voice capability—but I finally found one on the fringe of the Tank District on the edge of an abandoned lot. I stepped into the lighted box, my wet clothes sticking to my steaming skin, and dialed a familiar number.

"Spocarelli, Saint City Parapsych." She sounded hassled and tired. Behind her, frantically ringing phones and raised voices, shuffling papers. It sounded busy.

"Gabe." My voice was a husk of its former self. "It's me. Any news?"

One lone second of silence was all I got. Then, "Holy *fuck*," Gabe whisper-screamed into the phone. "Where the *fucking* hell are you, Danny? Eddie and I been looking everywhere for you! What the *fuck* are you doing? We thought Lourdes had taken you out too! What are you *doing?*"

This struck me as an excellent question. What was I doing? "Thinking. Been thinking. Look, the other four on the list—"

"Three," she said grimly. "It was a busy night. He got a Shaman named Alyson Brady last night and killed four cops to do it. It's like he has some sort of link with them, he's hunting them down like a bloodhound. We had all of them in safehouses. Now we're moving them every two hours. The holovids are having a field day. They're calling him the Psychic Ripper. Chief just got finished chewing my ass out over this. I sure hope you have a good fucking idea in that steel box you call a head, I have been worried *sick* about you, goddammit! Why didn't you call me? Goddamn you and your theatrics, Valentine!"

I closed my eyes. Four Spook Squad cops down, and Brady. I'd known Brady, even worked on a mercenary job or two with her. I might have even seen her wearing that spade necklace. We'd never discussed Rigger Hall at all, not even when we were crouched behind a pile of wreck-

age with three desperate bounties shooting at us, me
bleeding from my head and her bleeding just about everywhere else. That had been the Gibrowitz job; the bounties
were wanted for the rape and murder of the Hegemony
senator's daughter. We'd brought them in a little worse for
wear. Brady, in particular, did not like rapists.

The necklaces.

Instinct clicked under my skin. I actually gasped, cutting off Gabe's frustrated swearing.

If I hadn't been so tired, so physically and emotionally
exhausted, I might not have seen it. "Gabe." My voice
took on a new urgency. "Look. Do they still have the
spade necklaces?"

"I don't . . . I know Brady had one." Gabe's tone sharpened suspiciously. "Danny, what are you thinking?"

"Get those necklaces from them. Do it now. Take 'em
to the station, and *don't touch them* if you can help it.
Leave them on your desk for me and *clear out.* I think
that's how he's tracking them. Get all the necklaces together. I'll be there in an hour to get them. Draw him off."

"Danny, we still don't know what we're dealing with!"
The high edge of panic colored her voice. "If it's a *ka*—"

"I think I know what's going on. And he killed Jace because he couldn't kill me, Gabe. I'm the best equipped to
track him down, goddammit, if it's a *ka* I'll take my goddamn motherfucking chances." My voice was infused
with a certainty I didn't feel. Then something else occurred to me. "Why did you think Lourdes had taken
me out?"

"Your *house,* you idiot! Didn't you see the footage?"
Phones beeped and buzzed behind her. I heard someone
shouting about a Ceremonial trace. More shuffling papers.

Click of a lighter and a long inhale—she was smoking again.

I think that is the very first time you have ever called me an idiot, Gabe. "What footage?"

"Hades, Danny. It's been all over the news. Your house was wrecked and they have footage of you wandering off looking like you'd been hit on the head. Worrying the *fuck* out of me, I might add! I thought Lourdes was following you, I thought you might be *dead*!"

A slight, shaky laugh boiled out of me. "I *am* dead, Gabe. I just don't have enough sense to lie down and admit it. Get the necklaces. I'm coming to collect them, and I'll take care of Lourdes or Mirovitch or both or *whoever* this is. And Gabe, if you've got the necklaces there in the building and you start to feel hinky, *run*. Don't take him on."

"But—*backup*, Danny! For the love of Hades—"

"No fucking backup." My voice was flat and level. "You saw what he did to Jace, he's already killed enough of your people. I'm part *demon*, Gabe. If anyone can take this on, it's me; if I think I need backup or a goddamn thermonuclear strike I'll call in and *tell* you. Don't you fucking *dare* put anyone in danger by sending them after this guy. He's *mine*."

"Danny—"

"Your word, Gabe. I want your word."

Long crackling silence. If I had to worry about human psions behind me getting hurt my effectiveness would be halved, and I was, after all, stronger, faster, and able to take more damage. Gabe was in an unenviable position—throw more of her coworkers in the line of fire and hope this man, whoever he was, didn't kill them, or send me and trust me to finish the job. Trust the lying certainty in my voice. There was only one choice she could make. Sacrifice the many, or trust me to handle it.

"Fine. You're on." But Gabe's voice shook. Another inhale, a long exhale of synth-hash smoke I could almost taste over the phone line. "I'm glad you're alive, Danny."

That makes one of us. A choking laugh ripped its way free of my throat. "Thanks, Gabe. Be careful."

"You got it. Don't do anything stupid." She slammed the phone down. I rested my head against the metal and plasilica of the phone booth, laying the receiver back into its cradle. Hunger twisted under my breastbone. A wave of weakness slid over me.

Doreen. Eve. Japhrimel. Jace. The litany kept going under my conscious thought, the sharp spurs of guilt sinking in, poisoning all they touched.

"I need food," I muttered.

. . . feed me . . .

Can it be you have not resurrected him?

"Can't now even if I want to, sunshine," I said, with a kind of grim humor. "Look at this. I'm talking to myself in a phone booth. Come on, Danny. It's time to go get some food."

Another thought stopped me. I keyed in another number from my datband's clear plasilica display. It rang four times.

"The House of Love," a male voice purred out of the receiver. "What is your wish?"

"This is Dante Valentine," I said, low and fierce. "I need to speak to Polyamour. Now."

"Well, everyone has to—" The sound clicked off. I heard something, moving material, and then another voice.

Female, dark and smooth, and raising the hair on the back of my neck.

"Ms. Valentine. Lady Polyamour thought you'd call. Just a moment."

"Lady" Polyamour? I was too tired to even find that funny.

Another click. No hold-music, just staticky silence. I looked out over the abandoned lot and felt terribly exposed. The skin on my back roughened. The dawning gold of sunrise edged even the weeds in the empty lot with gold, touched the sky with blush. Thin cirrus clouds trailed across the sky—the night's rain was pushing eastward, inland, leaving a fresh-washed pale blue and pink in its wake.

Then another click. "—punishment. I told you to tell me if she called." Polyamour's voice. I smiled slightly, my skin feeling as if it was going to crack. I needed food, lots of it, and soon. "Ms. Valentine. I thought you would call again."

"I hate to be predictable. Look, Poly, I need to know something. The necklaces. The spade necklaces, the reminders. Where did you get those from?"

"Keller got them from a jeweler . . ." She was silent for a moment, probably trailing the name through memory. It didn't take long—a Magi-trained memory is a well-trained memory. "Smith. Bryce Smith. His uncle."

I let out a long, satisfied breath. The normal living in a house with excellent shields—what else does a psionic kid do for his loving uncle? I'd bet the shields were Keller's work, after the kid left school.

After he'd left school—and before Mirovitch had broken free of whatever deep psychic vault Kellerman Lourdes had locked him in, maybe believing him dead. "That's what I needed, Poly. Thanks. Lock your fucking doors and stay under cover, okay?"

"Thank you for your concern, but I'm quite well-protected. Dante?"

"What?" I leaned my forehead against the metal again. The clear plasilica windows were starting to steam up.

For once, she didn't sound disdainful or controlled. Instead, her voice was tinged with something foreign—respect. And not the fawning respect of a courtesan for her callers—*genuine* respect. "Thank you. You're welcome here anytime you choose to come."

Oh, gods above, don't tempt me. "Thanks." I hung up. *Food. I need food.*

In the Tank District there were eateries that still served real meat instead of protein substitute. I stopped at a taqueria, bought and wolfed two huge steak burritos; then went to the burger stand next door and took down three triple-cheeseburgers in ten minutes. Next was another burger stand and three more cheeseburgers, this time with soy bacon. Then, with the edge of the blowtorch hole in my gut slightly taken off, I walked into a Novo Italiano cafe and ordered spaghetti and garlic bread, with bruschetta to start off with, stuffed mushrooms, and a double order of calamari. I barely even tasted it. I would have ordered more, but they took too long to bring it to the table.

When I finished there, I stopped in a convenience store and bought a twelve-pack of plascanned weightlifter shakes, meant to help those with black-market augments keep their muscle mass. Ten minutes later, in an alley, I dropped the last can and wiped my mouth.

The hunger was only blunted, but I'd told Gabe I'd be

at the station in an hour and had only fifteen minutes left. Made it just in time, bolting up the stairs and reaching the third floor, whirling in through the door and finding Gabe's office empty. On her desk were four silver necklaces, their chains tangled together.

The entire third floor was eerily silent and empty. Of course, with a Feeder killing psionics—both cop and civilian—and the suspected trigger to his tracking on Gabe's desk, she would have little need for persuasion to clear the place out. They were probably watching, waiting to come back after I left the building.

I didn't blame them.

I scooped the necklaces up, looking around. Finding a blank piece of paper proved to be a little tricky. In the end I wrote on the backside of a laseprinted burglary report.

The first victim—the normal was Lourdes's uncle. He made the necklaces. I know where Lourdes is. I'm going to make him fucking pay. Do NOT send anyone after me!

I paused, then wrote, *THANK YOU.* Underlined and circled twice. It didn't seem enough, so I laid my hand on the paper and let a tingle of Power down, shaping stray ink into a glyph—*Mainuthsz,* a Greater Glyph of the Canons, shaped like the suggestion of a rider on a horse twisted into an inky line sketch. It meant unconditional love, a partnership—something she and Eddie had, something I had always wanted.

The swift dark stream of guilt roared under the surface of my mind for a few moments before I wrestled it down. I was going to expiate the guilt in the oldest of ways—with blood. But to do that, I needed to think clearly.

Revenge is best served subzero, because revenge is no fucking good if you don't *think clearly.* I was perfectly prepared to die, yes—but I was not prepared to waste myself. Before I was through, Keller or Mirovitch—or both—were going to be sent to Hell, with all the ferocity and cunning I could muster, and all the clinical coldness I was capable of.

I picked up the pen. There was nothing else that could have expressed what I felt for her, or what I had to do. I hesitated, scrawled one more word.

Goodbye.

I ducked out of her office. The place was deserted. I made it down the stairs and out of the station, the spade necklaces dangling in my hand before I remembered what and who I was, and stuffed them in my pocket.

Come and get me now, Mirovitch, I thought, waiting for the lash of pain down my back, waiting for the phantom wounds to reopen.

They didn't. Instead, an ice-cold wall of fury closed around me, impenetrable, shutting me away. My quarry was in front of me, the track clear, my revenge assured. I was going to make him pay, no matter who he was. Lourdes, Mirovitch, the fucking King of the Rats—I was going to kill him.

Now it was personal.

30

I still needed food. Seven restaurants later, the late-afternoon sun glittered in my eyes as I ended up in a pub in the eastern fringe of Saint City, sandwiched between the city and the lake. I was working my way toward the Bridge going east on instinct, from one meal to the next. The necklaces were a weight in my pocket. I hadn't precisely lied—I didn't know *exactly* where Lourdes was, but I could feel a little tingle in my subconscious. I'd hunted down too many psychopaths and criminals not to know that little tingle. It meant that I was close and on the right track. The bounty hunter in me was satisfied, and that was good enough for now.

I set down the pint of beer, wiping my lips with the back of my hand, and studied the demolished large-size pizza in front of me. I hate the taste of beer, but it provides a lot of carbs in a very short time, and I needed fuel. I felt like a goddamn glutton, but I was *hungry*.

I sighed. From a back booth, my eyes tracked through the dark pub. The holovid feeds were showing an advert for the newest series about a group of Ceremonials in East Los Dangeles-Frisco. *For hating psions so much they cer-*

tainly love to watch us on the holovids, I thought, as I always did.

Then the feed switched and it showed my house, the familiar grainy images of the column of flame rising. I watched, my fingernails tapping the table. Gabe had thought Lourdes and Mirovitch had gotten to me in my own house, or trailed me away from the burning wreckage. She must have been worried, worried sick. A better friend than I deserved; Gabe had never let me down.

I watched, my eyes nailed to the display. Inside the column of flame, something twisted.

Something dark and swirling like obsidian smoke.

A vaguely human shape stretched in the middle of the fire, spreading its slender black wings, hands upraised. Then the column of fire was sucked back toward the figure, a shockwave rattling the camera.

I watched, my jaw dropping. *What the fucking hell?*

The flames didn't stop, but they were pulled back in, wreathing around the dark figure, which lifted its head as if searching. Then, maddeningly, the picture stopped, dissolving in a burst of static. My face flashed on the holovid, a thumbnail up to the right of an announcer. I saw with a slight twitch of aggravation that it was my new face. Someone had managed to take a stillcam holo of me. My hair was pulled back, tendrils falling softly and beautifully in my face, so I would bet it was taken at the House of Pain.

The announcer was of the type always chosen for holovids—slightly androgynous, high cheekbones, sculpted mouth. This one had sleek blond hair and a pair of bright green eyes that made my stomach turn over. I paid and got out of there in a hurry, my boots barely touching the stairs that took me streetside. The pub's antique wooden door swung shut behind me.

What was in my house? Was it Lourdes? Had he somehow been there, stalking me while I was blind with grief, and my torching the house had taken him by surprise? My throat went dry, my right hand clenching into a fist.

But I hadn't sensed Mirovitch or Keller. And even crazed with grief I was sure I would have noticed the cloying psychic stench of the Headmaster.

It couldn't be. It *couldn't* be.

Can it be that you have not resurrected him?

"Impossible." My voice startled me. I glanced around, catching a few frightened looks from the normals who were giving me a wide berth. "Im-fucking-possible."

Figment of the imagination. Or, if not . . . Santino had used the Egg against Japhrimel, and Lucifer had finished the job by beating him to death once he was already wounded. Would fire and Power do what I'd thought blood *might* do, and bring a demon back to life? Rebuild a demon's shattered body from ash? Even a Fallen demon?

Don't get distracted, Danny. Every moment you delay is another moment he has to kill someone else.

But I had the necklaces, didn't I? I was the target now.

I walked down the street, my hands clasped around the scabbard. My sword hummed inside the sheath, a subliminal song of Power. After a while I noticed that people were spilling out of my way while I walked. When I passed into a belt of residential buildings and the sidewalks were empty under old trees turning red and orange and white for winter, it was a relief. I crunched through wet-smelling fallen leaves and kept moving.

The sun was setting by the time I made it to the Bridge.

With hovertraffic being what it was, the huge Bridge was in a state of disrepair. But slicboarders can't go over water, and foot or wheelbike traffic needed the Bridge. A thriving traffic rumbled over the lake, and there was a rail line to take land supplies that for one reason or another couldn't go by hover transport.

I needed to go east, and I wanted to walk, so it was the Bridge or nothing.

On the west side, the old main roads zigzagged down the hill. I cut through the bands of shrubbery and wished I'd thought to keep my slicboard, or rent one. The edge of the river curled away under the beginning of the Bridge, I smelled cold iron and the dead, chemical-laden water. There were colonies of homeless people living on the banks, renegade psionics, all sorts of human driftwood. It made the Tank District look like a *sedayeen* commune. I kept walking.

The Bridge lay on the surface of the glass-calm lake, an architectural triumph when it was made five hundred years ago, revamped every few decades. The original concrete was crumbling, but haphazard repairs are done every year, and plasilica and new steel had been hammered in a few years ago during a grand reconstruction funded by Hegemony grants and City Hall. Algae drifted thick on the lake, harvested and distilled by the biotechs or anyone with a chem degree and a few thousand credits' worth of equipment. The last wave of additive-laced Clormen-13 had come from here; tainted and cut with some thyoline-based substance to make it more harsh and addictive. Not like Chill needed any help.

I could have been over the Bridge in a short time if I'd gotten a slic or used some of my demon speed, but I shivered, continued walking. The pond that the boathouse on the Hall grounds stood near fed into the river, I was sure of it. Even being this close to water that had touched the grounds of that cursed place was enough to make my blood turn cool and loose in my veins.

The more I thought about it, the more miraculous it was that the Black Room had managed to meet anywhere on the grounds, especially in the same place more than once, even if Keller only took the members there one at a time. Mirovitch had been uncanny, sniffing out hidden stashes of contraband, seemingly always one step ahead of every upswell of rebellion in the student population, as well as any student conspiracies. No matter where you turned, someone was reporting to the stooges, or being punished, or simply withdrawing into their own little shell, just trying to survive.

What other secrets had Rigger Hall kept?

After an hour's steady walk I reached midspan, pausing to look over the dark algae-choked surface of the lake. I had no warning.

My left shoulder came alive with pain, as if a clawed hand had curled around and dug in. I went to my knees in the middle of the road, steel creaking under me. I found my claw-cramping right hand under my shirt, my fingertips touching the writhing ropes of scar that was Japhrimel's mark. The slight pressure—fingertips against scar—made the world swim as if a pane of wavering glass hung in front of me.

Saint City seen upside down, the lights shimmering on the TransBank Tower, hovertraffic zipping by. Need burning hot in the veins, dropping, wings furled, breaking the fall at the last moment, booted feet slamming into pave-

*ment. Following a scent that was not a scent, a sound that
was a touch, a fire of need in veins old and strong, drawing . . . eastward.*

I came back to myself, ripping my fingers away from
the scar. My knees dug into the Bridge, which swayed
like a plucked string. I heard yells from both ends, used
my scabbarded blade to lever myself up.

Can it be you have not resurrected him?

Lucifer's voice, taunting me. And the dark winged figure in the middle of the flames . . . Fire, enough fire to
perhaps feed a demon?

Enough Power to perhaps bring one back, rebuild a
demon's body from ash?

Ridiculous. Insane. If Japh—

If *he* had been alive, even just barely clinging to life, I
would have known when I clasped his burning body to my
chest. I would have known every time I touched the glassy
lacquered urn. I would have *known.* I was a Necromance,
death was my trade, and I was as exquisitely sensitive to
the spark of life and soul as a sexwitch was to Power.

But what about the *soul?* A demon's soul . . . or a
Fallen demon's soul, the soul of an *A'nankhimel* . . .

I wished again that I'd been able to study more about
demons. Or, more precisely, about *A'nankhimel,* Fallen
demons, and the *hedaira,* their human brides. But none of
the books had anything other than old legends garbled to
the point of uselessness. The demons didn't like to talk
about the *A'nankhimel,* for whatever reason; and the Magi
for all their fooling around with demons, didn't know
about anything the demons didn't care to talk about. The
Magi's natural jealousy and obfuscation surrounding each
practitioner's research and results didn't help. I couldn't

even *question* a Magi about demons, they wouldn't talk unless it was to members of their own circle, and even inside circles each Magi had his or her own secrets.

What if I turned back now? I could find out. I could touch my scar and go wherever it led me. I could leave this horrible circle of murder and death and foulness behind and look for my dead demon lover instead of revenging myself and every other soul who had suffered at Rigger Hall. And if my sanity snapped, I could look anywhere in the world for him, anywhere at all. I could spend my life uselessly hunting down something that didn't exist, fooling myself into believing he was still alive, around the next corner, just out of reach.

No. If he had not come back before now, he wasn't going to. All the longing in the world couldn't fool me into knowing otherwise.

I squeezed my eyes shut, hot tears dripping down to the Bridge deck. I was just hallucinating, trying to hoodwink myself. Japhrimel was dead, Jace was dead, and I was hunting a Headmaster who refused to die.

Where did Kellerman Lourdes fit in? Was he carrying Mirovitch like a poisonous seed in his own thoughts? Was he a mule for the Headmaster's twisted psyche and soul, his slime-drenched Feeder *ka?* Or had Mirovitch taken over completely, grown inside Lourdes's body, driven out of his own middle-aged body by the assaults of the other kids?

None of it made much sense. It was ridiculous anyway. I'd shattered his urn to remove the hope of Japhrimel coming back. It was my penance, and by every god that ever was, I was going to pay my penance and have my revenge.

I swayed on the middle of the Bridge. Another thought chilled me—maybe the Power I carried, like a plasgun over a barrel of reactive, was going to eat me up. Maybe the only reason I'd survived so long was because I hadn't used the full extent of my capabilities, wasting myself on grief, bounties, and torturing Jace. Maybe it was rising, and it would burn me to ash—just like Japhrimel.

Just like my house.

I'm going to take him with me. Mirovitch, Keller, whoever he is, I'm taking him with me when I go. If I go.

What if I managed to kill Mirovitch? What then?

I was so tired, weary with a weariness that went all the way down to my bones and even further. I had read about despair of the soul, and never thought it possible until now. Even the part of me that had fought all my life, the stubborn refusal to give in that had colored my entire existence, was dully muted, hanging its head. There comes a time when even simple endurance can't carry you through.

I knew what it would be like, laying my head on Death's black chest, feeling the weight of living rise away from me. The clear light would break out from the horizon of What Comes Next, and I would go gratefully into that foreign land.

But not before Mirovitch. Or Keller. Or whoever the hell he was.

I looked out over the algae-choked, glassy surface of the lake, reflecting the orange glow of the city on every shore. I lifted one foot, uncertain, and then put it back down. Remained standing where I was.

The last few dregs of light squeezed their way out of the sky. Night folded over Saint City and the Bridge—and me—with all the softness of black wings.

I shook my hair back, ash falling free of the black silky strands, and continued on.

31

Walking up Sommersby Street Hill at night was a strange experience. The last time I'd seen this place had been in broad daylight decades ago, when I'd walked to East Transport Station to board the transport that would take me north to the regional Academy for my specialized Necromance training. While at the Hall I had rarely seen the street at night; students weren't allowed off the school grounds after dark, and I'd never come east of the Bridge in all my after-Academy years of living in Santiago City. I'd been all over the world hunting bounties, but this place so close to home I'd avoided like the plague.

Given my druthers, I would have continued doing so.

Fog was rolling in off the bay and the lake, a thick soupy fog that glowed green near the pavement and orange between the streetlights. With the fog came the smell of the sea—thick brine—and the smell of fire, burned candle wax, and ash. Or maybe the smell of a burned, smashed life was only mine, rising from my clothes.

I paced up Sommersby Hill, my bootheels clicking, and saw with a weary jolt of surprise that the Sommersby Store was still open.

While I was at the Hall, the Store was where all the kids went in our infrequent free time. We bought cheap novels and fashion mags about holovid stars, candy bars to supplement the bland Hall food, and synth-hash cigarettes to be smuggled on campus. The Store used to have a counter that sold tofu dogs and ice cream and other cheap fare, but I saw that part of the building was boarded up now. With Rigger Hall gone, most of the Store's customers would be gone too. It was a miracle that even the main part was still there.

For a few minutes I stood, my hands in the pockets of Jace's coat, the sword thrust through the loop on the belt of my weapons rig. I watched the front of the Store, its red neon blurring on the dirty glass. The newspaper hutch standing to one side of the door was gone, a paler square of the paint of the storefront marking where it had stood; but the slicboard rack was still there. The boarded-up half of the storefront was festooned with graffiti, a broken window on the second story blindly glared at me. I stared at the glass door with its old-fashioned infrared detector, the plasticine sign proclaiming *Shoplifting Will Be Prosecuted* still set above the door's midbar, dingy and curling at its corners.

I finally slid my sword out of the loop on my belt. Holding it in my left hand, I crossed the street.

I'm about to be swallowed by my own past. It wasn't a comfortable feeling. After all, my past had teeth. And what would I become when it finished digesting me?

Will you stop with the disgusting thoughts? Please, Danny. You're even irritating yourself.

The motion detector beeped as I stepped into the warm gloom. It looked dingier and even more rundown, but there was the same ice machine and rack of holovid mags, shelves of crisp packets and junk food in bright wrappers, and a plasilica cabinet holding cheap jackknives and dat-band add-ons, gleaming like fool's gold. The floor was still white and black squares of linoleum, dirt and dust drifting in the corners. Memory roiled under my skin. I expected to look down and see my scabbed knees under a plaid skirt, feel the stinging weight of the collar against my vulnerable throat and scratchy wool socks against my calves.

"Help ya?"

The voice was a rude shock. Even more of a shock was the man—fat, almost-bearded, dressed in a stained white T-shirt, oily red suspenders, and a pair of baggy khaki pants. I let out a breath. My left hand, holding the sword, dropped. "Hi." My eyes adapted to the gloom. Red neon cigarette-brand signs buzzed in the windows. *Tamovar. Marlboro X. Gitanes. Copperhead.* "I'm here for a pack of Gitanes. Make that two. And that silver Zijaan, in the case." I picked up a handful of Reese Mars Bars—my favorite during school years. I rarely had any money left over from my state stipend after it was applied to tuition and my uniforms. Even though Rigger Hall was for the orphans and the poor, the kids with families usually had a little more pocket change.

A psion was state property, their upbringing supposed to be overseen by trained professionals, the family just an afterthought—nice if it was there, but not terribly necessary. Had I missed my family? I'd had beaky, spectacled, infinitely gentle Lewis, and my books. The pain of that first loss seemed strangely sweet and clean to me now, compared to the sick, twisting litany of grief and guilt caroling under the rest of my thoughts. I'd had Roanna, my first *sedayeen* friend, the gentle ballast to the harshness of my nature even then. And my connection with my god had sustained me; I had always known, from the moment I read my first book on Egyptianica, that Anubis was my psychopomp. Some Necromances reached their accreditation Trial without knowing what face Death would take, I was lucky.

The library, the hall where we were taught fencing, a few of the teachers that weren't so bad . . . there had been good things too, at the Hall. Things that had sustained me. I hadn't missed the mother and father who had given me up at birth. I hadn't known enough to miss them, and still didn't.

I shook myself out of memory. Couldn't afford to be distracted now.

What else? I cast around.

There, on the rack, was a holovid mag that showed a picture of Jasper Dex leaning against a brick wall, his bowl-cut hair artistically mussed. It was a retrospective issue; memory rose like a flood again. I pushed nausea and memory down, trying not to gag at the smell of unwashed human male.

Mrs. DelaRocha had been behind the counter in my younger years, balefully eying the collared kids from the Hall, suspiciously peering at you, following you down the two aisles of the store, breathing her halitosis in your face when you asked for cigarettes. I squashed the guilty idea that if I turned around I would see her right behind me, her skirt askew and her cardigan buttoned up wrong, lipstick staining her yellowed teeth, her hook nose lifting proudly between her faded watery hazel eyes.

I laid the candy and the magazine down on the counter. He looked at me curiously, but got the cigarettes and the lighter for me. "The Zijaan's full-up. You want lighter fluid?"

"No. Thank you." I paid with crumpled New Credit notes instead of my datband, because that's what I would have done as a kid. He pushed everything back over the counter at me, glowering as he counted out my change— three single credits, everything in the store was priced in whole numbers and the Hegemony never indulged in the antique custom of sales tax like some of the Freetowns did. They had other ways of getting your credits.

The candy and the magazine went into my battered messenger bag. My emerald glittered, a sharp green spark crackling in the dimness. The man jumped nervously. The sight of all that blubber quivering made a completely reprehensible desire to giggle rise in my throat. It was suppressed and died away with no trouble at all. His T-shirt was filthy and barely covered his hairy chest; stub-ends of cigars lay in a plastic ashtray shaped like a nude woman with her legs spread. No doubt a commemorative item, the ashtray was half-pushed behind a stand-up holoshell calender.

Today is (blank spot). The last two digits of the year blinked—*75*. I shivered. The calendar was a good twelve years slow.

The extra pack of Gitanes went into my pocket. I opened the first pack, took my change, and stalked out of the store, ignoring his sarcastic "Havva good evenin'."

It's extremely unlikely I'll have anything of the sort. I stepped out into the fog-laden street. My hands shook only slightly as I clicked the Zijaan with my free right hand and lit the first Gitane. The smell of synth hash rose up, nearly choked me. I blinked. My eyes watered. I walked across the street again, head down, dawdling like I used to do on the afternoons when we were free to leave school grounds. Then I glanced back at the Sommersby Store.

A chill ruffled my spine.

It was dark and boarded-up, no neon in the windows. Abandoned like all the rest. No sign of lights, of neon, or of the fat hairy storeowner.

32

$\mathcal{M}$y mouth went dry, and the gray of shock fuzzed around the corners of my peripheral vision. I forced it away, bent over, my right hand twisting into a claw once again. The red eye of the cigarette taunted me. I inhaled smoothly, down into the pit of my belly as I'd been taught.

"Holy shit. I just bought Gitanes from a ghost." My voice sounded high and childish even to myself. Did this mean that the gods were with me? Or was I hallucinating again? Both were equally likely.

I re-crossed the street. If anyone was watching, they would probably think I was a lunatic. I poked at the boards over the shattered glass door I'd just walked through whole, went on tiptoes to peer inside the cave of the store. A heady brew of wet decay and other garbage-laced smells poured out; my demon-sharp eyes caught sight of a magazine rack upended, a few holomags scattered, drifts of trash on the floor. The plasticine counter was shattered too, and I saw a scraped-clean circle off to one side and a blackened scorch mark on the floor. Probably a fire some transient had made inside the abandoned building.

I dropped the smoking cigarette, then opened up my bag. The magazine was gone, and the candy, but one pack of cigarettes was there. I fished the other pack out of my pocket and stared at them, turning the unopened one over to read its warning label; there was a sweepstakes to win a free hover blazoned on the back.

I crumpled both packs in my fist, feeling the sticks break inside, and dropped them heedlessly. Then I drew the silver Zijaan from my pocket.

The breath left me in another gasping rush. The lighter was battered and scratched with hard use, and etched into one flat side was a cursive *C* wreathed with another cursive *M*.

I blinked. Flipped the lighter open, spun the wheel with a click, and orange flame blossomed. I snapped it shut. I ran my fingers over the carved letters.

For once in my life, I was completely at a loss. I looked up at the boarded-up storefront again, smelled decay and that strange, indecipherable scent.

CM? Christabel Moorcock?

"Christabel?" I said, tentatively, my voice echoing against the soggy shredded interior of the abandoned store.

No answer. Except the memory of the scraping awful scream—*remember, remember.* The lilac smell of terror clinging to pale-pink paper as Christabel wrote her last message. The memory of her bed, neatly made; her bookshelves religiously dusted, her kitchen and bathroom spotless . . . Everything in its place.

In all my years of dealing with Power and the strange logic of magick, I had never come across anything even remotely like this. I held up the lighter. Swallowed dryly.

Then I slipped the lighter in the breast pocket of Jace's coat. *There's a circle being closed here. Just like a Greater Work of magick.*

It was vaguely comforting. It meant some other agency might be working with me to bring Mirovitch and Keller down. Maybe Christabel was helping out another Necromance. Who knew?

Or perhaps it meant I was to be offered as a sacrifice. That was a little less comforting. I blew out a long breath between my teeth, a tuneless whistle that fell flat on the foggy air. I backed away from the store, finally hopping down from the sidewalk and into the street. I decided to go up the Hill and—

"Valentine! Hey, Valentine!" A girl's voice, light and young, and the patter of quick, light, running feet on concrete. My ears tracked it, the footsteps sounded as if someone was running up right behind me. My neck prickled.

I gasped, whirling, my hair fanning out. Sommersby Street yawned, the abandoned buildings and boarded-up houses mocking me. The concrete pavement was cracked and pitted here, and no hovertraffic lit the sky. Without the Hall, this district had probably gone into slow decline.

A perfect place to hide.

My own voice caught me by surprise. "Christabel?" *Okay, that's it. I have had enough of this. Everyone out of the swimtank. No more voices, no more illusions, no more delaying.* I straightened, my jaw set, my right hand cramped around the hilt of my sword. When I could walk without staggering, I continued up the middle of the street in defiance of any streetside hovertraffic, my bootheels clicking on the pavement. Winter had come early here up on the Hill, and frost rimed the darker places where the sun didn't reach during the day. Under trees and in shadowy corners, winter was creeping in without the benefit of the rest of autumn.

I continued up Sommersby and turned right onto Harlow. At the end of Harlow the gates rose up, wrought-iron with plasilica panels, an *R* done in gothic script on one half, an *H* on the other. On the top of the gates, dagger-shaped finials lengthened up like claws.

I stopped in the shelter of a doorway, looking at the gates. *Be careful, Danny,* Jace's voice brushed my cheek. *It only looks quiet. Don't trust nothin' in there.*

"You don't need to tell me that," I muttered.

The first illegal job I'd gone on had been as a result of Jace's tutelage, a few months into our relationship during a dry period. I'd complained that I didn't have enough to make my mortgage even with the apparitions and bounties I worked on, and he'd looked at me, his head propped on the headboard of my bed, and said, *How would you like to make some* real *money, baby?*

I'd done bounties and I'd tracked down stolen objects, but I'd never done corporate espionage or thieving before. I'd never even thought of doing mercenary work, but the money was good and Jace and I were a fantastic team. At the time I hadn't wondered at it, but no doubt Jace's Mob Family connections had come in handy. Under his tutelage, I'd become so much better at tracking bounties it wasn't funny, spending just half the time it normally took to bring them in.

The memory was strangely fuzzy, even the sharp sword of pain at the thought of Jace was oddly muted. I stared at the gate I'd seen for years in my nightmares, and my hand tightened on the scabbard once more. My heart thundered in my chest.

"Okay, Christabel," I murmured. "You're still leading the dance. Let's go."

33

I wondered why the geography of a place I'd tried so hard
to forget was burned so deeply into me that I had no
trouble calling up a mental map of the entire complex.
Behind the gate, the driveway would curve up the gentle
hill, the pond to the right, the shack of the boathouse just
visible on the other side. The main house, with class-
rooms, the cafeteria, and the gymnasium, would rear up
in front of the driveway. An ancillary road would curve
off to the left, leading to the four Halls, each one shock-
shielded and stocked with supplies for practicing the standard Magi disciplines, intranet security and an automatic
fail-safe on each one.

Behind the main building were the dormitories, two for
girls, one for boys (since the X chromosome carries Talent far more often than the Y) and the fencing salle/dojo,
the swimtank building, and, in the very back, the Headmaster's House. Further up the hill and also to the left was
the Morrow building, containing the Library, more class-
rooms, and a fully stocked alchemical lab, as well as hot-
houses for the Skinlin trainees closed around a courtyard
that held a co-op garden for the Skinlins and hedgewitches.

The only thing missing was the stink of childrens' fear—and, of course, the tang of Power as well as the glimmer of a security net: deepscan, magscan, and a full battery of defensive measures. Not to mention the chain-link fence, six foot tall and topped with razor wire Mirovitch had erected inside the older, more aesthetically pleasing brick wall.

Who did that to you, Danny? Jace's voice, harsh with anger, during one of our old fights. *Who made you think you were worthless? Tell me who. Goddammit, who did that to you?* And he'd turned in a tight half-circle, jerking away from me as if the offender might be hiding in the living room.

"Jace," I whispered to the empty, foggy street. "I don't want to go in there again."

Whether I was caught in some magick of Fate or just too stubbornly, exhaustedly determined for my own good, I was called upon to finish it. And who, after all, was left to finish it if I couldn't?

My right hand throbbed and ached. I dropped it, touched the pocket holding the spade necklaces. If I was right—and I goddamn well hoped I was—Keller would be tracking me now. I would draw him like a lodestone draws iron filings, like a broken-down hover in the Tank District draws techstrippers. Like a fight in Rio draws the organ harvesters.

Thinking of this, I reached down into my pocket and drew out four necklaces, leaving one behind. I cupped them in my palm, examining them closely. There was no thread of Power I could detect. But of course, if it was only a passive charm keyed to Keller I might not be able to see it at all, even with a demon's acuity. When it came to tracking spells, passive usually meant *weak,* but it also usually meant *invisible.*

I closed my right hand into a fist, the sharp pricks of the spade charms digging into my skin. The trickle of Power slid down my wrist like a razor, heat welling up under my skin. It pooled in my palm, melting, swirling, straining to escape.

I stared at my hand, the trickle of superheated Power making my fingernails glow.

Memory rose.

Crack. *The worst thing about the whip is not the first strike, laid hot against the back. For the first few microseconds it is almost painless—but then the red-hot fléchette, fueled with Power, scorchsplits open every nerve, and the entire body becomes the back. Not just the back, but the entire* world *becomes the lash of agony. The scream rises up out of the deepest layers of the body, impossible to deny. No matter how much the will nerves itself not to scream, the body betrays begging, pleading, breaking.*

I opened my fist.

Valentine, D. Student Valentine is called to the Headmaster's Office immediately.

The fléchette gleamed in my hand, long and thin and razor-sharp. Made of Power and the metal in the necklaces, it rang softly as I touched it with a forefinger. I blew a low tuneless whistle between my teeth and looked up toward the gate.

It was open slightly, fog wreathing through the bars. *Come into my parlor, said the undead Headmaster to the wary ex-pupil.* The lunatic singsong sounded a little bit more like me. I grabbed at the thought, sucked in another

breath, and dug in my messenger bag. I had no sheath that
would fit the fléchette, so I wrapped a supple piece of
plasilica around it and stuck it in my pocket with the last
spade necklace.

I don't think I'm going in through the front door. I
melted out of the shadow of the doorway to vanish into
the fog.

34

*I*t was still there, the old drainage tunnel. Trash drifted in the bottom of the round concrete cave, looking a lot smaller now that I was at least a foot taller. Several years of fallen leaves were turning into sludge at the bottom. I examined it carefully, reaching out to touch the concrete. Here, where the drainage ditch went through a hummock under the fence, someone had once cut through the iron grating covering the school side. Generations of students had carefully covered the hole with rotting wooden scraps from the woodshop, enough to let the water drain and cover the fact that the metal grille was broken. Since the hole went underground, it didn't register on the shields, psychic or electronic—or if it ever had, it had been forgotten. As far as anyone knew, this was one secret the students had successfully kept. Sneaking out to roam the streets at night was a Rigger Hall tradition, indulged in even in the darkest days of Mirovitch's reign. We were, after all, only kids. There was nowhere else to go, not as a collared psion. We were Hegemony property.

After hearing about the Black Room, I wondered if other secrets were kept. I would have thought it was impossible to keep anything from Mirovitch or his stooges. Now, with an adult's sense of circumstance and complexity, I found myself thinking a little more charitably about the stooges and rats. They had just been terrified kids, like me.

But I'd never broken. I hadn't broken even when he'd forced me to watch Roanna die—and now I wondered if he had known she would slip through his old, hard fingers and fling herself at the fence after we had refused to betray each other.

I had never broken, not even afterward when Mirovitch dragged me back into his office to punish me, demanding to know just what my *sedayeen* roommate had told her social worker—and if she had told anyone else. I knew now that he had been almost frantic at the thought of losing his personal playground, not to mention the punishment that would have been meted out to him; swift execution, most likely in a gasbox. After that, he'd had it in for me. My defiance outraged him, but I was still only one small girl in a large school. I frequently managed to stay beneath his notice.

I ducked into the end of the tunnel, my boots slipping in the scudge. Water sloshed. The air was absolutely still, and the fog made it eerily quiet. Complete blackness made the tunnel into an abyss, despite my demon sight. There were no streetlights on either side of the concrete pipe, and the thick fog cut visibility even for my eyes.

I lifted my sword, thumbed it free. The slight click of the katana easing loose of the scabbard was loud in the cottony silence. Three inches of steel slid free, and a faint blue glow flowed along the metal.

I saw the tunnel, still sloping slightly upward, a knee-high spill of water and leaf sludge coating its bottom. Permaspray graffiti tangled along the walls, some of it even glowing with Schorn's algae when the light from my blade touched it. The concrete was crumbling, but still sound. I couldn't see anything blocking it, and the water was still coming, so I bent down to step cautiously into the opening.

Halfway through, I paused and lifted my blade, looking at the left-hand wall. My boots sloshed; I moved very carefully, peering through the dark.

There it was. In black permaspray, the crudely-done drawing of a slender Egyptian dog with long ears, reclining; a copy of an ancient statue. I remembered biting my lip as I marked the wall, the sharp chemical reek of permaspray, and the satisfaction I'd felt when it was done. It was the mark of my personal war with the school, my badge of honor for not breaking. I smiled, holding my sword up a little higher, shaking my hair back. In the dim light, shadows shifting and crowding, it seemed the dog's head dipped once, nodding at me. I set my jaw and nodded back, then carefully stepped away.

The tunnel was shorter than I remembered. At the end, I pushed aside a sheet of rotted plaswood, setting foot for the first time in decades inside the walls of Rigger Hall again. I took a cautious sniff, smelled only leaf mold, grass, and salty fog. Strained my ears, but heard only the thick silence of a cloud-wrapped night. I held the cloak of my Power close but sensed no shields on the walls; when they closed the school, a team of Hegemony psions had come out and dismantled the defenses, earthing the power. And there were no electronic countermeasures. If

Keller was here, he was counting on invisibility to keep him safe.

The familiar loose tension invaded my body, my heart-beat speeding up. *I chased down a demon even the Prince of Hell couldn't catch. I survived two run-ins with the Devil. I'm the best Necromance in Saint City. I'm listed as one of the top-ten deadliest bounty hunters in the Hegemony.*

That thought caused a sniggering little laugh to jerk its way out of me. One of the biggest hunts of my life, and I wasn't going to make a red credit off of it.

That was a very adult thought, and I was glad. I still had to check to make sure I wasn't wearing the plaid skirt, and every time the denim of my jeans touched my knees I had to suppress a guilty start.

The grass was no longer manicured but knee-high, weeds lying thick and rank and edged by frost in the deeper shadows. I saw the familiar bulk of the dormitories' roofs over the hill, decided to go uphill and angle toward the Headmaster's House. I could cut around the back of the dojo and avoid any possible patrolling teacher or stooge.

As if there was anyone here.

For all I knew, nobody *was* here . . . but just because I felt like I should sneak around to avoid Mirovitch's hounds didn't mean it was a *bad* idea to exercise a little caution.

I'm being eaten alive by my own childhood. Gods above. Why me? The answer came in a flash. Why not? Who, after all, was better equipped than me?

I reached the top of the hill and hunched down instinctively, the edges of my shields roughening. *Dust, offal, magick, aftershave, chalk, and leather.* I retreated, almost as if scalded, gasping and dropping flat as the wall of magick passed overhead. He was scanning the grounds.

Well, now I know he's here. I tried to remember if I had any consecrated chalk in my bag. Then it occurred to me that I was doing exactly what a scared teenager would do—hiding, and waiting for Lourdes to find and trap me like a rabbit.

Which brought up another glaring hole in my plan. I didn't even have one. I was operating on a sort of half-ass instinct I hadn't used since I was twelve. A miserable instinct that was just what any stupid kid would use. The fact that it was impossible to plan for something like this didn't exonerate me from feeling a little dumb.

Time to start thinking, Danny! A whisper that sounded like Jace's in my ear, hot breath touching my cheek, warm fingers on my nape. It felt so bloody *real* I gasped, throwing myself down and rolling, instinctively throwing up a flare of Power that stained the hillside crimson for a moment.

Well, I just blew any chance I had of secrecy. I made it to my feet and bolted away at a different angle. This would take me directly to the Headmaster's House, keeping me below the sight line of the hill.

I heard boots crunching on gravel, which told me two things: that he was on the other side of the hill and behind me, and also that he had been at the front gate or in the dormitories.

For a moment, I considered veering up and engaging him head-on; but I was already running soundless as an owl. I heard the footsteps on gravel slow and strained my

ears, suddenly and, for once, blessing my demon-acute
senses.

A short yell of pain and the sound of something falling,
hitting the ground hard. Then a mad gravel-crunching
scramble, and footsteps on grass. I didn't stop, came around
the side of the hill's breast, and found myself faced with
the track leading up to the Headmaster's House.

*Polyamour came this way, with a nine-year-old girl
and Keller. Bringing them to Mirovitch.* My gorge rose.
The track was paved, and I ran over it using all the speed
and silence my new body could give me.

I had just come over the slight rise, leaping over a pot-
hole, when I heard a hissing crackle. I threw myself aside
and the bolt flung past me, crackling and spitting as it
went, and buried itself in the Headmaster's House.

The prim, two-story neo-Victorian was clearly abandoned, plaswood over the windows. Uncertain foggy light
showed great cracks in the peeling paint—the same kind
of leprous blue light I'd seen in Sukerow's apartment.
Only this time, the blue light spread, crackling and hissing. I wondered for a split second if the unhealthy looking
glow would give me a radiation burn. It certainly *looked*
like the diseased glow of a coremelt.

The explosion was deafening. I ended up lying in the
long grass on the side of the road, the shockwave smashing me down, a warm trickle of blood coming from my
nose.

"Plenty more where that came from," I heard from my
right, down the hill in the bushes. The bolt had streaked
past me from my right, which meant that he'd been
scrambling behind me.

The fléchette, he's probably tracking the fléchette.

And the last necklace that I had in my pocket.

"Who are you?" The wheezing, slightly asthmatic voice came again. Chills worked up my spine, spilled down my arms. It sounded odd, strangely distorted, as if passed through a synthfilter—but I *knew* that voice. My entire body went cold and strained against shock at the sound, my fingers digging into the earth, the smell of crushed wet grass and damp earth rising around me and warring with the heady, spicy fragrance of demon.

The Headmaster's House was burning merrily, orange flames instead of blue now, casting a livid light up into the fog. I had only a few seconds before he crested the rise and saw me.

Then I heard a horrible, chilling scream. *"No! NO! Stop it! STOP IT!"* This voice was different, a baritone, with the unmistakable tang of Skinlin. I only heard one set of footsteps—but then I heard a thrashing, like a fight.

"Whoever you are, *run*! Run for your life!"

I intended to run, but not for my life.

I intended to run for *his*.

"—*down*," Mirovitch hissed. "And *stay* down. In your place, boy."

I didn't stick around to hear more. I ran.

35

I suppose the last place either Mirovitch or Keller would have expected me to go was the cafeteria. There was a wall of boarded-up windows on one side, two lone left-over tables stacked against the wall, and insulation hung from the ceiling in long swathes. It was tactically exposed, and I'd had to break open a door to get in here—and if the sound of screeching metal and my own jagged breathing didn't bring Mirovitch, what I was going to do next would.

I was only a few steps in before my foot came down on something soft. My sword whipped out, and I found myself looking at an innocuous sleeping bag, lying tangled on the floor. The smell of canned beef soup hung in the air, and I smelled candle wax as well. Candle wax and unwashed human—and the cold, fetid reek of Mirovitch, dust and magick and feces and chalk and aftershave.

I'd found a lair. The trouble was, I wasn't sure of *what*.

I dug in my bag with one trembling hand. My sword glowed blue. My frantic fingers couldn't find any chalk, though I knew I had some. I could almost feel time winding down, the clocksprings of whatever was going to happen ticking away, closer and closer, rising through the water to sink its teeth into my thrashing legs.

I pulled my hand out of my bag and took a deep breath flavored with human and not-so-human scents, my own smoky demon smell suddenly strong as a shield in my nostrils. Reached into my pocket, fingers closing around the fléchette in its plasilica sheath.

The touch of cold metal shocked me back into some kind of sense. I crouched down on the floor in the middle of the caf, a swordsman's crouch, my blade held out to one side, the fléchette in my left hand. *What do I need chalk for? I'm part demon.*

The circle swirled in the air, dust scorching as the fire in me rose, whipcracking in small, controlled bursts, a tattoo of Power burning into the concrete under the linoleum. It took bare seconds. By the time it was done, I had a tolerable approximation of a double circle scored around me with red-glowing Power—and between the two circles, the subtly altered shapes of the Feeder glyphs Kellerman Lourdes had created writhed. Every candle Lourdes had placed in here burst into flame, suddenly alive with fire, their glow warm and welcoming. The fléchette began to hum, metal glowing, heating up in my hand. My pocket, the one holding the leftover spade necklace, began to smoke. I didn't have a hand left to fish it out, so I just crouched, on guard.

One of the plaswood windows blew in. Then another. Another. Splinters skidded across the floor.

Silence descended. Here was where it would end.

Do you believe in Fate, Danny Valentine?

I gulped down air, the three phantom scars on my back alive. The vanished brand along my lower-left buttock began to ache, dully at first, and then with increasing pain. A curl of smoke drifted up from my pocket. I waited.

The door I'd wrenched open creaked as it was pulled wide, then ripped off its hinges. And into the cafeteria shambled Kellerman Lourdes.

Now that I saw him up close, I vaguely remembered him as a tall, gawky, acne-pocked Skinlin, always on the periphery of whatever activity was being conducted. His career at Rigger had been singularly free of rumors and whispers. It was as if nobody noticed him at all. The invisible man.

Part of the puzzle became clear as I studied him. He stepped into the caf and watched me, dead dark eyes sparking with blue pinpricks, his thick wattled cheeks quivering ever so slightly.

"You were a Feeder already." Breathless, I sounded like I was fourteen again.

And scared.

That was why he'd been invisible; and that was why he could get close to Mirovitch that fateful night with Polyamour and Dolores. He'd had a Feeder's camouflage; it was no use being a psychic vampire if you shouted it to the heavens. No, they were all-but-invisible, especially to children, which was what made them so bloody dangerous. In a normal Hegemony psi school he would have been tested, treated, and more than likely saved, free to live out a normal life as a psion. But in Mirovitch's kingdom he was left untreated . . . and so he used that camouflage to kill Mirovitch with the others, probably taking Mirovitch's death into his own psyche and sealing his own fate as a Feeder—or even worse, a Feeder's mule. A physical body for the *ka* of the dead Headmaster to ride.

He stared at me fixedly, his face slack and wooden. Then something swirled in the bottom of his eyes, crawled for the surface, and tried to speak. "You're . . . not . . . one. Of. Them." He cocked his head to the side, his throat swelling as he wrestled for control of his own voice. "Get. Get out. Out of here. I can't . . . hold . . ."

"He's riding you," I realized out loud. "You're a Feeder's mule. But you kept him down for ten years." I felt a thin burst of satisfaction at having guessed right, along with a flare of guilt for how stupid I'd been. It was all plain as day now.

"I *can't*—" Kellerman Lourdes gasped, spittle flying from his lips. He twisted, hunching down, some terrible battle being waged for control of his body. "I *can't stop him* now. You . . . run . . ."

Then his head jerked forward, like a snake's quick whipping strike. The fléchette in my left hand abruptly cooled, the cold stinging my fingers far more than heat would have. I held on, grimly. Waiting.

Then blue light bloomed from the circle of glyphs I'd scratched into the floor. The necklace, still in my pocket, fell as I shifted. It had burned a hole straight through the Kevlar-reinforced canvas of Jace's coat. It fell, the chain writhing like a live thing, and hit the floor with an oddly musical tinkle.

The circle cracked. Blue light flared like a thunderclap, and I saw Kellerman Lourdes's entire body jerk as ectoplasm streamed from mouth and nose and eyes and ears, a coughing mass of it. I dove back as Mirovitch's *ka* streaked for me, its inhuman hands turned into venom-dipped claws. Only this was not Mirovitch, the stoop-shouldered tweedy Feeder Headmaster who liked to prey on children.

This was the *ka,* grown monstrous and foul, Mirovitch seen through the eyes of a child, with claws and fangs and the leprous blue-burning eyes of a closet-hiding goblin.

I screamed, scrambling back, forgetting I was holding a sword. The backlash of the circle's cracking and breaking from inside poured up my spine and jerked a coughing yell from my throat as the Headmaster descended on me, his claws raking my belly, one catching in my ribs. A hot gush of demon blood boiled out, I convulsed, and Mirovitch dove for my open mouth, gagging reeking ectoplasm forcing down my throat.

36

*G*agging. Retching. Agony, as the claws tore in through my skin and organs, viscera spilling in a hot stream, my eyes bugging out as everything behind them *pushed* like depressurization.

"Student Valentine is called to the Headmaster's Office immediately."

Walking, every step a dread drumbeat, up the wooden stairs. Mirovitch's smile as his dry papery hand landed on my shoulder. We've got something special for those who break the rules today, Miss Valentine. *Meeting Roanna's eyes, feeling the sick thump of knowledge behind my breastbone. She'd told her social worker, and Mirovitch had found out.*

Jerking, crackling, her body on the fence, Mirovitch's fingers sinking into my arm as he dragged me back into Hell . . . and the brand, glowing red hot. Leather against my wrists as I screamed until my voice broke, after he was finished with me and the red-hot iron burned my skin as his semen trickled down my thighs; the chair's hard slat in my midriff, unable to breathe, the sound of his papery laughter filling the universe as that last shameful memory

*crashed out from behind the locked door—the door I'd
closed and locked when I left Rigger Hall, the door that
had to close so I could go on living. Surviving.*

Fingers. In my head. Scraping, tearing, ripping. *Burning.*
No wonder Christabel couldn't be brought back—

The alien thing in my mind recoiled. That thought
wasn't part of the feedback loop that would keep me helpless while it destroyed me. I grabbed onto it with the last
shipwrecked vestige of my strength, sank my mental teeth
into its hide, and began to *fight.*

*Polyamour, tilting her head so slightly. "You learn
early that your body betrays you—it's your mind that has
to stay impregnable. Your soul. To have that filthy old
maggot fingering inside your head . . ."*

It howled with rage, this thing bent on rape and destruction, and tore into me all the more savagely, battering
down even more mental doors, tearing great gaping holes
in my psyche.

And I fought back.

*Two dark eyes, the last flaring of emerald light in them.
Green eyes in a saturnine face, the demon's mouth warm
as he mouthed my neck, my shudder against him, spent,
his murmur in my ear.*

Memory, twisting and whirling, Putchkin Roulette
with the inside of my head, the *burning* as he forced his
way in, battering down doors, bursting locks, trying to
find . . . what?

*"Even the loa can't force a woman's heart . . ." If I
hadn't been part-demon, I would never have heard his
murmur. "I had to give it up, Danny. I had to. For you."*

It screamed, recoiling from that memory too. Of
course, the memory of Jace was underlaid with a clean

pure well of emotion, shame and love and guilt twisted together but still mine, still a source of strength, inimical to
the unholy thing. I had weapons, if I could just reach
them, find them, *use* them. Good things, anything.

Smoke belched up, the unholy sick blue light forcing
its way into me, lesions cracking on my skin, demon
blood boiling, trying to heal me.

A convulsive effort. I was winning, if I could only remember.

Remember, Christabel keened. *Remember everything.*

*Remember Jace's face, sleeping and peaceful in the
bed you shared with him so long ago. Remember Doreen's
soft touch, the light in her eyes. Remember Lewis's hand
in yours, so strong, so sure. Remember the books he gave
you, each one telling you that you were precious because
he trusted you. Remember Japhrimel's last sigh as he
sank down on your body. Remember reading under the
covers with your heart in your mouth and your breath
stale in your throat. Remember Gabe, doing for you what
you could not do for yourself. Remember Eddie, holding
your shoulders, remember Japhrimel throwing himself
between you and Santino, determined to protect you. Remember, Dante.*

Remember everything.

My fingers tightened on the fléchette. I gagged. Black
spots over my vision. Passing out. Oxygen . . . even a
demon needed some kind of air. And then what he did to
my mind would be done to my body.

—*fucker flayed her alive*—

Christabel's raw scream, the shattering of tiles as she
lunged for me. No wonder—even Death might not take
this agony from me.

But I would win. As long as I could *remember.*

Remember, Dante. Remember everything.

I flung the fléchette as I fell backward, the thing that was Mirovitch forcing its way into my mouth and nose, ramming its way into my mind. I struggled, the memories fading as I tried desperately to keep them, to keep them and to stand, to *endure.*

The splinter of metal and Power pierced the wall of blue glow, shone like a shard of ice, and glowed as it bulleted in a perfect arc—

—and buried itself in Kellerman Lourdes' neck. *Kill the mule and the Feeder should die, please, Anubis, please . . .*

It was the only way I knew of to kill a *ka.* I would win, if I could just hold on.

If I could just remember what mattered.

Falling, then. Falling, falling, *fell,* concrete smacking my head and back, its claws twisting in my belly but I could not scream, it was in my throat, pushed past my gag reflex, forcing its way in, my nose burning and stretching, it was tearing at my jeans with one probing finger of ectoplasm, *it'll get in any way it can,* convulsing, darkness not just spots but a glaucous sheet closing over my vision.

Remember, Dante. Remember. Christabel's voice, not insane with an apparition's flat terrible finality, but as if she stood next to me, a skinny girl with bruised knees and folded arms, terrible knowledge in her childlike dark eyes. *Remember. Remember.*

I could remember nothing but one last despairing cry. The name that beat behind my heart, inside my head, the prayer I had left when all else failed.

Japhri—

My left shoulder suddenly crunched with an agony even greater, as if my left arm was being torn out of its socket one hard millimeter at a time. I managed a strangled noise past the suffocating thing stuffing itself down my throat, black demon blood pattering on concrete, and then the world exploded.

Fire. Red fire.

I heard a sound like thunder smashing the jars of the universe, every star exploding and raining fiery destruction, the grinding of an earthquake and the crackle of ice calving on every mountainside at once. Then blessed cold air seared my throat.

Searing. It hurt almost as much as what Mirovitch had done, my body blindly scrabbling for survival, every demon-tainted, demon-strong cell fighting to *live*. The wet tearing sound as my battered viscera spilled back into my stomach cavity, bones crackling as the scream bubbled past ectoplasm in my throat, a burst of Power forcing its way along my skin.

Something had happened.

Remember, Dante. Remember. Christabel's voice, grown huge, a bell filling the world, as she stared at me with her dark eyes. *Remember. Remember.*

I rolled weakly onto my side, coughing, choking the smell of dust, chalk, and aftershave out of my mouth, blowing out through my nose, slick egg-white gobbets of ectoplasm streaming away and rotting in seconds. I retched again, but didn't throw up.

—*do part-demons throw up?* The thought made me laugh. I giggled, a high, thin sound of insanity, and made it to hands and knees. My belly ran with fire, tender tissues stretched and straining. Grabbed for my swordhilt.

Found it, my right hand curling around wrapped metal slick with noisome fluids, Power jolting up my arm with a force that made me cry out weakly. Then I collapsed again, my sword solid in my cramping right hand, my shattered shields trying to close over me, Power bleeding out into the night air. Another convulsion, my forehead smacking concrete, a grinding pain flared in my middle as my abused insides rebelled again.

"Dante." The voice was soft and full of fire, smooth like old brandy going down to ignite in the belly. "What have you done?"

I screamed again, weakly, scrabbling against the floor. Yet another convulsion racked me. I vomited a long jet of shuddering, writhing ectoplasm tinged with black, smoking demon's blood and immediately felt much better—only three-quarters dead and burning instead of all the way dead and insane to boot.

Warm fingers closed over the back of my neck, under my tangled hair. "Be still." And then an amazing bolt of Power lanced through me. My shields mended in one explosive flare, but the ragged bleeding wounds in my mind still smoked raw and deep.

On my side. Arms around me, the stroking of a warm hand on the side of my face. "Truly you are foolhardy, *hedaira*," he said softly. "I suppose you have your reasons. Be still, now."

But I struggled up, my body obeying me now, the tearing pain inside my chest now soothed. The whistling empty hole in my chest left by his absence, the hole I had stopped noticing, was gone. My left shoulder didn't hurt. Instead, the mark sent waves of hot, soft Power down my body, each a little warmer and deeper than the last. "No," I whispered, my voice a pained croak. Then I coughed and spat another amazing gob of ectoplasm to the side. It hit the floor with a dull *splat,* and my stomach turned violently again. "No. You *burned.*"

I raised my head.

His dark eyes met mine, just the same. A lean, saturnine face, his cheekbones balanced, his mouth a straight unforgiving line. The demon Tierce Japhrimel touched my cheek, his knuckles brushing my skin. The contact sent a shudder through me, my body recognizing him before the rest of me could dare to. "You burned," I managed, before another fit of retching and gagging shook me. "You burned—you were *ash*—"

"While you live, I live." The corners of his mouth turned down, an expressive movement that managed to give the impression of a grim smile. "I suppose nobody told you."

I shook my head weakly. His smell—the scent of a demon, cinnamon incense, amber musk—wrapped around me, filled my lungs. I felt like I could breathe again, without every breath being tainted by the stench of dying cells. The smell of him seemed to coat my abused insides with peace, and flow down into the middle of my body to spread through my veins. "I tried," I whispered. "Books—Magi." I filled my lungs again. While I could, before what was undoubtedly a hallucination vanished. Gasped again, a great rasping breath blessedly free of the stink of dying human cells.

Human. *Human* cells. The thought of humans reminded me of where I was.

I tried to scramble to my feet but he caught me, his

strength embarrassingly more than mine, especially at the moment. "Be still. There is no danger."

"But . . . the . . . *Mirovitch*—"

"Is that his name?" Japhrimel moved aside slightly.

Spread-eagled on the floor, coated with ectoplasm, was Kellerman Lourdes. He looked dazed, his eyes rolled back into his head, his body limp. I could see one leg was twisted the wrong way, it looked like a fracture of the lower femur. I flinched. The pool of goo coating him pulsed, and as I looked Kellerman opened his mouth to scream. The cracked bone started to mend itself, creaking and snapping.

Christabel's voice still echoed in my head like a gong, like the circuit of Fate completing itself.

Remember, Dante. Remember for us.

My stomach rose in revolt again, was ordered back down, and subsided. Japhrimel's hands were at my shoulders. "Dante? I suppose you would not care to explain." He sounded mild, but the fractional lift of one eyebrow told me he was very close to violence.

My eyes drank him in. If he was a hallucination, I wanted to store every detail. But there was no *time*— Lourdes gurgled, a sound of choked agony.

"Up. Help me up."

My hallucination of my dead demon lover stared at me, his dark eyes thoughtful. Once they had been a brilliant piercing green, like Lucifer's eyes. But when he had made me into whatever I was now, his eyes had gone dark. Without the incandescent light behind them, they looked like ageless human eyes, infinite in their depth and as familiar to me as my own. Hot tears rose, I pushed them down.

Lourdes curled into a fetal position, some inhuman effort pushing him over, up on his hands and knees. Then he collapsed, broken as a rag doll, his half-mended leg twisted impossibly to one side. He rasped out something indecipherable. The blue glow pulsed. Lourdes screamed with a human voice, the end of the scream trailing off into a writhing gurgle.

"Explain *later*," I said, every word an effort. "Help me up *now*."

As usual, Japhrimel wasted little time with human questions. Instead, he hauled me up effortlessly. The long, high-collared black coat he wore was the same, wings masquerading as clothing, but instead of black jeans he wore a very dark blue denim and worker's boots, new and unscarred. It was the same, yet different.

Flakes of the ectoplasm drifted to the floor, cracking and crackling on my skin and clothes. "You found me." The words broke on a sob. I had thought I'd destroyed any chance of his resurrection. That was my penance. What was I going to do now?

"Of course. You bear my mark. Did you think me dead, Dante?"

Yeah, for almost a year you looked pretty damn dead, you looked like a pile of fucking ash and Lucifer kept sending me letters. "You're going to have to explain this," I muttered, as if I believed he was real. He moved gracefully aside, I started limping toward Kellerman. My right leg dragged a little, not quite obeying me. I was in a sorry state. Hallucination-Japhrimel stayed on my left side, out of the way of my swordhand, his hand weightless on my shoulder, those soft intense waves of Power pulsing down my body. Repairing. Mending.

I wondered if Power alone could heal my mind.

I didn't allow myself to look up at Japhrimel. If I looked, would I find out he wasn't there, and this just another hallucination, my starved brain dreaming in color and holo before dying? Even demons needed air, I wondered if a strangled and mindraped almost-demon would have a deathdream.

Was I still alive? Or were starbursts of blood rising to the surface of my brain, so that when they autopsied me Caine would say, *A classic example of psychic assault resulting in death* in his dry disdainful voice?

Caine would probably enjoy cutting me open.

I looked down at Kellerman Lourdes. He convulsed again, his leg straightening, the bone sounding as if it was shattering to tie itself back together. My right hand twitched, bringing the tip of my sword up. Blue light ran down the blade, a healthier shade of blue than Mirovitch's diseased glow.

His eyes rolled back down, and it was Lourdes, craning his head up and to the side, looking at me with human eyes. He stared up at me. His lips tried to shape the word, *who?*

Oh, gods. "Danny Valentine," I husked. "Couple years behind you, Keller. We never talked."

Comprehension lit his eyes. He dropped his head. "Pl-please," he rasped. "Before *he* comes back . . ."

"You're a Feeder, and a mule," I said. "There's no cure. Not at this stage."

Weariness settled over his face. Weariness, and a bravery that hurt me a little to see. "Do . . . it. Are . . . any . . . left?"

"Polyamour—*Bastian*. And three more." I lifted my sword a little, paused. "One question. *Why?*"

I had to know.

"Revenge . . ." His eyes fluttered again. "I . . . Took *him*. The others . . . couldn't. I took . . . the last . . . piece. Should have . . . killed myself. Couldn't . . ."

Of course not. By the time Keller knew what he carried, knew that Mirovitch wasn't dead, the *ka* would have had its hooks in deep. Keller could not destroy himself once the *ka* reawakened.

I thought of Gabe at Jace's bedside, doing what I could not. One act of bitter mercy for me, one for Keller. Even, each side of the scale balancing. I swallowed, tasted bile. Filled my lungs. The smell of rotting ectoplasm, dying human cells, and the Headmaster's cloying reek warred with the smoky fragrance of demon. Japhrimel's aura, twisting diamond flames, covered mine, the mark at my shoulder spreading and staining through my battered shielding, melding together the rips and holes. When it finished, I would have a demon's shielding again.

Christabel's voice faded. *Remember,* she whispered. *Remember everything.*

Was she real, or a memory? Was she here, invisible to me? And if she was, who else was with her? Every child damaged by Rigger Hall, or just one?

Just me?

My sword swung up, both hands locked around the hilt. I braced myself, my right leg threatening to buckle. "It's over," I whispered. "Be at peace, Kellerman Lourdes."

How many times at hospital beds had I said those same words, now bitter in my mouth, tainted with death? Necromances were brought to the side of the dying, to offer comfort and ease the transition. And not so incidentally, to make sure the deceased didn't come back.

He must be wielded with honor, but more important, with compassion. Compassion is not your strongest virtue, Danyo-chan. Jado's voice whispered, memory bleeding through the present like sluggish water through a filth-choked ditch.

Compassion? For Lourdes or for me, or for both of us? Or for every damaged soul shattered by Rigger Hall?

For all of them, then. For Roanna, for Aran Helm, for Dolores. For Christabel, who had left me the clue for whatever reason, whether adolescent hubris or nascent precognition. Whether she was haunting me or whether some other intelligence had her voice and was spurring me to finish this didn't matter. It was the mercy that mattered. Mercy for all the survivors, for Eddie and Polyamour.

For all of them, and for me.

And for him most of all, the invisible kid who had thrown himself in harm's way to save us all just as Jace had thrown himself forward to save me. All accounts balanced, except for the low sound of a swordblade as it clove the air and closed the circle.

Lourdes closed his eyes. But then they popped open, the cold blue glow filling them; Mirovitch looking out through Keller's eyes.

Compassion is not your strongest virtue, Danyo-chan.

Yes, it is, I told myself. *Gods grant I don't forget it. For all of them. For all the children.* I swung my sword down. It was a clean cut, with all my force behind it, gauged with perfect accuracy. My *kia* rose, short and sharp as a falcon's cry or the deathscream of an alley cat. Blood fountained up; arterial spray. Japhrimel pulled me back as the high-tension jet bloomed from Lourdes' neck. The sword shrieked, sparking, an intense blue-white streak of living metal. Blood flew free of steel, the blade clean and shining, muscle memory carrying it back into the sheath with a click, all in one move.

A shattering psychic wail rose as Mirovitch scrabbled blindly for life, the *ka* frantically seeking something, anything to latch onto, to replicate itself, ectoplasm bubbling and burning. I sagged against Japhrimel's shoulder. He again didn't ask any useless questions, just stood watchful as the pressure behind the bloodspray lessened. The tide of blood mixed with the ectoplasm, and I smelled the reek of released bowels.

"Japhrimel." My voice caught. "Burn him. Please. Every bit."

I didn't have to ask twice. The Fallen demon raised his golden hand, and fire leapt to obey him. It dug into the concrete, red liquid demon flame, drops of blood spat and sizzled. A breath of sick-sweet smell like roasted pork filled the air. Shadows writhed and jabbed against the cafeteria's dark walls. Heat boiled up, making the linoleum char and the paint on the ceiling bubble and blister.

Finally, the flame died down. I turned my face into Japhrimel's shoulder. "You're going to disappear," I said into his coat, not even caring that I knew what it was made of. "Just stay for a moment, just please just for a minute, a second—"

"Dante." His fingers came up, tangled in my already-tangled hair. "I heard you calling me. I tried to answer."

"Just for a few seconds." I buried my face in his coat, his other arm closed around me. I inhaled the smell of cinnamon, of amber musk, the deadly smoky nonphysical fragrance of demons. Filled my lungs with the breath of life. "Before I have to burn this whole fucking place down."

"Be still," he answered. "I am here, I have never left your side. I told you, you will not leave me to wander the earth alone."

I closed my eyes. The strength spilled out of my legs. Mirovitch was dead, Kellerman Lourdes was dead.

Jace was dead. The circle, closed.

My knees buckled. Japhrimel caught me, murmured into my hair. I started to cry. The sobs shook me as if a vicious animal had me in its teeth. There, with the bloody smoke filling the cafeteria, the scorched ash that had once been Kellerman Lourdes stirred only by a faint breeze passing through the shattered plaswood-covered windows. I did not stop crying until, exhausted, I passed into a kind of gray deathly haze broken only by the slight murmurs of Japhrimel's voice as he carried me away from that place of death—and the sound of rushing flame as he did what I asked and leveled the whole nightmare of Rigger Hall to the ground.

37

Sunlight spilled through the station house windows, but in Gabe's cubicle the glow of a full-spectrum bulb painted the air. Paper stirred on her desk, and the two empty brandy bottles were in the wastebasket with a drift of frozen gray cigarette smoke turned to ash.

"You caused a helluva lot of damage," Gabe said, her arms folded. "You *razed* Rigger Hall, there isn't a stick left. We didn't even get to recover a body. We only have your word—"

"Have there been any more murders?" I asked. "No? Good."

She sighed. "I believe you, Danny. I just . . . god-dammit. Did you know? Did you know it was a Feeder's *ka* for sure?"

I shrugged, looking down at her desk. What could I tell her? The circle had been mine to close. Had I been the only one strong enough to close it, or had I just been picked by blind chance?

Did it matter? It was over. It was *done*. I no longer heard Christabel's whispering in my head. Wherever she was, I hoped she was resting more comfortably.

Phones rang in the background, I heard someone's raised voice—the punchline of a joke. Guffaws greeted the attempt. My nose filled with the scent of humans, and my own fragrance rose to battle the stench.

I knew enough to do that, now.

"I'm sorry, Gabe. He was . . . it was . . ." My sword, lying scabbarded across my knees, rang softly. I pushed a strand of inky hair back, tucked it behind my ear. "Anyone else would have been a liability instead of a help, you know that. He would have killed a hell of a lot of cops if you'd gone in to take him down." Amazingly, my voice didn't crack. I swallowed. "Keller must have been an incipient, natural Feeder. Taking from Mirovitch triggered that propensity, but the *ka* was dormant and he might have thought he was safe. He held out for ten years, thinking Mirovitch was dead, getting as far away from Saint City and Rigger Hall as he could. His uncle even went to work in the Putchkin under diplomatic contract—I'd guess to get Keller away." *Leaving no trail for us, because all diplomatic-visa workers have their personal information under blind trusts.*

"And then, Mirovitch finally breaks free." Gabe shuddered. "Hades."

I nodded. "The necklaces were an etheric link: nice, passive, and undetectable. Mirovitch would drive his mule right up to their doors. He didn't have to crack their shielding—that was done from inside, by the necklaces themselves. Fed by the very glyphs Keller had taught them. They thought they were protecting themselves from Mirovitch's echo—but that very defense killed them." *And Mirovitch pawed through their minds to get the pieces of himself they'd torn away. No wonder none of the*

*victims were able to talk—that kind of psychic rape right
before death echoes for a long time.*

That was what had saved me, the fact that there was no
piece of Mirovitch inside my head for him to retrieve, my
refusal to give in. The simple act of remembering.

That, and Japhrimel.

I shivered, thinking again of the clawed maggot fingers
blindly squirming inside my head. My skin went cold,
and the mark on my shoulder pulsed once, flushing me
with heat. I straightened in the chair again, looking down
at the lacquered scabbard. My reflection, ghostly and distorted, stared back at me with wide dark eyes.

"Why kill the uncle, then?" Gabe shifted her weight,
leaning back slightly and regarding me. I looked up and
saw without any real surprise the touch of gray at her left
temple. It was only a few strands, and she had a lot of
fight left in her.

I shrugged. "Here in Saint City, the uncle was a liability. If anyone started tracing former Rigger students, the
uncle probably knew enough for an investigator to get the
picture with the right questions. Either that or the uncle
found out. We'll never know. That's why the shields on
Smith's house were intact—Keller didn't need to rip them
to get out."

And without Christabel's clue, I might not have caught
on so quickly. Had she been looking over my shoulder? I
didn't care to guess. That was one mystery I was happy to
consign to the gray land of *just-don't-think-about.*

Silence stretched between us, a taut humming full of
other questions. Other things neither of us could ever say.
She didn't ask where I'd vanished to for three days after
Rigger Hall was leveled, didn't ask where I had washed

up, and especially didn't ask me if I was okay. Instead, she kept her distance, a brittle fragile professionalism presented to me during the two hours of my taped statement and this less-formal wrap-up. Case closed. Crime solved.

Game over.

"Danny." Gabe leaned her hip on her desk, regarding me with her pretty, serene eyes. "You're . . . different. I . . . Look, I know what Jace meant to you. If you want to talk, if you need anything—"

I nodded. "I'll call," I promised.

I saw the crows'-feet at the corners of her eyes, the fine lines beginning to take over her face. Gabe was getting too old for the Saint City Parapsych crap. She was a cop right down to her bones; she'd take it all the way up to retirement and probably do security work afterward—but she was tired. Too tired, even though she had her own deep share of stubbornness.

And me? I wouldn't age. I would look just the same. And when Gabe died, who would I have left that remembered?

When she no longer remembered *me,* would I be dead too?

"Gabe?" I made it to my feet in one movement, caught myself. My right leg was still a little unsteady, despite my body's fantastic ability to heal. I struggled to find the words I wanted, failed, tried again. "Look, I just . . . be careful, all right? Take care of yourself."

"You sound like you're going to your own execution instead of on vacation." She laughed, her shoulders had relaxed. She was possibly looking at a promotion from this case. The most tangible benefit she'd received was a gold medallion and a silver credit disc. The credit disc would get her into Nikolai's office building downtown if she ever needed help. The gold medallion was an award for "superlative police work." Add to that a fat raise she didn't need and the goodwill of the Prime Power of Saint City, and she was as well-off as I could possibly hope for. I could rest for a little while, knowing she was safe.

I had one last question. "How's Eddie?"

She shrugged. "Okay. Dealing with it, I guess."

I nodded. That was good news."Tell him . . . Tell him I killed Mirovitch myself. He isn't coming back." My stomach fluttered briefly, the papery whisper of Mirovitch's voice echoing in the darker corners of my mind. "Tell him Dante gives her word Mirovitch is *dead*."

It was her turn to nod, thoughtfully, the emerald on her cheek flashing. "Danny." Her voice was soft, as if she'd forgotten we were standing in her office. "Look, I . . . I'm really sorry. If you . . . I mean, you—"

I felt my face tighten. I stepped forward, balanced on both feet, and put my sword down deliberately on the chair I'd just vacated. Then I spread my arms. She stared at me for a second, jaw dropping, and then moved haltingly forward, flinging her arms around me. She was so short her chin rested against the top slope of one of my breasts, but I hugged her anyway, carefully. She squeezed me with all her wiry strength, earning a slight huff of breath out of my lungs for her efforts. "You're my friend, Gabe," I whispered, my ruined voice creaking and breaking. "*Mainuthsz*."

"*Mainuthsz*," she echoed. Then she sniffed, as if her nose was full. "You'd better believe it. Go on, go on your vacation. And if you need me, call me."

"Likewise. Give Eddie my best." We untangled ourselves. I scooped up my sword. Turned away. Took four steps.

Taking the fifth step, out of her cubicle, was the hardest thing I'd done so far.

I did it, and was just about to turn the corner when she called out.

"Danny? One last question."

I looked back over my shoulder, brushing my hair back with my left hand, the sword's scabbard bumping my cheek, my emerald spitting a single spark.

Gabe leaned against her desk again, her arms folded. Tears glimmered on her cheeks, her eyes were red and overflowing. She looked wavery through the welling water in my own eyes. "Why did you burn your house, Dante?"

What could I tell her? In the end, I settled for a simple answer.

"That was a toll. A toll paid to the dead." I felt the smile tilt the corners of my mouth up even as a tear slid down, touching my emerald and rolling across my Necromance tat. "Gods grant they stay there. Goodbye, Gabriele. May Hades watch over you."

Outside, the sky was cloudy, night falling early as it always does in winter. There were no holovid reporters—they were busy covering a scandal (having to do with a judicial candidate, three hookers, two million credits, and a plasgun) in the North District. I was now, to my profound and everlasting relief, yesterday's news and probably already forgotten by a great many people.

A gleaming black hoverlimo broke free of its holding pattern overhead and drifted down, landing with a sigh of

leafsprings, the side hatch opening. I barely waited for it
to open all the way before I climbed up, ducking through
the airseals into climate control and filling my lungs.

Inside, everything was crystal and pale pleather, gleaming softly. Fitted into a rack on the wall was a twisted,
scarred *dotanuki*, its blackened blade still seeming to vi-
brate with the last strike made against an enemy it had no
hope of defeating. If Japhrimel had been there, Mirovitch
couldn't have attacked me—and Jace would probably still
be alive.

The sharp pinch of guilt under my breastbone retreated.
I would pay my penance in my own way, in my own time.
For right now, I couldn't stand to think about it.

I made a slight sound, wiping my cheek with the back
of my right hand.

Japhrimel sat tensely on one side. I made my way over
to him as the hatch closed. The whine of hovercells
crested, rattling my teeth as it always did, and my stomach flipped as the hover ascended smoothly.

I dropped down onto the pleather seat next to him, letting out a sigh that seemed to crack my ribs.

"You are done?" He sounded as flat and ironic as he
had when I'd met him; he stared straight ahead, giving me
his profile. It had taken some doing to convince him to
stay out of sight in the hover while I finished the hunt I'd
started. He had remarked dryly and fiercely that after
coming back to physical life, tracking me through Saint
City, and finding me trying to fight off Mirovitch, he now
knew what fear was, having never felt it in all the long
time of his life as a demon.

The admission, pulled out of him as if by force, had

broken me into a sobbing heap. And he had agreed to let me finish up with Gabe alone.

"That was the last bit of business," I said. "The case is closed. Gabe can go on now. And nobody needs to know about you. It would just raise more questions."

"Hm." He opened his arm as I slid next to him. I settled against his side, letting out another deep sigh as his familiar heat and aura closed over me. I laid my head on his shoulder and was rewarded with the pressure of his cheek against the top of my head, a subtle caress. "And you?"

I shut my eyes. It seemed they were leaking again. I had thought I was done with crying. "I thought you were dead," I said for the hundredth time. "I keep thinking you'll vanish, and I'll wake up."

"I told you, while you live, I live." He sounded calmer now, the tension leaving him. He settled back into the seat, and I leaned into him, grateful. "I would not abandon you, Dante."

"So if I'd dumped the . . . the *remains* into a vat of blood, would it have . . . brought you back?" A flare of embarrassment stained my cheeks with heat. It had been hard to leave him in the hover while I went into the police station; I still wasn't sure he was real. The throbbing of his mark on my shoulder, sending waves of heat through me, had remained a steady reassurance. But I wanted to hear him tell me again, I wanted him to keep talking, and above all else I wanted to feel his arm around me and feel the proof and comfort of his skin on mine.

He repeated his answer for me, again. "Most likely. The first . . . resurrection . . . is always the hardest."

"The fire, and the shields on my house collapsing—"

"I am here, am I not?" Now he sounded amused. He

stroked my cheek, and my breath caught. It was almost enough to drown out the persistent scratching sound of Mirovitch's last scream. "It was not so long a time, Dante. Not for us."

"Long enough," I muttered, my heart twisting again. "And if I'd known—if someone would have *told* me— Jace would still be alive."

"You said yourself the god denied you entrance into death. Perhaps it was his time." Japhrimel now sounded thoughtful. His coat shifted slightly as he moved against the seat. The driver made one low swooping turn over the city, banking to head southeast. The setting sun glittered on the water, rippling on the bay's surface, the shadows of transport hovers like the shapes of great fish drifting against the ground. I sat up to look out the window past his profile, studying the familiar geography of Saint City falling away under the hover while he studied my right hand loosely clasped in his left, lying in his lap. "I am sorry. I should have sought to tell you more."

"There wasn't time while we were hunting Santino. It doesn't matter." It did matter, but who was I to tell him that? If he wasn't going to make a fuss over me leaving him for dead in a burning house, I wasn't going to blame him for not having a chance to tell me more about what I was. Even enough for me, for once. More than I deserved. "Where are we going?" And the more important question, "Are you . . . are you angry with me?"

Anubis help me, I still sounded like a kid. Could he forgive me for using Jace to remind myself of what I used to be? Could he forgive me for loving a human, even if it was no match for whatever it was I felt for him?

A demon.

My demon. One of the many. Only this one, I hoped, wouldn't hurt me.

He stirred slightly, freeing his left hand to gently cup my chin, forcing my eyes to meet his. A spark of green flared to life in his dark eyes, like a flash at the bottom of a deep, old well. "You are asking if I am jealous. I recall a certain swordfight not too long ago, and the outcome—and my warning you not to use me to make the Shaman jealous."

I was glad part-demons didn't blush. At least, I hoped I didn't. My cheeks were on fire. The green spark vanished, leaving his eyes dark and thoughtful as they had been since his resurrection; his skin on mine made pleasant shivers rill down my spine. Seeing him brought home how little I knew about him—and how little I knew about what he'd made me into.

A *hedaira*.

Whatever that was. Maybe now I could learn what it meant.

His thumb stroked my cheek. My eyes half-closed. When he spoke next, it was very softly, his voice an almost-physical caress against my whole body. My flesh tightened like a harpstring. I swallowed hard against the wave of liquid heat. "How can I possibly be jealous when I know you spent your time grieving for me, Dante?"

That reminded me of something else. "Lucifer," I reminded him. "He said he'd been trying to contact you. That was the first clue I had that . . . "

Japhrimel shrugged. "What do you owe him?" He leaned closer, a fraction of an inch at a time. My heart sped up, anticipation beating just under my skin with my pulse.

I swallowed dryly. My eyes were dry and grainy, and bright diamond needles of pain sometimes rippled through my head. I couldn't think of Jace without my chest hurting and my eyes filling—couldn't think of Rigger Hall without shuddering, my hands shaking like windblown leaves. It would take time for the effects of Mirovitch's mental assault to fade, time for my almost-demon body to heal. It would be quick, Japhrimel told me—but his idea of quick wasn't exactly mine. Yet.

And being near him would speed the healing even more. But the grief and the guilt, would those go away? Did I want them to, would I still be *human* if I no longer felt that pain?

"Dante?" Japhrimel asked.

"Last time I checked, I was even with the Devil. He got the Egg back." My breath hitched in, almost a silent gasp. *Though he's been sending me letters. If he sends another one, Japhrimel, will you throw it away? Or will you open it? And if he knows you're alive, what will the letter say?*

I couldn't bring myself to worry about it.

"Then let him wait," Japhrimel said, and his mouth touched mine. I didn't ask him again where we were going.

It didn't matter.

THE NINE CANONS: AN INTRODUCTION

Lecture at the Stryker Lee Hegemony
School of Psionic Arts

Are we all present, then? Or at least physically here? (*Faint laughter.*) Very well. Let's start immediately, shall we?

Writing is an old art, one of the oldest abstract arts known to man. We presently believe the Sumerians to be the first to practice it, but given the perishable nature of much written work we may have overlooked other civilizations entirely—including the theory that somehow demons learned writing first and taught it to humans. (*More faint laughter.*) I see the Magi students are not chortling. Good.

The cuneiform of the Sumerians represents for us a critical development in human understanding: the need to convey reality with symbols.

Ever since its inception, writing has been regarded as an art that smacks of the magickal. For example, a large part of Egyptianica sorcery was focused on writing. The *Book of the Dead* (here I refer to both the Egyptianica and Tibetan manuscripts of the same name) qualifies as an act of religion, which in several important aspects is indistinguishable from an act of sorcery, not the least in which it presumes that the written or spoken word—human language itself—can alter the behavior of an immutable law (namely, death), and another state of being, the afterlife. We are all familiar with the concept of Logos here, the magical act of naming to enforce one's will on the world? Good.

It is *critical* to understand one simple thing about the

Canons. This is a magickal law you have had drilled into you ad nauseum, and I will repeat it again.

There is no such thing as an empty word. Write that down, underline it, brand it into your memory. The psionic arts are tightly regulated and accredited practitioners are held to a high standard because of this simple fact. Word wedded to will—intent, that is—produces change in reality, which is the heart of even simple sorcery. Words are an extension of action; an action wedded to intent is sympathetic magick, the First Great Branch of sorcery. The Second Branch, encompassed by but distinct from the First, is runewitchery and other magickal writing. The propagandists of the twentieth century fumbled with this law, and their shortcomings as well as triumphs will be studied later this semester.

Let us take a short look at the Canon itself before we dive into theory, shall we?

The Nine Canons we have now had their nucleus in *one* Canon, from a manuscript dating to just prior the Seventy Days War. As you will no doubt recall, just prior to the War, the Awakening was beginning, and a renascence of occult knowledge as well as workable techniques for controlling Power were flourishing, both in the subversive stratum of noncitizenry in the Republic of Gilead as well as in what we now refer to as the Putchkin Alliance. This particular Canon, today known as the Jessenblack Runes and the first half-canto of the Nine, was codified by a nameless person in Stambul. It was first distributed among the ceremonial magicians in that city as a set of broadsheets, stapled together and extremely perishable. The great revolution in the Jessenblack Runes was their accessibility—they are never more than two syllables, and were distilled from several different occult traditions. They are more properly glyphs than runes—Question? No? Very well.

We know very little about who discovered the actual technique for distilling a rune, but history has provided us with some interesting candidates, any one of whom would be an excellent subject choice for your term paper, by the way. Let us explode one myth right now: Saint Crowley the Magi had nothing to do with the Jessenblacks, though his strain of magickal theory certainly fed the spirit of experimentation that bore such fruit during the Awakening itself.

The easiest and best theory is that the Jessenblacks were simply in the right place at the right time. Due to the explosion of psionic ability during the Awakening, any set of runes would have done just as well. However, the Jessenblacks were easy, they were simple, and they worked nine times out of ten—which is far more than many other pre-Awakening occult practitioners could say.

The rest of the Canons were added in dribs and drabs over the next century of magickal experimentation, leaving us with the Nine we know today, which encompass by themselves an entire branch of magick. Not only that, but the fact that the Nine have been used by so many psions for so long has given them a quantum increase in the amount of untapped Power each rune possesses.

This is of course a simplification. The Canons are not powerful in and of themselves. Like any symbol, they are fueled by human intent. Think of it this way, especially those of you talented as runewitches: The Nine Canons are a set of doors. It remains up to you to expend the effort of opening the door. Once opened, the door will stay open as long as you hold it, and the combined weight of expectation—of Power—built up over successive uses of the rune is there to be tapped.

Now, can anyone tell me what holds the door open? Yes, Miss Valdez? (*Indistinct murmur.*) Very good!

Your sorcerous Will holds the door open, which is why practice is so important to runewitchery. This is a feedback cycle. Your Will is strengthened and trained by attention and practice, allowing you to hold the door open and incidentally adding the weight of your expectation to the symbol countless other psions have used. This is the reason the Canons are required study for every psion, not just runewitches or Ceremonials.

Now, if you will open your books to page eleven, we will begin the first Canto . . .

(*Fadeout.*)

NEITHER FRIEND NOR FOE

Term Paper: Magi Studies 403

East Merican Hegemony Academy of Psionic Arts

Dacon Whitaker

The current strain of Magi thought has undergone a complete reverse in past years. This paper examines the attitudes most current among active Magi practitioners and touches on how this change came about.

The pre-Awakening view of demons was hazy in the extreme, tainted by the Religions of Submission. Of all spiritual practices, only Vaudun and Santeriana came close to a workable theory of interaction with noncorporeal or sometimes-noncorporeal beings. This had begun to change by the end of the twenty-first century, when a vibrant counterculture existed, most notably of those studying Saint Crowley's work. However, the Republic of Gilead interrupted most serious experimentation in this area, and the confusion of the Seventy Days War, as well as the social and economic dislocation caused by the Awakening, further interfered.

Between the Awakening and the advent of Adrienne Spocarelli's work, demons were defined as primarily noncorporeal as well as ethically unsound and morally capricious—in essence, trickster demigods, against whom humans are essentially powerless and can only beg for favors from. Magi theory at that time held that whatever place demons existed in prior to and after their visits to our physical plane was an environment unsuitable to flesh-and-blood beings. This attitude was widespread even though Broward, in his classic study, points out that demons do indeed seem to breathe and bleed (witness the woodcuts of the Sterne collection and the holostill captures of the Manque Incident.) Broward's observations were treated with the assumption that when demons enter our physical plane, they take on a physical body and so, can be hurt. (Adrienne Spocarelli, in her famous essay *What's Flesh Got To Do With It?*, remarked wryly that a thermonuclear strike might even work to kill a demon—with a whole lot of luck.)

It was Spocarelli's work with a reliable method of calling and constraining imps that finally answered the question. Spocarelli claims to have been able to induce an imp to write in Merican on the hardwood floor of her study inside a circle; the imp's claws would scratch out a word or two in response to her carefully-phrased questions. The complete transcript sounds like a conversation between a lawyer and a mischievous five-year-old, but several important points can be deduced.

First of all, whatever place demons come from, they *are* physical there as well as here. Much ink and breath has been wasted on trying to determine actually *where* they come from, whether different plane, dimension, planet, or simply state of being; Spocarelli's greatest revolution was declaring that she didn't care where they came from, she simply wanted to find out how they affected *our* home plane and planet—and why they seem so damn interested in it. As physical beings, they only seem to violate natural laws; in reality, they may well be made of a stuff that conforms to different laws only because of its basic alienness but conforms to laws all the same. In other words, just because hover technology superseded petrolo does not mean that either violated natural law. And just because demons supersede humans in magickal technology does not mean that human or demons violate natural laws.

Spocarelli's other great revolution is so simplistic as to seem obvious and is predicated on the first. While other practitioners looked upon demonic lying with several layers of shock and disapproving prudery, she pointed out that demonic *culture* may be so different from ours as to make their "lying" simply a different set of social interaction rules. If they are physical sentient beings, they have a culture; if they have a culture, they may even have prohibitions against whatever they define as "lying." All verbal brinksmanship on both sides aside, Spocarelli declared that she wanted to discover how and why demons are seemingly addicted to interaction with humanity, and that it might be worthwhile to apply anthropological and archeological tools as well as magickal theory to our interactions with demonkind.

The effect of this simple suggestion cannot be overestimated. At one stroke, Spocarelli disposed of any lingering superstitious worship of demons, reducing them to the level of beings that could be studied with scientific techniques; she also made it possible, though reactionaries loudly trumpet against her, to put the Magi in a position of power instead of supplication when it came to these beings.

The next thing that can be deduced from Spocarelli's transcript of the imp's replies is this: demons are as fascinated by humans as we are by them.

Spocarelli, while often scoffing at the notion of demonic involvement in human evolution, nevertheless does not completely rule it out. Again, she is utilitarian: whatever involvement demons might have had in shaping human genetic code is irrelevant at this juncture. What matters is that they are now seemingly enthralled by and disdainful of humanity at the same time, much as Nichtvren are. But while Nichtvren have the advantage of once being human, demons do not. Why, then, are they so fascinated?

Even pre-Awakening sources (Caplan, Perezreverte, Saint Crowley, Saint Goethe, and the anonymous author of the Illuminatis Papers, to name a very few) agree that demons are possessive and controlling in the extreme. A human who catches a demon's attention does not easily escape meddling. Even Spocarelli herself seems to have had some murky trouble with a particular demon, though reports of this are sketchy at best and mixed up with legends about other members of her famous family.

Perezreverte, in his classic *Nine Gates*, postulates that demons are hungry for human adulation, that it feeds them in some way. This is sound magickal theory and a good working hypothesis, even if demons presumably had other means of gaining Power before the advent of humanity. Perezreverte also seems to think demons are lonely, sometimes bored with their own kind, and turn to humanity for momentary diversion. He seems to give some credence to the ancient tales of fleshwives, though any mention of *that* myth tends to drive Magi to fits of frustration. Dealing with demons is hard enough without pulling in outright fabrication to muddy the issue.

This leaves us with something important to remember: We simply do not know what demonic motivation is yet. They are jealous and possessive when they deign to take notice of humanity, and the Circles working with Lesser Flight demons often note how one or more Magi within the circle will be singled out for positive or negative attention, often with almost-disastrous results on the Circle's cohesive magickal Will necessary to keep a demon under control (if such a thing can ever be said to be done.)

The logical extension to these new strains of thought is a deeper examination of reported instances of demon behavior, especially when the demon attaches himself to a particular human, whether as familiar or nemesis. Many Magi circles are reporting positive signs in dealing with imps and certain Lower Flight demons with anthropological cultural-sensitivity guidelines establishing their behavior. The amount of information available about demon anatomy and hierarchy has quintupled since Adrienne Spocarelli's time, and instances of severe harassment seem to be on the decline. However, this may not prove anything, as Circles are not likely to report ignominious failures, and actively demon-harassed Magi rarely live long enough to report their experience.

To sum up, having accumulated enough data since the Awakening, the Magi community was simply ripe for someone to put into words a few laws about dealing with demons in a way free of pre-Awakening superstition. Genius often consists of simply seeing what was there before, something Spocarelli seems to have excelled at. On the other hand, her utilitarianism has earned her severe criticism, mostly from hard-core academes who consider her as throwing the baby out with the bathwater and not practicing proper caution. On the other hand, Spocarelli survived far past the median age for actively demon-consorting, solitary Magi. She must have been doing something right.

We do not yet know why demons are so fascinated

with humanity, or whether they are at heart friendly or inimical to human interest. The gamut of opinion runs from
the ever-cautious old-fashioned Magi who think extreme
caution must be taken to defend the greater mass of
humanity from demonkind to those who insist that it is
humanity's prerogative to bargain with demonkind for su-
perior magickal training and technology, to the benefit of
both sides.

Whether friend or foe, demonic intervention in human
affairs does not seem likely to cease. And that is the
strongest reason for the Magi to continue research, to find
out exactly what they want from us.

Note: The electronic notation on this document reads:
"B-. Wonderful paper, Mr. Whitaker. Who wrote it for
you?"

Glossary

Animone: an accredited psion with the ability to telepathically connect with and heal animals, generally employed as veterinarians

Anubis et'her ka: Egyptianica term, sometimes used as expletive; loosely translated,"Anubis protect me/us"

A'nankhimel: (*demon term*) 1. a Fallen demon 2. a demon who has tied him/herself to a human mate 3. chained 4. shield

Awakening, the: the exponential increase in psionic and sorcerous ability, academically defined as from just before the fall of the Republic of Gilead to the culmination of the Parapsychic Act (codifying psionic power) and the Paranormal Species Act (giving protection and voting rights to paranormal species), a dual triumph for the alternately vilified and worshipped Senator Adrien Ferriman. *Note: After the fall of the Republic, the Awakening was said to have finished and the proportion of psionics to normals in the human population stabilized, though there are fluctuations occurring in seventy-year cycles to this day.*

Ceremonial 1. an accredited psion whose talent lies in

working with traditional sorcery, accumulating Power and "spending" it in controlled bursts 2. Ceremonial magick, otherwise known as sorcery instead of more-organic witchery 3. (*slang*) Any Greater Work of magick

Clormen-13 (*Slang: Chill, ice, rock, smack, dust*) addictive alkaloid drug *Note: Chill is high-profit for the big pharmaceutical companies as well as the Mob, being instantly addictive. There is no cure for Chill addiction.*

Deadhead: 1. Necromance 2. normal human without psionic abilities

Demon: 1. any sentient, alien intelligence, either corporeal or noncorporeal, that interacts with humans 2. the denizens of Hell, often mistaken for gods or Novo Christer evil spirits, actually a sentient nonhuman species with technology and psionic/magical ability much exceeding humanity's 3. any member of the previous definition's species 4. (*slang*) A particularly bad physiological addiction

Feeder: 1. a psion who has lost the ability to process ambient Power and depends on "jolts" of vital energy stolen from other human beings, psion or normal 2. (*Psion slang*) A fair-weather friend

Flight: a class/social rank of demons *Note: There are, strictly speaking, three classes of demons: the Low, Lesser, and Greater. Magi most often deal with the higher echelons of the Low Flight and the lower echelons of the Lesser Flight. Greater Flight demons are almost impossible to control and very dangerous.*

Freetown: an autonomous enclave under a charter, neither Hegemony nor Putchkin but often allied to one or the other in matters of trade

Hedaira: (*Demon term*) 1. an endearment 2. a description of a human woman tied to a Fallen (*A'nankhimel*) demon

Hegemony: one of the two world superpowers, comprising North and South America, Australia/New Zealand, most of Western Europe, Japan, some of Central Asia, and scattered diplomatic enclaves in China *Note: After the Seventy Days War, the two superpowers settled into peace and are often said to be one world government with two divisions. Hegemony Afrike is technically a Hegemony protectorate, but that seems mostly diplomatic convention more than anything else.*

Ka:1. (*Archaic*) soul or mirrorspirit, separate from the *ba* and the physical soul in Egyptianica 2. fate, especially tragic fate that can't be avoided, destiny 3. a link between two souls, where each feeds the other's destiny 4. (*Technical*) Terminus stage for Feeder pathology, an externalized hungry consciousness capable of draining vital energy from a normal human in seconds and a psion in less than two minutes

Magi: *Note: The term* "Magus" *is archaic and hardly ever used.* "Magi" *has become singular or plural, and neuter gender.* 1. a psion who has undergone basic training 2. the class of occult practitioners before the Awakening who held and transmitted basic knowledge about psionic abilities as well as training techniques 3. an accredited psion with the training to call demons or harness etheric force from the disturbance created by the magical methods used to call demons; usually working in Circles or loose affiliations

Master Nichtvren 1. a Nichtvren who is free of obligation to his or her Maker 2. a Nichtvren who holds territory

Merican: the trade lingua of the globe and official language of the Hegemony, though other dialects are rampant 2. (*Archaic*) A Hegemony citizen 3. (*Archaic*) A citizen of the Old Merican region before the Seventy Days War

Necromance: (*slang*: deadhead) an accredited psion with the ability to bring a soul back from Death to answer questions *Note: Can also, in certain instances, heal mortal wounds and keep a soul from escaping into Death.*

Nichtvren: (*slang*: suckhead) altered human capable of living off human blood *Note: Older Nichtvren may possibly live off strong emotions, especially those produced by psions. Since they are altered humans, Nichtvren occupy a space between humanity and "other species"; they are defined as a Paranormal Species and given citizen's rights under Adrien Ferriman's groundbreaking legislation after the Awakening.*

Nine Canons: a nine-part alphabet of runes drawn from around the globe and codified during the Awakening to manage psionic and sorcerous power. Often used as shortcuts in magical circles or as quick charms. *Note: Separate from other branches of magic in that they are accessible sometimes even to normal humans, by virtue of their long use and highly-charged nature.*

Novo Christianity: An outgrowth of a Religion of Submission popular from the 1100s to the latter half of the twenty-first century, before the meteoric rise of the Republic of Gilead and the Seventy Days War. *Note:*

The death knell of Old Christianity is thought to be the great Vatican Bank scandal that touched off the revolt leading to the meteoric rise of Kochba bar Gilead, the charismatic leader of the Republic. Note: the Republic was technically fundamentalist Old Christianity with Judic messianic overtones. Nowadays, NC is declining in popularity and mostly fashionable among the middle-upper class.

Power: 1. vital energy produced by living things, i.e., prana, mana, orgone, etc. 2. sorcerous power accumulated by celibacy, bloodletting, fasting, pain, or meditation 3. ambient energy produced by ley lines and geocurrents, a field of energy surrounding the planet 4. the discipline of raising and channeling vital energy, sorcerous power, or ambient energy 5. any form of energy that fuels sorcerous or psionic ability 6. a paranormal community or paranormal individual who holds territory

Prime Power 1. the highest-ranked paranormal Power in a city or territory, capable of negotiating treaties and enforcing order *Note: usually Nichtvren in most cities and werecain in rural areas.* 2. (*Technical*) The source from which all Power derives 3. (*Archaic*) any non-human paranormal being with more than two vassals in the feudal structure of pre-Awakening paranormal soceity

Psion: 1. an accredited, trained, or apprentice human with psionic abilities 2. a human with psionic abilities

Putchkin: 1. the official language of the Putchkin Alliance, though other dialects are rampant 2. a Putchkin Alliance citizen

Putchkin Alliance: one of the two world superpowers,

comprising Russia, most of China (except Freetown Tibet and Singapore), some of Central Asia, Eastern Europe, and the Middle East *Note: After the Seventy Days War, the two superpowers settled into peace and are often said to be one world government with two divisions.*

Republic of Gilead: theocratic Old Merican empire based on fundamentalist Novo Christer and Judic messianic principles, lasting from the latter half of the 21st century (after the Vatican Bank scandal) to the end of the Seventy Days War *Note: In the early days, before Kochba bar Gilead's practical assumption of power in the Western Hemisphere, the Evangelicals of Gilead were defined as a cult, not the Republic. Political infighting in the Republic brought about both the War and the only tactical nuclear strike of the War (in the Vegas Waste).*

Revised Matheson Score: the index for quantifying the level of psionic ability *Note: Like the Richter scale, it is exponential; five is the lowest score necessary for a psionic child to receive Hegemony funding and schooling. Forty is the terminus of the scale; anything above forty is defined as "superlative" and the psion is tipped into special Hegemony secret-services training.*

Runewitch: a psion whose secondary or primary talent includes the ability to handle the runes of the Nine Canons with more ease

Sedayeen: 1. an accredited psion whose talent is healing 2. *(Archaic)* An old Nichtvren word meaning "blue hand" *Note: Sedayeen are incapable even of self-defense, being allergic to violence and prone to feeling*

*the pain they inflict. This makes them incredible heal-
ers, but also incredibly vulnerable.*

Sekhmet sa'es: Egyptianica term, often used as obscen-
ity; translated: "Sekhmet stamp it," a request for the
Egyptos goddess of destruction to strike some object
or thing, much like the antique "*God damn it*"

Seventy Days War: the conflict that brought about the
end of the Republic of Gilead and the rise of the Hegemony and Putchkin Alliance

Sexwitch: (*Archaic*: *tantraiiken*) an accredited psion who
works with Power raised from the act of sex; pain also
produces an endorphin and energy rush for sexwitches

Shaman: 1. the most common and catch-all term for a
psion who has psionic ability but does not fall into any
other specialty, ranging from vaudun Shamans (who
traffic with *loa*) to generic psions 2. (*Archaic*) a normal
human with borderline psionic ability

Skinlin: (*Slang:* dirtwitch) an accredited psion whose talent has to do with plants and plant DNA *Note: Skinlin
use their voices, holding sustained tones, wedded to
Power to alter plant DNA and structure. Their training
makes them susceptible to berserker rages.*

Talent: 1. psionic ability 2. magickal ability

Werecain: (*Slang:* 'cain, furboy) Altered human capable
of changing to a furred animal form at will *Note: There
are several different subsets, including Lupercal and
magewolfen. Outsiders and normal humans are generally incapable of distinguishing between different subsets of 'cain.*

**Don't miss *The Devil's Right Hand*,
the sequel to *Dead Man Rising*
by Lilith Saintcrow
Here's an exciting preview . . .**

If I was going to visit the Devil, I wanted to be ready.
So I opened up the huge dresser in the corner of the
bedroom. Japhrimel was nowhere to be seen. I knelt on
naked knees, my hair drying in a thick braided rope
against my back. I pulled out the lowest drawer and saw
with faint surprise everything was still there.

*Well, why wouldn't it be there? You put it there, it
hasn't moved. You're being ridiculous, Danny. Get
moving.*

Trade Bargains microfiber shirt, sheds dirt easily and
doesn't smell no matter how long you wear it, thanks to
antibacterium impregnation. Butter-soft, broken-in jeans,
cut to go over boots and treated to be water and stain
resistant, patches tailored in to accommodate holsters and
with the crotch inset so side-kicks were possible. The old
explorer's coat, too big for me because it was Jace's,
supple tough Kevlar panels inset in canvas, one pocket
scorched where a silver spade necklace had turned red-
hot and burned its way free. The rig, still oiled and

spelled, not cracking like regular leather would. Knives, main-gauches and stilettos, and the two silver guns, cartridges neatly stacked off to the side. And in its deep velvet case, the necklace Jace had given me in the first days of our affair. I'd worn it all through the last job— tracking down Kellerman Lourdes. Even after I'd finished, that job had almost killed me.

I could admit that much now, if only to myself.

The necklace was beautiful. Silver-dipped raccoon *baculum* on a fine silver chain twined with black velvet ribbons and blood-marked bloodstones as well as every defense a Shaman knew how to weave, all twisted together in a fluid piece of art. He hadn't given any other woman something like this—at least, not that I knew of. He had spent months making it, a powerful mark of his affection for me.

If I went into Death again, if I took the necklace he'd worked so hard on or the sword that had twisted with his death and called his apparition up, what would it have to say to me?

Maybe something like "I loved you, Danny, and I was human. Why couldn't you love me?" Maybe something like that. Or maybe, "Why did you let me die?" Or "What took you so long to come find me, Danny?"

What would he say?

"I'm not brave enough to find out," I whispered, and picked up the necklace with delicate fingers. I fastened it, and spent a moment arranging it so the *baculum* hung down, each a curve of silver against my golden skin, its knobbed end pointing out. "Or am I?"

I felt as if some shell had been ripped away, as if my skin was hitting the air for the first time. I'd spent so long living on the edge of a sword, taking one bounty after another, taking jobs other Necromances wouldn't touch, honing myself into a weapon to still the voices whispering in my head. *Not good enough, not strong enough, not brave enough, not tough enough.* And now, instead of feeling properly terrified, I felt a kind of giddy glee. Soon I'd be facing down some new kind of danger, feeling as if my heart was going to explode from adrenaline. I had said that all I wanted was a quiet life, to be left alone.

I'd actually believed it when I'd said it, too.

Under the necklace were my rings, chiming as they tangled together. I lifted them one by one – amber rectangle, amber cabochon. Moonstone. Plain silver band. Bloodstone oval, obsidian oval. Suni-figured thumbring on my left hand. They began to glow, sullenly at first, then brighter as my Power stroked at them. I sighed, feeling the defenses and spells caught in each stone rise to the surface, tremble, and settle back into humming readiness.

I dressed quickly, my fingers flying as they hadn't for years. Buttoning up my shirt, my jeans, finding a pair of microfiber socks. My boots were a little cracked, but everything still fit. Living soft hadn't made me fat yet, though I'd lost the look of being starved. A demon metabolism, every girl's best friend.

I picked up the rig with trembling hands. Shrugged myself into it, fastened it down. Tested the action of the knives. They were still sharp. The plasgun went into its holster under my left arm. The projectile guns rode easy in their holsters, I slid clips in them both, chambered a round in each, and then looked down.

The only thing left was my tattered canvas messenger bag – the bag that had gone into Hell with me, had gone back to the nightmare of my childhood with me, the bag I'd carried on every job since Doreen had bought it for me and sewn in the extra pockets and loops of elastic to hold everything down.

I scooped up the bag and the six extra clips, paced over to the bed, and dumped everything out. Scraps of paper, containers—blessed water, salt, cornmeal mix, my lock-picking set, extra handkerchiefs and ammo clips and my athame, still glimmering with Power inside its plain black leather sheath. The bit of consecrated chalk—my fingers trembled, seeing that. I had been searching for it desperately in the abandoned cafeteria of Rigger Hall with Lourdes chasing me, carrying the poisonous seed of Mirovitch inside his brain like a cancerous flower. A silver Zijaan with a cursive-script 'CM' etched on it. A battered paperback copy of the Nine Canons—the runes Magi and other psions had been using since before the Great Awakening—that I'd had since the Academy. My tarot cards in a hank of blue silk. Rough bits of quartz crystal, a few more bloodstones, some chunks of amber. More odds and ends.

My hands seemed to know what to do. I laid Jace's coat down, my fingers moving, checking, stowing everything in its proper place. Then I picked up the bag, gave it an experimental shake, and let it settle. I ducked through the strap and settled the bag on my hip, under the holster carrying my right-hand gun. I rolled my shoulders back as everything settled in, then shrugged into Jace's coat. Picked up my katana.

"Ready for anything," I muttered.

The house was oddly quiet. I listened and heard nothing, not even servants moving. I realized how used to the sound of human hearts beating I'd become. The maids didn't talk to me—I didn't speak Taliano, and they didn't speak much Merican, so I let Japhrimel translate and was grateful none of them looked askance or forked the sign of the Evil Eye at me. And none of them set foot in the library unless it was to dust while I was sleeping or to leave a box of new books inside the door. Only Emilio seemed unafraid, both of me and of the demon who shared my bed.

I stood for a few moments, breathing, the room resounding with small sounds as my attention swept in a slow circuit, brushing the curtains of the bed, sliding along the walls, caressing the framed Berscardi print above the low table where Japhrimel usually kept a single lily in a fluted black glass vase. The lily was gone, the vase empty. The curtains on the window fluttered. I sighed.

Then I turned on my heel, my boots clicking, and strode out of the bedroom and down the hall. The doors rose up on either side of me, bedrooms that were never used, a small meditation-room, a sparring room with a long wooden floor and shafts of light coming in every window. I found the door I wanted unlocked, hit it with the flats of both hands. It was well-hung, and swung inward, banging against the wall. Dust flew out; this wasn't a place anyone entered often.

The room was long, and the wood floor glowed with layers of varnish. At the far end, barred by two shafts of sunlight, stood a high antique ebony table, and on this table lay a scarred and corkscrew-twisted *dotanuki*, its hilt-wrappings scorched.

Jace's sword. Still reverberating with the final agonized throes of his death.

A blot of darkness hunched on the floor in front of the table. Japhrimel, on one knee, his back turned to me.

Of all the things I expected, that was probably the last.

He didn't move. I strode up the center of the room and came to a halt right behind him, my boots sliding on the floor. I dug my heels in—going too fast. It seemed I would never learn how to slow this body down. My rings spat, swirling with color, each stone glittering.

I waited. Japhrimel's head was down, his black hair falling forward to hide his face. His black coat lay along the floor behind him; his back was utterly straight. He didn't speak. Sunlight fell like honey, but the sun was sinking down in the sky. We were going to go find this door into Hell soon.

I finally settled for stepping close and laying my hand on his shoulder. He flinched.

Tierce Japhrimel, Lucifer's assassin and oldest child, *flinched* when I touched him.

I didn't choke with surprise, but it was damn close. "Japhri—"

"I have been here, asking the ghost of a human man for forgiveness." His voice slashed through mine. "And wondering why he has more of your heart than I do."

I suppose it was the closest thing to jealousy I'd ever heard from him. I closed my mouth with a snap, found my voice. "He never did," I finally said. "That was the problem."

Japhrimel laughed. The sound was so bitter it dyed the air blue. "Are you so cruel to those you love?"

"It's a human habit." The lump in my throat threatened to strangle me. "I'm . . . sorry."

Even now, an apology didn't come easily. It tore its way out of my chest with razor glass studded along every edge.

Japhrimel rose to his feet. I still couldn't see his face. "An apology without a battle," he said. "Perhaps there is hope."

I knew he was using that black humor again, using it like a blade laid along the forearm to ward off a strike. It still hurt. "If I'm so bloody bad why don't you go back to Hell?" *Great, Danny. Lovely. You're really on edge, aren't you? This is really adult. No wonder he treats you like a little kid sometimes.*

"I would not go back even if they would have me. I seem to prefer your malice." He turned on his heel, away from me, the edges of his coat brushing my knee. "I will wait for you."

It was my turn to interrupt. "Don't run away from me, dammit."

He paused. Stood with his back to me still, his shoulders iron-hard. "Running away is your trick."

You little snot of a demon, why do you have to make this so fucking hard? "You're an arrogant son of a bitch," I informed him. The air turned hot and tight, and the twisted corkscrewed sword lying on the table rang softly, its song of shock and death cycling up a notch. Catching the fever in the air, maybe. We were both throwing off enough heat and Power to make the entire room resound like an echo chamber.

"You're right. I am what you make of me, Dante Valentine. I will wait for you outside the door." He strode away, every footfall a clicking crisp sound. Anger like smoke fumed up from his footprints. His coat flapped as if a wind was mouthing it.

"Japhrimel. Japh, wait."

He didn't pause.

"Please. Don't do this. I'm sorry. *Please*." My voice cracked, as if Lucifer had just finished strangling me again.

Two more steps. Then he stopped, just inside the door. His back was straight, rigid with something I didn't care to name.

"I'm being an idiot." I folded my arms defensively, the slim length of my sword in my right hand, a bar of darkness. "I'm *frightened*, Japh. All right? I woke up, you weren't here, and you drop this on me. I'm fucking terrified. Cut me a little slack here, and I'll try to stop being such a bitch. Okay?" *I can't believe it, I just admitted being scared to a demon. Miracles do happen.*

I thought he'd continue out the door, but he didn't. His shoulders relaxed slightly, the hurtful static in the air easing. It took the space of five breaths before he turned back to me. I saw the tide of green drifting through his eyes, sparks above a bonfire. His mouth had softened. We looked at each other, the Fallen and me; I tried to pretend I wasn't hugging myself for comfort.

"There is no need for fear," he said finally, softly.

Yeah, sure. We're about to go meet the Devil, for the third time in my life. I could have done without ever meeting him at all. He's probably got something special planned for us, and the Devil's idea of a little surprise is not my idea of a good time. "You've got to be joking." I sounded like I'd lost all my air. The mark on my shoulder turned to velvet, warm oil sliding along my skin from his attention. "It's the *Devil*, Japh." *I don't think Lucifer's likely to be in a good mood.*

He came back to me, each footfall eerily silent. Stopped an arm's-length away, looking down to meet my eyes, his hands clasped behind his back. "He is the Prince of Hell," he corrected, a little pedantically. "I will let no harm come to you. Only trust me, and all will be well."

Trust you? I've trusted you for a long time now. "Is there anything else you haven't told me?" I searched his face, the memorized lines and curves. He had his own harsh beauty, the beauty of a balanced throwing-knife or the curve of a katana, something functional and deadly instead of merely aesthetic. Funny, but when I was human I had thought him almost-ugly at first, certainly not *beautiful* by any stretch of the imagination. But the longer I knew him, the better he looked.

He shrugged. Gods, how I hate demons shrugging. "If I told you what I guess, or what I anticipate, we will never go. Until I am certain, I do not wish to cloud the issue with suppositions. Best just to go, and to trust in your Fallen. Have I not earned that, at least?"

You didn't answer the question, Japh. But he was right. Goddamn it, I hated having to admit he was right; even I knew that anticipating something from the Prince of Hell was likely to end in a nasty surprise. And most of all, Japh had never let me down. "I do." My voice dropped, the soft ruined tone of honey gone granular soothing the last remains of tension away. "Of course I trust you."

I thought he'd be happy about it. Instead, his face turned still and solemn as we looked at each other, the mark on my shoulder pulsing and sending a flood of heat down my skin. "Cut it out." I sounded a little breathless. A little? No, like I could hardly get enough air in to protest. It was as intimate as his fingers in my hair, as intimate as his mouth against my pulse. "Let's just get this over with."

A single sharp nod, and Japhrimel offered me his hand. It was another mark of trust that I let him take my right hand, my sword hand; it made me nervous as hell to know that he could very easily keep me from drawing just by tightening his fingers a little.

I don't want to do this. I don't. Japhrimel led me out of the room, and the doors closed behind us, silent on their maghinges. *But if I have to face down Lucifer, at least I've got Japh with me.*

It wasn't as comforting as I'd thought it would be . . . but I'd take it. After all, I had no choice.

BITTEN

Kelley Armstrong

Elena Michaels is your regular twenty-first-century
girl: self-assured, smart and fighting fit. She also
just happens to be the only female werewolf in
the world . . .

It has some good points. When she walks down a dark
alleyway, she's the scary one. But now her Pack – the
one she abandoned so that she could live a normal life
– are in trouble, and they need her help. Is she willing
to risk her life to help the ex-lover who betrayed her by
turning her into a werewolf in the first place? And,
more to the point, does she have a choice?

<u>GUILTY PLEASURES</u>

Laurell K. Hamilton

My name is Anita Blake. Vampires call me The Executioner. What I call them isn't repeatable.

Ever since the Supreme Court granted the undead equal rights, most people think vampires are just ordinary folks with fangs. I know better. I've seen their victims. I carry the scars . . .

But now a serial killer is murdering vampires – and the most powerful bloodsucker in town wants me to find the killer.

THE DRESDEN FILES

Jim Butcher

Look out for the case files of Harry Dresden, modern-day wizard:

STORM FRONT

Harry Dresden is the best and technically the 'only' one at what he does. So when the Chicago P.D. has a case that transcends mortal capabilities, they come to him for answers.

FOOL MOON

Business has been slow and you'd think Chicago would have a little more action for the only professional wizard in the phone book. But then along comes a brutally mutilated corpse, strange-looking paw prints and a full moon . . .

GRAVE PERIL

All over Chicago, tormented ghosts are causing trouble. Someone – or something – is purposely stirring them up to wreak unearthly havoc. But why? And why do so many of the victims have ties to Harry?

SUMMER KNIGHT

When Harry seems most down on his luck, the Winter Queen of Faerie offers him a job: all he has to do is clear her name of murder. It seems simple enough, until Harry finds out that the fate of the entire world rests on him solving this case . . .

DEATH MASKS

Harry Dresden should be happy that business is pretty good. But now he's getting more than he bargained for: vampire duels, hit men, the Shroud of Turin . . . And then his semi-vampiric ex-girlfriend turns up.

BLOOD RITES

Working in the world of film seems attractive – until the film producer claims to be the victim of a curse and the women around him start dying in spectacular ways. Then Harry discovers that his vampire friend has a personal stake in the case . . .

THE BLOOD SERIES

Tanya Huff

Look out for these razor-sharp supernatural thrillers:

BLOOD PRICE
Vicki is caught up in the deadly pursuit of a mass murderer with an inhuman appetite for mayhem and destruction. Her advisor on the case isn't reassuring, but then only Vicki Nelson would ally herself with Henry Fitzroy, a five-hundred-year-old vampire.

BLOOD TRAIL
Vicki is on the trail of an assassin hell-bent on wiping out Canada's last remaining werewolf clan. And with back-up from vampire Henry Fitzroy available on a strictly nocturnal basis, she's already regretting the decision.

BLOOD LINES
Vicki is investigating a bizarre double murder within the Toronto museum Egyptology department. No-one will talk and Vicki begins to suspect that minds are being tampered with. Then her vampire friend starts having visions of the sun – an unpopular vampire subject – and an unhealthy pattern starts to emerge.

BLOOD PACT
Death has struck close to home for Vicki Nelson PI, as her mother is the victim in a case that may become the most terrifying of her career. Vicki and her sometime lover, vampire Henry Fitzroy, have discovered something that will be difficult to lay to rest.

BLOOD DEBT
It began with a visitation from a ghost, a tormented soul hungry for vengeance. The wraith is determined that Henry and Vicki track down its killer, and is fully prepared to use the innocent inhabitants of Toronto to ensure their support.